Coralum

Ivana L. Truglio is a book lover. She always has been! Ivana made up her mind to be a writer when she was six years old and never looked back.

Through the years of learning to fly, studying archaeology and ancient history, and finally working in office jobs, she never stopped reading and writing. For 11 years, she worked for multinational publishing companies in the tax team (don't hold that against her!) and learned all the tricks of the trade to start her own publishing company.

Contact Ivana
linktr.ee/ivanaltruglioauthor
Facebook: @ivanatruglio
Instagram: @ivanaltruglioauthor

Also by Ivana L. Truglio

The Paradise Series
Rilla
Illaria
Crystal Dragons
Child of Paradise

Kora's Choice

The Guild Series
Inventrici
Sarti

Corallini

Guild Series

Ivana L. Truglio

First published in Australia in 2024
by Jonquil Press
ABN: 99871403756

A catalogue record for this
book is available from the
National Library of Australia

ISBN: 978-0-6483416-8-0 (paperback)

Cover illustration by Jane Green

Typeset in Adobe Garamond Pro 10pt/11.5pt

For my daughter,
who is just amazing in every way.

ACKNOWLEDGEMENTS

This book wouldn't exist but for the fact that when I was 10 years old, I went to Italy with my family, to my mum's home town of Torre del Greco. Tor'Esint is very loosely based on my memories of those days spent in Italy.

If I hadn't met my Zio Ciro Scognamiglio, one of the most famous corallini in the world, I would never have fallen in love with the art of corallo myself. Had I lived in Italy, I'm certain I'd have tried to follow in his footsteps, but it was near impossible to do that from Australia. So I researched everything I could about corallini and infused these pages with that knowledge. I hope the little details bring the story to life for you.

As usual, I'd like to thank my readers. Your kind words and enthusiasm keep me going!

Without the wonderful and supportive writing community on Discord, most notably Zola Hobbit, Dom The Wicked Captain and Kwara, I might not have the motivation to open my story file some days.

My unending thanks to my brilliant editor, Anicee Dowling. She notices the smallest of errors and helps shape the story into what I want it to be. I love how invested she gets in the characters' lives.

A special shout out to my mother who lent me all the pieces of coral and cameo jewellery in her collection for inspiration and research.

As always, thank you to my family for understanding that I cannot survive without writing and always give me the time I need with my stories.

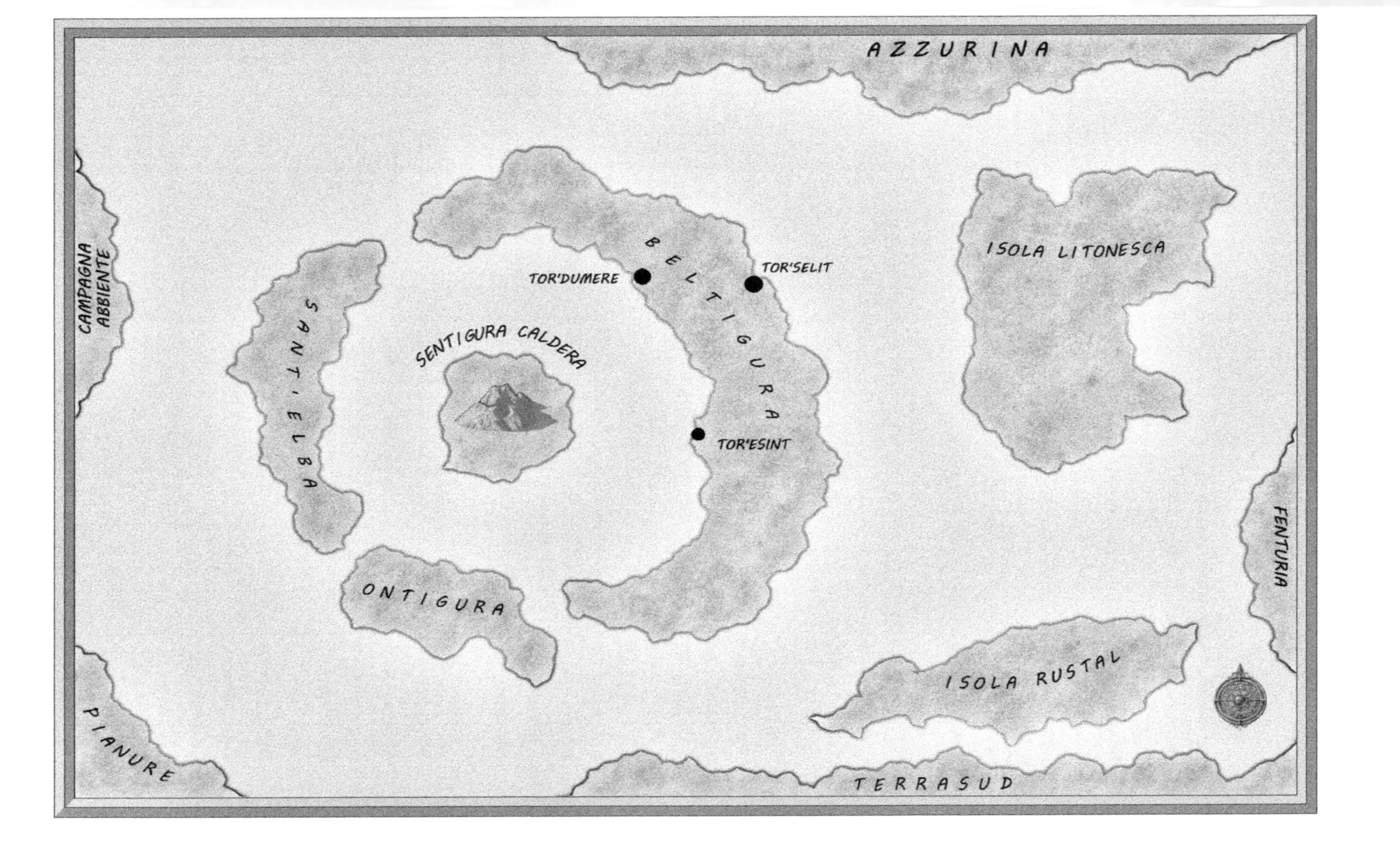
AZZURINA
CAMPAGNA ABBIENTE
BELTIGURA
TOR'DUMERE
TOR'SELIT
TOR'ESINT
ISOLA LITONESCA
SANT'ELBA
SENTIGURA CALDERA
ONTIGURA
FENTURIA
ISOLA RUSTAL
PIANURE
TERRASUD

LIST OF TERMS

GUILDS

Guild	Title
Mercantili Guild (merchants)	Mercantessa (f.)/Mercante (m.)
Alchimisti Guild (alchemists who also function as doctors)	Alchimista (n.)
Inventrici Guild (inventors of anything mechanical)	Inventrice (f.)/Inventore (m.)
Gioiellieri Guild (jewellers, specialising in gold, silver or coral)	Gioielliera (f.)/Gioielliere (m.)
Sarti Guild (seamstresses and tailors)	Sarta (f.)/Sarto (m.)
Musicisti Guild (musicians, including composers and singers)	Musicista (n.)
Falegnami Guild (carpenters)	Falegname (n.)
Calzolai Guild (cobblers)	Calzolaia (f.)/Calzolaio (m.)
Artiste Guild (artists, including painters and sculptors)	Artista (n.)
Fabbri Guild (smiths, including blacksmiths, goldsmiths and silversmiths)	Fabbro (n.)
Ballerini Guild (dancers)	Ballerina (f.)/Ballerino (m.)
Vetraie Guild (glassblowers)	Vetraia (f.)/Vetraio (M.)

MONEY

1 Gold	3 Electrums	60 Silvers	600 Coppers
1 Electrum	20 Silvers	200 Coppers	
1 Silver	10 Coppers		
1 Copper	smallest unit of money		

CALENDAR

Mercantili	First month	Autumn
Alchimisti	Second month	Winter
Inventrici	Third month	Winter
Gioiellieri	Fourth month	Winter
Sarti	Fifth month	Spring
Musicisti	Sixth month	Spring
Falegnami	Seventh month	Spring
Calzolai	Eighth month	Summer
Artiste	Ninth month	Summer
Fabbri	Tenth month	Summer
Ballerini	Eleventh month	Autumn
Vetraie	Twelfth month	Autumn

DAYS OF THE WEEK

Gildadi	Trading Day (Guild Day)
Ramedi	Trading Day (Copper Day)
Argentodi	Trading Day (Silver Day)
Legaramedi	Trading Day (Electrum Day)
Orodi	Trading Day (Gold Day)
Mercatodi	Market day, every second week for Guilds, every other week for regular vendors
Riposidi	Rest day

GLOSSARY

Amministratore (m.)/Amministratrice (f.)/ Amministratori (pl.)	administrators
Amore	love
Argentiera (f.)/Argentiere (m.)/Argentieri (pl).	silversmiths
Companion	life partners who have had a commitment ceremony
Coppola	flat hat
Corallina (f.)/Corallino (m.)/Corallini (pl.)	coral workers
Corso	course
Funicolare	cablecar
In bocca al lupo	good luck
Limoncello	lemon liqueur
Maestra (f.)/Maestro (m.)	Guild Mistress/Master
Mamma	mum
Marinaia (f.)/Marinaio (m.)/Marinai (pl.)	sailors
Miglio/Miglia	mile/miles
Nipotina	granddaughter
Nonna (f.)/Nonno (m.)	grandmother/grandfather
Orafa (f.)/Orafo (m.)/Orafi (pl.)	goldsmiths
Panettiere	baker
Pasticceria/Pasticcerie	pastry shop/s
Papà	dad
Piazza	square
Piede/Piedi	foot/feet
Pollice/Pollici	inch/inches
Ristorante	restaurant
Signora/Signore	miss/mister
Tesoro	treasure
Trinzale and lenza	decorative headwear
Vecchietta (f.)/Vecchietto (m.)/Vecchietti (pl.)	old people
Via	street
Zona	zone

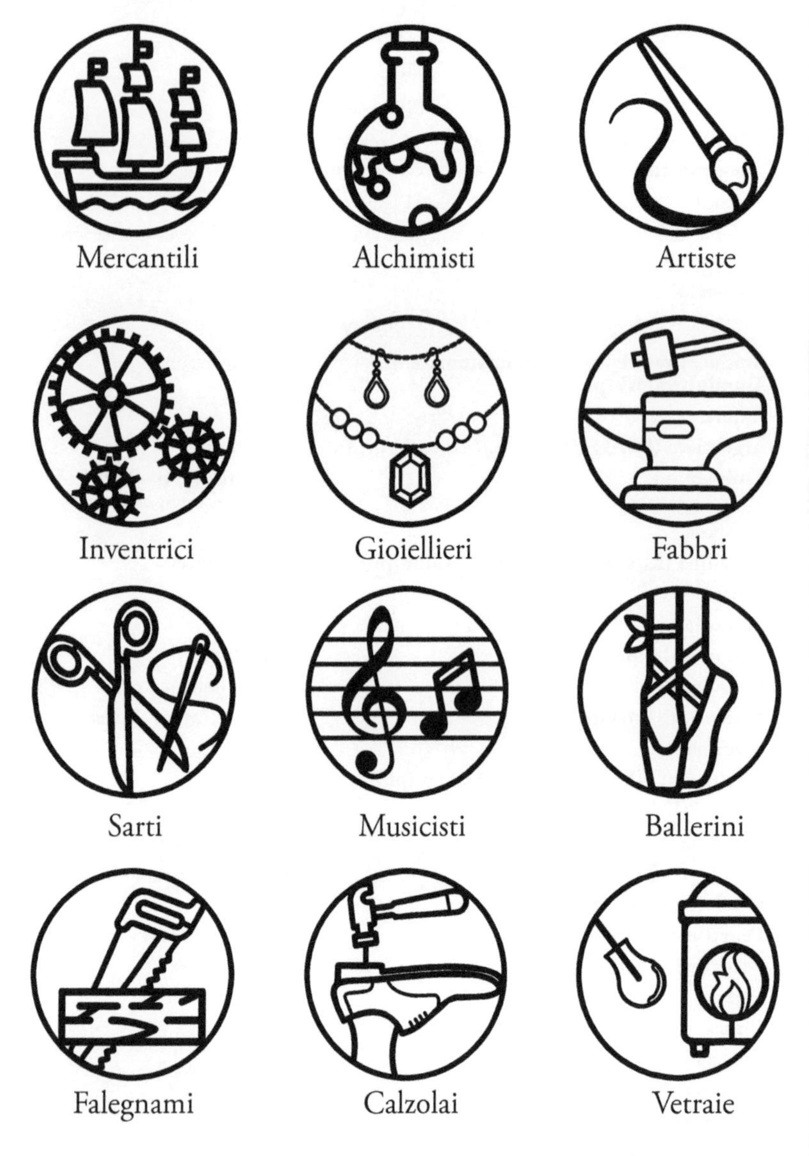

Author's note: For the sake of having a single version for each Guild name, I alternated between the feminine and masculine for those that weren't gender neutral, completely understanding that this is not how the Italian language works.

Chapter 1 – Gildadi 23 Inventrici 230 Years After Implosion

Ciro stood on the beach, staring out at the Baia di Beltigura as the briny breeze lifted strands of his thinning hair. Usually, he preferred to stand barefoot in the black volcanic sand, but this early in the morning, the sun had yet to warm the beach enough to his liking. He hadn't cared when he was younger. The feel of the sand between his toes had been worth the crisp winter chill stealing into his body.

These days, he almost always felt cold. Even today, with his shoes on, he would need to warm himself by the fire back at home. Seppe would have it lit by the time he returned. Ciro smiled. What would he do without Seppe?

"Zio Ciro!"

He turned and smiled as Loredana and Tania ran barefoot towards him, leaving little footprints in the sand.

"Look what we found!" They chorused happily.

The girls held out their small wicker baskets, filled to the brim with corallo branches. The branches were varying lengths, but all of them thin. Ciro patted the girls affectionately on the back.

He emptied their finds into the larger basket on his hip, secured the lid, and gave them a copper coin each. It was a good trade. Today's trove might yield him an entire necklace, which would easily sell for a gold coin.

Not every day was so successful. Ciro wished he could once, just once, find a piece of corallo big enough for him to carve into a real masterpiece. Something as long and thick as his forearm would provide a wonderful canvas. The girls sometimes found larger pieces, as big as their hands, and Ciro did what he could with those, but he longed for more. In Tor'Dumere, he'd once seen a carving in a trunk the size of his head and had studied it for hours.

Some days, he missed his youth, when *he'd* been the one trawling the beach for corallo for his Maestro. He'd happily spent hours combing the beach in search of the bright red branches his Maestro needed to make the precious necklaces.

"Will you be back again tomorrow?" Loredana asked hopefully.

"No, bella, not tomorrow. It's the monthly Guild meeting and I can't miss it. The day after, I'll be back then," Ciro explained patiently.

Little Tania's eyes grew so large and watery, Ciro feared she would start crying there and then and he wouldn't be able to stop her. He lay a hand on her shoulder and leaned in close.

"I tell you what, why don't you find whatever you can for me tomorrow and come past my shop? Seppe will be there. You might even convince him to make some of that lovely hot chocolate and twist his arm to give you a biscuit."

Tania tried to hide her smile at that suggestion, but Ciro could see straight through her. He patted her head and lightly brushed his fingers against Loredana's cheek before turning towards the docks.

He wished he could do more for the girls but their mamma wouldn't allow it. As it was, she only accepted the coins he gave them because they "worked" for him. Serafina was stubborn like that, and proud. The three of them were the only family he had left. At least Serafina had agreed to move to Tor'Esint with her girls when her mamma, Ciro's sister, had died. For that, he would be eternally grateful.

The walk to the dock was peaceful. Ciro walked past the small row boats towards the larger fishing trawlers and Mercantili Guild boats, waving at the marinai as he passed. He knew them all by sight, if not by name. Ever since his apprenticeship with Maestro Enrico, he'd walked along the beach and the dock almost every morning, looking for corallo and shells. Enrico had taught him how to select the best conch shells, how to find the flaws that would ruin a cammeo. By now, all he had to do was walk the dock and anyone who had something interesting for him to look at would call him over.

Some days, he made it all the way to the end of the dock and back without being hailed down. In the early days, it had disappointed him when that happened, but now there were so few Corallini that competition for good shells and corallo had all but disappeared. In truth, Ciro had enough shells at home that he could last months without needing to find more.

"Ciro Corallino, I've got something for you."

Ciro looked around to see Corrado waving him over to his old paddlewheel boat.

"What is it this time, Corrado?" Ciro asked with a sigh. Corrado always tried to sell him anything but the shell and corallo he wanted.

"Something special." Corrado winked. "I picked it up for you on the caldera."

Ciro paused. "Sentigura Caldera? *You* went to *Sentigura Caldera*?"

Corrado waggled his eyebrows up and down.

"What is it then?"

Ciro stepped closer to the boat despite his doubts. Corrado held up a finger and disappeared into the tiny compartment that served as his personal quarters. Ciro waited patiently for him to reappear, which he did – holding something larger than his cupped hands, wrapped in a white cloth.

Looking up and down the docks, Corrado carefully uncovered his treasure. Ciro saw a sparkle as the treasure glinted in the sun.

"What *is* that?" he asked curiously.

Corrado shrugged. "Some kind of volcanic rock. It's sharp as a razor, but beautiful, no?"

Ciro found himself nodding without meaning to. "I can't carve that," he pointed out. "It *is* beautiful though."

Corrado went an uncomfortable shade of red. His deckhand walked up casually and looked at the rock.

"He's hoping you can make a bit of jewellery with that, for a *signora* friend."

Corrado turned angrily to the deckhand. "Stuarto, what'd I tell you about yer mouth?"

Stuarto scrunched his nose. "To always keep it shut on account of me sticking my foot in it so often."

"Right." Corrado nodded. "Now, how about you check the boat over while I talk to Ciro."

Stuarto mumbled something inaudible under his breath but went to check the other side of the boat, leaving Ciro alone with Corrado.

"He's right though. I do want you to make something for a *friend* of mine. Then you could use the rest of it yourself, no charge!"

Ciro smiled knowingly. "And this *friend* of yours, what sort of jewellery were you hoping to give them?"

Corrado opened and shut his mouth a few times before staring glumly at the rock. Ciro covered up the rock with the cloth and took it from Corrado. He opened his wicker basket and placed it gently on top of the corallo branches.

"Don't worry. I'll figure something out," Ciro promised.

Corrado grinned. "Thanks, Ciro."

Ciro nodded amiably and continued his stroll to the end of the dock. Only one other marinaio hailed him down, but the shell he offered was not to Ciro's liking. It mattered not. With the unusual rock Corrado had given him, he'd keep himself busy figuring out what to do with it.

Ciro took his time walking back to his workshop. These old bones forced him to move slowly. He didn't mind it so much. Even if the rest of Tor'Esint was rushing around madly, at least he could still take his time.

The bitter aroma of coffee greeted Ciro upon his arrival. By the time he'd divested himself of his coat and wicker basket, Seppe was there, holding out a scalding cup of coffee. Ciro took it gratefully, blew on it carefully and sipped with puckered lips. Coffee always tasted better when it was hot, but he'd been burned often enough to always be cautious now.

"Did you find any treasures?" Seppe asked hopefully.

Ciro shrugged and passed him the haul. Seppe took out the cloth covered rock and placed it on a workbench before upending the basket and sifting through the small corallo branches.

"You know, these are all similar sizes. You could make a branch necklace this time, rather than shape all the balls. There's enough of those in the display cabinet as it is."

Ciro glanced at the cabinet. Seppe was right – there were at least five necklaces in varying designs, all with corallo balls. The branch jewellery fetched a higher price because they had more corallo, even if they took less time to make.

"Yes, fine. Will you make the holes? I've got something else to work on today."

He uncovered the cloth and Seppe peered at the peculiar rock.

"It won't go with the corallo. It's too abrasive. What will you do with it?"

Ciro shrugged. "If I knew that, I wouldn't need to spend all day on it. Now, leave me be so I can work."

Seppe shook his head but scooped the corallo back in the wicker basket and went over to the corallo piercer. It was of the same design that Maestro Enrico had used all those years ago. The only improvement Ciro had insisted on was the addition of the foot pedal over six years ago, so that either he or Seppe could work the machines by themselves. It should have cost a small fortune, but Telchide Inventore had insisted he only pay for the material. Ciro had agreed, but only on the condition that he would make a cammeo of Telchide's companion, Sebetine di Serenita.

The young signora had obligingly sat for him as he sketched her likeness so he could finish it in his own time. She'd been in her early pregnancy, belly just starting to round. They'd been such a happy couple. Ciro shook his head at the thought. Sebetine had disappeared years ago. Poor Telchide had been so heartbroken even Ciro hadn't been able to cheer him up.

When Sebetine had been declared dead almost two months ago, the news had been scarcely less shocking than the fact that Telchide had found himself a new signora. Ciro had only met her once, and briefly at that. Now the rumour was that she was pregnant with Telchide's child.

Ciro resolved to visit them one of these days. But not today. Today, he would occupy himself with the rainbow-tinged black rock. He brought it over to his cutting station and sat down to work pushing the pedal up and down to get the saw moving. The saw dipped into water at the back of the machine, keeping the blade cool. It wouldn't matter for one stone, but with the amount of corallo he usually cut, it was a necessity.

With steady hands, Ciro gently pushed the rock towards the saw, angling it so that it would cut with the grain. He cut off a section of the rock as big as his thumb, leaving a much larger section for other creations.

Grasping the stone with a pair of metal tongs, he held it up to the light. Every facet shone a different colour, creating a rainbow effect. Ciro stared at it for a long while, trying to decide what he could possibly do with such a stone. The jutting edges looked so sharp he daren't run his finger along them for fear of cutting himself.

Smoothing – that would need to be the first step. Ciro took the stone to his grinding wheel. This machine was generally used with corallo to make each cutting into a smooth ball, but it would work just as well for other stones or gems, and he had done so many times in the past. But this stone was too beautiful to smooth the rough edges entirely away. He would need to be careful with it.

As Seppe began washing the corallo in a corner of the workshop, Ciro painstakingly worked at smoothing the edges of his new stone without ruining the sparkling effect it had. When he felt confident that he'd worked it enough, he picked it up with his bare hands, testing the safety of the edges. To his delight, it didn't cut him, even when he slid the shaped piece from one hand to the other, letting it slip along his fingers.

He brought the rock over to the gioielliere workbench – the one he used for working with metal rather than corallo. Most of the time, Ciro worked with gold as it set off the corallo so well. But with *this* rock, he would use silver. He took a small ingot of silver, set up the rolling mill and fed it through over and over, making it thinner and longer until it was down to his desired thickness, pausing to anneal the metal every now and then as it became harder and more brittle as he worked on it.

The rolling process took such a long time that Seppe had already moved on to cutting sections off the corallo branches by the time Ciro finished.

Finally, the silver rod was ready for the draw plate. Ciro was quite proud of the improvements he'd insisted on for this process. As an apprentice, he'd had to draw through the metal rods with tongs. It had not been a kind process to his hands. When he'd saved up enough money, he'd insisted on a system to help him pull the metal through the draw plate. This contraption was set up along a narrow workbench. At one end were metal holders to keep the draw plate in place. At the other end was a long strip of canvas rolled up with a windlass. The end of the canvas was folded and stitched over a triangular bit of metal that hooked over the metal tongs.

Ciro fed the silver rod through the largest hole on the draw plate, clamped it with the metal tongs and turned the handle on the windlass to pull the metal tongs back and draw the silver rod through the hole.

It was a much easier and smoother process than doing it completely by hand. Every third or fourth hole, Ciro annealed the silver so it wouldn't break. He pulled the long silver rod through the draw plate until he got down to the smallest hole, a fraction of a pollice. It would give the pendant a nice, delicate feel.

He took the stone and the silver wire to his workbench and sat down with his pliers. Carefully, he bent the wire around the rock, gently wrapping it into place. At the top of the rock, he curled the silver into a loop with enough overlap to ensure a necklace could not slip out of it.

Ciro held up the pendant and smiled. It was one of the simplest ways to create a pendant, but in this case, it was also the most elegant, for any more metal around the rock would only detract from it.

Seppe stopped his drilling and came over to see.

"That's not bad. What are you charging for it?"

Ciro raised his eyebrows. "Nothing."

"Nothing?" Seppe narrowed his eyes. "Ciro, we can't live on *nothing*."

"My payment was the rock, Seppe. With what's left of it, I can create at least another twenty pendants the same as this, or forty earrings or rings. There are countless options that will bring in money. I don't need to charge Corrado for this."

He gestured dismissively to the pendant, as though it hadn't taken him all morning to create.

"How are you going with the corallo branches?"

Seppe, thankfully, knew when not to continue arguing. Instead, he showed Ciro his progress. It had been a good decision to show Seppe how to use the different machines. This way, Ciro could give the more repetitive and mundane tasks to Seppe so he could have time to concentrate on the more detailed work himself.

More than half the corallo had been cut so that the branches were now single spikes, all roughly the same size. It would still take another hour or so to finish the rest of them, and then drill holes through all of them.

"I need food," Ciro said suddenly. "I'll make you a panino. Prosciutto?"

Seppe looked up. "I can make it."

"I know," Ciro answered easily. "But you're busy and I'm not. I'll make it."

Before Seppe could argue, Ciro disappeared into the kitchen. It was a tiny little thing behind the workshop. The size had never bothered him. Small places were easier to look after. Less space, less mess. Besides, all he really needed a kitchen for was to prepare food and make coffee.

***

It was nearing four o'clock when the shop door opened. Ciro looked up in surprise. He wasn't expecting anyone today and orders had been steadily dropping off in the past few weeks. He wasn't sure if something had happened or if people were just not willing to spend money on luxury items.

A well-dressed lady with a Gold Sarti Guild Mark walked purposefully towards him with a white paper package. The brown curls escaping her braid softened her angular features. Overall, it was a pleasant visage, though so different from when she'd first set foot in his shop that it took him a moment to recognise her.

That day, her curly hair had been loose, held in place only with a lenza and trinzale. Even her manner of dress had been different then – a lovely green skirt and cream blouse with green sleeves and a brown leather corset. Today, she wore a much more functional work dress, though no less striking. She looked around for a clear workspace to place the package on and brushed a curl out of her face.

"Good afternoon, Signora Sarta." Ciro got to his feet and walked over to her. "Let me help you with that."

He took the package gently from her and set it on the glass-topped display case. Greta Sarta smoothed down her skirt.

"Thank you, Signore Corallino. Now, I know we said three weeks for the shirts, but I hope you don't mind I brought them to you early. I've moved workshops and have a lot of new orders. I didn't want your shirts to get lost amongst them. I can come back later to pick up the cammeo."

Ciro took her hand and pressed it gently. "Signora, please, slow down."

She instantly stopped talking and looked down at their hands. Ciro patted her hand gently and showed her to a chair on the other side of his workbench. She hesitated, but sat down. Ciro walked over to the glass-topped display bench and pulled out a drawer underneath it. He opened a few boxes until he found the one he was looking for.

He walked back to Greta and placed the box in front of her with the lid off.

"This is my part of the trade."

Greta stretched out her long fingers and gently touched the cammeo likeness of herself. It was set in a silver brooch with gold rope around the pendant, like most of the brooches Ciro made. He nodded, pleased with himself as the smile spread across her face.

"It's beautiful," she whispered.

"Well, yes. It's as beautiful as the model herself."

Greta blinked in surprise and blushed brightly before shaking her head. "No. It's too beautiful for our trade. You must allow me to make something else for you or pay you."

"Signora, no." Ciro shook his head firmly. "It was a fair trade. You likely spent more time on the sleeves than I did on the cammeo."

There was a loud clatter across the workshop as Seppe dropped a tray of corallo balls. Ciro watched in dismay as the balls scattered to all corners of the workshop floor.

"Sorry, Ciro. I'll pick them up! Sorry, sorry."

Ciro sighed. Perhaps he really ought to apply for an apprentice. He wasn't getting any younger, and Seppe ... well, Seppe wasn't even a Gioielliere to begin with.

"Signora, please excuse me. If we don't pick them up now, we'll lose some of them and I don't want you slipping on any stray corallo balls. Seppe, get the tray."

Ciro slowly knelt down only to realise Greta was already on her knees, effortlessly finding and picking up corallo balls. He thought to ask her not to, but she seemed stubborn and he was grateful for the help. Between the three of them, it took a surprisingly short amount of time to gather them all up. Greta had insisted she be the one to crawl under the workstations as she was by far the youngest and best suited to the task.

"Do you only make necklaces with these?" she asked, holding up the last corallo ball and studying it carefully.

"No." Ciro shook his head. "Some are used in brooches, others in earrings."

Greta dropped the corallo ball in the wooden tray with the rest of them. She had a spark in her eyes that Ciro mistrusted.

"Signora, if you're getting any strange ideas, I'll stop you now. We have a Gioiellieri Guild meeting tomorrow morning to discuss the Guild Ball and, I can assure you, I'll be too busy with those works to bend my mind to anything else."

Greta's eyebrows shot up at his words. "I wasn't going to make more work for you. I wanted to know if anyone has used them with clothing, as regular beads."

Ciro looked over at Seppe who only shrugged.

"Not that I know of, Signora."

"Well then, could I persuade you to let me purchase one hundred of them?"

"One hundred?" Ciro asked, confused by the turn of events. "You ... want to purchase one hundred corallo balls, by themselves, without a setting?"

Greta smiled broadly. "Yes, please. In different sizes if you have them."

Behind him, Seppe found an empty box and began counting out a selection of corallo balls.

"Signora, I don't mean to be rude, but they would still be almost as expensive as the necklaces you didn't want to purchase for your apprentices."

"Oh, yes," Greta said with a smile. "I can't thank you enough for the pendants for my girls. They love them so much they wear them every day."

Ciro shook his head. "Signora, are you certain about this?"

"Quite certain."

Greta opened her coin pouch and pulled out two gold coins. When Ciro did not move to take them, she put them on his workbench and went to watch Seppe as he continued counting out corallo balls.

Ciro hesitated a moment but tucked the gold coins in his own coin pouch. It was an odd trade. Even other Corallini didn't buy corallo balls from him, each preferring to make their own, as they should.

When Seppe was finished, he tied a piece of twine around the box to secure it. Greta took the box with a large smile.

"If these work out well, may I count on you for more corallo balls?"

Ciro's eyebrows shot up. "Signora, I don't think you understand how we obtain corallo. I cannot simply buy as much as I like – I can only use what the sea gives me, and she does not guarantee a steady supply."

"Very well. However, your store and your skills have impressed me." She grinned at him with a twinkle in her eye. "I don't know if I'll be able to keep away, even if you can't promise a *steady supply* of the corallo balls."

Ciro bobbed his head, bemused by this lady, and walked her to the door. She left with both boxes of treasures safely tucked into her pockets.

"That was a nice little exchange," Seppe said from his corner of the workshop.

"It would help us if she keeps buying corallo balls."

"True," Ciro replied, walking over to Seppe, "but I really will have a lot of work after tomorrow. Every Gioielliere will be expected to create Parting Gifts for the Guild Ball and, depending on how many they require, I may have little time for anything else."

Seppe patted his back. "You know I'm always here to help. You've taught me every part of the process for the corallo necklaces aside from the metalwork. I'm sure I can keep up with Signora Sarta's demands."

Ciro smiled at his companion's confidence and willingness to help. "You're right, Seppe. What would I do without you?"

Seppe shrugged. "Die from lack of coffee? Speaking of. I'm going to make another pot."

Chapter 2 – Ramedi 24 Inventrici 230 Years After Implosion

The Gioiellieri Guild Hall was one of the oldest in Tor'Esint. It was also one of the smallest. The Hall of Great Works did not need to house such large items as many of the other Guild Halls.

Ciro loved looking at the wonderful pieces on display every time he came here. It should have bored him, seeing the same pieces over and over again, but every time it instead made him marvel at the techniques people had taught themselves over time. Being a Corallino meant that he did not generally make the same types of jewellery other Gioiellieri made so his skills were a little different.

True, he still worked with metal, making necklaces, earrings, bracelets and brooches, even the occasional hair pin, but those items were different to other Gioiellieri who would make the majority of their items from the metals themselves. On occasion, they might use gemstones in some of their creations, but even then, it was different to using corallo.

Ciro took a seat in the Great Hall along with every other Gioielliere in Tor'Esint. Matteo and his sister, Lidia, came to sit beside him. Ciro appreciated the company. They were a nice young set of Gioiellieri who got along well enough to set up a workshop together. Both were on their Silver Guild Mark and had been for a few years now. They insisted on submitting their Great Works together, which meant they had to be worthy of a combined upscaling of Guild status.

"Did we miss anything?" Lidia asked as she shuffled closer to them.

Ciro shook his head. "They're still waiting for everyone."

"I don't know why they don't just run these at the end of the day's trading like every other Guild," Matteo complained.

Lidia hushed him quickly. Criticisms of one's Guild could cause any number of complications. Ciro was always careful to mind his own words. There were too many Gioiellieri who thought the Corallini belonged in the Artiste Guild rather than this Guild – there was so much sketching and sculpting involved in creating cammei and corallo statues. If they ever managed to get the Tor'Esint Amministratori to agree with them, Ciro would find himself either without Guild status at all or reduced to a Copper Artiste Guild Mark. It was a precarious situation for him and the other Corallini but there was nothing they could do about it. So he played by all the rules of his Guild – even abiding by ones his fellow Gioiellieri thought were ridiculous.

"May I have everyone's attention please!" Yvette's loud voice rose over the chatter. The room quieted. "Thank you. Now, as you all know, it's three months until the Guild Ball. We need to discuss and divide the work for Parting Gifts. So far, we have a total of four hundred attendees with a potential maximum of five hundred, not including our own members.

"Our Guild currently boasts thirty-five Gioiellieri, meaning you each have more than ten Parting Gifts to create. I would encourage everyone to create fifteen Parting Gifts, so that we don't run short. Play to your strengths and don't create anything worth more than two electrums each, for you will not be reimbursed more than that from the Guild. Please remember the Gioiellieri Maestri will decide how much each creation is worth, so do not attempt to swindle them."

A murmur went through the crowd. The Gioiellieri Maestri were well known for taking only the material into account and a fraction of the hours of work involved in each creation. Ciro kept his mouth shut. The materials for the cammei he created were not very expensive, but the Maestri were often happy to pay him a premium as he was the best Corallino in Tor'Esint. They had yet to realise that it only took him a day to create a cammeo, especially at this point in his career. When he was younger, and honing his carving skills, it would have taken him a week for each one.

"To ease the financial burden of creating the Parting Gifts, you may bring your creations to the Guild Hall each Mercatodi for reimbursement. They will then be stored in the vaults until the Guild Ball. If anyone requires any materials they cannot source themselves, please remain behind to speak with the Guild Amministratori. Anyone who would like to be more involved in the organisation of the Guild Ball is also requested to remain behind. Lastly, we ask the Corallini to remain behind. We have a special project for you to work on. That's all. Thank you for your time."

Ciro sat patiently while most of the Gioiellieri rose to leave.

"Do you want us to stay?" Matteo asked, leaning towards him.

Ciro shook his head. "You two go on. I'll meet you tomorrow night for dinner."

The Guild Hall quickly emptied until just the Corallini were left with Yvette. Ciro nodded amiably to them. There had been so many more of them when he'd first been apprenticed. Maestro Enrico had been one of eleven Corallini in his day. Now, there were only four of them – none of whom had any apprentices – and all at least in their fifth decade. Theirs was a dying art which would soon be dead if they didn't do something about it.

"Thank you all for staying," Yvette said, sitting amongst them. "I know the four of you don't usually work together, but I'm hoping you can make an exception for this. Well, unless you all agree that just one of you should work on it."

"Yvette, we're all getting on in years. Just tell us what you want."

That was Simone for you. He never minced words. His carvings lacked as much imagination as his life lacked spark. Yvette smiled thinly.

"We've come into possession of a rather large piece of corallo and would like it carved in time for the Guild Ball. It's to be the centrepiece of the Parting Gift table."

Ciro swallowed. "How large?" he asked, mouth suddenly dry.

"It's fourteen pollici by nine pollici," she replied, watching their reactions.

Ciro let out a low whistle, thinking back to the corallo trunk he used to study in Tor'Dumere. "I've never seen a piece so large in Tor'Esint."

"None of us have," Anna replied. "And *you've* seen the biggest of all of us. Don't think we don't know that the marinai all save their best pieces for you!"

Ciro raised his eyebrows at that but didn't reply.

"So, you want us to work together on it?" Simone asked. "Four sets of hands on the one piece won't work. We all have different styles. It will look horrible. Just pick one of us to make it."

"Speak for yourself!" Anna retorted hotly. "We all know she'll only pick Ciro if you force her hand and I, for one, would like to be part of this, even if I have to amend my style to match his."

"So would I," Sabrina added in her soft voice.

Yvette looked over to Simone. "Well, what's it to be? Do you want to work with the others, or are you happy to let them work without you?"

"Do we all still need to make fifteen Parting Gifts if we work together?"

"Of course." Yvette stared at him, unapologetic.

"Then no." Simone stood. "I don't have time to waste on this. Presumably, the Maestri won't even reimburse us for our time on this because they're providing the material."

There was no response. Simone waved a dismissive hand at them and walked away.

Ciro couldn't believe the man's stupidity. Who cared if the Maestri wouldn't reimburse them? This was their chance to create a true masterpiece. A treasure of epic proportions. It would live in the Hall of Great Works forever.

"Yvette, tell us what we need to know," Ciro broke the silence. "Where is this piece? Where will we work on it? Are there any guidelines we need to adhere to?"

Yvette waited until Simone had left the Great Hall before speaking.

"It's in the vault right now, but I'm not naive enough to think the three of you can work on it there. Which of you has the biggest workshop?"

Ciro exchanged glances with Anna and Sabrina. He was by far the oldest of the three of them but also had the smallest workshop.

"It doesn't matter which workshop is the biggest," Sabrina told her. "We all know Ciro's the best Corallino and his workshop will have the best tools for us. Not to mention if we have to wait for him to walk to one of our workshops every day, we won't get much work done."

Yvette pursed her lips but, when Anna nodded her agreement, she only sighed.

"Very well then, Ciro, I'll organise to have the piece of corallo moved to your workshop. I expect you to take great care with it. No one is to see it until the Guild Ball. There are no other guidelines."

Ciro rubbed the stubble on his cheek. "Keeping it hidden will be difficult, no matter whose workshop we use. Unless you have movable partitions for us to hide it behind."

Yvette frowned. "I'll arrange something. Make sure you clear space for it, Ciro. I'll organise for the piece to be transported to your workshop tomorrow. Please don't make me regret this decision."

Ciro patted her hand. "Yvette, when have any of us ever let you down? I've helped host six Guild Balls in my time. Anna and Sabrina have helped host at least four of those. We know what we're doing, and we know how important it is. We won't let you down."

Yvette nodded firmly then left the three of them.

"Now, signore, if you'll be so good, perhaps you can accompany me to my workshop and we can decide on a good space together?"

Anna and Sabrina shook their heads and laughed.

"Come on, vecchietto, let's go before the sun sets," Anna said with a laugh.

Ciro stood and tilted his chin up. "Who're you calling vecchietto? I'm not even twenty years older than you. Careful, or I might start calling you vecchietta and then where would we be?"

Anna opened her mouth to protest, but Sabrina stood between them.

"Let's not fight about our age," she said firmly. "Let's just go before they throw us out."

***

By the time they reached Ciro's workshop, Loredana and Tania had already been and gone. As he suspected, they'd managed to twist Seppe's arm to make them hot chocolate. He was still sorting through the collection of treasures they'd found along the beach.

"Seppe, time for coffee," Ciro said, disturbing him from his work.

"Good morning, Giuseppe," Sabrina said. "One sugar for me, please."

Anna nodded her head at Seppe. "Same for me."

Seppe quickly disappeared into the kitchen, leaving the small treasure trove in the back corner. Ciro helped the ladies out of their coats and hung them on the coat rack by the door. With the three of them in the workshop, there wasn't much room to move.

"Sabrina, I appreciate your concern for my wellbeing, but I'm not certain we can all work here."

Sabrina looked around the workshop thoughtfully.

"What are you planning on making for Parting Gifts?" she asked.

"Cammei brooches," Ciro answered with a shrug. "They're the easiest and quickest for me."

Sabrina walked over to his favourite workstation, where two thick wooden pegs were leaning comfortably in their nooks, both with cammei attached to them with wax.

"So you'll spend most of your time here, yes?"

Ciro nodded.

"Then we clear a space in the corner opposite the door to work together. Do any of your benches move?"

"No," Anna shook her head and pointed to the long bench along the wall opposite the window. "We just clear that end and work there."

"Anna, we won't all fit there," Ciro pointed out.

"I know that, vecchietto, but we can work on it one at a time. It'll be too difficult any other way. Rina and I can alternate coming over and you can work on it whenever we're not here. That gives us each two days in a row to work on our Parting Gifts."

Ciro raised his eyebrows at her tone, but did not disagree. It was a good idea.

"Sabrina, are you happy with that arrangement?" he asked as Seppe brought out a small tray with four coffee cups and handed them out to everyone.

The youngest Corallina nodded eagerly, took her cup and barely blew on it before drinking down the entire thing. Ciro blinked in surprise. He would never understand how some people didn't burn themselves drinking coffee that way.

"Shall we come back tomorrow afternoon, then, to have a look at the piece and decide how to carve it?" Sabrina asked.

"Yes. Now let's get back to our workshops. I detest these ridiculous Guild meetings at the beginning of the day," answered Anna before Ciro could open his mouth. She drained her coffee and placed the cup back on the tray. "Thank you, Giuseppe."

The ladies left before Ciro had managed more than two sips of his coffee. He stared after them for a moment, drained by their bustling about, then sat down at his workstation to enjoy the rest of his coffee in peace.

Chapter 3 – Argentodi 25 Inventrici 230 Years After Implosion

True to her word, early that morning, Yvette blustered into Ciro's workshop with a group of men. Two of them brought in the large piece of corallo, covered with a canvas cloth. Another two brought in a tall, three panel wooden partition, painted with a lovely view of Tor'Esint from the sea.

"Where do you want it?" Yvette asked, standing out of the way of her workers.

Ciro pointed to the clear end of the long workbench and stayed where he was until the men had finished setting everything up so that the screen hid the corallo from view. Yvette looked at it critically from all angles.

"Yes, that should do nicely. That will be all, signori. Thank you."

The four men bobbed their heads at her and left without a word to, or even a glance at, Ciro.

"May I look at it?" Ciro asked, walking behind the screen.

Yvette followed him and drew off the canvas. Ciro stared at the largest piece of corallo he had ever seen since leaving Tor'Dumere. It was indeed the height and length that Yvette had indicated, and as wide as Ciro's upper arm. It had a pockmarked exterior, as all corallo did when it came from the sea, but with a little work, that roughness would smooth away to reveal a flawless trunk.

"Where did you find this?" he asked, running a hand over it in delight.

It wasn't as vivid a red as the corallo branches he usually worked with, but the lighter shade did not detract from its beauty. From experience, Ciro knew the colour would lighten down to white at the centre of the piece. It was one of the things that made carving larger pieces of corallo both a challenge and a joy. If you understood the piece, you could create magnificent artworks. If not, you would waste the piece by creating something mediocre, not worthy of the red treasure.

"In the bay, of course," Yvette deflected. "Now, have you made arrangements with Anna and Sabrina? I don't want to hear that any of you have been talking about this with your customers."

Ciro stared at her until she looked away.

The spindle came to life in the workshop. Seppe was busying himself drilling holes in corallo branches. The sound of each machine was so familiar to Ciro, he didn't need to look to know which one was being used. Yvette, however, peered around the screen.

"Who's that?" she asked. "You don't have an apprentice, and he's too old even if you did."

Ciro shrugged. "It's Seppe. Giuseppe di Antonio."

"What's he doing here?" she persisted in hushed tones.

"He lives here, Yvette. Has done for years. We grew up together in Tor'Dumere."

"This hasn't been approved by the Guild," Yvette said, her manner becoming officious.

"What's to approve?" Ciro asked. "I'm not teaching him to be a Gioielliere or Corallino."

Yvette paused. "Do you mean to tell me he's been living here and working for you all these years like a *shop boy* and not registered on our Guild files?"

Ciro was glad the drilling was loud enough to mask her words. "Seppe is not a shop boy any more than any other family member of any other Guild member. Do you mean to tell me all household members need to be approved by the Guild when they have nothing to do with that Guild?"

"Of course not," Yvette snapped. "But *he* isn't registered as part of your family or your household, is he? And you've got him working here! It's reckless of both of you, especially with the smoking edicts the Mercantili have organised. They could try to convince the Maestri to strip your Guild Marks for that!"

Ciro felt his face go red with his rising anger. In his younger days, he would have shouted at the Guild Amministratrice. Instead, he spoke to her in a steady voice.

"Giuseppe di Antonio is my best friend – my most loyal and trusted *companion*. He has been for the better part of forty years. I do not need *your* permission, or anyone else's to count him as part of my family – my household. Understand?

"In all that time, he's been working with me. No one has batted an eyelid until *you* agreed to bring a corallo trunk and asked me to keep it secret."

Yvette stared at him lips pursed, shook her head and left without another word. Ciro refused to hide his relationship with Seppe from the world. That didn't mean he flaunted it either. Their relationship simply existed and that was all there was to it. They'd never wanted or needed a commitment ceremony to call themselves companions. Why should the Guild care about that?

He took a moment to calm himself before joining Seppe at the spindle. At his approach, the Seppe stopped working the pedal and the drill slowed to a halt.

"I didn't mean to disturb you," Seppe said, frowning. "Your guest didn't seem too happy to see me. Should I have waited until she left?"

"No," Ciro said firmly. "You were helping me, as you do every day. You didn't do anything wrong."

Seppe raised his eyebrows uncertainly. "Do you want me to thread these branches when I'm done drilling?"

Ciro shook his head and thought for a moment. "Seppe, does it bother you that you do all this work and don't get to use Corallino as your surname?"

For a long moment, Seppe was silent. "Does it bother *you*?"

"I'm ashamed to say I've never thought about it before," Ciro replied heavily. "I *should* have thought about it. When you first came to Tor'Esint, I should have asked you to join the Guild then."

Seppe shook his head. "I was already twenty-nine by then. I don't think your Guild would have let me become an apprentice. Do you?"

"I suppose not," Ciro replied. "But still."

"But nothing, Ciro." Seppe squeezed his hand gently. "I don't care what name I have, or what anyone thinks of me, as long as I have you."

Ciro softened at those words. He covered Seppe's hand with his other one and kissed him. "You'll always have me."

***

Just after trading, Anna and Sabrina arrived. Neither of them had an apprentice, though Sabrina had a companion and a grown family. Her children had declined to join the Gioiellieri Guild – Flavio choosing the Alchimisti Guild and Grazia favouring the Sarti Guild. It still meant her companion was around to keep the workshop open in her absence. Anna was not so fortunate.

"Let's see it then," Anna said, walking behind the screen without invitation.

Sabrina joined her and drew in a sharp breath. "It's marvellous! Just think of all the things we could do with it."

Ciro locked the door to his workshop and joined them behind the screen with his sketchbook and a pencil. Anna moved the large piece of corallo, looking at it from all angles.

"How will we know where the colour will change?" she asked. "That will make all the difference to what we carve, and how we carve it."

Both Corallini looked at him expectantly.

"Well, we could choose a small section to carve with the Gioiellieri Guild Mark. You know, leaving the Mark itself untouched but carving the inner sections down to the white, so we can see what happens."

The ladies looked at one another. Something passed between them and then they nodded.

"Yes, let's do that then. Ciro, pass me your pencil."

Ciro did as he was told. Anna might be almost twenty years his junior, but she was as bossy as an older sister. With the pencil, Anna sketched the Guild Mark in an unobtrusive section near the base of the corallo.

"Larger," Sabrina said. "If we're going to pay homage to our Guild, people may as well see it."

Anna smudged the lead with her fingers and re-drew the Guild Mark, larger than before. Both ladies then turned to look at him.

"Yes?" he asked, uncertain of the sudden attention on him.

"Let's face it, Ciro," Anna said, "You're the best able of the three of us to carve this quickly so we can see what happens with the colour.

Ciro shook his head. "I'm not going to rush myself with this beauty."

Anna opened her mouth angrily, but Sabrina laid a hand on Anna's arm to quieten her.

"Is there another way to see the colour, other than carving this Guild Mark?"

Ciro stared at the corallo thoughtfully. "Honestly, I don't think so. But I don't want to rush into this. Why don't we each come up with some ideas for carving it, no matter what the colour. Then when we begin, we'll see what we have to work with."

"Paper, then," Anna said, holding out her hand. "And a pencil each."

Ciro tore two sheets of paper from his sketchbook and handed one to each of the ladies. Seppe, always so helpful, brought over the small wooden box in which Ciro kept all his sketching materials.

Anna took her sheet from Ciro and sat down to begin. Sabrina did likewise, both of them behind the screen. Ciro stood and studied the piece of corallo. It looked fluid, like the branch of a tree floating in the rippling sea. His hand flew across the page, lines forming the picture in his mind of Sentigura Caldera smoking away in the middle of the sea, with all the fishing boats of Beltigura floating around it. He detailed the waves in the sea, the planks of wood on the boats, the plumes of smoke rising from the caldera.

On the next page, Ciro sketched out the view of Tor'Esint from the sea, the houses rising up to the ridge. It would be more detailed and difficult to get right. People would need to be forgiving if the view wasn't an exact replica. But they wouldn't be, he thought to himself.

In the space left on that page, Ciro began sketching away mindlessly, not thinking of the piece of corallo. He was best at people, so why not draw them. Before he'd realised what he was doing, he'd drawn the figure of a lady standing with a hand to her chest, smiling down at a rose being held out to her by a child, who in turn was holding the hand of a younger child. He looked at it carefully and recognised Serafina as the lady with Loredana and Tania as the children. He thought it was the most beautiful thing he'd ever done, but shook his head, knowing Yvette would not be pleased to know he had used his own family as the models.

Seppe came up behind him and looked at the sketch. "It matches the shape quite well."

"These others would be better," Ciro replied, pointing to the two landscapes, but Seppe shook his head.

"No, they look like you're trying too hard to please people. I never like your work when you do that. *This* one is much better."

Sabrina craned her neck to see the sketch. Ciro held it out for her to take.

"Giuseppe's right," she said. "It matches the shape and it's a beautiful image."

Ciro coughed. "Yes, well, what have the two of you drawn?"

Sabrina held out her sheet for all to see. It was a fishing boat with workers pulling in a net of fish. It would require a steady hand and a fine eye for detail to get it right.

"That's lovely," Seppe said. "Very true to Tor'Esint. After all, where would we be without our marinai?"

"In a city that stinks less of fish," Anna replied sourly.

"What have *you* drawn then?" Sabrina asked harshly.

Anna turned her page around for all to see. It was also a boat, but one held aloft from the waves by a sea monster. The detail on it was exquisite.

"That's remarkable," Ciro stated, slightly annoyed that such a sour lady could draw so well, even if it was a gruesome image.

"It *is* remarkable," agreed Sabrina, "but won't people think we're bringing bad luck to our marinai? I don't want to be punished for other people's superstitions."

Anna scowled and threw her pencil on the workbench. "Why should I care what other people think?"

"Leave the sketches with me," Ciro told them. "I'll take a walk down to the docks tomorrow morning to ask the marinai what they think of all the ideas. Now, Seppe and I are expected out to dinner with Matteo and Lidia, so if you'll excuse me, I need to get ready."

"What do two young pups like them see in a vecchietto like you?" Anna asked snidely.

"I don't know. Perhaps they wish to learn from my long years, or perhaps they're happy to dine with anyone who isn't a lavalump like you."

It was a cruel thing to say, and he instantly regretted it, but before he could make amends for his words, Anna had grabbed her coat and departed the workshop in a flurry of seething fury.

Sabrina looked from the door to Ciro with such disappointment on her face.

"I know," he said in a defeated tone. "That was too cruel. I don't know why Anna always brings out the worst in me."

Ciro did not miss the look which passed between Sabrina and Seppe, but neither of them seemed willing to comment.

"What do you two know that I don't?" he asked suspiciously.

Seppe shook his head. "Nothing you can do anything about. Now, why don't we try out those new shirts Greta Sarta made for us?"

Sabrina winked at Seppe and bid them both a good evening. Ciro couldn't help feeling like there was something he was missing, but there was little time to dwell on it. He did, after all, have evening plans with Matteo and Lidia and he enjoyed those evenings immensely.

***

A short while later, Ciro found himself walking down an alley with Seppe. It was so narrow they couldn't comfortably walk side by side between the crates along the walls. Above them, ropes were strung between windows where, during the day, washing would be hung up to dry. This quarter of Tor'Esint was not as opulent as other quarters. Here, few apartments had yards, and certainly not ones large enough to hang washing. The few yards that existed were planted with fruit trees or vegetable plots, to help keep the residents fed.

However, what it lacked in riches, it made up for in character. A few months ago, Lidia had found a hidden street with ristoranti all along it. You could barely tell what they were from a distance, but walking along the street, Ciro's senses were seduced by yeast-infused pizza dough, rich tomato sauces and melting mozzarella. His mouth watered as they found their way to Pizzeria di Marco.

"Ah, Signore Corallino, Signore Giuseppe!" A young man called out from the doorway. "Your party is seated and waiting for you. Please, let me show you the way."

Ciro walked ahead of Seppe, their fingers gently entwined, making sure he stayed close. Matteo and Lidia rose as they approached, kissing them both on the cheek in greeting.

"We took the liberty of starting off with a marinara and a potato pizza," Matteo told them as they sat. "They're quick here – we can order more soon."

Ciro hailed a waiter and ordered drinks. The waiter soon returned with two bottles. He poured them each a glass of wine along with a glass of lemon-infused water. These dinners with his friends were among the few occasions that Ciro allowed himself the luxury of eating and drinking whatever he liked. He was not so lucky as some Gioiellieri to have all the riches he could want, but a nice dinner every now and then was worth the expense.

"So, tell me, friends, have you decided on what to make for your Parting Gifts?" Ciro asked. The sound of the street musicians made it easy to talk in here without being overheard by other tables. It was one of the reasons Ciro so liked dining on this street.

Lidia glanced at Matteo and grinned. "I've decided to make earrings with small gems."

"A good choice." Ciro nodded. "And you, Matteo?"

"I wanted to make rings," Matteo replied, "but Lidia pointed out it would be too difficult to give them as gifts because we won't know the size of people's fingers."

"She's right," Seppe replied. "What about a cravat pin or cufflinks? There will be men at the Guild Ball as well. They'll need something too."

"That's right. You could even make necklaces or bracelets to match Lidia's earrings, that way couples can match with each other."

Matteo shook his head. "We can't guarantee who'll get which Parting Gifts. I don't want to make a match for something that may never be worn together."

The marinara and potato pizze were placed on the table and all conversation ceased as everyone took a quarter slice, folded it in half and began to eat. Ciro took a marinara first. The thick tomato sauce sprinkled with oregano, garlic and salt was one of his favourites. After devouring the slice, he took a mouthful of lemon-infused water to cleanse his palate. Next, he took the last remaining slice of the potato pizza, sprinkled only with rosemary and salt. Pizzeria di Marco made this better than most. He loved the slices of potato, just thick enough to provide a punch of flavour, but thin enough not to overpower the dish.

"What about you?" Lidia asked, after they'd ordered two Tor'Esint specials – tomato sauce, thin mozzarella slices, basil and garlic. "Have you decided what to make? Or do you not need to make anything with the special project Yvette had for you?"

Ciro laughed at her indelicate way of asking. "I can't tell you what the project is, Lidia. But I do still need to create Parting Gifts. I'm going to make cammeo brooches. I have all the materials I need, and they won't take me too long."

Seppe coughed as Matteo and Lidia's eyebrows shot up. Ciro realised his error.

"Well, what can I say? I've been making cammei for more than half my life. Let's just not tell the Guild Maestri how quickly I can carve them now."

Lidia tilted her head closer. "And how quickly is that exactly?"

"A day or two if I've nothing else to do." Ciro shrugged. "Mind, that's just for the carving. That doesn't include the actual gioielliere work. But if I have them all lined up and ready to go, it's easier to do them all together."

Matteo's eyes bulged. He looked at his sister who was equally surprised.

"You'll both get there," Seppe told them. "Ciro wasn't so fast as all that when he was younger. In fact, I remember more than one customer complaining when he didn't have their cammeo ready on time. My coffee was all that placated them. That's all I'm saying."

Ciro laughed at the memory. "Yes, Seppe, your coffee saved my business. What would I ever have done without you?"

The next round of pizze arrived and, once again, all conversation ceased. Ciro savoured his slices with small bites. The flavours were so simple and worked well together. When he was done, he washed down the final bite with a sip of wine.

"Now, tell me, what's happened since our last dinner? I want to know everything."

A large smile spread across Lidia's face, though she bit her lip to try to hide it. Matteo looked at her questioningly. She nodded.

"We're going to apply for an apprentice," Matteo told him.

Ciro clapped his hands together and held them to his chest. "Teo, Dia, That's wonderful news! I'm so pleased for you. Will you apply for one each?"

"Really, we just want one between us, but if the Maestri don't allow it, then we'll consider taking two. It might even come in handy to have one each."

Ciro nodded in agreement. Though he'd never had an apprentice himself, he could see how sharing one could cause friction within the household.

"Do you think you'll ever get one, Ciro?" Lidia asked.

"I don't see how I could," Ciro answered. "My little house only has one bedroom above the workshop. Where would an apprentice sleep?"

"In the workshop?" Matteo suggested.

"There's barely room to walk, let alone lie down to sleep." Ciro shook his head. "No, I don't see how I could."

"Couldn't you move to a larger workshop?" Matteo asked, desperately trying to find a way for Ciro to pass on his skills to someone.

"Teo, at my time of life, moving workshops is the last thing I want to do."

"What about Loredana?" Seppe suggested quietly. "She's nearly old enough now. I'm sure Serafina would agree to the girl sleeping at home during her apprenticeship."

"Loredana?" Ciro asked, baffled. "I don't think she'd be interested in spending her days with a vecchietto like me."

"Isn't she your oldest niece?" Lidia asked. Ciro nodded. "Ciro, I've heard the way you speak about her. If she adores you the same way, she'd love to work with you. You could at least offer her the option. It would be a terrible shame not to pass your skills on."

Ciro did not answer but sipped his wine until his glass was empty. He did not want them to know how tempting an option it was. By the sideways glances Seppe threw his way, Ciro knew he wasn't fooled.

***

As they walked home later that night, Ciro felt the odd tension in the air.

"Seppe, for Caldera's sake, what is it?"

Seppe was quiet for a moment longer. "You asked me earlier today if it bothered me not to be a Corallino. Well, now I'm asking you, does it bother you not to ever have had an apprentice because I take up space in your house?"

"Our house," Ciro said firmly. Seppe had never expressed any opinion on it one way or the other before, but from his question, it was clear that it had been on his mind for years. Ciro rented their house – his workshop – from the Gioiellieri Guild, so technically it was his alone. He had just always hoped Seppe didn't look at it that way. "It's *our* house. And no, it doesn't bother me. I might ask Loredana, I might not, but even if I do, she'll likely refuse."

"She won't refuse, Ciro. Especially if you promise to offer Tania an apprenticeship when she comes of age."

Ciro shook his head and continued walking. It was too tempting. He didn't want the art of the Corallini to die out with his generation. And to have his own family follow in his footsteps was almost more than he could bear. It would make him so very proud, but he couldn't let himself think like that when it would never happen. Even if Loredana was willing, Serafina would see it as an act of charity and refuse to allow it.

Chapter 4 – Legaramedi 26 Inventrici 230 Years After Implosion

Ciro found himself on the docks again, walking along with more purpose than usual. The lovely pendant he'd created for Corrado's *friend* sat in a little white box, tied up with twine. He really ought to pay the sailor for the rock. It would provide enough material for a decent number of pendants, earrings, brooches, and perhaps even rings.

The large paddle sailboat was there, in its usual spot. When Corrado returned from his recent trip with two Inventrici and an Alchimista, the Mercantili Amministratori had stripped the interior, looking for contraband items but found nothing. The identity of the Guild members had remained a mystery to everyone. Even Ciro hadn't managed to get Corrado to talk.

The only benefit of that trip, as far as Ciro could see, was that the ash-sucking marinaio Corrado had hired to help him for months beforehand had not returned with him. No one had asked why. No one liked him well enough to care. The new marinaio, Stuarto, seemed a decent enough man.

Ciro paused at the boat. Corrado was hanging over the side by a rope, chisel in his other hand, scraping barnacles off the wood. Stuarto was holding the rope steady.

"Good morning, Corrado," Ciro called out. "I have something for you."

Stuarto let slip the rope to wave a greeting. Corrado's yelp was cut short by a loud splash.

"Not again!" Stuarto groaned as he leaned over the side of the boat and hauled a soaking Corrado onto the deck. "Sorry, Corrado, sorry!"

"Stuarto, if I hadn't promised your mamma I'd keep you for at least a year, you'd already be back in their shop."

Ciro wiped the smile off his face as Corrado towelled his face dry.

"Ciro, I haven't got any shells for you, no corallo either," Corrado told him.

Ciro shrugged. "I have something for you though."

He held out the small white box. Corrado quickly dried his hands and threw the towel at a red-faced Stuarto. He took the box from Ciro and opened it reverently. The spark that lit his eyes was well worth the effort.

"It's perfect," Corrado said with a smile. "I like that you left it rough around the edges."

Stuarto laughed. "Matches her temper, don't it?"

Corrado turned and glared at him. "Take yer foot outta yer mouth and see to the rest of those barnacles."

Stuarto bobbed his head in apology and went to do his bidding. Ciro couldn't help but feel sorry for the young man. His heart was clearly in the right place, if he could only keep his mouth shut.

"Thanks, Ciro. Will the rest of the rock pay for this?"

Ciro nodded and took the sketches from the day before from his pocket. "Tell me, what do you think of these?"

Corrado took the sheets and leafed through them slowly, taking in all the details.

"They're all good, but I like the sea monster, and the woman with the flower best. What're they for?"

"Oh, just a little something I'm working on," Ciro told him. "You don't think the sea monster will be seen as a bad omen then?"

"Nah, marinai'll love it."

Corrado handed the pages back to Ciro, who folded them and hid them safely in his pocket.

"Thank you, Corrado."

He shook the marinaio's hand and began the long walk back along the docks to the black pebble beach where his nieces would be collecting corallo for him.

When he arrived at their usual meeting place, the girls were already there and waiting with overturned baskets of corallo branches. Tania was helping Loredana sort the branches into piles according to their sizes. He watched them for a short while, unobserved himself.

Loredana was ten years old now. The minimum age for apprenticeships was thirteen, though he'd heard of circumstances where a younger age was acceptable within families. In Tor'Dumere, it had been a common practice. All children of a Guild household began an unofficial apprenticeship when they were capable of doing anything useful in the workshop.

It would really all come down to Loredana and the Gioiellieri Guild Maestri.

Loredana looked up as he approached them. She smiled at him from where she was crouched, tucking a strand of her light brown hair behind her ear.

"Good morning, Zio," she said. "We're just sorting them for you."

"What good little workers you two are."

Ciro smiled down at them. He wanted to say more – to ask her to be his apprentice – but he couldn't bear the thought of her refusal. Loredana, always so perceptive, noticed something amiss. She wrapped an arm around her sister's shoulder, whispered something in her ear and then took Ciro by the hand and walked him out of earshot.

"What's wrong?" she asked. Ciro shook his head. Loredana put her hands on her hips and glared at him. "Zio, I know when you're worried or sad and you look both today. What's wrong?"

"Reda, tell me, do you like visiting my workshop? Looking at all the things in it?"

She smiled broadly. "Of course! I *love* your workshop. You know, Seppe sometimes lets me help him sort the corallo into sizes. That's why we're doing it here – to help him. I'm good at that."

Ciro nodded. "Hmm, well then, let me ask you this. Have you considered if you might like to join a Guild one day?"

She paused thoughtfully. "It *would* be a good option. Mamma can barely buy us food anymore now that we eat so much, even with her new position in the pasticceria. They've given her an extra two days, but it won't be forever. It's only until Giulia comes back with her baby on her back."

"I see." This was news to Ciro. At least she had extra days for the time being. "And have you given any thought to which Guild you might join?"

"No, not really. But I still have three years until I can even put my name on the waiting lists and then I have to hope someone takes me. Mamma told me not all Maestri are nice." She drew in closer. "I'll tell you a secret. I'm a little bit scared of what would happen if I put my name down and get a horrible Maestro who beats me and doesn't feed me."

Ciro's chest tightened. He drew her in for a long embrace and held her close.

"If you were my apprentice, I'd never let that happen to you, Reda. Never."

Her breath came out in a tremble.

"But you don't take apprentices, Zio. Mamma said so. You've *never* taken one."

"For you," he said, with a kiss to the top of her head, "I would."

She hugged him so tightly he could hardly breathe, and he let her, just to stop his heart from bursting.

"I'll talk to your mamma. If she agrees, I'll apply to the Gioiellieri Guild to let you start earlier because you're my niece. They've been known to agree once in a while."

"Thank you, Zio. Thank you!"

"Reda, I'm finished!" Tania called out. "Zio, can we come for a hot chocolate?"

Ciro pulled away from Loredana. "If your mamma isn't expecting you."

Tania shook her head. "She'll be at the pasticceria until after lunch."

"Come on, then, let's go. If you behave yourselves, Seppe might even let you help him a bit and I might find an extra coin or two for you."

Tania handed one of the baskets to Loredana and the two of them raced ahead to his workshop. He didn't mind lagging behind and Seppe would look after them until he returned.

***

At the end of the day's trading, Anna and Sabrina came past again. The girls had long since left the workshop, taking their happy sounds with them. Ciro found he enjoyed working with such joy in his workshop. Loredana was always mindful and helped in every way she could and even Tania was better behaved in his workshop than her own house.

Ciro disliked the idea of the two of them running about Tor'Esint or staying home alone. When they weren't in his workshop, he had no idea what they did. He couldn't help but wonder what Tania would do if Loredana was apprenticed to him. Surely Serafina wouldn't allow her to remain alone all day, would she? That was something he would need to discuss with her before things went any further.

"Did you ask the marinai then?" Anna asked without preamble.

"I did, and they liked these two."

Ciro set the two sketches Corrado had picked out on the workbench beside the large piece of corallo. He didn't think it necessary to tell them he'd only asked one marinaio.

"I like my sea monster," said Anna. "It matches the shape and it's a good subject matter that everyone can relate to."

"Didn't the marinai think it would be a bad omen?" Sabrina asked, hesitantly.

Ciro shook his head. "No, we can pick whichever one we like. Whichever will be the best option for this piece of corallo."

"I like the girls," Sabrina said. "It's a more pleasant image. The sea monster makes my skin crawl."

"That just means I drew it well." Anna sniffed and stuck her nose up in the air.

Ciro clapped his hands to halt the argument about to happen.

"There's only one way to settle this. I'll make a clay model of each picture so we can see which we like best. If I carve all the details, we'll have a finished model to work from so it doesn't look like three Corallini have worked on it."

He waited for a sharp retort from Anna, but it never came. She and Sabrina readily agreed. Ciro narrowed his eyes suspiciously at Anna.

"Unless you want to make a model of the sea monster and boat yourself while I work on the lady and children?"

Anna shook her head. "I'm not too proud to admit that you're the better sculptor of the two of us. How long will it take you?"

Ciro shook his head. "I'd say at least a week, maybe two."

"Fine then, you let us know when to come back. We'll work on our Parting Gifts until then," Anna told him. "Come, Rina, let's go home.

"You're taking on a lot of the work yourself," Seppe said, once they were alone. "Don't you think they ought to help a little more?"

Ciro sighed heavily. "Seppe, you know how long I've waited for an opportunity like this. If it means I work more on it than the others, so be it. I won't let that stop me from having a hand in it."

Seppe walked over and kissed his forehead. "I know, Ciro. I know. And I'll help all I can to keep the workshop going. I just don't want you getting too tired. You're not as young as you once were."

Ciro grinned at his companion and shook his head. There wasn't anything he could say to that.

Chapter 5 – Riposidi 1 Gioiellieri 230 Years After Implosion

Ciro knocked on Serafina's apartment door just past eleven thirty in the morning, Seppe by his side. He heard the shouts of excitement before the door opened.

"Zio Ciro! Seppe!"

He held his precious package up high as the young girls swarmed them for a hug.

"Girls, let them go before they decide to leave and take the desserts with them," Serafina called out.

They quickly let go, only for Tania to tug them in by their shirts and Loredana to close the door firmly behind them. Ciro grinned at Serafina. She certainly knew which threats to use on her daughters.

He placed the package on the table and kissed all three of them on the cheek. Seppe did likewise.

"It's so good to see you, Zio," Serafina told him, returning the kiss. "I feel like I barely see anyone other than at work these days."

"I wish you'd let me help you," Ciro said quietly, trying not to let the girls overhear. Seppe was trying, unsuccessfully, to keep the girls from peeking into the package.

Serafina gave Ciro an exasperated look. "You already help more than you should. Don't think I haven't noticed all the little jobs you think up to give the girls an extra few coins. It's not that I don't appreciate it, but I don't want them to come to expect it of you. They'll begin to see you as a source of income rather than their Zio. Now, come and sit down. Lunch is almost ready."

Ciro didn't bother replying. There'd be time later for their conversation. For now, he simply wanted to enjoy a meal with his family. He sat down next to Seppe, who'd given up his attempts to keep the contents of the package secret.

"Oooh sfogliatelle *and* cannoli!" Tania squealed in excitement.

"Yes, but remember you may only have one if you eat everything on your plate," Loredana said in a stern voice. "Right, mamma?"

"Yes, Loredana," Serafina said tiredly. "But remember *you* aren't her mamma."

Loredana looked as though she would retort, but Ciro caught her eye and she closed her mouth.

"Why don't you pour a drink for Zio Ciro and Seppe?" Serafina looked pointedly at her eldest daughter. "Tania, put the desserts on the bench and set the table while I finish preparing lunch."

"Yes, mamma," the girls chorused.

Within a few minutes, the table was laid out for lunch with steaming bowls of pesto gnocchi and a glass of water in front of everyone. Ciro dared not ask for anything else to drink for fear Serafina could not afford it. He hated the thought of embarrassing her.

"Buon appetito," Serafina wished them all.

At her word, the girls dug hungrily into their pasta. Seppe was not far behind them – gnocchi was one of his favourites and Serafina knew it. She also knew the two of them rarely had time to make pasta themselves and had taken it upon herself to cook gnocchi with a different sauce every Riposidi. Ciro loved her for that. Unlike the others, Ciro ate his gnocchi one piece at a time, savouring every mouthful.

At the end of lunch, after Tania had presented her empty plate to her mamma, Serafina brought the box of desserts to the table. The sfogliatelle had little pockets of ricotta and semolina. The cannoli were filled with sweetened ricotta mixed with chopped bits of chocolate that spilled out at either end. The girls waited patiently until Ciro and Seppe had both chosen their desserts. Seppe had bought enough of both sweets so that everyone could have one of each.

When everyone was finished, Ciro helped Serafina with the dishes while Seppe played cards with the girls. He waited until the dishes were done before drawing Serafina to one side, as far from the girls as possible in such tight quarters.

"Rafi, will you come for a walk with me?" he asked her quietly. "I need to stretch my legs. Seppe will stay with the girls."

Serafina's eyes darted to the three of them, still playing cards and nodded.

"I suppose some fresh air would be nice," she admitted. "Girls, will you stay here with Seppe? I'm going for a walk with Zio Ciro."

Tania barely paid them any attention, but Loredana glanced up and winked at Ciro. He gave her a quick smile before escorting her mamma out the door and down the dark stairwell.

Out on the street, Ciro offered his arm to Serafina. She took it with a smile, and they walked slowly together. By the time they were halfway around the block, Ciro had finally built up enough courage to speak.

"I want to talk to you about Loredana," he began.

Serafina gripped his arm tightly. "Did she let Tania break something in your workshop? I *told* her not to bring her sister there so often."

"No, nothing of the sort," Ciro said quickly, patting her arm reassuringly. "Your girls are always welcome in my workshop. In fact, that's what I wanted to talk to you about. I know Loredana's still young by conventional standards, but she's a very responsible child and already helps Seppe quite a lot. I ... was hoping you might agree to let me take her as an apprentice."

Serafina missed a step.

"An apprentice? But, Zio, she's only *ten*."

"True," Ciro admitted, "but back in Tor'Dumere, children begin their apprenticeship with their parents even younger than that."

"Zio, I know you're doing everything you can to help me, but *really*. We don't live in Tor'Dumere and Loredana isn't your daughter."

Ciro took a few steps to compose his answer. "Loredana may not be my daughter, but she is my *niece*, which is still family. With your permission, I'd like to petition the Gioiellieri Guild to allow me to take her on as a young apprentice. A normal Gioiellieri apprenticeship lasts five years, but hers would last eight years, to make up for her age.

"I'd only ask for two conditions. One, that she sleeps at your house as I have no room at mine, and I pay her a small amount each week to make up for that. Two, she brings Tania with her any day that you're working. I couldn't bear the thought of leaving the poor child by herself."

Serafina stared at him in silence. Ciro did not try to press her for an answer. He simply kept walking with her by his side.

"You've spoken to her already, haven't you?" she asked finally.

Ciro nodded. There was no point in hiding it.

"Whose idea was it?"

Ciro shrugged. "Does it matter? She's excited about the idea and I can't deny I'm longing to pass on my skills to her. I don't want to be one of the last Corallini."

"What will you do if I refuse?" Serafina asked. "Will you apply for another apprentice?"

Ciro shook his head before he could stop himself. "Serafina, you're the only family I have left. Corallo is in our blood. *Please*, let your daughter learn from me. I promise I'll be a good Maestro. I'll even leave her my workshop when it's time. Her and Tania, if they both join me. What do you say?"

Serafina huffed out a laugh. "What *can* I say?"

"Say yes," Ciro said simply. "I can't promise the Guild will agree to let me take her so young, but I won't bother asking them without your permission."

Serafina pulled on his arm to stop him walking. She leaned over and planted a kiss on his cheek.

"Thank you, Zio, for everything."

Ciro drew in a sharp breath and held it for a moment before whistling it out. "Is that a yes?"

"Yes," she laughed. "Yes."

***

When they returned to the apartment, Loredana jumped out of her chair and ran over to them.

"Did you ask her?"

Ciro nodded. Loredana hopped from one foot to the other as she looked back and forth between them.

"Well?" she pleaded.
Serafina stroked her daughter's hair and kissed the top of the head.
"If the Guild agrees, then so will I."
"Oh, mamma!" Loredana threw her arms around Serafina. "Thank you! I can't believe it! Thank you, so much! You too Zio!"
Ciro patted her back. "Don't thank us yet. We still need the Guild's permission."
"For what?" Tania called out from her seat.
"To let me become Zio Ciro's first apprentice ever!" Loredana squealed excitedly.
Tania frowned and her eyes filled with tears. Serafina hurried to her younger daughter and knelt down in front of her.
"Don't worry, bella. Zio Ciro will let you stay in his workshop with Loredana."
Tania's bottom lip trembled as she looked between Ciro and her mamma. She nodded bravely and sniffed back her tears. Within moments, her dismay was completely forgotten. Tania turned back to Seppe and played another card.

Chapter 6 – Gildadi 2 Gioiellieri 230 Years After Implosion

Ciro dressed himself in his finest clothes, completing the outfit with the new shirt Greta Sarta had made him, and looked at himself in the mirror. Seppe came up behind him and straightened the laces at the edge of his shoulder. Ciro held his hands in front of him and stared at them as they shook.

"Nervous?" Seppe asked, turning Ciro around to hold his hands.

Ciro nodded. "I shouldn't be. Even Matteo and Lidia are applying for apprentices and they're less than half my age."

"Yes, but they aren't asking for family, or for a young child. It's a simpler process."

"What if the Guild says no?" Ciro asked quietly.

"Then you apply for her again when she's thirteen. That wouldn't be ideal, but it's only a few years away."

"What if they say yes?" Ciro swallowed, his mouth dry. "What if I'm a terrible Maestro?"

Seppe laughed and kissed him. "Impossible. I know I'm not your apprentice but, even so, you managed to teach me how to do everything with corallo in just a few short weeks. Imagine how much more easily a child will pick it up."

"But what if she hates it here, if she spends all day every day with me?" Ciro leaned his head against Seppe's forehead. "I don't want her to hate me."

Seppe took him by the shoulders and looked him straight in the eye.

"Ciro, you're more scared the Guild won't allow it than anything else. Don't try to disguise your fears with me. I know you'll be heartbroken if they say no, but you won't know until you ask them. And just remember if they do say no, it's only for a few years until she's thirteen. Loredana can wait and so can you."

Ciro stared into those light brown eyes, which had seen him through all his trials, and nodded.

***

The Gioiellieri Guild Hall was only a few blocks away from Ciro's workshop. He took his time walking there, trying to form his request in his head. As the head Gioiellieri Amministratrice, Yvette was reasonable – most of the time. Her behaviour last Argentodi notwithstanding. Ciro had usually found her not too difficult to deal with though she could be prickly in temper. But this was too important, and he had to get it right.

Ciro walked up the steps to his Guild Hall and along the Hall of Great Works, paying less attention to the displays than usual. Yvette was at her desk, head down, reading forms and signing papers. She looked up at his approach in some surprise.

"What are you doing here?" She paused, before speaking more softly. "Did something happen with the project?"

Ciro shook his head. "No, nothing's the matter at all. I, erm..." He hesitated while Yvette looked at him expectantly. "I'd like to apply for an apprentice."

Yvette's eyebrows rose until they disappeared behind her dark brown fringe. "An apprentice? At *your* age?"

Ciro frowned. "Well, yes. You see, I'd like to take my niece as an apprentice, but she wasn't old enough until now." Ciro paused. "In fact, she still isn't actually of age, but I was hoping you'd make an exception."

Yvette held up a hand and flipped to a different section of her folder. She began to fill out a form.

"Name – Ciro Corallino. Age?" Yvette asked, looking up at him.

"Seventy-one," Ciro replied.

"Your niece's name and age? Is she on the apprentice list?"

"Her name's Loredana di Serafina. She turned ten last Fabbri. She isn't on the apprentice list."

Yvette wrote down the details then put her pen down slowly and looked up at Ciro again.

"You know the minimum age for an apprentice is thirteen years, Ciro. Why are you even asking this?"

Ciro sighed.

"You said it yourself – I'm a vecchietto. I want to pass on my skills and I'd like to pass them on to my family. In Tor'Dumere, children even younger than Loredana are apprenticed within their own families, but only complete their apprenticeships at the same age as other apprentices. I'm requesting the same thing.

"I'd like to take Loredana as my apprentice, but have her apprenticeship last for eight years rather than five. I'd also ask that she live with her mamma during the apprenticeship as I have no wish to take her away from her family so young."

Yvette signalled to another Amministratore to take her place and led Ciro into a small sitting room. She motioned for him to take a seat but paced the room herself.

"Ciro, I know you grew up in Tor'Dumere, and things were different there, but this isn't Tor'Dumere. The rules are stricter here. You *must* know I can't approve your request without first discussing it with the Guild Maestri."

She finally sat down across from him. Ciro looked at her expectantly.

"You want me to ask them *now*?" she asked incredulously.

"I'd appreciate it, yes."

Yvette shook her head and huffed at him. In the end, she stood and left the room, leaving Ciro to his own thoughts. At one point, a younger Amministratrice came to bring him a cup of coffee. Ciro sipped it slowly and sat patiently, waiting for Yvette to return.

Eventually, one of the Guild Maestri, Rosalina, appeared. She was trailed closely by Yvette.

"Ciro Corallino!" Rosalina kissed him on both cheeks. "It's always a pleasure to see you."

"Maestra Rosalina, it's been too long."

Ciro kissed her in return and held her hands fondly. Rosalina had been apprenticed at the same time as him, though with a true Gioielliere. It hadn't taken her long to rise through the ranks to become a Guild Maestra. They rarely spoke these days other than in passing, but only for lack of time.

Rosalina sat beside him and took the paperwork Yvette waved at her.

"Yes, thank you, Yvette. You may return to your other duties. Ciro and I will discuss this matter in private."

Ciro did not miss the irritated look Yvette threw his way before she left the room, but he nodded his head in thanks. He saw no point in rudeness. Only when she'd left the room did he speak.

"Sali, I know this is an unusual request, but I would ask you to at least *consider* it." The words rushed out before he could stop them.

She lay a hand on his arm, instantly quieting him.

"What makes you think I *won't* consider it?" she asked in confusion.

Ciro shrugged.

"Ciro, I think it's a wonderful idea. I don't want the art of corallo to die out with the four of you and you're the first to apply for an apprentice. Your niece, Loredana, would be lucky to have you as her teacher. Is she willing? Is her mamma?"

Ciro's eyes filled, and his vision blurred. The tears ran down his face as he blinked.

"Yes." Ciro coughed, to clear his throat. "Yes, in fact it was Loredana's idea. And Serafina said she'll allow it if you do."

Rosalina nodded and looked at the paperwork. "Now, Yvette tells me you wish for Loredana to remain living at home. Can you provide adequate reasoning for this?"

"There's no room," Ciro said simply. "I have a small workshop and only one bedroom. Besides, she'll miss her mamma and sister too much if she lives with me. I was thinking of giving her a few coppers a week to make up for the fact that I can't provide her board."

Rosalina tapped her pen against the paper a few times before scribbling a note.

"That sounds reasonable. Does Serafina know of your plans?"

Ciro nodded. "I also promised that Tania would be allowed to accompany Loredana to the workshop any day Serafina is working. She's only eight years old. I can't bear the thought of her staying home alone."

"Yes, well, I won't write that," Rosalina told him. "Best not to put too many conditions in this contract. Now, under these circumstances, we'll need both the mamma and child to be present to sign the paperwork. Can you organise that for tomorrow?"

"Tomorrow?" Ciro asked, baffled. "So soon?"

Rosalina smiled gently. "As soon as you can organise it. I believe the sooner Loredana begins her apprenticeship, the better. I'm certain the other Maestri will agree with me."

She stood and opened the door for Ciro.

"We'll be expecting you then. Try to come before trading ends."

Ciro nodded, trying to comprehend the turn of events. He walked through the Guild Hall and all the way home in a daze. He barely paid attention to the customer in the shop – Seppe had the transaction well in hand. Ciro walked straight through to the kitchen and stared at the stove, tightly gripping the edges.

He was still standing there when Seppe walked in.

"Did they refuse?" he asked, laying a hand on Ciro's shoulder.

Ciro released his grip and shook his head slowly.

"Rosalina wants to meet Loredana and Serafina. Tomorrow."

He turned to look at Seppe. Those sharp brown eyes saw everything.

"You're going to be a wonderful Maestro. Everyone knows it and so do you. Now, go on and let them know about the meeting. I'll keep the shop running until you return."

***

That afternoon, Anna blew through the door like a blustery sea wind. All the calm in the workshop descended into frazzled nerves.

"What's this I hear about an apprentice?" she asked without bothering to greet him.

Ciro raised an eyebrow at her.

Anna sighed heavily. "Ciro, it's all over the Gioiellieri Guild. You know how they love to gossip. Now, tell me the truth – did you apply for an apprentice today?"

Ciro crossed his arms in front of his chest. "I did."

Anna stared at him, open-mouthed. "Well, I say. *Really*?"

Ciro nodded.

"Well then. Let's hope the little lava-licker is grateful for the opportunity and that you don't die before the apprenticeship is up."

"I'd appreciate it if you don't talk about my niece like that," he said in a low voice. "Say whatever you like about me, but Loredana is off limits. Understand?"

Anna paused. "I understand," she said gently. "Sorry, Ciro. I didn't know that Loredana was the lucky one. I was only joking."

He stared at her coolly. "Your jest was not appreciated. Now is that the only reason you came?"

"Yes," she answered shortly. "But now that I'm here, I can help you with the sculptures if you're not done."

Ciro took a deep breath. "Of course I'm not done. I have the rough shape of your sea monster and boat. You can work on the details while I start on the other one."

Anna followed him behind the wooden panels. They worked in silence the entire afternoon. Ciro had taken the initial pictures and filled in as much detail as he dared on the pages. On the other side of the paper, he'd sketched in the reverse side of the image. For him, that was the main difference between cammei and corallo carvings. The cammei were single sided – no one would ever see the back of it and expect a carving. The corallo statue, however, would be viewed from all angles.

It was well past trading by the time they put their tools down. The sculptures were coming along nicely but would still need at least a few days' work.

"I'll walk you home," Ciro stated, looking at the dusky orange sky.

Anna shook her head. "There's no need."

Ciro put his hat and coat on, ignoring her protests. Anna had a hard head – he'd realised that at their first meeting in her youth. She hadn't changed much in all the years he'd known her. The bitter shell she'd formed around herself had only hardened over time.

On the street, he offered her his arm. She took it rather reluctantly. They walked side by side along the pavement. Ciro took the side closest to the road in case any carriages or blazermobiles went past and splashed in puddles or threw up dirt at them. Anna huffed when she'd realised what he'd done. Ciro shook his head.

"I can't do right by you, can I?"

"What are you talking about?" she snapped.

Ciro shook his head and pursed his lips. Anna glared at him until he spoke.

"I'm talking about the fact that you seem to find fault with everything I do, even when I'm trying to be nice to you. I don't know why in Caldera's smoke I bother when everything I do makes you angry."

A strange look flickered over Anna's face so quickly Ciro couldn't make it out.

"What is it that makes you so angry with me?" he asked in exasperation. "Did I do something to you years ago that I don't remember? Do you hold a grudge for so long with everyone?"

Anna drew her red shawl tighter around her shoulders with her free hand and looked away from him.

"Bah!" Ciro cried, exasperated. "I give up. I don't know why I bother trying."

He quickened his step, wanting the journey to be over quickly, but Anna held steadily to their slower pace, forcing him to return to it.

"In all these years, you've never noticed?" Anna asked, subdued.

"Noticed what?" Ciro asked in exasperation, throwing his hands up in the air. Anna flinched at his sudden movement. "Excuse me, Anna, but really, I've no idea what you're talking about."

"I suppose it never occurred to you to notice. After all, you've always had Seppe."

"What does Seppe have to do with this?" Ciro looked at her in confusion.

Anna huffed out a bitter laugh. "Everything! Seppe is the reason you never noticed me!"

"What? Of course I noticed you!"

"Yes, but not the way I wanted you to. I tried to find a companion for myself, but every time I found someone, I compared him to you and every one of them fell short. But I could never have you because Seppe had you."

Ciro's eyes opened wide at her statement.

"Oh. Well, Anna, I..."

"Forget it, Ciro," she said, speaking over him. "There's nothing either of us can do about this. The worst part is, the angrier I got about it, the nicer you were to me, to try to make me like you. You never realised how much I already loved you."

They arrived at her doorstep. Ciro still didn't know what to say.

"Would it help if I'm horrible to you?" he asked with a half-smile. "I can try."

Anna slapped his arm with the corner of her shawl and smiled sadly. Ciro bent forward and kissed her lightly on the cheek like he would any close friend, only he had never done so with Anna before. He heard her sharp intake of breath before she drew away and fled inside her house.

Chapter 7 – Ramedi 3 Gioiellieri 230 Years After Implosion

Ciro waited impatiently outside the Guild Hall for Loredana and Serafina. The Guild Hall clocks were loudly chiming three o'clock. They should already be here.

"Quick, mamma!"

Ciro looked up sharply at the familiar voice and let out a long breath. They appeared around the corner, Loredana tugging at her mamma's hand. Both were dressed in their best clothes, threadbare though they were. Soon, Loredana would have proper clothes. Part of her apprenticeship was to be clothed and fed, and Serafina could not object. Perhaps, knowing that, she might allow him to buy Tania a new dress as well.

"Sorry, Zio, I was held up at the pasticceria. We're not too late, are we?" Serafina asked, out of breath.

Loredana glared up at her, then turned her attention to Ciro. "I *told* her we'd be late if she didn't hurry. You'd better not be the reason I don't get to be Zio's apprentice, mamma!'

"Peace, Reda, you're not too late," Ciro said, placing a hand on her shoulder and smiling reassuringly at Serafina. "Let's go in now."

One niece on either arm, Ciro walked into the Gioiellieri Guild Hall for the first time with a prospective apprentice. It was the most nerve-wracking thing he'd ever done.

Yvette looked up at their approach and shook her head. Ciro felt Loredana and Serafina let go of his arms. He didn't care if Yvette disapproved of his decision – hers wasn't the opinion that mattered.

"Good afternoon, Yvette." He took off his hat and nodded slightly. "Could you please inform Maestra Rosalina that I'm here with my prospective apprentice and her mamma, as agreed?"

Yvette motioned for another Amministratore to take her place and left to find the Maestri. While they waited, Ciro sent Loredana off to look at all the Great Works. Serafina joined her curiously – neither of them had ever set foot in a Guild Hall. He sat on a bench near the reception desk and watched them pointing excitedly to anything that drew their attention.

Loredana came running up to him. "Zio, are *your* Great Works here?"

"Of course," he replied easily. "Every Gioielliere Great Work ever submitted is displayed in this hall."

"Show me!" she cried, pulling him to his feet. "Where are they?"

Ciro took her hand and walked slowly down the great hall, towards the Corallini section. They were kept separate from the rest of the Great Works. He'd always liked the fact that there was a clear distinction within the Guild for Corallini, orafi and argentieri, at least until the Inter-Guild Edict came into effect.

The Mercantili had pushed for this edict over four years ago and somehow got it past Ministro Ercolano. In effect, it was meant to ensure Guilds were sticking to their Code and not sharing secrets. While collaboration between the Guilds had not been explicitly banned, the wording of the edict had been loose enough that the Mercantili had been able to use it to prosecute anyone they felt were breaking the rules. It was now solely interpreted as a ban on any collaboration whatsoever.

The orafi and argentieri never needed to concern themselves about the distinction from other Gioiellieri. Corallini, on the other hand, sketched, carved, and sculpted as part of their daily work, like any Artista. They were constantly afraid of being stripped of their Guild Marks and being forced to join the Artiste Guild as Copper Artiste or worse. With the Inter-Guild Edict, there was even the threat of imprisonment.

"Here we are," Ciro said, pointing to his Copper Great Work. "This corallo pendant was my first Great Work."

He looked at it fondly. Maestro Enrico had been so proud of him. A flawless corallo teardrop set in gold with corallo balls expertly shaped to accentuate the pendant. It had taken him an entire week to make it. The gold work had been the most difficult part. It had taken hours for him to roll and draw down the gold, then twist it into a fine bezel setting for the corallo teardrop. But it had all been worth it to finish his apprenticeship and gain his Copper Guild Mark. To really join the Gioiellieri Guild and be allowed to practice as a Corallino for the rest of his life. A smile tugged at the corners of his mouth.

"Where's another one of yours?" Loredana asked, impatient to see everything.

Ciro wandered over to the cammei. He pointed out a cammeo carved on a sardonyx shell fragment. The picture was one of his favourites. His sister, Concettina, had come for one of her rare visits. She had been so tired from her day out, she hadn't realised he was sketching her until the deed was done. He'd made a copy for her, but kept the original sketch for himself. Countless times, he'd used her likeness to practise until he could carve her by memory alone.

"Who's that?" Loredana asked, pointing to the cammeo brooch. "She's *beautiful*!"

Serafina leaned closer and drew in a sharp breath. "Mamma? You immortalised her."

"Nonna Cetti?" Loredana asked in confusion. "But that doesn't look anything like her. She looks more like *you*, mamma."

Ciro shared a knowing look with Serafina.

"Bella, you only knew Nonna Cetti when she was older," Serafina explained. "People say I look just like her when she was younger, but this must have been years ago. She looks as young as I am now."

Ciro nodded. "She may even have been younger than you are now. I made this when she was pregnant with you. It was for my Gold Guild Mark."

Loredana pressed her hands against the glass, trying to get closer to the cammeo.

"Zio, will you teach me to do this?" she asked in awe.

"If the Maestri agree to let you apprentice with me, then yes. But not in your first few years. Cammei are very difficult to make – they take a steady hand, a keen eye and years of practise. Some Corallini never master them, others take a week to create one."

Serafina glanced over to him and said in a quiet voice, "How long does it take *you*?"

Ciro shrugged. "A day, sometimes two," he replied just as quietly, ensuring Loredana wouldn't hear.

Serafina's eyes widened at the admission. "Why in Caldera's smoke haven't you taken an apprentice before now, Zio? You must be the best Corallino in all of Tor'Esint!"

Ciro didn't get a chance to answer.

"Indeed, he is," Rosalina announced, striding towards them. "We all hoped he'd take an apprentice years ago. Now, you must be Serafina di Concettina and *this*," she said, leaning down, "must be the lucky Loredana di Serafina."

Loredana puffed up her chest and beamed happily. "Does that mean you'll let Zio Ciro be my Maestro?"

"Reda, quiet!" Serafina reprimanded her quickly. "Excuse me, Maestra, my daughter appears to have forgotten her manners."

Rosalina laughed. "It's quite alright. Why don't we adjourn to the sitting room and discuss the matter in private?"

She turned on her heel and walked back past the reception desk, leaving Ciro to follow with his nieces. They were led into the same room Yvette had shown him to the day before. Waiting inside were the other two Maestri, Adamo and Luca – both a great deal younger than Rosalina and Ciro. They rose when everyone else entered the room.

"Ciro Corallino, it's good to see you," Adamo said, with Luca nodding his agreement.

Ciro shook hands with both of them and introduced Loredana and Serafina. Everyone sat, Loredana close to her mamma's side.

"Now, Loredana, I understand this was your idea?" Adamo asked in a gentle voice.

Loredana nodded.

"I see and did you ask because you want to become a Corallina or because you want to help your mamma?"

Loredana bit her lip and glanced up at Ciro. He nodded encouragingly at her.

"Both," she replied confidently. "I love Zio's workshop and couldn't imagine apprenticing with anyone else. But I don't think I'd have even thought about it so soon if mamma didn't have to do everything for us by herself."

"Loredana!" Serafina covered her mouth with a hand to stifle a gasp.

The young girl shrugged. "Well, it's *true* mamma. If Zio didn't help us a little already, we wouldn't have enough food some weeks. With an apprenticeship, you won't need to feed me as much, or buy clothes for me. Zio would have to do that."

Adamo looked at his fellow Maestri with raised eyebrows.

"Is this the only reason you've applied for an apprentice, Ciro?" Luca asked. "To compel your family to accept your generosity?"

"Of course not," Ciro replied. "I'll admit that it will be nice to help out my family, but it's more that I don't want the art of corallo to die out and none of us have an apprentice. I'm the oldest, so I think it's high time I set a good example. As I told Rosalina, in Tor'Dumere, children even younger than Loredana apprentice with their families. I don't expect her apprenticeship to end while she's younger than other Gioiellieri."

"And it works quite well there," Rosalina said firmly. "I've visited the Gioiellieri Guild there a number of times and the quality of Great Works there is easily comparable to our own."

"What about the sister?" Adamo asked, turning to Serafina. "You have another daughter, do you not? A younger one."

Serafina nodded. "Tania. She's eight years old."

"What will happen with Tania?" Adamo asked. "I don't mean to pry, but when you're working and Loredana is in Ciro's workshop, who will look after her?" Adamo asked.

Serafina's cheeks reddened and her eyes filled with tears. Ciro lay a hand over hers to reassure her.

"She'll come to my workshop," he replied. "She's a good child, and perhaps when she's older, she might like to become my apprentice as well."

The Maestri shared another look. They appeared to be talking to each other without saying a word. Eventually Rosalina clapped her hands together.

"Ciro, you know I'm in favour of any conditions whereby you take on an apprentice, however, since Loredana is so young, we'll need her mamma's approval, in writing, before we agree to anything."

Silence fell over the room broken only by Loredana's little gasp.

"Wait, does that mean...? Are you saying ... yes?"

Adamo smiled pleasantly. "Yes, as long as your mamma agrees. She is, after all, the most important person in this room right now."

Ciro looked to Serafina as eagerly as Loredana. She bit her lip and looked between the two of them.

"It's binding, isn't it?" she asked, slowly. "If I sign now, there's no turning back?"

Ciro turned to the Maestri. Some sort of wordless communication passed between them again.

"It *is* binding, but any contract can be broken if there is enough reason," Rosalina told them. "If the Guild member treats the apprentice badly, or if the apprentice refuses to work or ruins things in the workshop on purpose."

"So, not if she changes her mind?" Serafina asked.

"Mamma, I *won't* change my mind." Loredana grasped her arm. "I promise."

Serafina looked down at Loredana then turned to Ciro, biting her lip.

"I have the paperwork here. Take a moment to read it and see if you have any questions."

Rosalina held out the contract to Serafina. She did not take it.

"I'll read it out," he said, "so Loredana can hear it too."

He took the contract and read through it quickly before reading aloud.

This agreement was made the third day of Gioiellieri, two hundred and thirty years After Implosion between Loredana di Serafina (hereinafter called "the Apprentice") a minor of ten years of age, and Serafina di Concettina (hereinafter called "the Guardian") and Ciro Corallino (hereinafter called "the Maestro").

The Gioiellieri Guild Maestri witness that, with the consent of the Guardian, testified by the latter's execution of this Agreement, the Apprentice has agreed to serve the Maestro and the Maestro has agreed to accept the Apprentice.

The Apprentice will, as from the fourth day of Gioiellieri, two hundred and thirty years After Implosion, be in service with the Maestro for a total period of eight years, ending on her eighteenth birthday.

The Apprentice shall faithfully observe and obey the Maestro and work to the best of her ability in the interests of the Maestro.

The Apprentice will not reveal any secrets of the Maestro; do any damage or injury to the property of the Maestro or his customers; absent herself, except in the event of sickness; or refuse to do any work which the Maestro may lawfully require her to perform.

The Maestro undertakes to teach his craft to the utmost of his ability and competence. Further, the Maestro undertakes to provide sufficient food, drink, apparel, laundering, equipment and all other such items necessary and fit for an Apprentice.

As the Apprentice cannot be accommodated at the Maestro's residence, the Maestro will provide a stipend of one copper per day to be paid to the Guardian of the Apprentice while the Apprentice continues to reside with the Guardian.

At the end of the Apprenticeship, the Maestro shall and will deliver unto the Apprentice, new apparel of good quality encompassing two outfits for Trading Days and one outfit for Riposidis.

Signed by the Apprentice, Loredana di Serafina

Signed by the Guardian, Serafina di Concettina

Signed by the Maestro, Ciro Corallino

Witnessed by the Gioiellieri Maestri, Rosalina Gioielliera, Luca Gioielliere, Adamo Gioielliere

As he spoke, Loredana became visibly sombre as did Serafina.

"This is a serious matter, Loredana. Did you understand everything? Are you certain you want to sign the contract?" Serafina asked her daughter.

Loredana nodded firmly.

"It means I have to listen to Zio and be a good apprentice. He'll teach me everything and buy me clothes and anything else I need."

Rosalina held out a pen to the child. She took it somewhat hesitantly, sticking her tongue out the side of her mouth in concentration as she laboured over every letter of her name. Serafina was not much better, but at least Cetti had taught her that much. Ciro took pride in being able to read and write well enough to successfully run his workshop. He would see to it that Loredana was also educated in her letters, like his Maestro had done for him.

He signed the contract and passed it to the Maestri, all of whom signed with ease.

"It is done," Adamo said. "Loredana, you are now Ciro's apprentice. Make sure you arrive at his workshop bright and early tomorrow morning to start your first day. Serafina, should you have any concerns or queries regarding the apprenticeship, know that our doors are always open to you and your daughter.

"I'll make it my personal business to visit Ciro's workshop on a regular basis to ensure your daughter is being treated well and doing her best to learn her new trade."

Ciro noticed both Rosalina and Luca raise an eyebrow at this, but neither of them objected. Ciro didn't mind. It *was* an unusual circumstance, after all, and anything the Gioiellieri Guild needed to allow Loredana's apprenticeship to continue was fine by him.

They all stood and exited the room. Adamo insisted on escorting them to the street, pausing momentarily by the reception desk to hand the paperwork to Yvette.

Ciro drew Loredana's attention to the Great Works as Adamo slowed his pace to speak quietly with Serafina. The way he lingered with her reminded Ciro of the way he used to prolong his conversations with Seppe when they were younger, just to keep him nearby that little bit longer. The Guild Maestro was notorious for caring more about the Guild than his personal life, but Ciro could see the unaffected smile Adamo gave Serafina, the interest he showed in her, and Ciro saw no reason to get in their way. After the death of her companion and her mother, Serafina had focused her whole attention on the girls and supporting their little family. It might be good for her to focus on something else for a change.

When she caught up to them, Ciro escorted them both back to his workshop, where Seppe was looking after Tania. They made arrangements for Loredana to come alone the next day, as Serafina wasn't working and could look after Tania herself.

Chapter 8 – Argentodi 4 Gioiellieri 230 Years After Implosion

Ciro walked downstairs early, as usual, ready for his daily walk to the beach and along the docks. His head was full of all the things he would need to teach Loredana. Before he reached the door, Seppe called out to him.

"Coffee's ready."

Ciro turned in confusion. "Seppe, you know I take my coffee when I return from my walk."

"Not today," Seppe replied. "Loredana will be here soon. You can go for a walk then. She can't start the first day of her apprenticeship without her Maestro here now, can she?"

Ciro shook his head at his own foolishness and headed to the kitchen instead for a cup of coffee. At least he'd have a warm belly out in the crisp morning breeze. Taking a seat, he sipped the coffee as slowly as he could, taking his time with the liquid gold. Thankfully, there was a plantation of coffee trees just outside Tor'Esint so coffee was one of the only items, other than fish, not to have increased in prices since the Trading Edict.

As he waited for Loredana to arrive, Ciro began sketching cammei concepts for the Parting Gifts to calm his nerves. Four ideas were committed to paper by the time the door opened. Seppe helped Loredana with her coat and Ciro looked up as she approached his workstation.

"Good morning, my little apprentice!" he said with a spark of excitement.

She grinned broadly at him. "Good morning, *Maestro*."

Ciro chuckled at that. "You can still call me Zio, you know."

"I will." She nodded seriously. "On Riposidi, when you come for lunch."

He shrugged. It was probably a good idea, being formal in the workshop. Covering his sketches, he got to his feet.

"Let's take a walk," he told her. "It's the first thing I do, almost every morning."

Loredana nodded eagerly and ran to get her coat.

"First rule, Loredana," he called out after her. "No running in the workshop. It's small and there are a lot of things you can hurt yourself with or break."

"Yes, Maestro," she replied, big eyes darting around to take in her surroundings as though it was her first time in the workshop.

Ciro handed Loredana her coat and patted her on the back before putting on his own. He strapped on his wicker basket, with Loredana watching him closely.

"We didn't go to the beach to find corallo for you this morning," she told him in a worried voice.

"No matter, I still need to walk the docks. The marinai know to keep their best items for me."

***

On the docks, Ciro introduced Loredana to his favourite marinai and explained to her why he refused to purchase most of the shells they offered him. Antonino Marinaio had the only reasonable item today. It was a large sardonyx shell so perfect, Ciro could probably use it to carve an entire scene rather than divide it into smaller sections for cammei. It was an exciting prospect. He hadn't been able to do that all year.

Walking back to the workshop, Loredana turned to him with a frown.

"Maestro, how will you get enough corallo to work with if Tania and I don't gather it for you?"

Ciro patted her hand on his arm. "You can still gather corallo for me, with Tania if you like. I used to do the same for my Maestro during my apprenticeship. Then, if you see me, you can walk the docks with me or go straight back to the workshop and wait for me there."

Loredana thought it over for a few moments.

"I'll meet you on the docks the days I don't have Tania with me. She's little, you know, so she'll run up and down the docks knocking marinai into the sea. Then they'll get all angry and not want to sell you anything and *that* would be dreadful."

Ciro tried hard not to laugh at his niece's train of thought as they continued their slow walk back to the workshop.

At their entrance, curious eyes turned on them. Anna and Sabrina came out from behind the wooden panels and Seppe emerged from the kitchen with freshly brewed coffee.

"Good morning," Ciro greeted them in surprise, gently ushering Loredana in front of him.

Bossy as she was with her sister, she'd become uncharacteristically shy in the face of the older two Corallini.

"Is this the lucky Loredana, then?" Anna asked, looking the girl up and down. "She is rather young, isn't she?"

Ciro fought the urge to roll his eyes.

"Indeed, but as I've discussed with the Guild, she'll still finish her apprenticeship on her eighteenth birthday. Now, please excuse us. It's Loredana's first day and she has much to learn."

Anna quickly disappeared behind the wooden panels, but Sabrina took a moment to congratulate him.

"I'm sure Loredana will make a wonderful apprentice. May she bring you good fortune and increased business."

Ciro nodded in thanks and ushered Loredana to his favourite workbench. He instructed her to wait for him there while he spoke to Anna and Sabrina. Behind the wooden panels, they were quietly arguing about the clay models.

"To what do I owe the pleasure?" he asked them.

Sabrina raised her eyes in mock innocence. "We thought you'd be busy with your new apprentice and might like a hand with the sculptures, didn't we Anna?"

"Indeed. Why you chose to take an apprentice *now*, of all times, is beyond me. But we'll do our best to help," Anna replied magnanimously.

Ciro smirked at them. "I see. And your generosity has nothing to do with the fact that you wanted to meet my new apprentice, does it?"

They glanced at each other guiltily and avoided his eyes.

"Come on then, meet her properly and then go back to your workshops. I'll have the sculptures done by Riposidi. We can start working on the corallo next week."

He covered the corallo with its cloth and ushered the ladies out from behind the wooden panels and over to his favourite workbench, where Loredana was patiently waiting.

"Loredana, this is Anna Corallina and Sabrina Corallina. The three of us are working on a special project together, behind that wooden panel. From next week, you'll be seeing them quite often. I expect you to be respectful towards them and not to go peeking behind that panel. It's very secret and very important."

Loredana nodded eagerly and shook Anna and Sabrina's hands in turn, her eyes darting to the wooden panel. Ciro would have to keep an eye on her. It would not do for their secret to be shared by an excited child. The Guild wouldn't care who shared it, only that their surprise for the Guild Ball was ruined.

"Now, Anna, Rina, if you don't mind, I really do have a lot to show Loredana today. Come back on Gildadi evening and we can discuss things then."

He waited for the Corallini to leave and then carefully deposited his large new sardonyx shell on the workbench and looked at his waiting apprentice. Ciro rubbed his hands together, trying to warm them, as he thought how to begin.

"Well, I suppose the first thing is to show you the types of things I create and how the machines work."

"Will I get to use the machines today?" Loredana asked excitedly.

"Erm, no. Not today," Ciro answered carefully. "Today is for looking and learning."

"Tomorrow then?"

Ciro raised his eyebrows at her insistence but didn't answer. He did not trust a ten-year-old to use the machines safely. What would her mamma say if she cut off her finger?

"Come, look in the display cabinet. Tell me what you see."

He stood behind her as she peered into the glass-topped table.

"Necklaces, brooches, rings, earrings and lots of pendants."

She looked up at him expectantly.
"Is there anything else you can tell me about them?" he asked patiently.
Loredana grimaced and turned back to the cabinet.
"Well ... the necklaces are all corallo balls, with gold clasps. Some of them are single chains, some of them are multiple chains twisted together. Some of the brooches are cammei and some are corallo. All the earrings and pendants are corallo with gold." She turned to look at him. "Maestro, why do you only use gold?"
Ciro lifted the lid of the cabinet and handed her a cammeo.
"You didn't look closely enough. Try again."
Loredana carefully took the cammeo from him and examined it, emitting a soft gasp.
"Oh, it has gold *and* silver."
Ciro nodded. "Now, turn it over."
Loredana did as she was told and started laughing.
"A brooch *and* a pendant! You tricked me. Why is it both?"
"It's how I was taught," Ciro replied with a shrug. "One never knows how a signora will choose to wear her cammeo – why not give her all the options? It doesn't take much more effort to add the extra bits when you're already working with the metal."
Loredana ran her fingers over the cammeo, turning it over and over in her hands.
"When will I learn to make these?"
"When your drawings are good enough."
"My drawings?" she asked hesitantly.
Ciro walked over to his workbench, retrieved his sketchpad and turned to the latest sketches.
"I'll be making these for the Parting Gifts for the Guild Ball. Each one will be carved into a cammeo. This is where it all begins. One must learn to draw before working with cammei."
Loredana bit her lip. "I ... don't know how to draw."
Ciro lifted a finger. "Yet. You don't know how to draw *yet*. We can work on that. All it takes is practise. I'll get you a sketchbook of your own and some pencils. If you draw every day for an hour, I guarantee you'll be better than Seppe in a month."
Seppe grunted at that, which only served to make Loredana laugh.
"Do you have a sketchbook too, Seppe?" she asked.
Seppe stopped what he was doing and looked up at them with mock annoyance.
"I do. It's the one Ciro bought me when I moved to Tor'Esint – a welcome present."
"No," Loredana shook her head. "I mean one you haven't finished yet."
Seppe huffed. "What makes you think I ever filled all the pages? There are plenty left."

"I have it!" Ciro grinned triumphantly. "The two of you can learn to draw together."

Seppe turned to him sharply, prepared to protest, but when Ciro motioned to the excited child between them, he only shook his head and rolled his eyes.

"Now, Loredana, let me show you the making of corallo necklaces because this is something you will be able to help with immediately."

Ciro spent the rest of the morning showing his new apprentice the entire process involved in creating corallo balls, separating them into sizes, and threading them with cotton.

He left her to thread a string of corallo balls. Every minute or so, a loud *plink* betrayed the difficulty she was having keeping the balls on her tray rather than the floor. Ciro nodded happily to himself because each time it happened, she only sighed, picked up the escaped ball and tried again. She had a fighter's spirit which boded well for her apprenticeship.

Chapter 9 – Mercatodi 7 Gioiellieri 230 Years After Implosion

Ciro's nieces tugged him forward, holding one hand each. It was a long walk to Piazza Mercantile, but they showed no sign of tiring. If anything, the closer they came, the faster they walked.

"Hurry, Maestro! We don't want to be late!" Loredana whined.

"How can we be late when she doesn't know we're coming?" Ciro asked, out of breath. "Girls, slow down or you'll be the death of me!"

The threat of death worked ... for a mere block. Then the tugging began again, in earnest. Ciro did his best to keep up with their pace but in the end, they slowed to his.

As they neared Piazza Mercantile, Ciro took out the little card with Greta Sarta's address on it. When she'd brought the new shirts to his workshop, the card had been carefully tucked inside the package. It was a clever idea. Ciro didn't have cards like this. He did what every other Gioielliere did – ordered boxes with his name and address printed on top, so his customers would always remember where to find him.

"We're nearly there!" Tania shouted. "I can see the stalls!"

She let go of his hand to run, but Ciro quickly caught it again and held tightly. Mercatodi brought out large crowds and Serafina would never forgive him if he lost her daughter.

"Tania, stay close to me. You too, Loredana."

"Yes, Zio," they chorused.

They slowed to a halt when they entered the markets. Stalls were set up all over the Piazza, around the sides and in the middle. Ciro didn't often come to the markets anymore. He and Seppe had used to go at least once a month when they were younger. These days they found what they needed closer to home, in the little alleys leading up from the docks where they had daily food markets.

Tucking the card in his pocket, Ciro led the girls through the markets, looking at all the street signs until he found Via del Corallo. Greta's shop was quite fortunately situated on one of the busiest corners of the Piazza. A table was set out in front of the shop with two girls seated at it, talking with two young men.

Loredana pointed at them excitedly. "Zio, look! They're wearing your pendants!"

"It's rude to point," he whispered, and she immediately put down her hand.

One of the girls looked over to them as they approached. Her dimpled smile was so genuine, Ciro couldn't help but return it.

"Good morning, Signore Gioielliere," she said, her eyes lifting from his Guild Mark pin. "How may we help you today?"

Tania laughed loudly. "Zio's not a Gioielliere. He's a *Corallino*."

The girl frowned momentarily. "Not *Ciro* Corallino?" she said, touching the corallo dragonfly that hung on a chain around her neck.

Ciro nodded politely. "Indeed, Signorina. I was wondering if you could help me with some dresses for my new apprentice." Tania tugged at his sleeve and glared at him. "For both of my nieces, actually."

"Of course, Signore Corallino," she said, getting to her feet. "Let me take you inside. I'm sure Maestra Greta would like to talk to you while I take your nieces around the shop."

She spoke a few words to the apprentice beside her, then held out her hands to the girls.

"My name's Sofia. What are your names?"

"I'm Loredana," his niece said, slipping her hand into Sofia's. "Ciro Corallino's first ever apprentice! This is my little sister, Tania."

Tania quickly took Sofia's other hand as they walked up the stairs.

"I'm very pleased to meet you both. Let's go inside so I can show you some designs. Signore Corallino, is there anything in particular you need Loredana's clothes to have? Pockets, aprons, skirts, pants?"

Ciro heard her, but was so stunned by the sight of the workshop that he could not answer. It was at least five times as large as his own. He spied another apprentice inside and three Copper Sarti all at their own workbenches. The walls were lined with bolts of fabric and makeshift stands were lined up in rows towards the front of the workshop, full of dresses and coats. A fully dressed mannequin stood in every window, facing the street, each displaying a different style of clothing – some suits, some dresses. The effect was overwhelming.

"Signore, why don't you take a seat?" Sofia asked, gesturing to one of two large armchairs set up near the door with a small table between them. "I'll ask Annika to fetch you a cup of tea and call for Maestra Greta. Girls, have a look around, I'll be back in a moment."

Ciro sat and tried to recover from both the exceedingly long walk and the shock of walking into something that looked more like a Sarta factory than a workshop. He lost sight of his nieces in amongst the racks of clothes. Every now and then, their squeals of delight gave away their position, but he could not see them.

"Ciro Corallino, what a pleasure to see you!"

Greta walked over to him, resplendent in a cream and brown work dress, and shook his hand. He rose and kissed her on the cheek. After all, they were old acquaintances now. She pressed his hand firmly and took the seat beside him. Ciro returned to his own seat and kept still while Sofia set a tea tray between them.

"Signore Corallino has come to order some clothes for his new apprentice and her sister," Sofia told Greta. At her quizzical look, Sofia explained. "They're his nieces."

"Gather them up for me, Fia, dear." Greta turned to Ciro. "What I like to do for children is make their clothes with plenty of room to grow. That way you won't find yourself buying new clothes for them every few months when they hit a growth spurt. Now, it's up to you, but if you're happy for my apprentices to make the clothes, there will be a considerable discount as it will take longer and the quality won't be Gold standard. Of course, that's not to say the quality will be bad – I still have my reputation to uphold, you understand. Otherwise, they might find something to their liking from our ready-made clothing."

Ciro tried to take in all the information but found himself simply staring at the Sarta. It was the same every time he met her. She did not seem to be able to slow down.

When he didn't answer, she took a moment to pour them both some tea. Ciro did his best to hide his contempt for the diluted tasting liquid as he took a sip from the dainty cup.

Sofia returned with the children, both glowing so brightly he couldn't help but smile. He glanced at Greta and saw her taking in their secondhand, threadbare clothes.

"Loredana, Tania, say good morning to my friend, Greta Sarta."

"Good morning, Greta Sarta," they chorused.

"You have such a wonderful shop!" Loredana exclaimed excitedly. "Zio, I mean, Maestro, will you *really* buy our clothes from *here*?"

"Of course," he replied. "Now, Tania, don't be upset, but I really don't think I can convince your mamma to let me buy you more than one dress, so choose wisely. Loredana, you can have two I think. Good, practical work dresses like Greta, with pockets. Or trousers if you prefer."

"What about a leather apron like you and Seppe?' she asked hopefully.

Ciro shook his head. "You won't be using the fire-gun any time soon. I'll get you a leather apron when you're older."

Greta stood and walked around Tania. "Fia, why don't you take Tania to the third rack from the back. I think we have some dresses that can be taken in and hemmed up for her."

Sofia took Tania and left Loredana standing there, staring up at Greta with big eyes. Ciro sipped his insipid tea and watched Greta. She was deep in thought – he could almost see her mind swirling.

"Loredana, tell me, you don't wear a corset yet, do you?"

Loredana stared at Ciro, turned bright red, and looked quickly away.

"No," she whispered.

"No need to be embarrassed," Greta said kindly, noting the sudden discomfort of the young girl. "I ask all girls your age just in case. It makes a difference for the dresses, you see.

"Ciro, will you permit me to make one dress for Loredana in a timely fashion and let my apprentices make the other one? That way she'll have proper work clothes within a week or so. I can take her measurements now and have a work dress ready in a little over a week. We have plenty of patterns for work dresses, as we make all of our own. Loredana could choose her preferred designs."

Ciro nodded and took Loredana's hands.

"Reda, what do you think? Greta is the best Sarta in all Tor'Esint. You can have a dress just like hers, or one of her apprentices."

Loredana bit her lip and looked Greta up and down. Slowly, a smile crept onto her face. She nodded shyly, but enthusiastically. Greta patted her on the back and gave her a little nudge to guide her to the back of the shop.

"Let's get you measured up then. Follow me."

In the time it took Ciro to finish the entire pot of tea, Tania had finally chosen a dress in a lovely blend of orange and red sunset colours. Sofia allowed her to try it on and pinned her in so many places, Ciro couldn't keep track of the number of little yelps that came from the dressing room. Eventually, she emerged, with a large grin on her face.

"Oh Zio, it's the prettiest dress! Sofia says she can have it ready in just a week. Won't that be wonderful?"

Ciro nodded and held out his hands to her. Tania obligingly snuggled up onto his lap to await Loredana.

They weren't left waiting much longer. Greta followed his new apprentice back to him with a book held close to her chest. Loredana stood next to Ciro as Greta took a seat and showed him the designs Loredana had picked out. Both were simple work dresses in different styles. One looked just like the dress Sofia was wearing – a long, simple skirt with a pocketed apron stitched into the front. The other had no apron, but Ciro could see there were pockets sewn all around the waistline of the skirt, even around the back. Both appeared very practical.

"Seems I was right to bring my nieces here," Ciro said, leaning back in his chair and patting the hand Loredana lay on his shoulder. "Girls, why don't you go back outside with Sofia for a moment while I finish up with Signora Sarta?"

With a look from Greta, Sofia obligingly took the girls by the hand and led them back out to the stall on the street. Ciro waited until the bell tinkled for the second time, signalling the door closing.

"Forgive me, Greta," Ciro said, turning to face her directly. "I did not wish to discuss the cost with the girls around. They would feel forever in my debt if they knew your prices."

Greta frowned. "*You* don't know my prices," she reminded him. "You've ordered three dresses without asking."

Ciro shrugged. "Whatever it is, I'll pay. Those poor girls haven't had new clothes since their papà was lost at sea years ago. And, as you so kindly offered to make them with plenty of room for growth, they should last a good long time."

Greta faltered, her eyes darting to the window where she could probably see her stall and his nieces.

"That's exceedingly kind of you," she finally said. "Not everyone is fortunate enough to have family like you. Let's sort out the price and then get to other matters. For Loredana's first dress, my standard fee for a simple work dress from our existing patterns is usually one gold. However, as you are purchasing more than one dress, I'll bring that down to two electrums. Her other dress, if you'll permit an apprentice to make it, can come down as low as one electrum and ten silvers. Tania's dress was apprentice made, so is much simpler, and it only needs minor adjustments, so let's call that one electrum."

She wrote the prices down and did a quick calculation.

"That brings the total to four electrums and ten silvers."

Greta looked at him, almost defiantly, daring him to argue with her. He ran through her words in his mind again.

"It's a clever idea, giving your apprentices more experience and allowing your customers to purchase cheaper clothes from a Gold Sarta workshop. Have any of your fellow Sarti realised what you're doing yet?"

He winked conspiratorially and was rewarded with a light laugh. Greta lifted her cup and drained her tea, sighing happily as she sank back into the chair.

"I'm careful to keep most of my competitors out of my workshop," she admitted, smoothing her skirt over her knees, "but I cannot stop those who engage in dubious activities to spy on me."

Ciro heard a slight tremor in her voice and chose not to pursue that line of conversation.

"Should I bring the girls in for a fitting next Mercatodi?" he asked.

"Yes, that should work well. Tania's should be done by then and Loredana's may require two fittings at the most." Greta paused and looked thoughtfully at him. "Actually, Ciro, I was wondering if you might do me the honour of accompanying me for a meal one evening? I've heard the Exploding Beakers is quite the place to go these days. We could have dinner with Telchide and Aveline. What do you think?"

Ciro smiled at the thought. "That would be lovely, Greta. I must say, I'd like to get to know Telchide's new friend."

"Aveline Inventrice is my best friend," Greta told him with a smile.

He raised his bushy brows at that, momentarily doubting his resolve to join the dinner. A Sarta being so friendly with an Inventrice was dangerous these days. He'd only met Aveline once, the day of Sebetine's death declaration hearing and knew very little about her.

"A fellow Guild member must be nice for Telchide. Sebetine was good for him, but I always thought Telchide would have been happier if she'd joined a Guild. Any Guild."

Greta clasped her fingers tightly on her lap.

"You ... don't agree?" Ciro asked hesitantly. "Is he not happy to have found a fellow Guild member?"

Greta took a deep breath and spoke carefully. "I can tell you that she is happy with her situation and in her workshop, and loves Telchide and Teresina a great deal. But she isn't his companion."

Ciro frowned. Her words were very carefully chosen. "Companions" meant different things to different people. For Ciro and Seppe, it meant they'd found the person they wanted as their companion for the rest of their life, no formalities required. For others, they only used the term once a Commitment Ceremony had taken place. He'd never understood the need for such formalities. At least Aveline was happy, which meant so should Telchide be. And little Teresina.

"Well, I think dinner would be a lovely idea. If you organise it with Telchide and Aveline, I'll come. I'm sure Seppe won't mind a night to himself."

Greta frowned momentarily, tilting her head to the side, and then nodded. "Why don't you bring Seppe, I'll bring Domizio, and we'll make a night of it."

Ciro got to his feet and kissed Greta goodbye, gathered his nieces from the watchful Sofia and walked around Piazza Mercantile until he finally convinced them he needed to return to work.

On the way home, they passed by Pasticceria Delfina to pick up some sfogliatelle to celebrate Ciro's seventy-second birthday. He no longer cared for big celebrations, but insisted on at least a small dessert on his special day.

Chapter 10 – Gildadi 9 Gioiellieri 230 Years After Implosion

Ciro heard the clatter of beads behind him and sighed quietly. It was the second time just that afternoon that Loredana had knocked over the tray of corallo balls she was working with. It happened on a daily basis, usually more than once. At first, he'd dropped everything, every time, to help her pick them up. Until Seppe had pulled him aside a few days ago.

"She's your apprentice, Ciro, not your daughter," Seppe had told him firmly. "You can't waste your time picking up after her or she'll never learn to be more careful."

He was right, of course, so Ciro had stopped helping. He noticed the little smile creep onto Seppe's face as he realised Ciro had taken his advice. He was working on the first of the cammei Parting Gifts, waiting for Anna and Sabrina to arrive.

Ciro had spent all week with his hands covered in clay, creating models of what they might eventually carve into the corallo. There was no room for error. He had painstakingly carved every detail exactly as it was in both his and Anna's drawings, in clay replicas as large as the corallo itself. They were due to come this afternoon to decide which model to use. Ciro secretly hoped they would choose Anna's design so that if he ever found another piece of corallo all of his own, he could carve Serafina and the girls into it by himself.

"Can't I see?" Loredana asked, looking up from her corallo necklace. "If I look before they get here, they'll never even know."

"No," he repeated himself for the hundredth time, not bothering to look up from his cammeo.

"I won't tell anyone," she insisted. "*Please*, Maestro. Surely it's part of my apprenticeship to see something like this. You said yourself you've never seen a piece of corallo so large here. How many more years until you see another one? And you might not even be able to teach me then!"

Ciro hesitated. He was saved from answering by the arrival of his fellow Corallini.

"Anna, Rina, so nice to see you. Don't mind my young apprentice, she was just about to begin her drawing practice for the day." He leaned his wooden peg into one of the notches in his workbench and pulled out a sheet of paper. "Loredana, take this sheet of flowers. I want you to copy each one ten times into your sketchbook, then show them to me."

Loredana groaned audibly, but dutifully took the sheet and went to find her sketchbook. Without needing to be told, Seppe put down his own work and drew up a chair next to Loredana to sketch alongside her. Ciro left them to their work and followed Anna and Sabrina behind the wooden panel, adjusting it so the three of them could fit and still shield the corallo from view.

The clay carvings stood on either side of the corallo. Ciro looked from one to the other unhappily. There always seemed to be some small detail he'd forgotten, or that didn't look quite right. He saw one on the ship and reached out towards his tools.

"Don't!" Anna slapped his hand away. "You *always* do this. Leave the carving be. It's finished now."

Ciro shook his head. "Just one little thing..."

"No," Anna said, more gently. "Ciro, they both look magnificent. If you keep touching them, you'll eventually ruin them."

"Yes," Sabrina joined in quickly. "Let's just choose one now and then decide whether anything else needs to be changed."

Ciro, overpowered by their joint argument, withdrew his hand and crossed his arms.

"Decide then," he said, a little more gruffly than he intended.

"I still think the sea monster and boat is the better choice," Anna said, tilting her nose proudly into the air.

Sabrina rolled her eyes. "You only think that because it's yours. I think the lady is the nicer subject matter."

"We don't want the nicest subject matter but the better carving," Anna said. "And why do you always take Ciro's side?"

Ciro laughed at that. "Actually, I think the sea monster is the right choice."

Both of them turned and stared at him, open mouthed. He pulled the sea monster closer to the corallo, without looking at either one of them, and positioned it so that it matched the raw corallo more closely.

"See, the shape matches the branches reaching up here. If we turn the corallo upside down, we have different options. This way up, the monster is bigger at the bottom with tentacles reaching up to the broken boat. The other way, we have the boat intact with the tentacles rising up, but without the monster's body."

Anna tilted her head, trying to see it from the other angle. Sabrina followed her lead, but scrunched up her nose.

"I don't see it," Sabrina complained.

Ciro carefully jostled his way between them and picked up the corallo with a grunt. It was heavier than he'd expected. No wonder Yvette had two men bring it in. He put it back down before it slipped from his fingers. He did not even want to imagine what the punishment would be for dropping and breaking it.

"I can make another model, if you don't mind waiting another week to begin."

Anna shook her head. "We don't know how long it's going to take us to carve this, and we don't have the option to postpone the deadline. The Guild Ball won't wait for us. Let's just decide on one and make a start."

They both turned to Sabrina. She pursed her lips.

"I don't want to carve a sea monster," she said angrily. "Our first large piece of corallo and you both want to carve something so grotesque into it! What in Caldera's smoke is wrong with you?"

Anna placed her hands on her hips. "I'm not carving a simple statue of a lady and her children. If you don't want to carve the sea monster, we can do it without you."

Sabrina gasped angrily. Ciro turned sharply to Anna.

"That was *never* our agreement. The Guild gave this opportunity to all of us."

"Well then what do *you* suggest?" Anna said, returning to her usually bitter self.

Ciro searched for an answer. Any answer.

"We ask the Maestri. It's *their* corallo, after all."

It felt like a coward's way to escape a difficult choice, and it probably was, but Ciro refused to force one person off the project because of a disagreement as to the subject matter.

"That won't solve the problem," Anna said in annoyance. "All it will do is make one or the other of us unhappy."

Ciro closed his eyes briefly. This was meant to be a joyous occasion.

"Then we come up with a new idea altogether."

Sabrina squared her shoulders. "What about *my* design? The boat with the fishermen pulling in their haul? It's a compromise of both."

"It will still take me another week to make the model, but I can do it." Ciro shrugged. "I don't think that'll solve the problem, though. I still say we ask the Maestri to come see the clay models next week to help us decide which to make."

"And if we're not happy with their choice?" Anna snapped.

Ciro bunched his fingers together and wrung them in front of his face.

"Anna, what do you expect me to say?" he asked angrily, losing his patience. "At that point, you decide if you want to be part of something magnificent, no matter the subject being carved, or if you want to walk away because you don't feel like carving what the Maestri decide!"

"They won't choose my sea monster if we give them the choice!" she opined loudly.

"You don't know that," Sabrina said deceptively mildly. "They may think it's the better carving; or just want to cause a shock at the Guild Ball."

The last was said almost snidely. Ciro glanced at Sabrina in disapproval. There was never any cause to be so cruel to someone. Not on purpose.

"I've got work to do," Anna said, narrowing her eyes to thin slits. "I'm not going to waste any more time on this than I have to."

Ciro followed her around to the coat rack and took her gently by the arm.

"Anna, please say you'll come next week," he said quietly. "Don't let a small disagreement ruin the chance for us to work on this project together."

"Yes, you wouldn't want to miss a chance to work with Ciro now, would you?" Sabrina said slyly from behind him.

Ciro turned on her angrily, but the damage was already done. Anna wrenched her arm free and fled the workshop faster than a lava stream. He watched her go in dismay and heard a satisfied exclamation from behind him. He turned slowly to face the usually timid Sabrina.

"I think it's time you left," he said to her, and walked towards his apprentice and companion without waiting for her to go.

"What changed, Ciro?" Sabrina asked, putting on her coat. "Did she tell you her big secret so now you feel sorry for her and need to please her however you can? Is that it?"

Ciro sat down next to Loredana and opened his sketchbook. Without needing to be asked, Seppe stood to show Sabrina out. Ciro heard a muffled argument, but the door finally closed and Seppe returned to his seat. Even Loredana didn't ask what had happened – she only looked up at each of them once then continued her drawing.

"You're getting better," Ciro praised her. "Look, this little rose here is almost the same as mine."

Loredana brushed a light brown lock of hair from her eyes and studied the two drawings.

"Yes, but you gave me the simple rose, not the ones *you* do in your sketchbook. I *know* you give me easy pictures to copy."

Ciro shrugged unapologetically. "One must learn to walk before running. Flip to the front of your sketchbook and tell me if you can't see the difference."

Grudgingly, Loredana did as he instructed. He saw the small smile creep onto her face as she realised the truth of his words.

***

The Guild Hall clocks chimed four times and Loredana startled, spilling her remaining corallo balls on the floor again. She groaned in frustration, but at least this time she remembered to carefully lay the necklace she was working on in such a way that it would not come undone. Ciro glanced up from his cammeo but said nothing.

"I'll take Loredana home and get some fish and bread on the way back," Seppe said, setting a cup of coffee on Ciro's workbench.

"Could you pick up some clay for me, while you're out?" Ciro asked, breathing in the sharp aroma. "If not, I'll get some tomorrow instead of walking the docks."

"I can walk the docks for you tomorrow," Loredana piped up from the floor.

Ciro raised an eyebrow at her. "All the marinai know I'm your apprentice now, Zio. They won't try to sell me anything you wouldn't buy. And I'll just tell them you'll pay them on Argentodi if I get anything. Please!"

Her eyes grew so large, Ciro thought they would pop out of her head.

"Very well," he relented. "As long as you promise not to take Seppe the long way home today. His legs are even older than mine."

Ciro winked at Loredana and she hid her face when Seppe turned towards her giggles. Carefully, she replaced all the dropped balls on her tray, threaded the last few balls onto the necklace and tied the corallo-coloured string into a knot to secure them in place.

"Will you show me how you make this into a real necklace tomorrow?" Loredana asked, putting it gently in the drawer of unfinished works, alongside the branch thread Seppe had made the previous week.

Ciro nodded absently, his attention dedicated to the flowery cammeo he was carving.

Chapter 11 – Ramedi 10 Gioiellieri 230 Years After Implosion

The door flew open and Loredana ran towards Ciro, heedless of the fact that his hands were covered in clay.

"Zio! You need to come to the docks!" she shouted at him between gulping breaths. "Hurry! Now, now, now!"

Without pausing to even take her hat off, she tugged Ciro by the arm, preventing him from continuing his work. He shrugged free of her.

"Zio?" he said, raising an eyebrow. "My young apprentice, you convinced me yesterday that you could deal with anything on the docks. What's the big hurry?"

She shook her head and pulled his arm harder.

"You don't understand, *Maestro*. Antonino has the biggest piece of corallo I've ever seen! Bigger than my head!"

Ciro froze. She must have seen the disbelief in his eyes for she stilled and looked at him seriously.

"Maestro, bigger than my head, with branches from my wrist to the tips of my fingers all over it and a whole basket of smaller branches, but all of them bigger than I've ever seen on the beach. I couldn't carry it all if I tried and Antonino said he wouldn't trust me with it anyway. He's hiding it on his boat, under a pile of potato sacks, just for you."

Her words washed over him like a cloud of ash, suffocating him with hope. He cleared his throat, as though that would help him breathe.

"Wash your hands," Seppe told him. "I'll wet a cloth and keep the clay damp until you return."

Ciro nodded and went to wash up. The clay was being stubborn and did not want to wash off. He did the best he could and dried the rest. Before joining Loredana, he went upstairs and took a handful of gold coins from the secret cache under the floorboards next to his bed. If Antonino really had the treasure Loredana told him of, it would be worth more than he could possibly afford – he selfishly hoped Antonino didn't realise that.

***

Loredana ran ahead of him on the docks, weaving her way in and around the ropes tethering boats to the wooden planks. He hurried along behind her but could not match her pace. As it was, he was out of breath just from the brisk walk here.

As he approached the berth, Antonino waved him over. For the first time in their long acquaintance, the marinaio allowed him to board his boat. Ciro's eyes darted all over the deck until his eyes came to rest on a pile of potato sacks, clearly hiding something.

"Is that it?" he asked, not daring to move close.

Antonino nodded. "I was closer to shore than usual because of the Mercantili Blockade. Guess that's a good thing, or they'd have tried to make me pay a tariff for it."

Ciro listened with half an ear. All his focus was on the pile of potato sacks, but that snagged Ciro's attention.

"Mercantili Blockade?" He turned to face the marinaio. "*What blockade*?"

Antonino stared at him, eyebrows raised high. "Ciro, have you been hiding under a rock? The Mercantili Guild put up a blockade last week. Said there'd been too many goods getting into the city around their dock inspections. They left us just enough room to fish, but that's all. Anyone wanting in or out of Golfo di Tor'Esint needs to have special permission!"

Ciro looked out to sea. In the distance, he could just see a row of boats surrounding the gulf. They weren't so close together that no one could get past, but any who did would likely be punished if they didn't stop.

"Anyway, good for you that I stayed close to shore. There's a little area I know of that has corallo not too far below the surface. That's where we sometimes get you the longer branches." He looked up and down the dock, making sure no one was close enough to hear him. "But I got a friend, see, who helped me with a sort of water suit that lets me stay underwater for a while. Long enough to make a cutting if you get my drift."

Ciro had no idea what the marinaio was talking about but nodded all the same. All he knew was there was a treasure under the cloth and he couldn't wait to see it. Antonino glanced over to Loredana.

"Keep an eye out. Let me know if anyone's coming, right?"

Loredana nodded seriously and turned her back to them. Ciro could barely contain his excitement as Antonino drew back the sacking. His eyes grew wide. Loredana hadn't exaggerated – in fact, she'd *underestimated* how large it was.

Standing next to it, the trunk of the corallo reached his knees, but the highest branch reached as high as Ciro's waist and others spread out the length of his arms on either side. Next to it was a large wicker basket filled to the brim with large branches of corallo, easily each as long as his fingers, some as long as his hand.

Ciro's eyes blurred with tears. He'd never seen such a treasure before. Looking closer, he saw one of the smaller branches towards the top was cut short.

"What happened here?" he asked, pointing to the stump.

Antonino scratched at his beard. "A piece snapped off while we were hauling it up onto the boat. Didn't realise how delicate those smaller pieces were. Still, I'm sure you can work around that, no?"

Ciro nodded. Even with this imperfection, it would still make a magnificent statue.

"Thank you for saving it for me, but what will it cost?" he asked, reaching out to touch the beauty. "I can't promise I have enough."

Antonino covered it over again and drew Ciro to the small side panel where they could sit.

"Listen, Ciro, you've been my best customer for as long as I've been fishing. I always saved the best shells and corallo for you because you paid the most. One day, I thought to myself, I wanted to see what you did with it all. I snuck into your workshop when only your companion was there and snooped around. I ain't proud of it, but there it is, and I'm glad I did too. I went to the others' workshops after that to see if you're all the same, but they pale in comparison. I mean, have you ever gone into their workshops?"

Ciro shook his head. "I've only seen what they show me, or what they submitted as Great Works."

Antonino patted him on the shoulder. "I went to the Guild Hall too. You must know, even just from those works, that you're the best. Even Errico Corallino wasn't as good as you. I saw his works there too.

"Now, I'm going to sell you this basket here at a fair price. What we're going to do with the big bit there is you take it just as soon as you can figure a way to move it. When you carve and sell it, you pay me my cut then. Agreed?"

"I don't know," Ciro said, pursing his lips. "Who would ever be able to afford such a carving? And if they couldn't choose the subject themselves, who would want to pay for it?"

Antonino shrugged. "You have a bidding war. It's what we do with a big haul of vongole or fish. We bring it all to the front of the docks and have a bidding war. The right people find out about it and they bid. Simple as that."

"It could be a few weeks before I'm able to pay you if we do it that way," Ciro sighed. "Are you sure you trust me with it until then?"

Antonino got to his feet and pulled Ciro along with him. "Guess I'll have to. There ain't no one else in Tor'Esint I'm gonna trust with it. Let's call it five gold for these branches and we'll figure out the other one later."

Ciro stood and shook Antonino by the hand, clasping his shoulder at the same time. "Thank you, Toni. You'll never know what this means to me."

Antonino shrugged him off, embarrassed, and bent to pick up the large wicker basket. He went to pour the corallo into Ciro's own basket only to realise it wasn't big enough. Shaking his head, he poured as much as would fit and covered his own basket with a canvas cloth.

"Loredana, if I let Ciro take this basket home, can you bring it straight back again?"

She turned and nodded, jumping from one foot to the other. Ciro laughed at her excitement – it was obviously the most fun she'd had as an apprentice so far. He paid Antonino the five gold, feeling the loss keenly, and started the walk back home.

***

They entered the workshop to a loud argument between Seppe and Simone. Ciro motioned for Loredana to take Antonino's basket into the kitchen before anyone could snoop at the contents.

"It's not your workshop, now let me pass!" Simone shouted. "I've every right to see what they're doing!"

Seppe stood firmly in front of the wooden panels. "It may not be my workshop, but it's more than my life is worth to let you behind here. Ciro told me you decided not to work with them, so you've no business here. Please leave."

"I'm not leaving until you let me see," Simone said, pushing Seppe roughly aside.

Ciro coughed loudly and strode towards them.

"Take your hands off my companion," he said in a dangerously low voice, "and move away from the panel."

Simone rounded on him with lava in his eyes.

"I'm as much a part of the Gioiellieri Guild as you. I've every right to see what you're doing."

Ciro held out his hand to an unsteady Seppe, looking anxiously over him to make sure he wasn't hurt, and barely spared Simone a glance.

"You were offered the same opportunity as the rest of us," Ciro told him. "It was your choice to turn it down. You don't get to see it. Now, leave my workshop or I'll send my apprentice out to call the Tor'Esint Amministratori."

"Apprentice?" Simone sounded startled.

Ciro, satisfied that Seppe was unharmed, turned to stare at Simone, not answering.

Loredana calmly entered the workshop from the kitchen carefully carrying two cups.

"Coffee before we start today, Maestro?" she asked, walking slowly towards them. She handed one cup to Ciro and one to Seppe with a wink. "Did you need me to go to the Town Hall now? Or the Gioiellieri Guild? Didn't you say they wanted to know if there was any trouble?"

Ciro considered her offer.

"They *did* indeed say that. And Yvette would be furious if she knew." He turned to Simone. "Well, Simone, should I send my apprentice to the Gioiellieri Guild or the Town Hall? Either way, you'd be stuck in a lava stream. What's it to be?"

"Bah!" Simone threw his hands up in the air. "It's not worth it. Not like you'll get paid for your work anyway, so what do I care?"

He stormed out, slamming the door so hard in his wake that it rattled in the wooden frame. Ciro took a deep breath, set his cup down and rested a hand on Seppe's back.

"Are you alright?" he asked in a worried tone. "Did he hurt you?"

Seppe shook his head and sipped his coffee slowly with trembling fingers, obviously trying to calm his nerves. "He came in a little while before you and demanded to see the project, like it was his right. I held him off as best I could but, Ciro, I really don't think this is the safest place for you to work on it. What if he comes back again? What if he hires someone to steal it from you? What then?"

Loredana hugged Seppe with such force, he almost spilt his coffee on her. Ciro took the cup from him to forestall an accident.

"I don't know," Ciro admitted. "I need to ask the Maestri to help us decide what to carve next week anyway. I suppose it can't hurt to tell them what happened today."

"I'll tell them," Loredana volunteered. "I've got to go out anyway to bring Antonino his basket. On the way back, I could give the Maestri a message from you if you like. Will that help?"

"Will that help?" Ciro laughed. "My little apprentice, you've already done so much to help. Who knows what Simone would've done without your threat? But yes, it's a good idea. Wait a moment while I write a note. Don't let anyone read it except one of the Maestri – not even Yvette. Understand?"

Loredana nodded solemnly. Ciro gave Seppe back his coffee and patted Loredana's cheek. She smiled affectionately at his attention, which in turn made him smile. He went to his workstation, blew on his coffee and took a small sip before taking out a sheet of paper and a pen. Ciro quickly wrote to the Maestri asking them for a meeting at his house next Gildadi and explaining the problem with Simone, wording it in such a way they should not take action against him.

He handed Loredana the sealed note with instructions to go straight to the docks, then the Guild Hall and back again. No side routes, no stopping anywhere else. She promised and tucked the note in her pocket. Only once she'd left did Ciro finally finish his coffee, watching Seppe. His faithful companion turned towards him, seeming to feel eyes upon him.

"I'm fine, Ciro. Really."

Ciro only nodded. Seppe shook his head, knowing full well Ciro would not stop worrying for him.

"Tell me what happened with Antonino."

Ciro put his hand down to the full basket by his side. He hadn't had time to take it off since returning. Carefully, he undid the strap and put the basket on the largest workbench. Lifting the lid, he gestured at the large corallo branches. Seppe picked one up and turned it over, studying it closely.

"It's good quality. Is it all like this?"

Ciro nodded. "And there's more in the kitchen. I don't know where Loredana put it, but we'll need a new basket for all of these. There's too many for our usual spot."

"I've got some baskets out the back. I'll find something," Seppe replied. "Are you happy to keep them in the workshop?"

"I've nowhere else to keep them." Ciro shrugged. He really could do with a slightly bigger workshop. "But we've got a bigger problem. That piece of corallo, well, it's even larger than the one the Guild gave us to work with. I don't know where we're going to keep it. Or how to find a customer for it. Antonino suggested a bidding war, but I wouldn't know where to start."

Seppe smiled. "Oh, but I think you do. Your new Sarta friend – I've heard people talking of her lately. She made a dress for Signora Loyola, of all people, and as a result has many more wealthy customers. Aren't we meant to be having dinner with her soon? You could drop in a quick request for an introduction."

"Seppe, I do believe you've been eavesdropping." He kissed Seppe with a laugh. "Good for me! I'll make sure to ask her. In the meantime, we've got to figure out a way to get the corallo here without anyone seeing. We'll have to just keep it in the kitchen until we have a better spot. It'll be too heavy for us to keep moving around."

Seppe drained the rest of his coffee and took Ciro's empty cup.

"Who do we know that owns a blazermobile?" he asked, walking to the kitchen. "Doesn't Telchide's new companion have one? I'm sure I heard she does."

Ciro sighed heavily. "She's not his companion, and I don't like asking favours from so many people."

"Then you should have started charging more for your wares a long time ago," Seppe called out from the kitchen. "Just because it doesn't take you as long to make things anymore, doesn't mean you shouldn't still charge a lot for them. People are paying for your skills, not the amount of time it takes you to make something."

Ciro grunted. Seppe had made the same argument many times over, but Ciro had always refused. Just because his skills were unsurpassed in Tor'Esint didn't mean he had to charge through the nose for his wares. He thought it unfair that poorer people should not afford his goods. They deserved just as much finery, for he was certain they worked just as hard, or harder, than wealthy people.

He recalled his discussion with Greta about the options she gave her customers to purchase cheaper clothes. Of course, he charged only what he needed to for his pre-made corallo jewellery items and more for the custom ordered pieces, but cammei were different. Not many people would purchase a pre-made cammeo – they wanted them custom made for their loved ones, so he had little choice but to charge the same price to everyone. Either he sold them all for a fortune, or just what he knew the poorer people could afford.

Seppe returned, carrying a large basket containing the corallo Loredana had left in the kitchen. Ciro poured his own stash into the basket, which was now half full with corallo.

"I saw some trolleys down at the docks," Ciro told him, "Antonino might have one we can use. I'll ask him tomorrow morning if I can borrow one. I really do need to work on this clay model now. What a morning!"

Chapter 12 – Argentodi 11 Gioiellieri 230 Years After Implosion

Ciro woke early and set about rearranging the workshop. If Antonino agreed to let him use the trolley, he'd need somewhere to store the corallo until he figured out what to do with it. The kitchen, he had quickly realised, was out of the question. There was barely enough room to move let alone store the large trunk of corallo.

The workshop, though, he could manage. There was a corner behind his favourite workbench that would be perfect for the trunk, if he could just clear the space. He lost himself in the manual work of rearranging his workshop.

Small baskets of shells were added to a larger one on the other side of the workshop, in the corner next to the larger machines. The shell fragments, which had already been cut and shaped for cammei, were stowed in the second drawer of unfinished works. Technically, they *were* unfinished works, he reasoned with himself. Once moved, he could see that the stone floor was covered in a carpet of tiny corallo fragments, either from small branches or balls that had rolled there to be forgotten and lost over time. What a mess!

He was well into sweeping up the area before Seppe walked in with a cup of coffee and a biscuit on a saucer.

"You make enough noise to rouse a petrified man!" He passed the cup and saucer to Ciro, taking the broom from his hands. "Drink, eat, and go to the docks."

"Sorry, but look, it's the perfect spot!" He gestured to the newly cleared area. "And no one will see it while I sit here. We'll just cover it with a cloth and then we're set."

Seppe just glowered at him until Ciro walked away and ate his breakfast. Seppe was always grumpy if something woke him earlier than usual. Ciro had learned early on that he should never operate any of the noisy machinery before trading. It had quickly gotten to the point where Seppe had practically banned him from using the machinery at all, preferring to choose when he had to deal with the noise.

The only thing Ciro insisted on doing himself was cutting the sardonyx shells into cammeo shapes. They were precious to him, and he did not want to entrust any part of that process to someone else. The corallo, while also precious, was simpler, much more repetitive, and it almost didn't matter if a mistake was made because corallo could always be changed into another shape to add to a different collection. Fewer people would notice blemishes on their corallo balls than would notice them on cammei.

"I'm going down to the docks. Antonino should be back with his haul by now and can help me put the corallo on a trolley."

"Oh yes, and is he going to help you move it too?" Seppe said, shaking his head. "It'll be too heavy for you. You'll stop halfway home and need help getting it back."

Ciro waved a hand at him angrily. "Bah! I can't talk to you when you're like this. I'll be back later. If Loredana arrives before me, ask her to start with her drawings."

Before Seppe could reply, Ciro took his coppola and coat off the wall and left the workshop.

The walk down to the docks calmed him. The pavement became more crowded the closer he got to the docks. Marinai were set up all over the streets with their wares in barrels. Some had fish, others thin razor clams, vongole or cuttlefish. Ciro tried to stay away from the fish-filled barrels. If he was sprayed with water as tails flicked around, he'd stink of fish all day and, much as he loved the taste, the smell on his clothes was more than he could bear.

On Corso delle Gilde, the main road along the docks, there was barely room for a carriage or blazermobile to pass. It was always like that early in the day, but by midday, most goods had been sold and the marinai cleared away. People like Antonino had a bevy of workers selling his wares so he could remain with his boat and fix things for the next day's work.

Ciro wound his way through the marinai market and down to the actual docks. Antonino was mending a fishing net when he arrived.

"Good morning, Toni," Ciro called out from the dock.

Antonino looked up and waved, needle in hand.

"Here to pick up your special item?" Antonino asked.

Ciro nodded. "I've cleared space for it in my workshop, but I was hoping you'd lend me a trolley to move it?"

"By yourself?" Antonino laughed. He called out to someone on his boat and waited until they appeared.

"Tiziano, help me move this corallo trunk and then take over the mending for me. I'll be gone for a half hour or so." He set the needle and net on a nearby box. "Don't go wasting time. I know how long it should take to do this and I'll know if you've been slacking off while I'm away."

Tiziano nodded, with a look that clearly showed he'd heard the same speech a thousand times. Antonino jumped over the side of the boat and positioned his trolley in place. It was a little thing, only a few piedi in size – just big enough to move two barrels of fish. Unlike many of the other trolleys Ciro had seen, this one had short wooden sides all around except where the moveable handle was, so it wouldn't impede movement.

"Keep it steady," he told Ciro as he jumped back on board and worked with Tiziano to carefully lift the corallo.

Ciro stood behind the trolley, to make sure it wouldn't move when they placed the corallo on. It looked heavy. Ciro wondered if he and Seppe would be able to move it by themselves. At least Antonino would be able to help him get it up the stairs to his workshop in the first place.

Antonino and Tiziano positioned the corallo atop the trolley, tying it in place and ensuring the cloth covered it completely from prying eyes. Antonino had taken the extra precaution of tying a rope around the bottom of the cloth so it wouldn't slip. With a final warning to Tiziano, he lifted the trolley handle and began to tug at it. Ciro quickly caught up and pulled on the other side of the handle, easing the burden for Antonino.

Together, they navigated their way through the throng of marinai.

"It's a good thing you're near the docks, Ciro, or I'd never have agreed to help you," Antonino said jovially.

Ciro grunted in agreement. Though his workshop was only four blocks away from the dock entry, Antonino's berth was halfway along the docks, adding at least another five hundred piedi to their journey.

It was a strategic position – Ciro had purposely selected a workshop as near the beach and the docks as he could at the time. If he was to walk there every day in search of materials, he didn't want to be on the other side of Tor'Esint. It had worked in his favour many times.

By the time they returned to the workshop, Loredana had arrived with Tania. Ciro hesitated for a moment. He'd forgotten it was one of her days. That could make things more complicated, but not impossible.

"Zio Ciro!" Tania squealed, running down the stairs and hugging his legs tightly. "What's in there?"

"*This* is a big secret," Antonino answered before Ciro could reply. "Your Zio can't even tell *you* about it."

Ciro nodded in agreement. "Yes, Guild secrets, Tania. Sorry. Now, be a good girl and practise your drawing with Loredana."

Tania scrunched up her face as though she would argue, but changed her mind and raced back inside.

"It will be kept a secret, until you've sold it, won't it?" Antonino asked, warily. "I don't want anyone finding out about it and stealing it. And I don't want many knowing it was me who sold it to you. The fewer people who know about it, the better."

"Yes, of course," Ciro reassured him. "I have a plan to find some bidders, then I'll give you your share as soon as it's sold. No one needs to know where it comes from. But should there be more of a market for this than I think there is, or even the larger branches I took yesterday, is that something we can discuss?"

Antonino rubbed his nose along his arm, sniffing as he did so. Ciro tried not to scrunch up his nose in distaste at the sight.

"I reckon so. Just you come see me when you run out." He paused for a moment. "And if you don't mind your Corallini friends knowing about those branches, send them my way. *Those* I can pass off as getting without my new special water suit."

Ciro easily agreed to the plan and went inside to call Seppe. The three of them unfastened the ropes, lifted the corallo off the wooden trolley and navigated their way up the stairs, careful not to bump the wider branches against the doorway. Once inside the workshop, it was trickier, as all three couldn't all hold the corallo at the same time and navigate between the narrow spaces. Ciro and Seppe took it in turns to hurry around the workbenches and display cabinets to help on the next section.

Eventually, they managed to manoeuvre it all the way to the spot Ciro had cleared just behind his workbench. Only then did he realise the corallo was larger than he'd remembered. There was barely enough room left for him to sit. Seppe found the cloth they had put aside to cover it and quickly switched it for Antonino's canvas cloth without allowing Tania to see what was underneath.

Once Antonino had left, Loredana glanced up from her drawing and smiled proudly at Ciro. She'd done a marvellous job in getting him down to the dock yesterday. If not for her, Antonino may have relented and sold the corallo trunk to the Gioiellieri Guild, or to another Corallino. She picked up her sketchbook, brought it over to Ciro and showed him her flowers.

"Zio, when will I do something other than flowers?" she asked, not quite pouting.

Ciro shrugged. "You can try sketching your sister if you like. Mind, don't expect it to look like my portraits, but you need to start sometime. Otherwise, I can draw some small birds for you. Your choice."

She considered her options. "Tania won't be here tomorrow, so I'll sketch her today. Can you draw some birds for me to copy tomorrow? Or fish?"

"Fish?" Ciro asked in surprise. "Why fish?"

"I like fish," she said simply.

"Well, fish it is then," Ciro huffed. "And birds. Birds are important. They're pretty and people like them. They make nice carvings and you'll need to be good at them."

"Fine – birds and fish. But Tania today."

She returned to the display desk, which she and Tania had converted to a sketching station and proceeded to stare at her sister. Ciro left the two of them there and returned his attention to the corallo trunk. It was more than three times the size of the one the Gioiellieri Guild had given him to carve. If the Guild found out about it, they'd insist on using it instead. Ciro hoped it didn't come to that – he knew he'd refuse and that would be the end of the entire project.

"How are you going to stop Anna and Sabrina from snooping back here?" Seppe asked quietly.

"They've been too busy arguing with each other to notice anything other than what's behind that wooden panel," Ciro replied, disgusted with their behaviour. "And with the Maestri coming on Gildadi to decide on a design, they won't have eyes for anything else. Now, let me get back to that last clay model or I'll have nothing to show them."

Chapter 13 – Mercatodi 14 Gioiellieri 230 Years After Implosion

Every second Mercatodi, Piazza Mercantile was crammed with Guild stalls of every kind, many of which often spilled out into Via dell'Oro and Via Mercato. Every other Mercatodi, the cafés and pasticcerie opened their doors wide and brought tables and chairs out to line the Piazza. Ciro loved it – the bitter aroma of coffee, the sweetness of the desserts – it was enough to make him salivate.

"Zio, can we get a pastry?" Tania asked, skipping along beside him. Loredana tried to shush her, but Tania just opened her eyes widely, innocently. "I'm hungry and they smell so nice!"

Loredana pinched her arm, which caused Tania to squeal, hurting Ciro's ears.

"Loredana, what was that for?" he asked, dragging her around to his other side, away from her sister.

"Mamma specifically told her not to ask you for anything today," Loredana said loudly enough for Tania to hear. "She's already annoyed that you're buying Tania a dress, she doesn't want her spending all your money."

Tania gripped Ciro's hand tightly. "*You're* getting new clothes, so why can't I?"

"Because *I'm* the apprentice, not *you*!" Loredana snapped.

"Girls!" Ciro said, loud enough to make passersby turn their heads. "Girls," he repeated more quietly, "enough fighting or I'll tell Greta we've changed our minds about the dresses."

The effect was instant. Silence, pure and sweet. Ciro only wished he'd thought of it earlier in the week. They'd been at each other's throats half the time. Tania was not impressed that Loredana was taking up more of Ciro's attention than she was. It was a problem to which he had no solution.

By the time they arrived at Greta's workshop, Tania was gripping his hand so tightly, it actually hurt. He shook free of her to open the door and let them in. Loredana followed Tania inside. They immediately walked to opposite sides of the showroom – Ciro could no longer think of it as a workshop when it had so many outfits on display.

The young apprentice, Sofia, came to greet him with her beautiful dimpled smile.

"You look like you could use a drink," she said, showing him to a large armchair. "Tea?"

Ciro tried not to scrunch his nose at the idea, but clearly didn't manage. Sofia laughed lightly.

"I'll put on a pot of coffee for you," she said conspiratorially. "Greta hates the smell, but many of our customers prefer it, so she'll just have to grin and bear it."

"Thank you, Sofia." Ciro pressed her hand between his before sinking into the armchair with a sigh. "You've no idea how much I need one."

Sofia's eyes darted from one young girl to the other. "Don't worry, we'll fix them both up so they'll be smiling for days and not have anything to fight about."

Ciro watched the harmony of the Sarti in this workshop and wished for such peace in his own life. The Copper Sarti spoke jovially as they worked closely at a cluster of workbenches. He could not see Greta from where he was because of the fabric panelling in front of her workbench. Off to the side of the work area, two girls barely older than Sofia herself, probably also apprentices, were working on separate items.

Sofia spoke to the older one who glanced over to Tania and put down her work. The older apprentice walked over to a rack near the change room and flicked through the clothing until she found the item she was searching for then called Tania over. Loredana looked over her shoulder as Tania ran to try on her new dress.

Ciro waited until Tania was behind the curtain before beckoning over Loredana. She didn't wait to be asked, but sat on his lap and snuggled into his shoulder, legs curled up under her.

"I know you're going to tell me not to be mean to her," Loredana said, in a trembling voice, "but I'm not trying to be. Mamma was very clear this morning. She knows all you're doing to help us and doesn't want to be more of a burden than she already thinks we are. Especially with Tania coming to the workshop every day that mamma's working."

"Shh," Ciro whispered as he stroked her hair. "I'm not angry with you. We just have to find a way to entertain her when she comes, so she doesn't feel left out. Can you help me with that? Try to think of something, and so will I. We can give her a special project to work on while I teach you all you need to know."

Loredana nodded into his chest. Ciro wrapped his arms around her and held her tightly until the tension released from her body. He kissed the top of her head before letting her go.

Sofia arrived at that moment with his coffee and a pot of tea, which she set down on the small table between the two armchairs.

"Are you ready to try on your first dress?" Sofia asked Loredana. "Greta worked on it for days, just for you."

Loredana's eyes lit up. She hopped off Ciro's lap and placed her hand trustingly in Sofia's. The apprentice Sarta winked at Ciro as she led his niece away.

Only after they were both out of his hair did Greta make an appearance. He rose to kiss her cheeks. She took the seat next to him, helping herself to a cup of tea. Ciro followed her lead and picked up the cup of coffee, savouring the bitter aroma and the first moment of peace he'd had all day.

"It gets easier," she told him. He looked at her inquisitively. "The apprentice situation, I mean. It *does* get easier. You just need to find your rhythm, that's all."

Ciro raised an eyebrow doubtfully. "The apprenticeship isn't the problem. It's the other one coming along when her mamma's at work. Otherwise, there wouldn't be a problem."

Greta looked across as the girls came out of their respective change areas and admired their new dresses.

"You know, Telchide's daughter seems about your littlest one's age. Do they know each other?"

Ciro shrugged. "I've barely seen Chide these past few years. I don't think the girls have met Teresina."

"You might like to introduce them," Greta suggested casually. "Apparently, she's quite the precocious child. Telchide says she's teaching his apprentices to read and often helps her nonna around the house. I'm sure she'd appreciate a friend."

Ciro grunted noncommittally. Greta smoothed her dress over her knees.

"Have you spoken to Giuseppe about dining at the Exploding Beakers?" she asked, a little too casually. "You could always mention introducing the girls to each other to Telchide then. I was hoping we might go this evening or tomorrow."

"This evening would be lovely. Could we make it for an hour after trading?" he asked hopefully. "I don't think we can walk there any quicker than that."

Greta broke into a large smile, softening her angular features. "Well, yes, five o'clock would be fine, but I won't have you walking all that way. My new blazermobile arrived just the other day and I've barely had a chance to use it. Would you permit me to drive you?"

Ciro sat up straighter. "A blazermobile? Seppe would murder me if I gave up the opportunity for the two of us to ride in one."

"It's settled then," Greta said with a laugh. "I'll pick you up at half past four. Nestore won't mind if we're a little early and have a drink before the others arrive. I've heard his Smoking Limoncello is to die for."

"A ... *Smoking* Limoncello? What in Caldera's smoke is that?"

Greta leaned in close. "Aveline says it's a zesty, lemon-flavoured liqueur, served in a chilled beaker with thick, lemon scented smoke rising out of it."

"Well then, a Smoking Limoncello we must have. Now, let me see these dresses my nieces look so happy about."

***

Loredana gathered up Tania at the end of day's trading and together they cleared away their mess from Ciro's workshop. Both had refused to take off their new dresses when leaving Greta's shop, so Ciro gave them a little basket to take their old dresses home. Threadbare though they were, he knew Serafina would not allow them to be discarded. He hated that she always had to be so careful with her money. Perhaps that would change when the money he gave her for Loredana began to make a difference.

They left at a quarter past four, giving Ciro just fifteen minutes to freshen up before Greta arrived. Seppe was already laying out their new shirts upstairs. They got ready as quickly as they could, which wasn't nearly fast enough. Greta knocked on the door before Ciro was even halfway down the stairs.

"Coming, coming," he called out loudly.

The knocking ceased. Ciro wove his way through the workshop and opened the door just as Greta's hand was poised to knock again. She quickly dropped it with an apologetic smile.

"I'm not sure how to get the blazermobile's engine to stop running. I've got the brake on, and Domizio's holding it steady, but we don't know how long that'll work. Are you ready?"

Her words swirled around him like a gust of wind. He found himself nodding, just to stop her talking.

"Seppe, our ride's here!" he turned and called out loudly.

Seppe hurried down the stairs, always that little bit sprightlier than Ciro himself. Greta greeted Seppe politely, only to be surprised when he too kissed her cheeks. Flustered, Greta opened the front door to the blazermobile and shuffled over to the steering wheel, taking over from Domizio. Seppe opened the back door and quickly climbed in, drinking in every detail of the new contraption. Ciro smiled to himself as he locked the workshop door behind them and hopped into the blazermobile, squashing up close to Seppe.

"Good evening, Signori," Domizio turned to greet them. Ciro and Seppe replied in kind as they settled in.

"Ready?" Greta asked, her hand on the brake lever. Everyone nodded. "Let's go!"

She tugged the lever up and then eased it down. The blazermobile roared to life and the vehicle screamed down the street. Greta held the steering wheel with both hands, peering carefully out the front window and weaving her way around the evening couples in their horse-drawn carriages. Ciro felt slightly perturbed by the jolty drive, but whenever he chanced a sideways glance at Seppe, his companion's eyes were as sparkling as his smile.

By the time they reached Viale del'Alchimisti, the blazermobile's engine had started to sputter and jolt them forward in small bursts.

"Oh, Lucrezia warned me about this!" Greta groaned. "I've let it run too low on blazer solution. I don't suppose you're happy to walk the half block to the tavern? Aveline will know how to fix it. She can help us on the way home."

"That was amazing!" Seppe exclaimed, making everyone jump. "Blazermobiles are fabulous, aren't they?"

Ciro didn't answer. He wasn't quite as enthused as Seppe and didn't want to hurt his feelings. Instead, he opened the door and hopped out, helping Seppe from the blazermobile as Domizio did likewise with Greta. They were on the border of the Alchimisti and Inventrici Quarters, quite close to Telchide's workshop.

Ciro held out his arm for Greta and was pleased to see Domizio hold out his arm for Seppe. The lovely Sarta looped her arm in his and strode off down the street with Domizio and Seppe following close behind.

They arrived at the Exploding Beakers as a cloud of bright blue smoke billowed out of every crack in the building. Ciro looked at Greta hesitantly, but she walked straight ahead, into the smoke. He had no choice but to follow. Once inside the blue cloud, Ciro took shallow breaths, until he recognised the scent of lilac. That sweet, heady scent – it was all around him. He breathed in deeply and let out a laugh.

"This is marvellous!" he cried as they walked through the door with Greta. "Lilacs, Seppe! It's lilacs!"

"Who guessed it?" a loud voice boomed from within. "Who guessed lilacs? Come to the bar!"

As the smoke dissipated, Ciro found dozens of eyes staring at him. He took his hat off and nodded politely before hanging his things on the wall rack. Seppe nudged him towards the bar where Greta and Domizio were already waiting for them.

"Which one of you two fine signori guessed lilacs?" the burly man behind the bar asked them, as Ciro and Seppe approached.

"That would be me," Ciro said proudly.

"Well, then, your first drink is on the house. What'll it be?"

Ciro looked at Greta who nodded encouragingly. He gave a small shrug.

"I've heard the Smoking Limoncello is the drink of choice."

The man nodded knowingly. "Coming right up. Take a seat and I'll bring it over when it's ready. What about your friends?"

"We'll have the same to begin with," Greta said. "We're here to have dinner with Telchide and Aveline."

The man looked at her closer. "Of course, Greta Sarta! I should have recognised you sooner. And who are your friends?"

"Nestore, meet Domizio Sarto, Ciro Corallino and Giuseppe..." Greta paused and blushed brightly. "I'm so sorry, Ciro only ever calls you Seppe."

"Giuseppe di Antonio," Seppe replied quickly. "But almost everyone calls me Seppe. You should too."

"Well, friends, why don't you take that booth in the corner?" Nestore gestured to the very back corner, sparsely lit by lanterns on the wall. "The six of you should fit in snugly. I'll bring four Smoking Limoncelli in a moment."

A stylishly dressed lady walked through the door, with Telchide a step behind. Ciro wasn't entirely certain, but he thought it was Aveline – he'd only met her once before, at Sebetine's inquest. Telchide helped her off with her coat, took off his own and hung them on the wall rack.

"Make that six, Nestore. I've had a craving for one of your drinks all week!" Aveline said, waiting for Telchide before walking over to them.

Greta leaned in to hug her. "Veli, you look so much better than the last time I saw you!"

"Yes, well, Crez's ginger tablets are doing wonders for my stomach."

Ciro stood by with Seppe, waiting for someone to properly introduce them. He doubted Aveline would remember him.

Telchide finally looked up and saw him. His eyes widened with his smile.

"Ciro! It's been too long!" He came over and kissed Ciro and Seppe on both cheeks, then hugged them close. "And Seppe! I've missed you both so much!"

"Well, no one stopped you from coming to visit," Ciro said, before he could stop himself.

Seppe elbowed him in the ribs.

"We could just as easily have visited Chide," Seppe said quietly, catching his gaze and holding it. "No matter. It's good to be together now, and we hear you have some news for us."

Telchide frowned in confusion. Ciro nodded towards Aveline.

"Oh, yes, forgive me. Ciro, Seppe, this is Veli. Aveline. Inventrice."

Telchide stumbled over the introduction like a child learning to walk. He was just like his father, Alberto Falegname. Ciro followed along easily, having grown up with Alberto.

"Aveline, it's a pleasure to meet you," Ciro said, shaking her hand.

She gave him an easy smile, and shook his hand firmly, doing likewise with Seppe. "Chide's told me all about you. I feel like we're friends already."

Nestore waved them all away from his bar. "Go, sit, or I won't be able to make your drinks."

Ciro followed the others to their booth and slid in between Telchide and Greta. Seppe was across from him between Aveline and Domizio.

"How's the new arrangement working, Greta?" Aveline asked.

Greta smiled broadly, glancing at Domizio. "Very well indeed. Mizi recommended some fantastic Copper Sarti and I *think* they like working with me."

"We *love* working for you, Greta," Domizio replied quickly. "And your apprentices have come so far now you have more time to spend with them."

"Your young one, Sofia, seems to be a great asset," Ciro added in. "My nieces absolutely adored her. They couldn't stop discussing what Sofia said about their new dresses. We barely had a quiet moment all day."

Domizio raised his eyebrows in a way that suggested he'd mentioned something similar to her himself.

"Yes, well, Fia is a lovely girl. I don't deserve such an apprentice, but there you have it." She paused for only a moment before launching into another topic. "Telchide, how old is Teresina now?"

"She's six."

Aveline huffed. "Yes, but she acts like a teenager already. You should see the way she orders around Chide's apprentices when they let her. I tell you, Chide, she needs friends her own age."

Ciro could practically feel Greta glowing beside him.

"Exactly what I thought." Greta clapped her hands together. "You know, Telchide, Ciro's youngest niece could be a good friend for your daughter."

"Niece?" Chide asked in confusion. "I didn't know you had a niece. Well, not here anyway."

Ciro tried not to shake his head. "Seems we both have news. My sister's girl, Serafina, came here with her daughters just a year or so ago, when Cetti passed. I've taken her eldest, Loredana, as my apprentice. She's ten. Tania is eight."

"Congratulations!" Chide clapped him on the shoulder. "I always hoped you'd get an apprentice. Does she pay attention?"

"Chide, dear, I think Greta was trying to find a playmate for Teresina," Aveline said gently. "Do you think she'd like to play with a child only a couple of years older than her?"

Telchide blinked a few times. "Well, I don't know. She never has before. We could ask her."

"Or we could just set it up," Aveline countered. "It would give Serenita a nice break from entertaining her. When will you see Tania next, Ciro?"

"Tomorrow. We go to Serafina's house every Riposidi. A sort of tradition if you will."

"To be fair, I think she wouldn't mind a break either," Seppe said. "Poor girl works hard and then has us to cook for every Riposidi. Doesn't seem fair."

Greta adjusted her position next to Ciro, sitting up straighter.

"We could have a little celebration," Greta said. "I've got my new workshop going nicely, Aveline's pregnant and Ciro has a new apprentice, not to mention Telchide's two apprentices, though they aren't quite as new. All our apprentices hardly get time to spend together. We could all go out for lunch."

"No," Telchide said firmly. "You'll all come to my house. I insist. Ciro, Seppe, bring the family. Veli's right – it will be good for Teresina to meet a few children close to her age and that way they can play in her room."

"Chide, I'm not so sure about that," Aveline said gently. "That will be sixteen people for Serenita to cook for; assuming you come too, Domizio."

"Which means she'll be too busy to bother you," Telchide said softly, kissing her cheek. "Well Domizio, do we count you in?"

"How could I give up the chance to spend more time with Greta?" Domizio asked, looking fondly across the table at the Sarta.

Ciro saw the light blush rise on her cheeks, but he doubted anyone else noticed with the arrival of their Smoking Limoncelli. Nestore set the tray down in the middle of the table, which quickly filled with a layer of smoke. Ciro breathed it in deeply. The scent of lemon was strong, even before he took a sip. Zest exploded on his tongue, making his eyes water, but he couldn't stop drinking. It was the most marvellous thing.

The same was not true for everyone. As soon as Aveline picked up her drink, she put it back down forcefully, turning a sickly shade of green.

"Excuse me," she mumbled, pushing Seppe and Domizio out of the booth and running to the water closet.

Greta excused herself to go after her friend.

"I don't know how she does it," Telchide said softly. "She's sick most mornings and can barely keep anything down the rest of the day. I don't know why she agreed to come tonight. I mean, I know she wanted to meet you properly, Ciro. Greta's spoken of little else since she first walked into your workshop."

"It's true," Domizio agreed when Ciro raised a doubtful eyebrow. "The girls love their corallo pendants and wear them every day. But Greta's cammeo ... I can't even begin to tell you how much she loves it. I'm sure you noticed, she wore it tonight, as she does with every outfit she can match it with. Always on the opposite side to her Guild Mark brooch."

"Well, I must admit, I'm pleased to hear it," he said, with a final long sip of his Smoking Limoncello. "After so many years, I thought people might be bored by the art of a Corallino."

Greta returned, with menus from the bar, and sat next to Domizio, pushing Seppe over to Aveline's seat.

"Aveline will just be a moment. She's freshening up. I'll just order her a broth and hopefully she'll feel better soon. Now, Ciro, I wanted to ask you, is the Gioiellieri Guild planning anything particularly special for the Guild Ball? Other than the usual Parting Gifts? Any ... spectacles or such?"

"Signora, I've lived through enough Guild Balls to know that *anyone* who speaks of them beforehand is severely punished. That will not be my fate. I'm sure you'll thoroughly enjoy yourself. More than that, I will not say."

Greta shared a look with Telchide, but the Inventore shook his head at her. She sighed and sat back to enjoy her drink. By the time Aveline returned, they'd already ordered their food. Ciro had swapped seats with Telchide, to allow him to comfort Aveline.

Later that evening, after Greta had graciously stopped off at Serafina's apartment building so Ciro could tell her the change in plans for the next day, they pulled up in front of his workshop. Aveline had explained the finer workings of the blazermobile to Greta, so there was now no fear that it would run away without her or run out of blazer solution during a drive.

"Greta, I wondered if you might be able to help me," Ciro said, his hand on the door handle of the blazermobile. "I'm in a position I've not been in before and have an item I'm not entirely certain I can sell. I understand your client list is ... well, your clients move in affluent circles. Is this correct?"

"Yes, I would say that's correct," she replied curiously.

"Yes, well, do you think you could help me organise a sort of bidding war, or an auction of sorts, with only one item? I realise it's an odd request and if it's not possible, that's fine. I just thought I'd ask."

"Of course it's possible," Greta said easily. "But you don't need my help for that. You can advertise it in the newssheets and get a nice turnout."

Ciro immediately shook his head, as did Seppe.

"A secret auction, then?" Domizio asked. "For an item you don't want to tell everyone about?"

"Yes, exactly!" Ciro nodded. "Really, I don't even know if I can show it to them before they agree to buy it. I'll need to check with ... my supplier."

Greta frowned. "Ciro, this isn't something that's going to get you in trouble, is it? The Mercantili Guild's been on the lookout to hurt any Guild members they can after the Alchimista trials went so badly. They put up a blockade around Tor'Esint because they thought people were trading around them. Even passenger ships are being stopped on their way in and out."

"I don't think it will," he said. "It shouldn't. Will you help me?"

"Of course," she agreed easily. "You figure out how you want to do it and let me know. I'll spread the word among my most affluent customers, and they'll do the rest. Your item, whatever it is, will be sold before you know it."

"You see, Ciro, I told you she'd be able to help," Seppe said, proudly puffing up his chest.

"So you did. Clever man." Ciro kissed his cheek. "Thank you for the lift, Greta. It was lovely to meet you, Domizio. See you tomorrow with the rest of the family at Chide's house."

Chapter 14 – Riposidi 15 Gioiellieri 230 Years After Implosion

They stood outside Telchide's house, the five of them, ready to go in. Loredana and Tania both wore their new dresses. Serafina was fussing over her own outfit. It was clean and tidy, but so awfully plain. She had agreed, after much convincing, to wear one of Ciro's corallo branch pendants on a thin gold necklace. It drew attention away from the rest of her plain bodice.

"Now girls, be on your best behaviour, *please*!" Serafina said in a quiet voice. "Don't make me regret bringing you here. And Loredana, don't forget that your behaviour also reflects on Zio Ciro."

"Mamma," Loredana sighed. "We've been perfectly well behaved every time you've ever taken us out anywhere. Why would this be any different?"

Serafina didn't answer, but fussed with Tania's hair, trying to untangle it by running her fingers through the messy curls to no avail. Ciro shared an exasperated look with Seppe and knocked on the door. Loudly. There was already such a racket coming from inside.

"I'll get it!" yelled a young girl.

They heard her footsteps pounding up to the door. A child opened the door, barely younger than Tania, in a lovely yellow dress with so many pockets, Ciro couldn't count them.

"Are you Ciro Corallino and family?" she asked in a prim and proper voice.

"Indeed," Ciro answered with a little bow. "And you are Teresina di Sebetine?"

She smiled from ear to ear. "Yes. Come in. We've been waiting for you. Are your nieces here too?"

Teresina peered around him, trying to see who else was there, but eventually gave up and cleared the doorway for them. She stood up on a chair and took their hats and coats as they came in, depositing them on the nearby stand. When Loredana and Tania walked in, she went very quiet and very still.

Ciro gave Loredana a little nod. She returned the gesture and held out her hand to Teresina.

"I'm Loredana di Serafina. This is my sister Tania. We've very pleased to meet you."

Teresina shook their hands firmly. "Would you like to come up to my room? We can play there until lunch is ready."

The girls nodded eagerly and ran off with Teresina, up the stairs and out of view. Aveline walked over and lay a hand on Ciro's shoulder.

"That seems to have worked well," she said with a sigh of relief. "One never knows with Teresina. She's so used to adults that I thought she'd never agree to play with other children."

"My girls usually only have each other for company, and it can get a bit trying," Serafina said, edging closer to Ciro.

He took the hint.

"Aveline, may I introduce you to my niece, Serafina di Concettina. She lives in Zona Gioiellieri, not far from my workshop." He lay his hand on Serafina's back. "Serafina, this is Aveline Inventrice, a brilliant Inventrice by all accounts."

They exchanged pleasantries and Aveline led Serafina away to acquaint her with everyone else. Seppe took the opportunity to lead Ciro to a workstation laden with antipasti where the older apprentices were already making themselves at home. Ciro ate a few mouthfuls, taking the time to reacquaint himself with Telchide's workshop. It had changed a great deal since he'd first started renting it. The oddest thing was a contraption by the stairs.

"Chide, what's that on the handrail?" he asked, walking over to take a closer look.

Telchide came over and excitedly pulled down a little platform and patted it with his hand.

"Sit, I'll show you!"

Ciro made himself comfortable and waited. Telchide then placed a box in his hand.

"Wind this up and hold on tight!"

Everyone in the room stopped to look. Ciro did not like to disappoint them, so he wound up the little key on top of the box. With a sudden jolt, the entire chair began to move effortlessly up the stairs. Ciro watched the ground fall away below him and held on tightly. At his age, a fall down stairs could be catastrophic. Finally, and without incident, he stopped at the top of the stairs. It was a marvellous contraption!

"How do I come back down?" he called from the top floor.

Little footsteps came pattering down the hall. Teresina, closely followed by Tania and Loredana, ran up to him.

"I'll show you, if you say we can have a go next," she said, waggling her eyebrows up and down.

Ciro had to laugh. "But of course, Teresina. How could I ever deny the three of you a chance to use such a wondrous invention. Is it one of your papà's?"

"Caldera's smoke, no!" Teresina shook her head vigorously. "This was Aveline's project. Papà did help her a little, but it was her idea."

"Oh but, Zio, you should see the lightbox Signore Telchide made!" Tania said, jumping up and down. "It's the most wonderful thing! Come have a look before you go back downstairs."

"Very well."

With more ease than he expected, Ciro dismounted from the chair and followed the girls into Teresina's room. It was larger than the room he shared with Seppe, but instead of being taken up by a large bed, Teresina's small bed was firmly wedged up against a wall and a slew of inventions littered her floor.

She closed the blind and made an adjustment to the box by her feet and it started glowing – actually glowing – bright yellow.

Ciro went in for a closer look and realised the entire light box was filled with liquids in different compartments.

"Papà made it for me because I couldn't sleep properly with all my nightmares. They won't let him submit it as a Great Work because of the Inter-Guild Edict, you know, but it could have earned him a Gold Guild Mark otherwise. As it is, he's earned his Electrum and will probably get his Gold one soon." She turned up to Ciro and looked him up and down. "Where's your Guild Mark?"

"I only wear it on Trading Days," Ciro told her. "No need for it any other time."

"But how will anyone know what Guild status you hold if you don't wear it all the time?"

Loredana bristled at that. "Zio Ciro is the best Corallino in Tor'Esint. Anyone who knows anything about corallo knows that. What difference does it make if *you* know his Guild status? It's *Gold* by the way."

Ciro lay a hand on Loredana's shoulder, bringing her in close to him. The yellow light faded and Teresina opened the blind.

"You don't have to get angry about it," Teresina said haughtily. "*All* the Guild members I know wear their brooches or pins any time they leave the house. Or even if they don't, they wear them as long as they're in their workshop. The only time papà doesn't wear his is when he's sleeping because he works *all the time*. I hardly ever see him anymore. He's got so many projects to work on and another workshop on the other side of town where he works with Aveline sometimes."

She hesitated and closed her mouth, but the damage was done.

"Why does he need *another* workshop when this one is so big?" asked Tania. "You should see Zio Ciro's workshop. It's *tiny* compared to this. Barely any room to sit and draw, which is what I do almost the whole day when I go. I get so bored. Bet you never get bored. Wish I could come play with you instead."

"Oh, that would be fantastic!" Teresina jumped up. "Can she, Ciro? Can she come play instead of staying in your workshop?"

"It's not up to him," Loredana said firmly. "That's mamma's decision, and I doubt she'll say yes for a snobby little girl like you. You don't need to boast about how fabulous your papà is or how many workshops he has! Didn't anyone ever teach you to mind your manners?"

Before Ciro could say anything, Loredana had fled the room. Teresina stared after her, open-mouthed.

"I can see why you'd rather play with me than her," she said to Tania.

Only Ciro seemed to notice the struggle on Tania's face of whether to defend her sister or make fast her budding friendship with a rich Inventore's daughter. In the end, Teresina won. Ciro tried not to care, but a little part of him shrivelled at the sight. He left the girls to their games and went to find Loredana.

She was sitting on the stone step at the back door, angry tears coursing down her face. Ciro eased himself down beside her, pulled out a kerchief and dabbed it on her cheeks before placing it gently on her knees.

She sniffed and breathed out a long trembling breath, like she was trying not to make a sound. Heart breaking, Ciro put his arm around her and held her close. There was nothing to say that would make her feel better. As he looked at the small courtyard, full of fruit trees and herbs, he knew their situation in life could not change so completely that he could give her everything that richer families had. Or that more complete families had.

Teresina may not have a mamma, but she had Serenita and Aveline, who had very deftly taken over that role, even from afar as the case appeared. Her mamma had disappeared so long ago, Ciro doubted she even remembered her anymore. Not so for Loredana.

Her father had died at sea, shortly before Concettina passed on. He knew they'd been close. So close that Loredana could still barely speak of him. It was Serafina who'd told him the hurt caused by her companion's passing. How Loredana had adored him to the point of idolisation. How she'd crumbled when he hadn't returned from his fishing expedition.

"Did I ever tell you the story of how I came to live in Tor'Esint?" he asked. Loredana dabbed her cheeks and shook her head. "When Nonna Cetti and I were a little older than you, our parents took us to all the Guild Halls one day to show us all the Great Works. They were determined we would be Guild members but refused to force either of us into a Guild we didn't choose for ourselves.

"It was a kindness not many parents showed their children. Back in Tor'Dumere, I'm sure you know, children follow in their family's footsteps, or they are no longer part of the family. The same happened with Telchide, you know. His parents tried to make him a Falegname like them, but they quickly realised his passion did not lie with wood working. I knew his father well – we grew up together. I was already here when he told me of Chide's passion for inventing. So, I helped to find him a place with a Maestro, which suited all of them."

Loredana looked up at him with red eyes. "I thought you were going to tell me how *you* came to live here. Not how *Telchide* came to live here."

"Yes, yes," Ciro nodded. "I get distracted thinking about the past. Where was I?"

"Guild Halls." She snuggled into him a little closer.

"Ah, yes, so we went to all the Guild Halls and in every one they asked us each what our favourite Great Work was and wrote down the list. At the end of the day, we went to mamma's favourite ristorante and went through the lists, mamma with Cetti and papà with me. We struck out any I had no interest in. By the end of dinner, I'd narrowed it down to two Guilds – Gioiellieri and Artiste. I was already good at drawing. I had sketchbooks full of portraits, mostly of my family, but some of my friends as well.

"So, the next day, papà took me back to those two Guild Halls and watched me. Papà said I only stayed a few moments in front of the paintings in the Artiste Guild Hall, but longer in front of the statues. But when we got to the Gioiellieri Guild, I went straight back to the tiny section they had for Corallini and spent the entire time looking at everything they had.

"But, you know, there was only one Corallina left in all of Tor'Dumere and she already had a full complement of apprentices with a waiting list years long. I would've been too old before she even had time to start working with me. It wasn't feasible.

"My parents gave me a choice then. I could join the Artiste Guild in Tor'Dumere with a friend of the family who wouldn't charge them too much to take me. Or I could move to Tor'Esint, where there were seven Corallini to choose from, all of whom had room for another apprentice. I chose the Artiste Guild."

Loredana sat up suddenly. "You what? Why?"

"I didn't want to join that Guild, because they *never* work with corallo. But I didn't want to disappoint my family by leaving. My mistake was that I didn't tell them. I told Cetti." He shook his head at the memory. "And you know what she did then? She told mamma and papà that *she* wanted to join the Artiste Guild because she knew they could only pay for one of us to join and I wouldn't challenge her for the spot. But she was a year younger than me and wouldn't be able to join a Guild yet.

"So, papà told me he'd put my name down on the Gioiellieri Guild in Tor'Esint for a Corallino, all done by correspondence. It was only after I left that Cetti changed her mind and said she'd rather be a shop girl than an Artiste. Eventually, they convinced her to join a Guild. She chose the Musicisti Guild."

Loredana's breathing slowed and her tears stopped as she listened.

"So, if she hadn't done that, would you really have stayed in Tor'Dumere and joined the Artiste Guild?"

Ciro nodded. "Unless my parents figured out that I really preferred corallo. In fact, I'm not sure now that it was all because of Cetti. I always blamed her and, eventually, thanked her for what she did. But maybe it wasn't all her idea."

"I'm glad she did," Loredana said, nudging him softly. "Otherwise, I'd never have gotten the chance to become a Corallina and it's what I want to do more than anything else."

"Yes, but I have a feeling it's not what Tania wants to do."

"Bah, Tania's still a baby!" Loredana threw up her arms in complete imitation of Ciro himself. "She'll change her mind a hundred times before she's old enough to apprentice with anyone."

He nodded and shrugged. "Perhaps. Now, what do you say we dry the rest of those tears and go inside? You know, you're not the only new apprentice. Telchide got his two just a few months ago."

Loredana smiled bravely, wiped her face with the handkerchief and passed it back to Ciro, who took it with the tips of his fingers and tried not to think how wet his trouser pockets would now get with the soggy cloth.

Chapter 15 – Gildadi 16 Gioiellieri 230 Years After Implosion

Loredana came in earlier than usual that morning. Ciro looked up at her arrival and frowned when he realised that Tania wasn't with her.

"Mamma organised to leave her at Telchide's house," Loredana informed him. "*Apparently*, Teresina offered to teach her to read alongside Florio and Gaspare in the mornings. Then they can play until mamma finishes work and picks her up."

Ciro watched her expression closely. She was being very careful to keep her face completely blank.

"Can you read at all?" he asked her.

She shrugged. "I can read and write my name and a few others like mamma's, Tania, yours and Seppe's, but not much else. Mamma tried to teach us our letters, but she was never very good at them herself. Nonna Cetti said it was impossible to teach mamma to read."

Ciro frowned. He wished he'd known how much trouble Serafina had learning how to read.

"But you don't want to learn from Teresina, am I correct?"

"Well, *honestly*, who would want to learn from that snot-faced little brat? Thinks she's so amazing because her papà is a rich Inventore who makes anything she asks for and buys her all the pretty dresses she wants. Well, our papà loved us too, even if he wasn't rich!" Loredana practically shouted. "And now Tania's going to learn to read before me and become just as much of a snot-faced brat as Teresina!"

Ciro looked over to Seppe, who nodded his agreement to the unspoken plan.

"No, she won't," Ciro said. "I promised to teach you to read as part of your apprenticeship, and I will. We'll start today. It can be before your drawing practice."

"Really?" she asked with the hint of a smile.

"Absolutely. Now, go sort out the corallo with Seppe while I quickly finish this little section of my cammeo, then we'll get started. How does that sound?"

Loredana ran over and hugged him tightly, burying her face in his chest. Ciro kissed the top of her head before nudging her away.

"Come now, we've a lot of work to do today before the Maestri arrive. What time did they say they were coming?"

Loredana pulled away from him and went to empty her little basket of corallo on the counter.

"They said they'd come just before trading ends. Do Anna and Sabrina need to come too? I can let them know when we finish my lessons if you like."

"Yes." He nodded. "Do that. Now, let me finish what I'm doing so we can start your lessons."

***

Later that afternoon, a full quarter hour before trading ended, Anna arrived. She was unaccompanied by Sabrina, which did not bode well. Seppe made her a coffee and Loredana drew her portrait while they waited for the others to arrive. Ciro had told Loredana she could ask the Maestri themselves if she was allowed to see the project, so she'd insisted on staying until they arrived. On her way to tell Anna and Sabrina to come that afternoon, she'd left a picture note for her mamma explaining that she would be staying late at the workshop.

Sabrina arrived just before the Maestri, and kept herself as far from Anna as possible, which was ridiculous in Ciro's cramped workshop. They'd need to do something about their fragmented relationship if they were to work together on this project.

Rosalina entered ahead of Luca and Adamo. All three were wrapped up in winter coats, but there was little room left to hang anything on Ciro's hat stand. Loredana noticed as well and went to take their coats to hang them over the back of her chair.

"Ah Loredana, how are you enjoying your apprenticeship so far?" Adamo asked her.

Loredana proudly puffed up her chest. "I'm enjoying it very much. My Maestro is a talented Corallino and is teaching me a lot."

"I'm pleased to hear it," he told her with a genuine smile. "And is your mamma happy with the new arrangement?"

"Yes, Maestro." Loredana cast a sideways glance at Ciro confirming she had permission to ask questions. "I'm glad the three of you have come today. You might be able to help us settle a disagreement."

Rosalina joined them. "A disagreement? In such a short amount of time?"

"Oh, not that kind of disagreement," Loredana quickly reassured her. "It's just that I know this project is a secret, but I think it's important that I get to watch the work. After all, how often does an opportunity like this come along?"

Rosalina looked sharply at Ciro. "You've told her?"

"Barely anything," he replied. "She knows there's a special project behind the wooden panels and she's not allowed to go there."

"And you've been making clay models," Loredana chipped in.

Ciro nodded. "Difficult to hide everything about the project from my apprentice, but I'm doing my best."

"I think it's safest not to show her," Luca said. "Apprentice she may be, but she's still a child. What if she has a slip of the tongue and word gets out?"

"Who would I tell?" Loredana asked brazenly. "Almost everyone I know is in this room. Aside from mamma and Tania, of course."

"Loredana!" Ciro said sharply. "I said you could ask the Maestri, not be rude to them."

She looked down, shamefaced. "Sorry, Maestro."

"I apologise, Maestri, for my apprentice's candour. She will not speak out of turn again."

"She's still a child, Ciro," Adamo said calmly. "Don't make promises you can't force her to keep. I actually agree with her. Opportunities like this *don't* come along often. It would be remiss of us to deny her the opportunity to learn. Rosalina?"

The oldest Maestra walked over to Loredana and leant down to be face to face with her.

"I agree, it's important for you to see the process, but I also remember what it was like to be a child with a secret. What should your punishment be if you tell? And your reward for keeping the secret until such time it is no longer necessary?"

"My punishment could be letting Teresina teach me to read instead of Maestro Ciro," Loredana said easily. "I can't imagine anything worse! And my reward..." She looked at Ciro questioningly.

"Your reward could be to make your first cammeo," he suggested. "It won't be perfect, and I can't guarantee you'll be happy with it, but it will be quite an achievement."

Loredana's eyes lit up, her mouth gaped open.

"Well then, we have our terms," Rosalina said, standing upright again. "Luca, do you agree?"

Luca shook his head. "I still don't think it's the best idea, but I can see the need for it. Signorina, you'd better keep this secret like your life depends on it."

Loredana gave him a withering stare. "Have you *met* Teresina? My life *does* depend on it. I wouldn't want her to teach me to read if she was the last person in Tor'Esint."

Adamo laughed lightly. "That's settled then. Let's see these clay models so we can make a decision."

Ciro, with Seppe's help, moved the wooden panels to allow everyone behind them and still not allow others outside the workshop to view everything.

"Now, as most of you have seen, this is the corallo trunk we've been given to work with. Simone refused to work on it, so we're left with myself, Anna and Sabrina. The three of us came up with some designs and narrowed the choice down to these. From here, we cannot decide."

He withdrew the cloth from the corallo and positioned the three clay models so everyone could see them. It hadn't taken him as long to carve Sabrina's model as he'd anticipated, so it too was ready for inspection. He heard Loredana's little gasp from beside him. Had she recognised herself on his model or was it feigned amazement at such a large piece of corallo when she knew his other one was larger?

"I've attempted to utilise every branch of the trunk without wasting any of it," he said, standing back to allow everyone a good view.

Anna stood beside him, watching the Maestri like a hawk. They would determine the course of this carving. If either of the other Corallini didn't agree with the choice, they had only two options – withdraw from the project or go ahead even though they disagreed. It was not a position he envied either of them. Ciro could detach his feelings from the carvings. They were all works of art and that was all that mattered to him.

"Much as I think the intricacy of the sea monster is the best of all three, I wonder if it's the best subject matter for the Guild Ball," Luca said after a lengthy session of studying them.

"I disagree," said Rosalina. "Not that it's the best – it is – but that it's not the best subject matter. Tell me any Marinaio you've ever met who hasn't told you some story or other about a sea monster. Every child in Tor'Esint must have heard at least a dozen different stories about them. They're part of our lives, part of our culture, and this design makes such a vivid display of them. It's wonderful. I cast my vote here."

All eyes turned to Adamo. He looked closely at all the models, turning each one around so he could see all sides, not caring that everyone was waiting on him.

"Though I personally like the statue of the lady holding a flower, I think the sea monster is technically better. It showcases more skill, and depth of design. If the corallo changes colour as many do, that change will be showcased in a better light."

"But how many people will want to see such a carving at the Guild Ball?" Luca asked in exasperation. "It will turn them off the food and drink."

"It will do no such thing," Anna snapped. "It hasn't turned your stomach now, and it won't turn theirs then. This sea monster was tastefully done. The grotesque nature shows through without the viewer being repulsed. In corallo, it would be considered the best of all Great Works, were it ever submitted as one."

"It's repulsive," Sabrina retorted. "Who wants to go to any event, let alone the Guild Ball, with such a grotesque statue taking pride of place on the Parting Gifts table? Only a person as bitter as you could create it in the first place, Anna."

"I beg to differ, fellow Corallina, but Ciro created this masterpiece, I only drew the picture for him. And did you not notice that *your* carving isn't even an option in anyone's mind, your stupid, peaceful fishing boat."

"Enough!" Rosalina didn't shout, but her voice carried over their bickering and immediately silenced them. "If the two of you cannot work together on this, we'll take both of you off the project and give it to Ciro alone. Is that what you want?"

"No, Maestra," they both mumbled, apologetically.

"Right, then I'll ask you both to help Giuseppe in the kitchen to make everyone a cup of coffee while we decide. Our decision will be final. If you disagree with it, you are free to leave the project, though you will still be bound to silence. Understood?"

Seppe took his cue and escorted the Corallini into the kitchen. Ciro stood out of their way, his arms clasped lightly around Loredana, keeping her still and quiet. He kept his peace as they discussed the matter back and forth. By the time the coffee was ready, a decision had been reached.

"We've decided on the sea monster," Rosalina said. "It is the best carving and we do not believe it to be inappropriate for the Guild Ball."

Sabrina glowered angrily. Ciro could see this going badly, but was distracted by Loredana tugging on his sleeve. He tried to brush her away, but once she had his attention, she pointed to the basket where he had the larger branches of corallo.

"Might I offer a compromise?" he asked, before Sabrina could say anything to make the situation worse. The Maestri turned to him as one. "I have recently come into possession of some branches of corallo, large enough to carve into something decent, rather than just jewellery. If the Guild is willing to purchase some of these pieces, I don't mind handing them over for Sabrina to carve while Anna and I work on the main trunk."

Sabrina opened her mouth to snap, but slowly closed it as she took in his offer. The Maestri quietly discussed the matter amongst themselves, while Ciro motioned for Loredana to bring out just one of the larger branches. All eyes were on his apprentice as she placed the bright red branch on the display table. It was longer than her hand.

"How did you come into possession of such large pieces?" Luca asked. "We searched for months to find a piece big enough for the Guild Ball but couldn't find anything even as large as that branch until this piece fell into our laps."

Ciro shrugged. "Antonino Marinaio. He found them along the coast. Said he wouldn't have found them, but the blockade prevented him from fishing as far out as he usually does, so he worked harder to find some corallo for me. For us."

"How many of these pieces do you have?" Rosalina asked.

"How many do you need?" Ciro countered with a cunning smile.

She laughed and shook her head at him.

"Sabrina, are you happy to work on the smaller pieces alone?"

The younger Corallina nodded.

"Then let's start with one and see what you come up with," Rosalina told her. "Ciro, we'll pay you one gold for this piece. Sabrina, you carve it and bring it to the Guild Hall when you're done. If we're happy with the work, we will negotiate how many you can carve. Agreed?"

Sabrina hesitantly picked up the corallo branch and turned it over. "I suppose so. It's better than carving that monstrosity."

Ciro lay a calming hand on Anna's arm before she could rise to the bait. It mattered not what Sabrina thought – the Maestri had chosen Anna's design and it would be spectacular. He kept his hand there while Rosalina, Luca and Sabrina made their farewells. Adamo had begged the pleasure of seeing Loredana's sketchbook before walking her home.

While the two of them were occupied, Ciro brought Anna back behind the wooden panels.

"I've been thinking, it's going to be a lot more work with just the two of us. So, if you're happy with this arrangement, you could come three days a week and Seppe can mind your shop so you don't lose orders. He's good with customers and won't mind helping."

"I heard my name," Seppe said, joining them behind the panels – the Gioiellieri Maestri seemed to assume he had already seen the project, so what difference did it make now? "What are you volunteering me for?"

"Running Anna's shop in her absence," Ciro said with a wink. "Of course, her shop won't be anywhere near as busy as mine and you'll get awfully bored."

"Well, that'll just give me time to shape and polish all her corallo," Seppe told him. "I'll come tomorrow, before trading and you can tell me everything I need to know and anything you want me to help with while I'm there."

"Out of the question," Anna snapped. Seppe gave her an injured look and she hastily replied as she realised her error. "I don't mean I don't trust you, Seppe. Caldera knows you've helped Ciro for years. I know you're capable. I just meant you aren't obliged to help me just because I'm working with Ciro on this project."

Seppe took both her hands and looked at her earnestly. "Anna, I insist. I refuse to sit and idly wait for customers. If you don't give me something to do, I'll probably find something anyway, so it may as well be something you need me to do."

Anna sighed heavily. "Fine. Come by at half-past seven. That'll give me plenty of time to explain everything to you. Now, I'll be off."

"I'll walk you home," Seppe offered. "And don't even think about arguing. I've been here all day. I need to stretch my poor legs and buy some dinner or we won't eat tonight."

Ciro bid Anna good night and went to join Adamo and Loredana.

"Her sketches are coming along quite nicely," Adamo told him. "Especially the flowers. She insists on sketching my portrait now that she has me."

Ciro chuckled as Loredana reprimanded Adamo for turning his head. He walked over to look at the sketch. Her portraits needed work, but considering she'd only just begun drawing in earnest less than two weeks ago, the improvement was impressive. She finally finished and held it out to Adamo proudly. He took it and pursed his lips. Ciro wished he had some way to tell him to be kind to an amateur.

"The eyes have a lovely shape, and the curve of the nose is quite pleasing," Adamo said with a studied air. "Overall, a very good effort I think. Don't you, Ciro?"

"Indeed, I think it's time we add a portrait a day to your sketching practice," he replied, waggling his eyebrows at her.

Loredana groaned as the workshop door opened. Serafina walked in with a grumpy child in tow.

"Reda, what are you still doing here?" she asked, leaving Tania to sulk by the door. "We found your note and had to walk all the way back here. Tania is fit to scream at all the walking today."

Loredana was unapologetic. "Maestro Ciro had an important meeting and, as his apprentice, I couldn't miss it. It's not my fault if Tania's too tired from her day of playing with Teresina, *snot-faced brat that she is*." The last was added in such a low mumble that Ciro doubted anyone but himself heard it.

"It's true Rafi, I really did have an important meeting with the Guild Maestri. Adamo here can attest to that."

Serafina's eyes widened as Adamo turned to greet her.

"My apologies, Maestro Adamo," she said, blushing furiously. "I was just worried about my daughter. Loredana, get your things. It's time to go."

Ciro glanced outside. Twilight was already fading to dark. He caught Adamo's gaze and the Maestro took his cue.

"To be so concerned for your daughter only shows how loving a mamma you are, Signora Serafina." Adamo got to his feet and walked to her side. "Now, please allow me to accompany you home. If your little one can't make it, I'm certain she'll beg to break your back instead of walking, and I simply couldn't stand for that."

"So what? You'll let her break *your* back instead?" Loredana snorted. "Don't give her the idea or she'll beg for a lift all the way home!"

Tania's head snapped up. "I can walk just as far as *you* can. Don't think you're better than me because you're an apprentice now. At least *I'm* learning to read." She stuck out her tongue at Loredana.

"Shows what you know," Loredana retorted, hotly. "I'm learning to read too."

"Girls, *please*!" Serafina clapped her hands together. "Zio, no more late nights this week or she'll be unbearable for days."

Ciro held his hand over his heart and nodded. "I promise. Goodnight everyone and thank you, Adamo."

The Maestro shook his hand and departed with Ciro's family. Once they were gone, Ciro heaved a long sigh and went to put on a pot of coffee.

Chapter 16 – Ramedi 17 Gioiellieri 230 Years After Implosion

Ciro met Loredana on his way back from the docks. She'd gathered a little basket of corallo, but Ciro told her not to collect any more for a while.

"We have more than enough, and with the extra corallo Antonino sold me, I won't have time to work on anything else for longer than I care to imagine. You can meet me on the docks if you like, or you can go straight to the workshop."

Loredana skipped along beside him. "Okay," she said easily. "But I have *news*! You'll never guess what happened last night."

"Last night?" Ciro asked in confusion. "You were with me last night."

"*After* that, Zio. Guess!"

Ciro scratched his stubbled chin. "Adamo walked you home and carried Tania the entire way?"

"Well, yes, but that isn't it," she replied, jumping up and down. "Mamma invited Adamo in, well she really didn't have a choice because he had to carry Tania to bed because she fell asleep in his arms. But *then* she offered him a cup of coffee and he ended up staying for hours! I don't think he was gone by the time I went to bed."

Ciro tried not to react. It was up to the two of them what they did, and Caldera knew that Serafina deserved to have someone care for her, but there were two young girls in the mix. Loredana was older – she missed her papà terribly and had placed him on a pedestal above everyone else. Tania had been so young when he was lost at sea, that any new man in her life would quickly feel like a papà to her. He couldn't help wondering if it was a wise decision to move so quickly.

"I'm glad your mamma has a new friend. She doesn't usually allow herself to have fun. Perhaps Adamo can convince her to go out once in a while."

"He already did!" Loredana squealed. "He asked her to accompany him to the Guild Ball!"

Ciro's step faltered. "He did what?"

Loredana frowned. "Isn't that a good thing? Mamma blushed so brightly I thought she'd faint! And of course she said yes. But this morning she was already worrying about a dress. You *know* she doesn't have anything nice enough for the Guild Ball."

"Yes," Ciro said softly. "I'm surprised Adamo didn't realise the same thing."

He remained silent the rest of the way back to the workshop, happy to let Loredana ramble on about whatever she wanted. His thoughts were otherwise occupied.

Anna was waiting outside when they arrived.

"Thank you for sending Seppe," she said. "It feels like he already knows his way around my workshop."

"Seppe is a treasure," Ciro said with a knowing smile. "You won't know what to do without him when this project is over."

"We'll see about that!" Anna huffed. "Now, I'll put on a pot of coffee while you get your apprentice sorted for the morning. Then we can start."

Ciro let them all in and settled Loredana down at his workbench and flipped through her sketchbook.

"Your flowers are coming along nicely. It won't be long now before you move onto birds and fish."

He caught the grin on Loredana's face as he pulled out his sketchbook and flipped to a new page for her.

"Copy these flowers out and today you can add in the vines," he told her. He drew an oval, roughly the size of a standard cammeo. "Then why don't you try your own flower design inside this oval."

"Really?" she squealed, excitedly. "Will I get to carve that design if I keep the secret?"

Ciro laughed. "Perhaps. If you can draw the same design every day until it's perfect."

Loredana nodded solemnly and took out her sketchbook and pencil. Ciro watched her at work until Anna brought out the coffee. She peered over his shoulder.

"She's getting better," Anna said. "I think she's lucky to have you as a Maestro."

"You'd do just as well with one." Ciro nudged her softly.

Anna sighed. "Well, I might consider it after the Guild Ball. I don't think it's fair of me to request one now when I'm not going to be in my own workshop half the time."

They disappeared behind the panel to begin work. It was slow progress. Mistakes couldn't be fixed, so they had to be so careful not to make any.

"Should we start on opposite sides of the corallo and meet at the edges?" Anna asked, looking at it from all angles.

Ciro shook his head. "Every time I've tried that in clay carvings, one side ends up higher than the other and I can't match them up. What if we work on one branch section each?"

"That could work," Anna agreed.

Ciro brought over a range of chisels and different sized hammers. They chose their tools and got to work. Ciro was lost in the complexity of it, trying to exactly replicate what he'd done in clay. It was more difficult than he thought it would be. The coral was much harder than the clay, but also more fragile. If he wasn't careful, he'd accidentally chip off a section he didn't mean to.

When Loredana poked her head around the panel, Ciro hammered his thumb and cried out, clutching the injury.

"Careful, Maestro!" Loredana chided him. "One must always be careful with tools."

Anna laughed and threw an arm around Loredana. "I like this one. She has a good sense of humour."

Ciro only rolled his eyes at them. Loredana took his hand and kissed his thumb.

"All better," she said. "Can we do reading lessons now?"

"Yes, you can begin by writing out the letters, like I showed you yesterday, a whole line of each. I want you to sound out the letters for me and Anna as you write them. Can you do that?"

Loredana nodded and went to get her things. Instead of sitting at Ciro's workstation, she positioned herself at the nearest clear spot to the two of them. She began with the first letter and sounded it out every time she wrote it.

"Is that a mandatory part of her apprenticeship?" Anna asked in a whisper. "Or did you take it upon yourself to teach her?"

Ciro picked up his tools again to resume work. "Not mandatory, no, but I thought it an important skill for her. At the very least for taking orders. Wouldn't you teach your apprentice to read if you had one?"

"I'm not a great reader myself," she admitted. "As you say, I'm good enough to take orders, but not much else."

Ciro only nodded and continued his work, trying not to show his surprise. He'd naively assumed all Guild members were taught to read and write, though perhaps not everyone needed to.

When Loredana was finished with her letters, Ciro allowed her to watch them work until she began to fidget, then he set her to working on another corallo necklace. At the rate she was going, he'd need to take an afternoon to make clasps for a handful of necklaces, or there'd be nowhere to put them. He toyed with the idea of giving them as Parting Gifts for the Guild Ball, but decided people would rather the cammei or intricate pendants than a simple corallo necklace.

At noon, Loredana ran down to the nearest pasticceria and returned with three panini. Ciro barely noticed the time fly by. He found he enjoyed working with Anna, even with Loredana's interruptions. It was a shame that would all be over when this statue was complete. But at least then, he'd have Seppe back in his workshop every day.

Chapter 17 – Argentodi 18 Gioiellieri 230 Years After Implosion

It was late in the afternoon when Greta strolled into the workshop, holding a large white box. Ciro had spent half the morning with Loredana, teaching her how to read, then giving her some new fish and flowers to sketch before positioning himself so that she could draw his portrait while he worked on his latest cammeo. The rest of the time he'd spent continuing the work he and Anna had started the day before on the statue.

"Signora Sarta, how lovely to see you!" Loredana ran to greet her, proudly swishing in her work dress. "What's in the box?"

Ciro came out from behind the panel as Greta put the box down on the display table. He noticed how careful she was not to bump any of Loredana's work.

"It's your other work dress," she replied. "I thought I'd save you the trip of coming to get it on Mercatodi. If you try it on now, we can make sure it doesn't need any further adjustments."

Loredana looked to Ciro who motioned for her to use his bedroom. She grinned, took the box and ran upstairs.

"You didn't need to bring it today," Ciro told her. "We could have come for a walk."

Greta's eyes darted to the panel from behind which Ciro had appeared. He followed her gaze in momentary confusion.

"We're alone," he said, frowning. "Just you, me and Seppe. Why did you really come?"

"As you requested, I asked my most affluent patron, Signora Loyola, if she could help with your bidding war. Today she came to me with a list of potentially interested people."

She handed Ciro the list. He read it over, recognising a few names.

"We think it'd work best if you send invitations to them all for an evening event. You could provide antipasti or desserts and alcohol while they mingle, to loosen their purse strings. Then show them the item in question and explain what you intend to do with it before the bidding begins."

He followed along as best he could – she always spoke so quickly!

"Show them the item?" he asked. "But I can't move it – it's too large and heavy. They'd all have to come here."

Greta looked around, assessing the workshop. "We can work with that. If you'll allow me, of course. And, you know, when they're here and looking at all your pieces of jewellery, they might just decide to purchase an item or two, whether they win the bidding war or not."

Ciro wagged his finger at her with a smile. "You're a very cunning Signora, you know that? No wonder your shop does so well."

Greta shrugged demurely and smoothed out her skirt, though it wasn't wrinkled in the least bit. Seppe joined them, with a cup of tea in hand. Ciro had told him how the Sarta appeared to prefer that insipid drink over coffee and Seppe was eager to please, as usual.

"We'll need more help than you imagine," Seppe told her. "Ciro may be able to read and write, but his script is not the prettiest I've ever seen. If we're going to do this properly, we may as well do *all* of it properly. Now, after you measure Loredana, I'll take her home so you and Ciro can speak freely and organise everything. Do you have time? I'll help when I return."

Greta didn't even check her pocket watch before agreeing and not a moment too soon. Loredana came racing down the stairs in a lovely pale blue work dress with a completely different design to the first one. Where the first had been in forest green, with a simple long, narrow skirt and a pocketed apron sewn in front, this one had a slightly fuller skirt with pockets sewn all around the waist and a simple bodice and cream-coloured sleeves. Loredana was holding another pair of sleeves in her hands.

"You left these in the box by accident," she said, holding them out to Greta.

"No, bella, it wasn't by accident. They're spare sleeves, in case you need them," Greta explained. "And they'll work just as well with your green work dress, just as the light green sleeves will work with this blue dress. I matched the colours so you can mix them as often as you like."

Loredana's eyes grew wide with delight. Before Ciro could stop her, she'd thrown her arms around Greta and was hugging her tightly. Greta laughed and hugged her back before pulling her away and turning her around.

"Now, let me see how it fits before Seppe takes you home."

As Greta performed her routine checks, Seppe gathered up Loredana's things to take her home. Ciro slipped behind the panel and covered up his work with a cloth. Should Greta happen to peek behind it, he didn't want her to see. After all, it was meant to be a secret from everyone, including his friends.

In the end, Greta had done her job so well there were no adjustments necessary. Loredana refused to change back into her green dress to go home, so Seppe fetched that for her and bundled her out the door.

"She's such a lovely girl," Greta said, looking out the door after her. "It's good that she's appreciative of the things you give her."

"Yes, well, it's also good she doesn't know how much her dresses cost or she'd tell her mamma who's already worrying about..." Ciro stopped himself and shook his head.

Greta narrowed her eyes. "What's Serafina worrying about?"

"Nothing, nothing." Ciro said quickly.

"Ciro, you know I'm acquainted with her now. If you don't tell me, I'm likely to go and ask her myself."

Ciro startled and laughed. "I believe you would too."

"So, out with it."

"Well, she hasn't told me herself, but I understand she's been invited to the Guild Ball and, well, you saw her best dress on Riposidi when you met her at Telchide's house."

Greta clapped her hands together. "I'll make her something! Send her to my shop."

Ciro was already shaking his head before Greta finished speaking. "She'd never dare walk into a Gold Sarta's shop. She knows she can't afford even the simplest of your gowns."

"But I won't charge her Gold fees. I'll let one of my apprentices make the dress, or at least that's what I'd tell her." Greta shrugged as though it were the most natural solution.

"She'd never accept your offer, trust me. She'd see it as charity and outright refuse it."

Greta frowned. "Do you think she'd consider hiring a gown? It'd be an absolute fraction of the price, and she would return it afterwards."

"You do that?" Ciro asked in surprise. "I've never heard of a Sarta hiring out gowns before."

"There's always a first time." She winked. "What do you think? Will you suggest it to her? I'd do it myself, but don't want her to feel obliged just because I offered."

"Of course," Ciro agreed. "Now, come, sit. Let's discuss this bidding war."

He drew out a chair for her and they sat at the display table with a notepad between them. Ciro wrote down *Invitations* at the top of the page and placed the list of names beside it.

"We'll need to decide the best day and time," Greta said. "If we give them enough notice, they should be able to schedule other things around it. An Orodi, in the evening, should work best."

"Next week?" Ciro asked.

Greta shook her head. "We'll need to write up the invitations and send them out with enough time for people to reply and then again enough time for us to organise food and drink for them."

Ciro took the wooden calendar from the long workbench and fiddled with it, getting the dials to the right sections.

"What about Orodi, 9 Sarti?"

Greta held out her hand for the calendar. Ciro passed it over and watched her do the mental calculations. She nodded.

"That should work. Shall we say six in the evening? That will give me enough time to come here after trading and help you set everything up. My apprentices might even come to help, and Domizio can take them out to a ristorante then bring them back afterwards to help clean up."

Ciro raised an eyebrow. "You really don't need to help so much," he told her. "Nor do your apprentices."

Greta took the pen, wrote the time and then laid the pen down carefully.

"Are you afraid the Mercantili Guild will accuse us of inter-Guild relations or are you simply too humble a person to accept a friend's generous offer?"

"Inter-Guild relations?" Ciro breathed in a whisper. "I hadn't even thought of that!"

"Well, don't," Greta said firmly. "As long as I don't profit from the evening, they'll have nothing to base any accusations on. Now, stop your protests because, if you hadn't noticed, I'm going to help you whether you ask me to or not. You came to me in the first place with a query and, I'm sorry, but you can't exclude me now. After all, you don't have the addresses of these clients and I may just have to withhold them unless you agree."

Ciro laughed, long and loud. He was rewarded with seeing Greta's face melt into a smile.

"You have me over a barrel then. Let's discuss the food. Savoury and sweet or just one or the other?" he asked, moving right along.

"We could do a mixture of both," Greta suggested. "I'll order some desserts from my favourite pasticceria if you organise some antipasti. Something easy to eat, without getting their fingers messy. These clients won't want to accidentally make a mess on anyone else's outfit, which would be all too easy for them to do in cramped quarters."

She paused, eyes wide, and covered her mouth with her hand.

"I'm sorry, Ciro. I didn't mean to offend."

Ciro laughed. "No offence taken," he reassured her. "They *are* cramped quarters. If we could have it anywhere else, I probably would. Now, don't worry. I can ask Seppe to make something during the day." Then he saw the look on her face. "Or I'll ... find somewhere to order some from. I wonder, where are we going to place these delicacies? On the display table?"

Greta looked around the workshop thoughtfully.

"That will prevent people from seeing your works. What about on the long workbench?" she suggested. "Or, they could be in the kitchen and Seppe and I can bring them around on little platters until the bidding begins, leaving you to talk to the potential clients about your work as a Corallino."

"Yes, that could work," Ciro agreed. "Now as far as the alcohol, I wonder if I could buy a bottle of Nestore's Smoking Limoncello or would grappa and vermouth suffice?"

"I don't think Nestore sells his alcohol in bottles. From what I understand, he makes them himself as people request them, because of the alchemical reaction. Grappa and vermouth will have to do. They can't expect much when the food and drink is free, after all."

Ciro read the list as Greta finished writing their tasks.

"You have a lovely script, you know – neat and beautiful. Would you consider writing the invitations yourself?"

Greta blushed at the compliment and nodded.

"Good, then. I'll purchase some elegant cards for you. Then we have one thing left to decide."

"What's that?" Greta asked, looking at the list.

"Which of us will conduct the bidding war itself? You know the clientele better, but I know the product better."

The door opened and Seppe walked in with a small basket of fish, parsley, potatoes and bread.

"Let me get dinner on and then I'll come help. Won't be a moment."

Ciro leaned into him as he walked past, closing his eyes momentarily. When he opened them, he saw Greta watching him with something akin to sadness. He took her hand gently in his and patted it with the other.

"What's the matter?"

She smiled and shook her head. "You know each other so well, and you're so happy. I don't think I'll ever have that."

Ciro raised his eyebrows at that. "I'm sorry, but you already have that. Don't think I didn't notice how Domizio looks at you. The young man worships the ground you walk on. And, I've got to say, you seem rather fond of him yourself."

"He'll tire of me soon enough. Or I'll tire of him. One or the other. It always happens." She shrugged. "Better that way, I suppose. I don't want anyone tying me down. That's all a man can do for me."

Ciro choked out a laugh. "That's *all* a man can do for you? My dear, I think you may have been doing things wrong if that's all he can do for you. Besides, I think you've forgotten a few key things this man has done for you.

"Sofia and Loredana got to talking at Telchide's house last week. Seems your young apprentice told *my* young apprentice of the dangers of trusting anyone outside your immediate circle. She heard all about that deceitful spy and the damage she could have caused. And of course Loredana told me everything.

"She even told Loredana how Domizio carried her home one night when things went badly, and how he stood up for you to that ungrateful whelp you tried to help.

"No, my dear. From the sounds of it, he's already done much more than tie you down. It sounds like that's the furthest idea from his mind."

Seppe returned, drying his hands on a cloth. "Fish is in the oven. Potatoes are on the boil. What're you two up to?"

"We only need to decide who will run the bidding war itself," Ciro replied, allowing Greta to gather her thoughts. "Do you have any suggestions?"

Seppe tucked the cloth into his pocket. "Honestly? Anna. She'd be perfect for it. No nonsense, straight to the point, knows the product and doesn't care a fig for how rich someone is – she won't ever let them cow her."

"Not possible," Ciro told him. "My source was quite firm about keeping the item secret from other Corallini, at least until it was sold and we knew what it would sell for. In truth, Greta, even *you* shouldn't be involved but I needed your help finding the correct clientele. I'm certain my source will forgive me for that."

"Anna? I don't think I've met her." Greta picked up the pen again and wrote the name down on her list. "But if she's all Giuseppe says she is, then perhaps a discussion with your source is in order. I don't know the product well enough, or I'd offer to run the bidding myself."

Ciro could only think of all the things they'd need to work out for Anna to agree, even if Antonino agreed. She'd likely insist on a similar piece of corallo for herself, or cheaper prices on large branches. Perhaps even a percentage of this bidding war, depending on how well it went.

"I'll think about it," he promised. "Now, Greta, did you drive here or shall we walk you home?"

"I drove. What's the point of having a blazermobile if you don't use it?" She stood up and smoothed down her skirt. "Now, don't forget to ask Serafina if she'd consider hiring a gown for the Guild Ball. I'll keep pestering you about it until I have an answer – you know I will."

Ciro nodded and showed her to the door, kissed her farewell on both cheeks and waited until she was safely away in her blazermobile before locking the door.

"Guild Ball?" Seppe asked immediately. "What did I miss? Why is Serafina going to the Guild Ball?"

Ciro drew him into the kitchen, so they could keep an eye on their dinner. "Loredana told me this morning that Adamo asked Serafina to accompany him to the Guild Ball. I'm yet to hear it from her own lips."

"The Guild Ball is still six weeks away," Seppe mused. "If that's true, he must like her a great deal to not think he'd meet anyone else to his liking in that time."

Ciro chewed his lip. "The thing is, have you ever heard of Adamo asking anyone out before? I don't just mean to a Guild Ball, I mean, anywhere. He's a handsome, eligible bachelor. News of his taking a liking to *any* young lady would be in society gossip before the week's end."

"Then perhaps he likes her more than you assume he might." Seppe checked the fish and stirred the potatoes.

Ciro didn't reply. His thoughts strayed to Serafina's first companion. He'd been a good man. Reliable, kind, loving. Much like Adamo, but not a Guild member. Marinai didn't have a Guild and all the protection and security they provided. Is that what Serafina was looking for, or did she truly like him? Or was she just too surprised to refuse when he asked?

He cast his mind back to the times he'd seen them together. Serafina had coloured at Adamo's attention and was clearly pleased to see him that night in Ciro's workshop. From what Loredana had told him, Serafina certainly seemed to like Adamo, though perhaps not quite as much as he liked her.

Chapter 18 – Legaramedi 19 Gioiellieri 230 Years After Implosion

"Toni, it's not the worst idea ever," Ciro called out from the dock. Antonino had refused him access when he realised why he was there.

"What part of 'secret' didn't you understand?" the marinaio asked angrily. "Bad enough you've got a Sarta involved, but a Corallina too! No."

"Toni, be reasonable," Ciro sighed. "I needed the Sarta for the contacts. And I need Anna for the bidding war. Just picture if *I* was the one doing it. We wouldn't get half of what it's worth."

Antonino crossed his arms, pacing back and forth along the deck, as though that would provide some solution to their dilemma.

"You bring her down here, today, before you show her what it is, and we talk to her *together* about it," he said firmly.

"No." Ciro shook his head. "Not today. She's busy. Tomorrow, Mercatodi."

"Out of the question," Antonino turned on him as though he were crazy. "Mercatodi is the busiest day on the docks! I won't have time for you or her. Bring her on Gildadi and not a word to her before that. Understand?"

Ciro agreed. He had no other choice.

***

That evening, Serafina came in with Tania in tow. Ciro had asked Loredana to beg her mamma for a visit. Loredana had been all too ready to agree when he'd promised Seppe would make his famous hot chocolate for the girls while he spoke with their mamma. And possibly a walk down to Cinzia's Pasticceria if they were good. It hadn't taken much convincing at all.

"Right, girls, help Seppe with that hot chocolate you were apparently promised," she said with a tired voice. Ciro helped her off with her coat and watched as she practically fell into a chair.

"Rafi, you look tired," he said softly.

She glared at him. "Well, thank you, Zio. And you look as well-rested as a lizard dodging lava."

"Now, now, Rafi. There's no need for that," he chided. "It was only an observation."

"Well, it doesn't help when I have to come past here on one of my days off because you want to talk to me. Couldn't it have waited until Riposidi?"

Ciro sat beside her. "No, I made a promise and tomorrow is the perfect day to keep it, if you are willing to hear me out."

She motioned for him to go on, a curious look etched in her tired eyes.

"Now, don't be upset, but Loredana mentioned you might be going to the Guild Ball this year. Is that true?"

Her eyes narrowed as she fought the rising blush on her cheeks. "It might be," she admitted. "What does that have to do with you?"

"Yes, well, she also mentioned you've been fretting about a dress and I have an offer."

"Zio, no," Serafina said firmly. "I won't allow you to buy me a dress alongside my daughters. I'll figure something out."

"I know that, Rafi. I'd never have offered. Not that I wouldn't want to – only I know you'd never accept it." He shook his head. "No, this is an offer from Greta Sarta, you remember her from Telchide's house? Well, she wondered if you might be interested in renting a gown for the event. At much cheaper rates than actually buying one."

Serafina paused, mouth open and ready to protest.

"We could go for a walk there together, you and I, tomorrow. We don't get to spend much time alone anymore."

"I'm certain it will still be more than I can afford," Serafina replied sadly. "She's a Gold Sarta after all."

"We won't know until we ask. I doubt Greta would have made the offer if she thought you couldn't afford it. What do you say? Seppe can watch the girls. If it's a nice day, he can take them for a swim at the beach. They won't mind at all."

Serafina sat deeper into her chair. "That *would* be a nice break, if nothing else."

"I can take you out for lunch, like I did when you used to visit with Cetti all those years ago."

"That'd be nice," Serafina sighed. "I'll bring the girls tomorrow morning then. If you're sure Seppe won't mind."

Loredana burst through the door. "Seppe said he's going to take us to the beach tomorrow! Zio, Maestro, does that mean I won't be your apprentice for the day and I get to just have fun?"

Ciro laughed. "Yes, although I hope you have fun in my workshop as well."

Loredana threw her arms around his neck. "Of course I do." She kissed his cheek. "But it's the beach and it's been such a long time since we went swimming! I can't wait!"

Chapter 19 – Mercatodi 21 Gioiellieri 230 Years After Implosion

Ciro walked arm in arm with Serafina. His niece didn't seem to mind the slow pace he set and was glowing with the freedom derived from someone else looking after her children on her day off.

They stopped at Caffe Ermenegildo. Ciro took a standing coffee, as did Serafina, with a sfogliatella to go. He was pleased when she didn't argue the point but simply enjoyed his spoiling her. In Piazza Mercantile, Serafina even stopped by a few stalls to look at all the items on display. Ciro pointed out the corner where Telchide now kept his stall, side by side with Aveline Inventrice.

When they arrived at Greta's workshop, Serafina almost refused to go in, daunted by the glamour of it. But Sofia, perceptive girl that she was, saw them from the street stall and swiftly left her fellow apprentice, Annika, to greet them.

"Signore Corallino, I was wondering when we might see you next," she said with her large, dimpled smile. "And Signora Serafina. I must say, I found your daughters absolutely enchanting. Especially Loredana. Please, come in. I'm sure Greta would love to see you."

She bundled them both inside without a care for Serafina's discomfort, or perhaps, in fact, to distract from it. On the small table between the two big chairs was a jug of water with lemon slices and mint leaves. She poured them both a glass and pressed them into their hands before they could protest, not that Ciro had any objection to the cool drink on such an unseasonably warm day.

"Maestra, you have special guests," Sofia called out over the array of workbenches.

Greta's head immediately popped up from behind a fabric screen. A smile spread over her face when she saw them. Ciro waved a greeting while, beside him, Serafina nervously sipped her water. Greta joined them, a kiss on each of their cheeks, and immediately began to talk Serafina's ear off. Ciro was left at a loss as the two of them wandered off to the clothing racks.

He took the opportunity to watch the Sarti at work. Each was consumed by their own project. Contrary to what he assumed, the suits and dresses weren't being worked on solely by the usual wearers of those items. Domizio and the hired Sarta were working on a dress together, while the hired Sarto and one of the apprentices were collaborating on a suit. It was an interesting process, one that looked as consuming as his own work – each a true craft in their own right. Sometimes repetitive, sometimes with room for imagination. The end result was always a work of art.

Domizio saw him watching and called him over.

"Signore Corallino, have you met Nicolina Sarta?" Domizio asked. "She was quite enamoured of the pendants Greta bought for her apprentices and the cammeo you made of Greta herself. Weren't you, Coli?"

The girl nodded enthusiastically. "I thought perhaps I might come by one day to purchase something for my mamma. Her eyes aren't as good as they used to be, but she says she sees just as well with her fingers."

"I'd be delighted to bring a selection of things directly to your house if your mamma would prefer to choose for herself," Ciro offered. He knew not all vecchietti were as mobile as he was and it seemed unfair to punish them for it.

"Oh, Signore Corallino, she'd love that! Would you really?"

"But of course," Ciro replied easily. "You jot down your address for me and times that suit you and I'll do my best to arrive within a week."

Greta came up behind him and tapped him on the shoulder. "Already making friends, I see."

Ciro turned to face Greta and looked behind her for Serafina.

"She's trying on a selection of gowns," Greta informed him, "after quite a vigorous discussion on price. She's a proud girl but saw reason in the end. I think we've come to a very profitable arrangement for both of us. Now, come with me so we can help her choose the best one."

Ciro followed Greta to a part of the workshop concealed behind a fabric panel, with a curtained-off area where, presumably, Serafina was trying on a gown. It took longer than Ciro had anticipated, with Greta disappearing behind the curtain to help with the fastening. He didn't ask questions or want to know exactly what was going on behind there.

When Serafina finally stepped out, she was resplendent in a sea-green dress. It had a full skirt, with a low neckline. Behind her was a full-length mirror. She turned this way and that, trying to see every angle of herself.

"It's beautiful, Greta. Is it ... the current fashion?"

Greta tapped the side of her nose. "The current fashion is anything you want it to be. I've made so many different designs for this Guild Ball that no one will look out of place. Full skirts, narrow skirts, high necklines, low necklines. Anything you can imagine will be there. So all that's left is for you to decide which of these gowns you like best."

"What do you think, Zio?" Serafina asked, hesitantly, pulling up the material at her bust.

"It looks beautiful, Rafi, but you don't seem comfortable in it. Try another."

Serafina pursed her lips and nodded. She disappeared behind the curtain and began the process for another dress.

"You shouldn't have said that to her," Greta whispered. "Ladies can be sensitive about their gowns."

"I know her better than you, Greta," Ciro replied just as quietly. "If she was tugging at the bustline now, she'd be tugging it all night at the Ball and draw attention to her discomfort. She wouldn't have done credit to your gown."

Greta huffed indignantly, but did not answer. Instead, she waited patiently until Serafina called her in for help.

The next dress was bright red, with black lace. The neckline was higher, so Serafina didn't tug at it, but the colour was just awful on her. Ciro tried to smile at it, but even Serafina was looking doubtfully at herself. It didn't take long for her to disappear behind the curtain for the next dress.

This time she emerged with a gorgeous dress, orange and yellow like autumn leaves. It had a fitted bodice and long flowing skirt in a crushed silk that rippled around her ankles. It was the most beautiful thing Ciro had ever seen her wear. And she looked comfortable in it, which was equally important. The capped sleeves over her shoulders kept up the modest neckline.

"That's the one, Rafi." He clapped in delight. "That's the dress for you."

"Do you think so, Zio?" she asked, smiling so broadly it must have hurt her cheeks. "I wasn't sure about the colour, but it does look like it works, doesn't it? What do you think, Greta?"

The Sarta smiled. "It's as though I made it specifically for you, which is what everyone will think when you wear it at the Guild Ball. I wouldn't bother trying on any of the other dresses. They'll all pale in comparison to this one. I'll set it aside for you and you can pick it up a day or two before the Guild Ball, then return it whenever you get a chance afterwards. Agreed?"

"Agreed," Serafina said happily. "Thank you, Greta. I don't know what I would've done without you."

Greta smiled and ushered Serafina behind the curtain once more. Ciro noticed the slight blush on her cheeks.

"Am I correct in thinking you may be one of those extremely talented people who shies away from compliments, my young Sarta?"

Greta glared at him.

"Well, that makes sense. There's no other way so many qualified Sarti would agree to work for you otherwise. Nor any way you could possibly have such a large and wealthy set of clientele who would all bend over backwards for you."

"None of them are bending over backwards for me," Greta said pointedly. "But I have their ears. Which is why I'll be hand delivering each of your invitations this afternoon. I'd ask you to join me, but it seems you are occupied with your family today."

"This morning," he corrected her. "I'm occupied with them this morning only. I'd be happy to accompany you, if you think it will help our cause."

"I'll pick you up at two o'clock then," she said with a smile.

***

Back out in the Piazza, the noise levels had not reduced at all during the time they'd spent in Greta's shop, but that didn't appear to concern Serafina at all. She happily navigated her way through the Piazza, stopping at every stall to take in the merchandise. Ciro led her to Telchide and Aveline's stalls. Teresina was sitting on her papà's lap, happily chatting to Aveline. When the young girl saw them approaching, she jumped up and looked around, confusion clouding her face.

"Where's Tania?" she asked with a pout.

"She went to the beach today, with Seppe," Serafina told her.

"Papà, why don't *you* ever take me to the beach?" she demanded.

Telchide ran his hands over his face. "Resi, you know I don't have time. Veli and I are very busy with our project, not to mention our usual orders. When would I ever have time to take you to the beach?"

Teresina crossed her arms. "Florio or Gaspare could take me, couldn't they? Tomorrow?"

"You may ask them, Teresina, but they may refuse," Telchide told her patiently. "After all, it's their only day off. They might prefer spending time with their fellow apprentice friends."

Serafina bent down to Teresina's level. "We could have a picnic at the beach tomorrow. If your papà or Aveline drop you off at my apartment, you can join us at the beach for lunch. If that's alright with you, Telchide?"

Telchide looked across at Aveline, who nodded.

"That would be lovely, Serafina. We'll bring her to your apartment on our way ... we'll bring her by eleven-thirty. Will that work?"

"Oh, thank you, Signora Serafina!" Teresina said, hugging her tightly. "I can't remember the last time I went to the beach. Papà is *always* too busy to take me and my nonna hates the sand. She says it gets everywhere and refuses to take me."

Serafina patted the girl on the back and took Ciro's arm to walk back through the Piazza.

"Are you sure that was a good idea?" Ciro asked her, when they were far enough away.

"Why ever not?"

Ciro cleared his throat. "You, er, do know that Loredana doesn't like Teresina, don't you? I mean, I don't mind having a beach lunch with her, myself, but not everyone may be as keen."

"What could Loredana possibly have against Teresina?" Serafina asked in confusion. "They've only met once."

Ciro didn't answer. Instead, he pointed out a pizzeria that looked promising. He wasn't done spoiling his niece just yet.

***

At five minutes to two o'clock, Ciro heard Greta's blazermobile pull up outside his workshop. She appeared to be getting the hang of driving it now, not running out of blazer solution, nor putting in so much that she feared the contraption would run off without her.

Seppe immediately went out to greet her and fawn over the blazermobile. He'd often spoken of it since their ride last Mercatodi. If Ciro could have afforded one for him, he'd have bought it in a heartbeat.

Greta walked through the door with Seppe close behind her and passed Ciro a small bundle.

"Have a look at the invitations, Ciro. Are you happy with them?"

He slipped one out from the ribbon holding them all together and studied it carefully. The details were all correct and the script was lovely. He slipped it back in and passed the bundle back to her.

"I couldn't have done it better myself," he told her with a grin. "Seppe, we shouldn't be more than an hour or two, I'd guess. Do you mind watching the shop while I'm out? I don't suppose we should have it closed all day long."

Seppe nodded easily and sat himself down to start cutting and shaping more corallo balls. Greta clapped her hands.

"That reminds me, Seppe! I'm running low on corallo beads. Could you set aside another hundred for me by the time we return? I've a few gowns in progress I'd like to use them on this week. Lots of different sizes, if you can – makes it easier to do different patterns."

Seppe pulled out a little white box from under the workbenches and winked at her. She brushed a curl out of her eyes and smiled.

"Thank you, Seppe. You're a treasure!" She walked over and kissed his cheek, then nodded to Ciro. "Let's go then."

The first on their list was Signora Loyola. Greta drove up the steep hill to the large villas on top of the crest. Loyola's villa was made almost entirely of stone and marble. Ciro stared up at the house a little uncertainly.

"Do you think that someone who lives in a house like this would really be interested in a bidding war?"

Greta laughed. "Ciro, Signora Loyola's the one who suggested all the other clients. She wouldn't want to miss out on the opportunity to outbid her friends and rivals. Can you imagine the shame of it?" Greta placed a hand over her chest and heaved exaggerated sighs.

Ciro shook his head at her antics. "Fine then, let's get this over with."

Together, they walked up the marble steps to the massive double wooden doors. Ciro pulled on a large rope to the side of the door and heard a series of bells ringing throughout the house. It was an ingenious invention that would ensure visitors would be announced all over the large villa.

Soon after, the door opened and a young maid stood there, red-cheeked and puffing.

"Oh, Signora Sarta, it's you again," she said, clearly unimpressed. "I didn't know she'd ordered *another* gown."

"Good afternoon." Greta gave her a forced smile. "I'm actually here with Signore Corallino to invite Signora Loyola to an exclusive event. Would you be so good as to ask her to the door?"

The girl rolled her eyes at the request but went to fetch her mistress.

"Charming young lady, isn't she?" Ciro said, sarcastically. "Is she always like that?"

"Unfortunately, yes. I don't think I've ever had a genuinely kind word from her."

They weren't left waiting long. The girl might have a bad attitude, but at least she attended her duties. Signora Loyola came into view and the full force of her personality was immediately apparent. Ciro fought not to take a step back.

"Oh, Greta, how lovely to see you." She kissed the air next to Greta's cheeks. "And with a friend! Whom do I have the honour of addressing?"

"Signora Loyola, this is the most talented Gioielliere in all of Tor'Esint, Ciro Corallino."

Ciro took off his coppola and bobbed his head slightly to the side. "Pleased to meet you, Signora."

He handed her the invitation and was ready to walk away, but Greta's hand on his arm made him pause.

"Ciro has a rather remarkable item to offer, which even *I* have not been so fortunate as to see. He'll be hosting a bidding war and inviting everyone you so generously listed to me. The item in question will only be revealed on the night. We sincerely hope you can make it."

Signora Loyola read the invitation, right there in front of them. Her eyes went back and forth over the details before she finally looked up at them. Ciro felt the sweat drip down his back as she scrutinised the invitation.

"Count me in. And if anyone on my list tells you they're busy, you just let me know and I'll make sure their schedule frees up."

Ciro frowned in surprise. "That's, erm, very kind of you, Signora."

"Not really," she told him. "I don't want any of them complaining to me that they missed the event of the season afterwards. It'll save me trouble later. Besides, I'm very curious to see what this special item is – if I feel like bidding on it, I want them all there to see what I've secured for myself and what they've missed out on."

Ciro's mouth gaped open. He only realised it when Signora Loyola laughed, and Greta pushed his chin up with a finger.

"You get used to her," Greta said, winking at Signora Loyola. "In fact, she rather grows on you the more time you spend with her. It's the oddest thing."

Signora Loyola narrowed her eyes. "Now, Greta, don't go spreading those vicious rumours about me. There are very few people I grow on, and I never expected *you* to be one of them."

Greta only laughed and shook her head. "We'll see you on Orodi, 9 Sarti then. Don't be late!"

She pulled Ciro down the stairs with her and back into the blazermobile. Only after they drove off did she explain.

"Signora Loyola has built up quite a reputation for herself of being extraordinarily difficult to deal with. She finds it paves her way to getting what she wants with the minimum fuss and the lowest prices." Greta kept her eyes on the street while she spoke, gesticulating with one hand. "There are apparently very few people who stand up to her.

"Telchide and I are the only ones I know of for certain. In our cases, we were lucky, or talented, enough that it gained her respect rather than her ire. I'm not certain everyone's been so lucky as we have. So, in practical terms, it's good for you that I have such a good relationship with her, or she might never have agreed to help us with this bidding war."

Ciro felt buffeted about by her words like a sail in a strong wind.

"Well, it seems to me as though I'll be in your debt when this bidding war's over. And what's a common Corallino like me to do to repay such a favour?"

Greta shot a withering glance at him and the subject was not raised again. They delivered the rest of the invitations, Greta throwing her pitch at them each time as "Signora Loyola's representative". The mere mention of her name made people straighten their spines and push back their shoulders. Each and every one was miraculously able to attend, even if their calendars had been terribly full before the mention of her name.

By the time they returned home, Ciro was exhausted. He thanked Greta for her help and promised to have everything ready the night of the bidding war, including Anna. It was a risk, promising something he had little control over, but all he could do was hope that Antonino, and Anna herself, would agree. If he could just make the offer enticing enough.

Chapter 20 – Gildadi 23 Gioiellieri 230 Years After Implosion

"Anna, really, it's a short walk," Ciro insisted. "I'm sure you'll enjoy yourself if you only agree to come. Please."

Anna sighed. "What's so important down at the docks that you can't tell me here?"

Ciro shook his head. They'd already been over it so many times. He refused to tell her without Antonino lest he say something he shouldn't.

"Why in Caldera's smoke did I ever agree to work with you? If you keep disrupting our progress for your own purposes, we'll never get this done and the Maestri will punish us somehow – I just know they will!"

Ciro only raised his eyebrows at her, expectantly.

"Fine." Anna threw her hands up in the air. "Let's go then. But after this, *no more interruptions*!"

"Agreed!" Ciro said, passing her coat over.

Down at the dockside markets, most of the barrels were still full of seafood. Ciro carefully navigated Anna around them, ensuring she didn't get splashed by fishy water and have cause to complain of the stench all day. They arrived at Antonino's boat to find him yelling at a deckhand. Ciro tactfully stood back until he was done.

"It's not a good day, Ciro." Antonino rounded on him when he was done with the deckhand. "Come back tomorrow."

"No," Anna said firmly. "We're just as busy as you and don't have time to come down to the docks when it suits your mood. Now, Ciro said he can't tell me whatever he needs from me without you, so suck ash and tell me!"

Ciro's eyes widened in surprise. He'd not often heard someone outside of the Guild on the wrong end of Anna's temper. It was a sight to see!

Antonino narrowed his eyes at her and glared for what seemed an eternity, then finally hopped over the side of his boat to be closer to them.

"I came across a rather large trunk of corallo and Ciro's holding a bidding war to see how much we can get for it. For some reason, he wants *you* to run the bidding war."

"Why should I?" Anna asked, hands on hips. "It's not like you offered the trunk to *me* now, did you?"

Antonino threw his hands up in the air. "You see, *this* is the reason I didn't want to tell her. Now she's angry."

"Toni, be reasonable," Ciro said calmly. "She'd have been angry as soon as she found out whether we asked her to run the bidding war or not. All you have to do is offer her the next trunk."

"Next trunk?" Anna asked, leaning in. "There's another one?"

Antonino glared at Ciro, who studiously avoided his gaze.

"There could be," he admitted, "depending on how the bidding war goes. And apparently that all depends on you."

"Fine. I'll run the bidding war, at a cost of one gold piece. And *you'll* sell the next trunk to *me*. Agreed?"

"Yes, fine, agreed." Antonino jumped back onto his deck. "Ciro, I don't want you to sell it for less than ten golds, you hear me? I know you'll want a large cut of that yourself for the carving, but I expect forty percent for the material itself."

Ciro nodded and bundled Anna away before she and Antonino could clash any further. They were well away from the docks when Anna stopped, forcing Ciro to halt alongside her.

"You did that on purpose," she accused him. "Why?"

"I need you for the bidding war," Ciro replied, tugging her back along the street.

"You could run the bidding war yourself. Why won't you?"

Ciro took a breath. "Anna, I may be a good Corallino, but I'm not proud enough to toot my own horn and certainly not in front of wealthy clientele. You, on the other hand, don't seem to have a problem with it. So, as I said, I need you."

"But you knew I'd insist on the next trunk, and a fee."

Ciro shrugged.

"Well, thank you," she said brusquely. "Now, let's get back to the workshop so you can show me this trunk, and why in Caldera's smoke we need a bidding war for it."

***

Ciro and Seppe held up the cloth, shielding the trunk from the window. Anna's eyes grew so big, Ciro thought they might pop out of her head. They covered it up quickly, Seppe re-tying the ropes around the base.

Loredana helped Anna to a chair and brought her a glass of water.

"Well, yes, I see now," Anna said, when she was over her shock. "When's the bidding war?"

"Orodi, 6 Sarti. Just under two weeks away." Ciro told her. "Greta Sarta will be coming to help on the night and, before you ask, she hasn't seen it yet. But she organised the clientele with help from a contact of hers, so I had no choice but to involve her."

"You do make odd friends, Ciro," Anna said with a small laugh. "Who'd have ever thought you'd have so many new things to occupy you so late in life. Just make sure the Mercantili Guild doesn't get wind of it."

Ciro only shook his head as he began to get things together for Loredana. The threat of the Mercantili Guild was always enough to sour his mood.

"Drawing first, then reading. After that, you can thread another necklace or watch me at work. Your choice."

Loredana nodded and got out her things. His sour mood lightened when he saw Seppe pulling out his own sketchbook to join her. Who knew all it would take was an apprentice to get Seppe to draw again?

Chapter 21 – Argentodi 25 Gioiellieri 230 Years After Implosion

Ciro and Seppe were the first to arrive at their regular dinner with Matteo and Lidia. The choice this week was Gianni's Ristorante. Ciro ordered a bottle of red wine and a jug of water. They were halfway through their first glass of wine when Matteo and Lidia finally arrived.

"Sorry we're late," Matteo puffed. "Our apprentices..."

Lidia glared at him when he didn't finish. "They were fighting. Again. Those two are at each other's throats so much, they barely have time to learn anything from us. Caldera forbid we try to swap them to teach them different things. Then they just try to pit us against each other by saying the other is a better teacher. It's exhausting!"

Ciro exchanged worried glances with Seppe.

"Couldn't you have asked for siblings?" Seppe asked. "Like yourselves?"

Lidia barked out a laugh as she sat. "They *are* siblings. We thought that'd make things easier, but it's only made things worse. I don't know if we'll be able to keep doing this."

They paused to order and drink a glass of wine.

"We don't really have a choice, Dia," Matteo said, watching the wine as he swirled it around his glass. "It's not like we can send one or both of them back."

"I don't want to talk about them anymore." Lidia waved her hand angrily. "What's happening with the two of you? How's your new apprentice working out?"

Ciro felt a gnawing in his stomach. It wasn't fair for him to have it so easy.

"Well, Loredana is a hard worker. Her first two tasks every day are to sketch for an hour, then practise her letters. Only after that is she allowed to work on anything else." He paused, trying to find something negative to say, to soften the blow of the terrible apprentices they seemed to have gotten.

"It's tricky with her being so young – I don't know how much of the machinery is safe for her to use. I wouldn't want her to cut her thumb off or sand her fingertips. And with the Parting Gifts and project the Guild have me working on, I've little time to spend with her. She spends most of her spare time just watching me or helping Seppe where she can."

Lidia sighed. "She sounds like a dream. Don't worry about teaching her everything too quickly. She'll have plenty of time to learn the trickier things as she gets older."

"At least we don't need to teach ours their letters," Matteo countered. "Their parents taught them that much. Too bad they didn't teach them to get along!"

"Teo, really, I don't want to talk about them," Lidia snapped. "What other news do you have, Ciro, Seppe? There must be something."

"We had dinner at the Exploding Beakers a few weeks back," Seppe told them. "Have you been?"

Lidia frowned. "Isn't that the Alchimista's bar?"

"Well, yes, but it has other patrons," Ciro pointed out carefully. "We went with a friend and some of his acquaintances. You remember my old friend, Alberto Falegname. I'm sure I've mentioned him dozens of times. His son, Telchide, joined us with his new lady friend and some Sarti."

"Lower your voice, Ciro, for Caldera's smoke!" Matteo hissed. "Do you want everyone in the ristorante to know you've been mingling with other Guilds?"

Ciro blinked, stunned. "I wasn't *working* with them, Matteo. It was only dinner," he said softly. "Just like this one."

"No," Matteo replied just as softly. "Nothing like this one. We can't be accused of anything if we're all in the same Guild. Haven't you heard about the raids?"

Ciro glanced at Seppe who only shrugged.

"What raids?" he asked, leaning in.

"Have you been hiding underwater, Ciro?" Lidia asked, astonished. "After the Alchimista Trials went so badly for them, the Mercantili Guild ordered a blockade of the Port."

Ciro nodded. "Yes, I'd heard about that one."

"Well, they've taken things further. They were certain that some Guilds were still interacting. I heard they tried to have the Inter-Guild Edict tightened last week, with the introduction of not even being able to buy goods from each other without paying a Mercantili Guild fee, but Ministro Ercolano refused to allow it.

"Now they've started raiding random ristoranti to try to catch people out having inter-Guild relations. If they find you at dinner with anyone outside their Guild, they've said they'll charge you as though you were working together."

"What?" Ciro sat up straight. "Why didn't I know about that? Did you know, Seppe?"

His companion frowned and shook his head.

"It's no surprise," Matteo said, still talking softly. "They purposely didn't advertise it, in the hopes of catching out more people."

"So how do *you* know about it?" Ciro asked, sceptically. "Do you have friends in the Mercantili Guild?"

Lidia rolled her eyes. "Of course not, Ciro. We were at a ristorante when they raided it. Thankfully, it was just us and our apprentices. But they arrested a Musicista and a Ballerina just for having dinner together. They tried to plead that they weren't working together, simply sharing a meal as old friends, but they were taken away for questioning anyway."

Their meals came and they ate in silence. What was there to say at this point that wouldn't cause more trouble? When they were leaving, they agreed to meet every fortnight instead of every week until the Guild Ball. There was just too much work to be done and so little time.

On the way home, Seppe kept glancing at Ciro, but he only spoke when they were finally behind closed doors.

"This bidding war of yours. If the Mercantili Guild finds out about it, and that Greta is helping you, how much trouble will you be in?"

Ciro leaned against him. "I don't know. I suppose we just hope they don't find out. Honestly, I think I'm in more danger of them finally deciding I shouldn't be in the Gioiellieri Guild if my main activities are carving cammei and corallo. Technically, that's more something an Artista does, not a Gioielliere."

Seppe kissed his forehead. "The Corallini have always been part of the Gioiellieri Guild. You should be in no trouble there. Unless they plan on extending their control even further than they already have."

"Things were so much simpler before the edicts." Ciro sighed heavily and shook his head. "I'm too tired to worry about it now. Let's just go to bed and worry about it tomorrow."

Chapter 22 – Orodi 6 Sarti 230 Years After Implosion

The day of the bidding war arrived. Ciro woke in a cold sweat. There was so much to be done. Anna had decided to stay in her own workshop today to keep out of their way. As soon as Loredana arrived, she was sent on an errand to confirm the antipasti and alcohol to be delivered that afternoon.

While she was gone, Seppe and Ciro worked to clear as much of the workshop as they could. Anything that could be moved into the kitchen, upstairs or even outside, was relocated. They managed to create a small area for their guests to mingle. Ciro looked at it critically.

"We should move the display table in the centre of that area and put the corallo trunk on top – tonight of course, not now. It's too heavy for just the two of us to lift."

Seppe joined him in surveying the room and shook his head. "If it's there, then some of them will have their backs to the trunk while Anna conducts the bidding war. Better, in fact, to place it on your cammeo workbench and conduct the bidding war from here, so all eyes are on the trunk and Anna can see all the bidders."

It only took Ciro a moment to realise Seppe was correct. He threw his arm around Seppe's shoulders.

"Really, Seppe, what would I ever do without you?

Seppe pursed his lips thoughtfully. "Lose all your clients, fall behind in your corallo necklaces and go out of business." He smiled as Ciro huffed out a laugh.

"Now, you'll need to wear your best work clothes tonight. And why not wear the shirts Greta made us? It's a good way to show our support for other Guilds in this difficult time, no?"

Ciro agreed, but refused to change until later that day. He did not wish to accidentally dirty his best shirt and have nothing left to wear.

Loredana came back with confirmations of the deliveries. Now all they had to do was wait. It was the longest day of Ciro's life. He could barely settle down to do anything which required a focused mind. So instead, he decided to make hook and eye clasps in the shape of a fishhook and a hooked fish for some of the necklaces Loredana had made. He showed her the tiny bit of gold they would need for the clasp.

"That's too small," she told him authoritatively. "How will you ever make a clasp out of *that*?"

"Watch and learn." Ciro winked. "If you're lucky, I might even let you help with the fire-gun."

Loredana jumped up. "The fire-gun? Really?"

Ciro nodded. "If you behave yourself and be careful."

"Oh, I will, Maestro. I promise!"

They began the process, Ciro methodically flattening the metal. When it was just at the right thickness, he positioned the metal on a marble block and helped Loredana aim the fire-gun in the right direction. Together, they heated the gold until it was just soft enough to shape into a hook and fish.

Loredana stood aside and watched the intricate process, asking questions at times, but mostly staying silent and allowing Ciro to work. He brought her close and involved her in any part of it he thought she could possibly help with.

By the end of the process, they'd created three hook and eye clasps for attaching to either end of a corallo necklace. Ciro attached the hook to one end of the necklace that Loredana had painstakingly strung earlier and the fish to the other.

"There you have it," Ciro said, holding up the first finished necklace for Loredana to see. "This will easily sell for three gold pieces – one for each strand of corallo balls – see it has three all twisted around each other. *You* made it possible."

Loredana held it reverently, studying every detail. She looked up at him with wide eyes that suddenly filled with tears. Ciro knelt down in front of her.

"Reda, what's the matter? You did such a wonderful job of it. Why are you crying?"

"It's *real*," she said, sniffing back her tears. "I mean, my apprenticeship. It's really real. I'm actually helping and learning and, oh Zio!"

She threw herself at him and buried her face in his chest. Ciro took the necklace from her and held her close.

"Yes, Loredana. It's all real and you're going to be a fine Gioielliera or Corallina. Whichever you prefer, I will teach you everything I know and the choice will be yours for what you decide to create for your Copper Guild Mark. But you have years to decide that. No rush."

Still hugging him, she moved her head to look up at him. "I'm going to be a Corallina. I'd never want to be anything else. And everyone will want to know me because Loredana Corallina was Ciro Corallino's first ever apprentice."

Ciro laughed and tousled her hair. She finally unlocked her hands from around him.

"Maestro, can I stay tonight and watch the bidding war?" she asked hopefully. "I'll stay out of the way, I promise!"

"I'm sorry, Reda, but I don't think it's a good idea. I don't know what time it will finish nor how late your mamma will allow you to stay."

She crossed her arms angrily. "If I was a proper apprentice and lived here, I'd be at the bidding war and it wouldn't be a problem. I'll leave a note for mamma telling her I'll sleep here tonight."

Ciro rubbed his forehead trying to decide what to do. Seppe came up behind him and whispered in his ear.

"Yes, alright," Ciro relented. "You can stay. But you can't sleep here, Loredana. There's no space. One of us will take you home after the bidding war."

She looked ready to argue, but changed her mind and nodded instead.

***

It was late in the afternoon by the time they'd tidied away everything from making the necklaces. The deliveries for the antipasti had arrived and were being kept cool in the marble cold-box. When the alcohol arrived, Ciro put it in the kitchen too and belatedly realised he didn't have enough wine glasses.

"We'll ask Greta when she comes," Seppe told him, when Ciro began to fret. "I'm certain she'll either have enough or be able to source some very quickly with her blazermobile."

Greta arrived just after trading, with all her apprentices and Domizio. They bundled out of the blazermobile and barged in with platters of desserts, putting them all in the cold-box as directed by Seppe.

Ciro pulled Greta to one side. "We appear to have slipped up on one of the finer details. Wine glasses. I only have four. Do you have some we could borrow?"

"Yes," Greta laughed, "but only because Maestro Ranieri liked to hold little gatherings in his workshop. I'll send Domizio to get them while we set up everything else."

"Thank you, Greta. It's much appreciated," Ciro said. "But before he goes, we'll need his help to move the item."

Between the four of them, they managed to lift the corallo trunk to Ciro's workbench. He refused to uncover it until later, to keep it as secret as possible.

Domizio left in the blazermobile with Annika to help him. As they were leaving, Anna arrived. She looked around the crowded room and shook her head.

"Ciro, there are already too many people here and I'm assuming none of them are your potential clients."

Greta walked up and shook her hand. "You must be Anna Corallina. Ciro told me all about you. Don't worry, Domizio will take my apprentices away before the bidding war begins."

The look Anna shot at Ciro was murderous. But Greta quickly stole her attention away.

"Now, for the bidding war, we've set up the item on Ciro's workbench over here. If you stand behind it, you'll be able to see everyone. Beforehand, we can all mingle among the potential bidders to discuss the item and hopefully loosen their purse strings with some alcohol and food."

Anna glared at her. “I’m not here to serve them. I’m here to perform a service to Ciro and secure the next such item for myself. Don’t expect me to do anything else.”

Ciro was not sure how much longer Greta would be able to handle Anna, so he swiftly stepped between them and motioned to Loredana.

“Loredana, why don’t you show Anna what you helped me make today?”

She quickly came and took Anna by the hand and lifted the lid of the display cabinet to take out her first necklace. When Ciro was certain the Corallina’s attention was fully occupied, he looked around the workshop to see if there was anything else he could do before the wine glasses or the bidders arrived. Greta came to stand beside him.

“Can we move the wooden panels?” she asked. “Or remove them altogether?”

“I’m afraid not.” Ciro shook his head. “There’s a special project behind there which must remain secret, even to the bidders. Only Anna, Loredana and myself are allowed back there.”

Greta raised an eyebrow. “Are you telling me even Giuseppe hasn’t seen behind the panels?”

Ciro didn’t answer and Greta didn’t press him. There was no point forcing himself to lie to her.

When Domizio and Annika arrived with the wine glasses, there was a scant fifteen minutes to spare. Sofia took charge of Loredana, without being asked. Loredana seemed perfectly happy to stay with her so Ciro let them be.

They carried everything into the kitchen, made the final preparations with the antipasti, then Domizio left with all of Greta’s apprentices, promising to return in an hour or two to help clean up and be an escort for anyone requiring one on the way home.

Ciro was helping Seppe pour the vermouth and grappa into glasses and arrange them on silver trays when the first bidders arrived. Anna called him out to greet them. Ciro was shuffled into the workshop with a tray of drinks as all the people he’d invited came through the door. He handed each a full glass upon their arrival.

“Welcome, welcome,” he said, over and over again, not remembering any of their names except for the illustrious Signora Loyola.

When his tray was empty and the workshop was full, Signora Loyola handed him a handful of wooden sticks with chalkboards on top. Each one had a different number.

“I took the liberty of bringing these for the bidding war. I don’t suppose you’ve run many before and it will make it easier to identify people,” she told him quietly. “It would please me if you’d use them.”

Ciro took the sticks with a confused smile. “Erm, yes, thank you. I’ll bring them to Anna now. Please excuse me.”

Ciro found Anna hiding in the kitchen with Seppe and Loredana. He handed her the wooden sticks.

"Apparently, these will help you run the bidding war," he told her. "I've no idea how. Do you?"

Anna turned them over and shrugged. "We'll figure it out or they'll tell us. Go back out there and mingle. You'll have to unveil it soon."

"Good luck, Maestro," Loredana said, bouncing in excitement. "In bocca al lupo!"

Ciro patted her affectionately on the cheek and returned to the noisy workshop with a platter of antipasti in one hand and a platter of pastries in the other. He manoeuvred his way to the longer workbench and set both trays down.

He cleared his throat and held his hands up for their attention.

"Signori and Signore, if you'll all turn your attention to the display table, you'll see the type of work a Corallino does. Each corallo item has been carefully handcrafted to perfection with skills honed for over fifty years. Now, with that in mind, I will unveil the item on offer tonight."

He walked over to his favourite workbench and untied the rope from the bottom of the trunk. When he was certain he had their full attention, he pulled back the cloth cover to reveal the largest corallo trunk ever seen in Tor'Esint, or likely anywhere else. There was a collective intake of breath at the sight. Even Greta, who must've had some indication of what it was, put a hand up to cover her open mouth.

"Imagine, if you will, any design you desire carved into these flawless corallo branches. The winning bidder will have the honour of choosing a design and be the proud owner of the only corallo trunk of this size ever carved. Please, come up for a closer look before the bidding begins."

He vacated the area, intending to seclude himself to a quiet corner until the bidding war. But every time he moved, he was accosted by a bidder, asking detailed questions of what he realistically could carve into it. His answer was invariable.

"Anything you can imagine," he replied to one and all. "I could carve the members of your family, the wonders of the sea, a forest of birds. Whatever you wish to choose. I'd make a clay model first, to show you what the finished product would look like, and then change any part of it you're not happy with."

The amount of times he said it, his throat was beginning to feel raw. All he really wanted was a cup of coffee, or a large glass of wine. But both Seppe and Greta had forbidden him from drinking alcohol while his guests were there, and coffee was out of the question as the smell would permeate the room. He permitted himself a glass of water then brought Anna out to begin the bidding.

She looked around the room with disinterest, her eyes only catching a sparkle when she looked at the magnificent corallo trunk. Ciro saw her lay out the wooden sticks on the display table.

"Everyone, please take a number. The bidding will now begin."

The pitch of conversation rose in excitement. Ciro wiped his sweaty palms on his pants. Greta had suggested the two of them walk around the room, trying to increase bidding, but he didn't know any of these people and had already answered their questions. Instead, he stood with his back against the wooden panels, well out of the way.

"Let's begin the bidding at five gold pieces," Anna said loudly.

"Five," said a short lady, sticking her wooden pole up in the air.

"That's five to number eight."

"Six," called out two people at once. They glared at each other.

"Seven," yelled one of them.

"Seven to number three. Do I hear eight from anyone? Thank you, number seven. And nine? Yes, thank you, number three."

Ciro watched the wooden poles going up and down as Anna increased the price by fives and then tens. After a minute, the bidding began to slow, but Ciro was barely breathing by this point. He'd shifted to lean on his long workbench to have something solid behind him. Greta was now right there beside him.

"We're at fifty gold coins now," Anna advised them all. "Do we have any takers for sixty? Sixty will be a bargain for such a large trunk of corallo to be carved into your design of choice by the most talented Corallino in all of Tor'Esint. Sixty anyone?"

Number five raised her stick and nodded.

"That's sixty gold to number five. Do I hear seventy signori and signore?"

"Seventy," called out a man in a deep tenor, raising his stick.

"Thank you, Signore. That's seventy. Will anyone go to eighty?"

There was a long pause. Anna looked around the room and shrugged.

"Seventy, going once, going twice." She held her hands up, ready to clap them to close the auction.

"Eighty." Signora Loyola calmly raised her stick.

The man glanced over to her.

"Ninety," he said, raising his stick.

"One hundred," Signora Loyola countered nonchalantly.

"Signora, let's not play these games," he said in a bored voice. "One fifty."

Ciro heard a gasp beside him and tightened his grip on the workbench. He felt a wave of nausea pass over him.

"No, Signore, no games," Signora Loyola replied. "One eighty."

"Two hundred," he growled, red in the face.

"Two fifty," Signora Loyola said smoothly.

Anna stepped in to regain control. "That's two hundred and fifty gold pieces for this magnificent corallo treasure from number six. Do I hear two hundred and fifty-five? Two hundred and fifty-five, anyone?"

She paused, a picture of perfect composure, waiting for anyone else to bid. "That's two hundred and fifty, then. Going once, going twice. Sold for two hundred and fifty gold to bidder number six. Thank you, signori and signore. That closes the bidding for tonight. But that doesn't mean anyone needs to leave empty handed. Right here in Ciro's display case is a wonderful array of jewellery suitable for any one of you. I'm certain you can find a lovely bargain there. Name your price and the Corallino will consider it."

Ciro marvelled at Anna's skills and tact. After selling an item for *two hundred and fifty gold coins* he'd be willing to almost give away everything else in his shop. That meant one hundred gold coins for Antonino, another one for Anna's services which left a total of *one hundred and forty-nine gold coins* for Ciro himself. It was more than he made most years, all in one sale.

Greta clutched Ciro's hand and shook it firmly.

"Well done, Ciro. Well done!"

Signora Loyola walked over to the corallo trunk and stood possessively close to it. Anna had a few words with her, then walked over to Ciro.

"I'm going to get Seppe to come out and help with sales. You get off your arse and start helping."

Startled into action by her language, Ciro went to mingle with his potential customers. They had propped up the display cabinet and were practically fighting over the items within.

Seppe and Anna both helped him with the sales. Anna didn't bother asking what he usually charged for his pieces – he was happy for her to make her own call. By the time all the customers had been served and had departed, the display cabinet held only a single corallo branch pendant. He searched in his drawers until he found a little white box – they were almost out of those too! He put the pendant in the box and tied it with a corallo coloured ribbon.

Still dazed by the events of that evening, he walked over to Signora Loyola. She grinned proudly at him, one hand resting on the base of the corallo trunk. He held out the box to her.

"A small token of my appreciation, Signora," he said softly. "Please don't offend me by not accepting. It's all I have left, and I won't have time to begin your carving until after the Guild Ball. But we'll have time to discuss the design. Whenever you'd like."

Signora Loyola smiled and caressed the corallo, like a lover.

"I always intended to outbid my friends, you know," she told him conspiratorially. "True, I didn't expect the price to go quite so high, but I would've gone even higher had one of them tried to outbid me again. I cannot bear the thought of any of them being the first to have ... well, anything really. Greta and Telchide can attest to that."

Ciro stared at her open mouthed as she placed five heavy pouches into his unsuspecting hands, and then more onto the workbench when his hands were full.

"I'll think of some ideas, or let my friends tell me their ideas, and then come to see you again. Farewell, good evening."

"Good evening, Signora Loyola," he managed to say as she walked away.

She had a quiet word with Greta before departing, but Ciro was too stunned to care what they were discussing. Seppe came over and quickly scooped the pouches into the basket Ciro usually took to the beach with him. They barely fit! He would need to go down to the Guild Hall tomorrow to make a large deposit.

Anna and Greta tactfully stayed away until Seppe had disappeared with the money.

"Well, that was a rather successful evening," Greta said with a smile.

Anna glared at her. "Don't know what *you're* so happy about. *I'm* the one who got them to bid so high and clean out Ciro's entire shop. Not *you*."

"Then I suppose you won't want my help finding any wealthy clients when you have your own corallo trunk to auction off?" Greta said lightly. Anna narrowed her eyes, but didn't reply. "Now, Ciro, Domizio arrived during the flurry. I shooed him off to the kitchen, but I think I ought to let him drive me home now. We could take Loredana home, if you like."

"No, you can't," Seppe said, walking back into the room. "She's fallen asleep. I laid out some blankets on our bedroom floor. She can sleep there tonight. But if you could let Serafina know her daughter won't be coming home tonight, that would save me a walk."

"Yes, of course." Greta turned to Anna. "We can offer you a lift home as well if you like."

Anna accepted the lift, though Ciro could see she'd have preferred not to. He cared not at all, still reeling from the events of the night. When they left, Seppe locked the door behind them and looked around the room.

"I'll clean up tomorrow morning. It's not like I'll have much else to do with everything sold out from under our noses. Loredana and I will need to clear the mess before we start working on more corallo necklaces."

Ciro shrugged. They would need to work on more necklaces than usual if they expected to have a full display cabinet, but it really didn't matter – not with the amount of money they'd made that night.

"I'll go down to the Guild Hall first thing tomorrow morning. I don't feel safe with all that money in the house."

They went up to bed, tiptoeing around Loredana. For all the success of the evening, Ciro fell into a troubled sleep, tossing and turning all night.

Chapter 23 – Mercatodi 7 Sarti 230 Years After Implosion

Ciro walked down the street, towards the Guild Hall. One hand held Loredana's – he'd promised to take her home straight afterwards. The other was firmly clasped around his wicker basket, trying to keep it from bouncing and making a jangly noise so that any passerby could hear how much money he had on him.

"Zio, can we walk a little slower please? I'm so tired."

"Huh?" Ciro turned and saw her slumped shoulders, dark rings under her eyes. "Yes, sorry Reda."

He slowed down to match her painfully slow pace. The Guild Hall clocks chimed eight o'clock and they were still two blocks away. Ciro's chest tightened at every passerby who came just a little too close or jostled him or Loredana.

Eventually they reached the steps and Ciro practically dragged Loredana up them.

"Zio, your hand is sweaty." She pulled her hand out of his grip and wiped it on her skirt. "Is something the matter?"

He said nothing but shook his head, stepped into the Guild Hall and took a deep breath, his shoulders relaxing from the hunch he hadn't realised was there. Loredana looked up at him suspiciously but didn't ask after him again.

Feeling much calmer, Ciro walked up to Yvette at the reception desk, Loredana close behind him.

"I need to make a deposit," he told her.

"Fill in this form," she said and handed him a piece of paper from a small stack on her desk without looking up.

Ciro took the form and a pen from the jar on top of the desk and filled in the details, his hand shaking slightly. He passed the form back to Yvette and returned the pen to the jar.

Yvette read the form with disinterest until she reached the amount.

"One hundred and forty-nine gold pieces?" she asked in disbelief. "Ciro, you've never handed in more than ten gold coins at a time. What're you playing at?"

He shrugged, trying to ignore Loredana's gaping mouth. "I had a big night last night. Lots of customers. They cleaned out my display cabinet and some placed future orders."

"Did any of them see the special project?" she asked, eyes widening.

He glared at her. "Of course not. What do you take me for? A fool?"

"Well, I'll have to call one of the Maestri to count the money into the vault for such a large amount before they sign off on it. Wait here."

She rang a small copper bell and another Amministratrice came to take her place.

Loredana tugged him away from the desk and pulled him down towards her.
"Was that true?" she asked. "I couldn't stay awake until they left. Did they really buy everything? Including the trunk?"
Ciro covered her mouth and quickly looked around to see if anyone had heard. There were only a few Amministratori walking around and none of them paying any attention to a Corallino and his apprentice.
"Yes, it's true. You saw the display cabinet this morning, didn't you? Wasn't it *empty*?" he whispered. She nodded, eyes wide. "One paid handsomely for the *special item* and the others bought everything they could see. I'll need your help next week to thread as many corallo necklaces as you can with Seppe. As soon as I've time, I'll make the clasps for them so the cabinet doesn't stay empty. Do you think you can do that? There may be a special little something in it for you if you thread as many as Seppe."
Ciro winked at Loredana as her eyes grew even wider.
"What kind of special little something?" she asked, curiously.
"Well, you already have a dress. What else would you like?"
"A music box," she said, barely thinking before she spoke. "Like the ones Telchide Inventore makes."
"That sounds like a good trade. Mind, I'll only buy you one if you thread as many as Seppe."
He held his finger up to make his point. She grabbed it and shook it, laughing.
"Follow me, Ciro," Yvette said, behind him.
She walked off without even waiting to see if he would follow. Yvette had never been the friendliest of people, but Ciro thought her manner had deteriorated since she'd delivered the corallo trunk to his workshop.
With all he'd heard about the Mercantili Guild recently, he supposed Yvette had every reason to be annoyed with him. With the special Guild project in his workshop, he was under closer scrutiny than he had ever been, and Ciro knew he had been bending the rules – not that anyone cared before that his companion was off the books and working alongside him.
Loredana held his hand tightly as they walked past the reception desk, past the room where the decision regarding her apprenticeship had been made, and to the vaults. Ciro had never been here before. His weekly or monthly deposits had never required the Maestri to sign off on them, nor warranted a large area for counting.
Adamo was waiting for them outside. His eyebrows shot up when he saw them.
"Ciro! I didn't expect to see *you* here," he said with some surprise. "And with your young apprentice."
"Good morning, Maestro Adamo," Loredana said with a curtsey.
Adamo returned the courtesy with a small bow, smiling pleasantly at the young girl. "So lovely to see you, Loredana. Is your mamma well? And your

sister?"

"Yes, thank you. I'll tell mamma you asked after her."

Adamo looked as though he was about to say something else to her, but turned instead to Ciro.

"Let's count this money, then."

Adamo brought Ciro over to a counting machine and turned it on. Ciro tipped the contents of his basket into it. He watched in growing anticipation as it counted the coins in case he had miscalculated. Loredana's face got closer and closer to the bowl into which the coins were falling.

"Um, Zio ... I mean, Maestro, this looks like more than one hundred and forty-nine coins."

Ciro looked to where she was pointing and frowned. He was certain it was one hundred and forty-nine. He'd counted it himself.

"Oh." He swallowed. "I may have been mistaken. It may, in fact, be one hundred and *ninety-seven*."

"What?!" Loredana squealed.

Adamo looked from the young girl to Ciro, frowning in confusion.

"One hundred and ninety-seven? Ciro, I hate to ask this, in front of your apprentice as well, but you haven't been doing anything illegal now, have you?"

"Of course not!" Ciro snapped. "I held a bidding war last night, for a special item. It went for a much higher price than expected, and the rest of the clientele cleaned me out. I haven't a single piece of jewellery left in my display cabinet. Loredana can attest to that."

The girl nodded. "The workshop was still a mess this morning after last night. I'll be making corallo necklaces with Seppe all next week!"

Adamo paused and looked thoughtful. "What was this special item then? Because I'm going to guess, with your miscalculation, that it was one hundred and forty-nine gold coins."

"It's a secret." Ciro shrugged unapologetically. "I promised not to tell until the item was sold and technically, the transaction isn't complete until the item is finished and delivered."

"Come, now. If there were bidders at your house, the secret is out. I must insist you tell me." Adamo took a deep breath. "You know I hate doing this, but as a Maestro of the Guild, I cannot knowingly remain ignorant of such things."

Loredana tugged on Ciro's shirt. "Maestro, remember, the secret was only from other Corallini until it was sold. It's sold now, and Maestro Adamo isn't a Corallino so ... it's alright to tell him, isn't it?"

"I ... suppose so." Ciro rubbed his stubbled cheek. "It was a corallo trunk and it wasn't one hundred and forty-nine gold – that was just my cut. The rest goes to my supplier and Anna as she ran the bidding war for me."

Adamo's frown grew increasingly dark. "Just your cut? Exactly how big is this trunk?"

Before Ciro could stop her, Loredana was measuring it out from the floor with her hands, trying to encompass the enormity of it. Adamo looked on in disbelief.

"But, the one we gave you to carve for the Guild Ball is less than *half* that size and took us months to source! How did you just happen to come across one so large? And sell it for so much?"

To that, Ciro put his hand up and shook his head. "I'm sorry, Maestro, but I swore not to reveal my source until they were ready to make another deal. They had to promise their next piece to Anna to convince her to run the bidding war for me."

"Very well then, but you can expect a visit from me next week to view this item." Adamo said. "I'll have to tell the Maestri. They may not be altogether pleased to discover that their centrepiece for the Guild Ball could be overshadowed by a private sale."

He corrected the figure on the deposit form, witnessed Ciro's signature of it and emptied the bowl into Ciro's vault.

"You know, Ciro, you've enough here to hire a larger workshop when you want to. I know we agreed Loredana would sleep at home for now, but when that arrangement no longer works, know that you now have the resources to change your circumstances. You might even be able to buy something outright."

Ciro was taken by surprise. He hadn't thought anyone would take notice of his circumstances or fortune.

"Thank you, Adamo. I'll keep that in mind. Now, we've got to be on our way. Serafina will be expecting Loredana – it was a late night, as I said, and she didn't manage to return home."

At Adamo's sudden alarm, Ciro patted his shoulder. "Don't worry, we let her mamma know. It's fine."

Loredana tugged at Ciro's shirt as Adamo led them back to the Hall of Great Works.

"Is that true, Zio? Did someone tell mamma I fell asleep?"

"Yes, bella, but it was already quite late. I think we're both going to be in a world of trouble when we arrive."

Loredana bit her lip. "Would a cannolo cool her temper?"

Ciro chuckled. "Yes, I believe it might."

***

After an uncomfortable exchange with Serafina about the previous night, along with a dessert peace offering, Ciro found himself down on the docks. It was busier than he'd like, but Antonino's coins were burning a hole in his pouch. He wanted to hand them over as quickly as he could.

He waved down the marinaio from the selection of barrels he'd set up along the docks. Though Antonino had a crew of marinai working with him, he was still run off his feet with all the people trying to buy seafood for the end of the trading week.

"Not now, Ciro," Antonino yelled at him. "I don't have time for a few gold coins."

Ciro squared his shoulders and weaved his way around the barrels to Antonino.

"I don't care if it's your busiest day of the year. I need to talk to you. *Now*."

Antonino tried to push him away, but Ciro stood firm. With an angry shout, the marinaio called over one of his crew to take his place. He shoved Ciro out towards the quieter section of the docks.

"This had better be worth my while, Ciro!"

Ciro took a deep breath to prevent himself from slapping the man. Instead, he undid the final pouch from his belt and handed it out to him.

"Your cut, from last night."

Antonino rolled his eyes and held out his hand. Only when he felt the weight of the pouch did he startle and stare at Ciro.

"What're you playing at Ciro? They'd better not be copper coins!"

He opened the pouch and drew in a sharp breath. Looking around furtively for curious eyes, he closed the pouch and tied it to his own belt.

"How much is it?" he asked, his voice suddenly strained.

"One hundred. Gold," Ciro clarified. "Anna took her one gold and I kept one hundred and forty-nine. Though I suspect any others will sell for less than one hundred. This appeared to be more a matter of pride to have the first one than anything else."

Antonino paused, counting under his breath. "Two hundred and fifty? It sold for two hundred and fifty gold coins?" he asked, his voice reaching an unusually high pitch.

Ciro shrugged. "I told you Greta Sarta knew wealthy clientele. They clearly have more money than sense. Anyway, I've got work to do. They cleaned me out last night. Remember you promised to sell the next one to Anna. She won't forget."

Antonino nodded dumbly as Ciro left him and walked back to his workshop.

Chapter 24 – Gildadi 9 Sarti 230 Years After Implosion

The door slammed open so hard it rattled on its hinges.

"Careful!" Seppe called out, shuffling towards the door.

"Are you Ciro Corallino?" a deep voice asked.

Ciro put his tools down and shot Anna an apologetic look before stepping out from behind the wooden panel.

"I'm Ciro," he said, taking in the man's muscular form and severe features. "How can I help you?"

The man pointed to the pin on his shirt. "Tor'Esint Amministratore. Is it true you held a bidding war last Orodi?"

"Well, yes," Ciro admitted, warily. "There's nothing illegal about bidding wars."

"No, but questions are asked when an item so expensive is sold without the knowledge of the Mercantili Guild," the man replied. "You've never dealt with the Mercantili Guild before, so how did you acquire an item so valuable without them?"

Ciro saw Anna step out from behind the panel and tried to shoo her back.

"I'm a Corallino, Signore. Everything I acquire is local, mostly from the sea or the local Fabbri for my metal. I don't sell outside of Tor'Esint, so have never required the services of the Mercantili Guild. Again, that is not a crime."

The Amministratore walked around the workshop, peering into the empty display cabinet, opening every drawer. Loredana edged away from him, holding her sketchbook close to her chest. The man picked up an oval shaped shell fragment.

"What's this?"

Ciro held out his hand for the item, but the man did not give it to him.

"What is it?" he growled.

"It's part of a sardonyx shell," Ciro replied stiffly. "For a cammeo."

The man raised an eyebrow but said nothing. Instead, he continued his inspection of the workshop, noting the baskets of corallo branches, the drawers of corallo balls.

"Where's the jewellery?" he asked, picking up the cammeo Ciro was currently working on for a Parting Gift.

"I sold it all. Last Orodi, at the bidding war," Ciro said, much more calmly than he felt.

"What's all this about?" Anna asked. "We've work to get on with. Like he told you, he was cleaned out at the bidding war and needs to make more items. Besides which, we're busy getting things ready for the Guild Ball. Be off with you!"

The Amministratore turned his attention from Ciro to Anna. "Who are *you*?"

"None of your business," snapped Anna.

"*Everything* in this workshop is my business," he said, staring her down. "Including this."

He snatched Loredana's sketchbook from her grasp and flicked through the pages.

"What's an apprentice Gioielliera doing sketching?"

"I'm not an apprentice Gioielliera," Loredana said before Ciro could stop her. "I'm an apprentice Corallina and if I can't draw, I'll never be able to create a cammeo."

"Sounds to me like you should've joined the Artiste Guild, girl," the man growled.

Loredana drew back and hid behind Ciro. His heart was hammering in his chest so violently, he thought it might explode.

"Amministratore, the Corallini have always sat within the Gioiellieri Guild as we create items of jewellery. You wouldn't find an Artista creating a brooch, or a set of earrings or a necklace now, would you?"

"I don't see any of that here," he said, finally noticing the cloth-covered corallo trunk behind Ciro. "What's under there?"

"This item has been sold," Ciro told him, without moving.

"Uncover it."

Ciro stood firmly in front of it. The man pushed him out of the way so forcefully, Ciro fell on top of Loredana. The girl squealed, but didn't appear to be hurt. She'd saved Ciro a broken hip.

Anna and Seppe came to help him up as the Amministratore uncovered the large corallo trunk. There was a quick intake of breath and a short, sharp laugh.

"You can't tell me *this* is an item of jewellery," he said. "Where'd you get it?"

Ciro refused to answer. The man loomed over him and struck his face. Loredana screamed behind him.

"Leave my Zio alone!" she yelled.

"Where?" he asked again.

Ciro remained silent, his temper rising like lava. The man raised his hand to strike Ciro again, but the Corallino still refused to answer.

"Antonino," Loredana shouted. "Antonino Marinaio."

Ciro's shoulder's crumpled at the vicious smile on the Amministratore's face.

"Very good. Now, what're you working on behind that panel?"

"That item belongs to the Gioiellieri Guild," Anna said firmly. "If you dare look behind it, I will be forced to tell the Maestri about the incursion."

The man stuck his face close to Anna's and sneered.

"Go ahead."

Ciro watched helplessly as the man walked behind the wooden panel.

"So, this is what you'll do with that piece, is it? Carve it up like a statue." He came out from behind the panel and glared at Ciro and Anna. "Now, tell me again exactly why you think we shouldn't charge you for breaking the Inter-Guild Edict when you're clearly carrying out the work of an Artista rather than that of a Gioielliere?"

Ciro clenched his fists. "I've already told you, this is only a small part of what a Corallino does. *Most* of it is the work of a Gioielliere."

"And yet, you can't show me a single item of jewellery. Shame," he tutted. "I'll be off now. But don't think this is the last you've heard from me."

The man left the shop, slamming the door behind him just as hard as before. Ciro felt his legs give way beneath him and struggled to reach a chair before he collapsed. Seppe was instantly by his side, stroking his hand.

"It's going to be fine, Ciro," he said in a trembling voice. "The Guild will save you."

Anna huffed. "The Guild may have no choice."

Seppe shot her a look, but Anna only shrugged.

"It's true. And if they do anything to Ciro, they'll try to do it to all of us."

"It's all my fault," Loredana cried out, bursting into tears. "I shouldn't have said that about drawing and Antonino. I'm so sorry, Zio."

Ciro drew her close. "No, Loredana. It's not your fault. You were truthful and you were trying to save me from harm."

"By throwing another man to the wolves," Anna hissed quietly. "We need to warn him."

Loredana looked up at her tearfully, but there was nothing Ciro could do to comfort her. Anna was right.

"I'm a fast runner," Loredana said, sniffing up her tears. "I'll go down to the docks and warn Antonino."

Ciro nodded, as much to get her out of the way as to warn Antonino. As soon as she left the workshop, he crumpled in on himself.

"I'm finished," he said, head in hands, tears stinging his eyes.

Much as he knew it to be true, it still hurt that neither Seppe nor Anna contradicted him.

"We need to minimise the damage," Ciro said, wiping the tears from his eyes and sitting up. "They might have everything they need against me, but we can still save the rest of you."

"And just how are you going to do that?" Anna asked, her voice thick with emotion. He couldn't tell if it was anger or fear.

"Well, first, I'm going to send you home, with Seppe, to collect as many carvings as you have and bring them here, or to the Guild. Perhaps they can store them in the vaults. Only leave everything that rightfully belongs in the realm of the Gioielliere and cannot possibly be attributed to the Artiste Guild.

"Then, I'll pay Sabrina and Simone a visit. Tell them to do the same thing. With any luck, the Amministratore will be trying to find Antonino, not worrying about the other Corallini ... yet."

Anna bit her lip and gave him a quick kiss on the cheek.

"Be careful, Ciro," she said, clutching his arm. "If he finds you at their workshops, who knows how he'll punish you."

Seppe shook his head. "It's too dangerous, Ciro. You don't have to do this."

"I do," Ciro said firmly. "Especially after giving Sabrina all those corallo branches to carve. I imagine she's working on those now and if they catch her, she'll be in as much trouble as I am. I'll wait for Loredana to return and then I'll take her with me."

Anna tugged at Seppe's arm until he finally agreed to go. Ciro could hardly bear to look at the fear in Seppe's eyes as he turned away.

***

"Sabrina, I'm not trying to take your moment from you," Ciro said angrily. "If you don't let me store these corallo branches or, at the very least, take them to the Guild Hall for storage, you'll be in as much trouble as I am."

"How do I know you don't just want all the glory for yourself? You and Anna, the conniving little ash-sucker!"

Loredana gasped. Sabrina looked down guiltily and had the decency to apologise to her, but not to Ciro.

"We're here to help you, Sabrina, believe me," Ciro pleaded. "You don't have any other items in your workshop that could get you in trouble, but *these* certainly will. Especially the ones you've already carved. Let us help you by taking them to the Guild Hall and I'll explain the mess I'm in while I'm there.

"They might even let you keep carving them in one of their rooms if they still want them for the Guild Ball, after this."

At the last, Sabrina's eyes narrowed. "You think they won't want them anymore?"

"I don't know." Ciro shook his head. "If they think all these carvings will get the rest of you in trouble, they might not, no matter how grand they want the Guild Ball to be."

Sabrina paused and looked at them properly, finally noticing Loredana's red-rimmed eyes and the bruise forming on Ciro's cheek.

"You're not joking, are you? This isn't all a prank to get you and Anna all the limelight, is it?"

"I only wish it were." Ciro sighed. "If you allow me to return these to the Guild Hall, I'll be asking them to take possession of the corallo trunk we're working on too, so nothing happens to it while we wait and see what the Amministratori do to me."

Loredana leaned against him. He put an arm across her chest and felt her little heart beating rapidly. All the pain he'd caused her. If only he could take it away.

"Fine then," Sabrina said sharply. "Take them away. But I want your personal guarantee that you won't be asking for them back, for your own personal use."

"You have it." Ciro placed his hand over his heart. "Now give me the corallo."

***

The walk to the Guild Hall was short and silent. Ciro held the precious cargo like his life depended on it – Loredana walked beside him, head down. From what she'd told him, Antonino had quickly packed up his ship and was planning to leave Tor'Esint until things quietened down. That could be a very long time indeed. Ciro was suddenly relieved he'd already given the marinaio his share of the profits.

Loredana opened the Guild Hall doors for him and offered to take the basket. Tired as he was, Ciro knew she wouldn't be able to lift such a heavy load. He shook his head and they proceeded to the reception desk.

"I need to speak to the Maestri," Ciro said, placing the basket on the desk, "and give them this."

Yvette looked up at him with a sour expression.

"You are in a world of trouble. Come with me."

She rang a bell and another Amministratore quickly came to take her place. Ciro followed her, with Loredana close behind. Yvette deposited them into the same room where Loredana's apprenticeship had been decided and left them there.

"What's going to happen?" Loredana whispered.

Ciro put the basket on the small table in the centre of the room and held out his hands for her. Loredana took them, tears in her eyes. He drew her in close and sat her on his leg, her forehead against his unbruised cheek.

"I don't know, Reda," he said truthfully. "But I'll do everything I can to make sure your apprenticeship doesn't end."

Silent tears streamed down her face. "If I can't stay as your apprentice, no one else will take me. Why would they when I make such blunders without knowing it?"

Ciro wiped away her tears with his fingers, only to have them instantly replaced.

"I'm going to say this one time, and I want you to listen carefully." He waited until she was looking at him. "You're a wonderful apprentice. Anyone would be lucky to have you. But, most importantly, I need you to understand that *none* of this is your fault.

"Your comment about the drawing would have made no difference once the Amministratore saw the corallo we were carving. And with Antonino, yes, it may have taken them longer to realise who my supplier was, but you warned him quickly enough that he could get away safely.

"You are a smart, resourceful, talented and kind-hearted person, Loredana.

Don't ever let anyone tell you otherwise, understand?"

Loredana nodded and hugged him fiercely.

They were not left waiting for long. Soon, the door opened and all three Gioiellieri Maestri entered with the same Tor'Esint Amministratore who'd abused him. Ciro's heart skipped a beat. He stood to greet them, but no one offered their cheek, or even their hand. He swallowed, hard.

"Ciro Corallino, you're accused of breaking the Inter-Guild Edict," the Amministratore said in a harsh tone. "A thorough search of your workshop revealed no evidence that you should be part of the Gioiellieri Guild. You are hereby stripped of your Guild Marks. You will return your workshop to the Guild and cease to charge for any work becoming of a Gioielliere. Your assets will be confiscated. Your apprentice is no longer yours. If we find *any* of these conditions are not met within the week, you will be imprisoned for a period of no less than three months."

"We did not agree to allow you to confiscate his assets," Rosalina said firmly.

"That's not your decision," the Amministratore told her. "Anyone stripped of their Guild Marks has their assets confiscated."

"And who is this money awarded to, pray tell?" she asked, hands on her hips. "There are no wronged parties to be compensated, nor injuries to pay for."

The Amministratore shrugged. "Not my area."

"Well, until this matter can be clarified and accepted by the Gioiellieri Guild, we will freeze his assets. Neither Ciro himself, nor the Tor'Esint Amministratori will be able to access them."

Adamo and Luca stood shoulder to shoulder with Rosalina and nodded their agreement. Ciro fell back in his seat, legs giving way beneath him. Only a few days earlier, he'd been offered the option to rent a larger workshop and now he was losing everything. *Everything*.

Loredana held his hand, patting it gently until the Amministratore left.

Rosalina rushed to Ciro and took him by both hands.

"I'm so sorry, Ciro. It was all we could do to stop him from stripping all Corallini of their Guild Marks. Anna and Seppe got here not a half hour before the Amministratore and explained it all. We managed to placate him by agreeing to strip *your* Guild Marks. Though that hardly seems a fair trade now. He'll be paying a visit to the other Corallini to verify they do indeed have jewellery in their workshops rather than only carvings."

Ciro didn't answer. Even though he'd suspected this might happen, he still couldn't quite grasp the enormity of it.

"We brought the basket of corallo branches from Sabrina's house," Loredana said in a quiet voice. "To save her. Will that help?"

Adamo lay a hand on Loredana's head. "Yes, that will help a great deal. And from what we understand, Simone doesn't usually deal with larger pieces of corallo anyway, but Anna is on her way there to warn him nonetheless."

"A week," Ciro finally said. "A week to move. I've nowhere to go. And only a handful of coins in my pocket."

"We won't leave you destitute, Ciro," Rosalina told him, tightening her grip on his hand.

"I'm afraid we must," Luca told her. "If we are found to be helping him, the penalty could be quite severe. They will accuse us of dealing with people outside the Guild and challenging their authority. It could be detrimental to the entire Guild to help just one person. I'm sorry, Ciro, but that's the truth of it."

"What of Loredana?" Ciro said, remembering his promise to her. "I want her apprenticed to Anna. Of the remaining three Corallini, she's the best and she's seen enough of what I do with Loredana to continue on from where I must leave off."

"But, Zio, I don't want to apprentice with anyone else," Loredana said, shaking her head violently.

Ciro held her face gently. "Reda, bella, we have no choice. I cannot continue to support you, or your mamma, anymore. Anna has space at her house. You can live with her and ease your mamma's burden more than I ever did."

Adamo stepped in. "Have you spoken to Anna about this? She may not agree."

"I doubt she'll object." Ciro shrugged. "She'd already been considering an apprentice but was going to wait until after the Guild Ball."

"We'll still need to check with her," Adamo said firmly. "And Serafina. She may not agree with her daughter living with a complete stranger."

"Anna's not a stranger," Loredana said quietly. "She's Zio's friend."

Adamo held out his hand to the girl.

"Ciro, will you allow me to watch Loredana and escort her home at the end of day's trading? One of us will need to explain the situation to Serafina and find an acceptable solution to the apprenticeship situation."

Loredana looked up at Ciro. He only nodded and gently pushed Loredana towards Adamo. He took her away, leaving space for Ciro to cry.

Rosalina stayed with him, while he shed his tears, offering only a hand to hold.

***

Ciro returned home late in the afternoon. Before he'd left the Guild Hall, Rosalina had asked for his Gold Guild Mark pin. His heart faltered as he handed it over. He'd never expected this could actually happen to him. Not really.

How could he have been so blind? There were signs everywhere that things had been getting worse, but Ciro had stuck his head in the sand and tried not to take notice. Fat lot of good it did him now. He'd have been better off paying attention and not taking any risks, no matter the reward. He'd ruined his and Seppe's lives, all for the chance to carve a magnificent piece of corallo!

Seppe was sweeping the floor when Ciro arrived. He paused, broom in hand, and looked him over, noticing the missing Guild Mark pin. Without either of them saying a word, he instantly understood. He put the broom down and held Ciro close. Ciro couldn't help the tears that soaked Seppe's shoulder – couldn't help shaking and crying out at the unfairness of it all.

"What are we going to do, Seppe?" he asked, finally wiping away his tears. "We've nowhere to go and I'm not allowed to perform the work of a Gioielliere anymore. I can't even work with Anna, even supposing she'd have me."

"No." Seppe shook his head. "But I could, if she'll have me. I could do what I always did for you, and she could pay me. I don't expect it would be much, but any little bit would help, no?"

"I should've paid *you*," Ciro said. "All those years, if only I'd insisted on paying you. Then at least we'd have *some* of our money."

Seppe shrugged. "It never mattered before now. Besides, where would I have kept any money? Under the rug upstairs with your secret cache?"

"You don't understand," Ciro told him. "They've frozen my assets. All we have left is the few gold coins in that stash. The Guild will be taking back the workshop at the end of the week. We'll have nowhere to live and no way to afford a new home." He gestured around the room. "Nowhere to put any of this."

Seppe glanced around him. "We could sell it," he said.

Ciro took in a sharp breath and immediately shook his head. Seppe took his hand and kissed it.

"Tomorrow, Ciro. Let's sort it out tomorrow," he said, standing up. "I've cooked fish and rice. Let's just eat and go to bed."

Ciro wanted to object, but his stomach grumbled, reminding him he'd barely eaten that day. He swallowed his protests and followed Seppe into the kitchen.

Chapter 25 – Ramedi 10 Sarti 230 Years After Implosion

Ciro stared at the ceiling, listening to the Guild Hall clocks chiming eight o'clock. He'd never stayed in bed this late on a trading day. There had always been work to do. But no longer.

Seppe wasn't beside him. When they'd woken at seven o'clock, as usual, Seppe had gotten up, put on warm clothes, and turned to wait for him. Ciro had seen the expectant look in Seppe's eyes, but he'd remained in bed. Pursing his lips and giving a short nod, Seppe had gone downstairs to make a pot of coffee. Even the smell hadn't enticed Ciro out of bed. He closed his eyes again, and began drifting off to sleep, though he really wasn't tired.

Eventually, Ciro heard one of the machines starting up. He could tell from the sound that it was the one they used that sawed larger corallo branches into smaller sections, ready to be shaped into balls. There was no sleeping with that thing going. He counted down from five and threw the sheets off himself to get ready for the day, whatever it brought.

Seppe had left him a cup of coffee that had gone cold, and he was busily working as though nothing had happened. As though the plan for the week was still for him to thread as many corallo necklaces as possible.

"What are you doing?" Ciro asked, sipping his coffee with a grimace in the doorway. He couldn't stop the frustration that bubbled away inside him that Seppe could muster any enthusiasm to get through the day.

Seppe paused his work. "We still have a lot of material. I thought to polish off as many pieces as possible, then perhaps Anna, or one of the others could buy them. We could use the money. Perhaps even Greta would buy some more beads, for her gowns."

Ciro said nothing, but continued to sip his coffee, his frustration turning into determination. It was as good an idea as any. But they'd only have this week to do it – after that, the Amministratori would punish them for performing Guild activities. He swallowed down what was left in his cup.

"Do you have any ready for drilling?"

Seppe opened the drawer between the saw and the drill. It was half full of corallo balls, ready for drilling. Ciro sat down at the drilling machine and worked seamlessly beside Seppe. It had been a long time since they'd had the luxury of working side by side. They hadn't routinely done that since those first years after Seppe had joined Ciro in Tor'Esint. At first, Seppe had watched from the doorway, as Ciro worked away at his tasks.

That had only lasted a few days. Seppe had always had a keen eye and it hadn't taken him long to realise that Ciro was so busy he could barely keep up with his orders. He'd asked what he could do to help and Ciro, knowing it might be against the rules but not really caring, had taught Seppe to use all of the machines that couldn't technically be classed as Gioielliere equipment because it was specifically only for Corallini.

No one had ever complained, though it was plain to everyone that Seppe was helping him in his Guild work. They'd probably only gotten away with it in the first place because there were so few Corallini in Tor'Esint that they didn't want to give him a reason to quit the Guild. And it hadn't mattered so much then – there were no Trading or Inter-Guild Edicts to worry about. The Mercantili Guild didn't have their hooks in everything back then. Ciro swallowed down his burning anger at the Mercantili Guild and the devastation they were causing. That anger couldn't help him now.

They worked together in silence for hours, pausing only to stretch their legs or give their eyes a break. At one point, Seppe made another pot of coffee. Ciro found he was actually enjoying himself.

They paused around midday for a quick panino and then got straight back to work. By the end of day's trading, they'd made hundreds of corallo balls, ready for beading or threading. Ciro looked into the basket where he kept the corallo branches – it was still more than half full. That would easily keep them busy another day or two. After that, Ciro could work on the sardonyx shells if he still had time.

He chose to ignore the fact that they really ought to be looking for a place to live. After all, he could only really sort that out when he had at least a small amount of money. He went to bed that night feeling more optimistic than he had any right to be. And it was all because of Seppe. Without Seppe, Ciro would fall apart and they both knew it. Ciro wished he could find some way to repay him. For everything.

Chapter 26 – Legaramedi 12 Sarti 230 Years After Implosion

Ciro divided the boxes of corallo balls into four piles – one for each of the remaining Corallini, and one for Greta. He put all the sardonyx shells and cut pieces into a basket, hefted it onto his back and took two of the boxes, putting them in a smaller wicker basket attached to his waist. He pushed the other boxes towards Seppe.

"You go to Sabrina and Simone. I'll go to Anna and Greta."

"Shouldn't *I* go to Anna?" Seppe asked. "After all, I'm the one who needs to ask her for a job."

Ciro shook his head. "I want to see her. And ... I want to see if she'll agree to take Loredana as her apprentice."

"You really should've visited Serafina," Seppe told him. "That would have been the decent thing to do."

"I couldn't ... I can't. How can I possibly face her after convincing her to let Loredana apprentice with me and then have this happen?" He shook his head again and adjusted his baskets. "Anyway, Adamo said he'd have to talk to Serafina about everything. I'll ask Anna about hiring you. Then tonight, we'll see how much money we have all together with what's upstairs and figure out where we can stay."

Before Seppe could protest again, Ciro walked out the door with his load of corallo balls and oval shell cuttings.

His first stop was Anna's workshop. It was only a block or so away, which was lucky because the baskets weighed him down more than he'd anticipated. The door was open for trading, so he walked right in and stopped in his tracks.

Loredana was there, holding a fire-gun all by herself, annealing metal with Anna peering over her shoulder in supervision.

"What are you doing?" he asked furiously.

Loredana turned off the fire-gun and looked up guiltily. Anna turned to face him, unfazed.

"What's the matter with you?" Anna asked in annoyance.

"*Me*?" Ciro asked angrily. "What's the matter with *you*? Letting a ten-year old child use a fire-gun by herself!"

Anna placed her hands firmly on her hips. "I believe *I'm* Loredana's Maestra now, so *I* get to make decisions about her apprenticeship myself. I don't need to consult you or anyone else about it. Besides, how will she ever learn to do these things if I never let her try?"

Ciro paused. "Her ... Maestra?" he choked out, the words sticking in his throat.

Loredana put the fire-gun down and hopped off the chair. "Isn't that what you wanted, Zio? For Anna to become my Maestra? That's what you told Maestro Adamo, isn't it?"

Ciro nodded, suddenly lost for words. He hadn't expected it to happen quite so quickly. He took the basket off his shoulders and put it on the floor.

"What's in there?" Anna asked. Lifting the lid, she peered in closer and gasped loudly. "Is this ... are they ... blank cammei?"

"And whole sardonyx shells, though I could just as easily cut and shape them for you if you like," Ciro told her. "I've no use for them anymore and I'd rather sell them to you than Sabrina and Simone. Would you care to purchase them?"

Anna looked carefully through the treasure trove. "Ciro, there must be a hundred blank cammei, and I can see at least another four whole sardonyx shells. It must have taken you years to find these. I can't take them."

"I'm not asking you to *take* them," he laughed wryly. "I'm asking you to *purchase* them. My assets have been frozen. I have no money left. Oh, I have these too."

He undid the smaller basket on his hip and opened the lid to take out the boxes of finished corallo balls and pierced branches.

"These are all perfectly shaped and pierced, ready for pendants or necklaces. Whatever you wish to do with them."

Anna poked her fingers through the boxes and smiled. "How much do you want for them?"

"Well, I think five gold for those boxes is fair. They'll make you at least ten necklaces, which you can sell for 2 gold each, easily."

Anna got out a sheet of paper to write it down.

"Two boxes of corallo, five gold each."

Ciro shook his head. "That's not what I said."

"But it's what *I* said," Anna told him. "Now, what about the shells? I think they're easily worth thirty gold, but I don't have that on me right now. Will you take it in instalments?"

"Forty gold pieces?" Ciro asked incredulously. "Anna, be reasonable. You can't afford that!"

Anna nodded. "As I said, not right now. But I'll pay you over time. Is there anything else I can help you with?" she asked.

Before he answered, Anna went to get him his ten gold coins. "This is for the corallo."

Ciro stood, back straight, trying not to think of this next request as the embarrassment it was. He winced at his past self as he suddenly and irrevocably knew how Serafina felt when he helped her financially.

"Will you hire Seppe? The edicts have nothing to do with him. He's so useful, and so skilled. He can thread corallo necklaces, cut and shape corallo balls, pierce corallo balls and branches. He can do virtually anything, other than metalwork and carvings."

Anna returned, ten gold pieces in her hand, and handed them to Ciro.

"Are things really so bad, Ciro?" she asked softly. "Are you sure you wouldn't rather keep him with you?"

Ciro barked out a short laugh. "To do what exactly? Anna, they stripped my Guild Marks. They'll be evicting me in a matter of days, they've frozen my assets and banned me from doing anything remotely connected to the Gioiellieri Guild. I only hope they won't charge me for selling you raw goods!"

"What does evicting mean?" Loredana asked worriedly.

"It means I won't be able to live in my own home anymore. After all, it never belonged to me. I only ever hired it from the Guild. I don't even know if I'll be able to keep my machines, not that I'd be allowed to use them anyway. But there's only three other Corallini and they all have their own equipment."

"You could keep them for me," Loredana said earnestly. "For when I'm a Corallina myself. I'll need a workshop and machines and tools."

Ciro smiled briefly at her enthusiasm. "I'd like nothing better than that, Reda, but I doubt I'll be able to hire rooms large enough to keep them all. They'll probably have to go to the Gioiellieri Guild for whatever they'll pay me for them."

Anna shook her head. "No, Ciro. We all know your equipment is the best. I don't have room for any of it myself, but if the Guild can't store it for you, they can certainly store it for me – for my apprentice. Leave it with me. I'll sort it out."

"And Seppe?" Ciro pressed the point, tears in his eyes.

Anna placed a hand on his shoulder. "Send him from next Gildadi. I'm sure you'll have more than enough to occupy yourselves until then. I'll find out the going rate for a hired hand."

"Thank you, Anna," Ciro said, voice thick with emotion. "I don't know what we'd have done without you. And ... thank you for taking Loredana. I can't begin to tell you what it means to me."

Anna hugged him. "I know," she whispered in his ear.

Ciro turned to leave, but found Loredana tugging his sleeve.

"Will you still come on Riposidi?" she asked. "Mamma is ever so worried about you."

"I don't think so, Reda. I need to find a new place to live and move everything in the next few days. I won't have time to spare, and I won't be able to bring you the desserts you look forward to so much. I'm sorry."

"I don't care about the desserts," she said a little too loudly. "I care about *you*. We all do. *Please* come for lunch."

Ciro sighed heavily and hugged her tightly. "I'll try, Reda. But if I'm moving that day, I can't promise to make it."

"If you don't come this week, I'll expect you next week," Loredana told him.

Ciro marvelled at how quickly she'd grown up. It was such a shame she'd had to, but he was so proud of her.

He left Anna's workshop, with more than just a small weight off his shoulders. He found he could breathe that little bit easier. There were ten gold coins in his pocket, another thirty to come, and whatever Anna decided to pay Seppe each week. It was a start.

The streets were busy leading up to Piazza Mercantile. Though it wasn't Mercatodi, every cafe had tables and chairs outside, making use of the Piazza. Ciro envied them all. Mammas and daughters taking coffee and cake together, couples sharing a pot of tea, friends giggling over the latest bit of gossip. Few of them could be Guild members, or they'd be hard at work.

He walked slowly to Greta's workshop, holding his hip-basket close. He shouldn't be asking his friends to purchase things from him – it felt like forced charity – but he didn't know what else to do. At least he'd never waited until Serafina had to ask for help before offering it. Though he was coming to understand that both situations were terrible.

Outside her shopfront, Ciro stopped and looked at the gaiety inside. Everyone was working hard, but all of them were so happy. He had no right to bring his misery inside there, even if he desperately needed the money. Heaving a sigh, he turned and walked away. He was halfway through the Piazza when he heard someone calling his name.

Ciro looked up and searched for the owner of the voice. He saw Sofia walking towards him smiling her dimpled smile, carrying a large brown package.

"It's so lovely to see you," she said brightly. "I'm just returning from Pasticceria Delfina. Won't you join us for a scroll? I bought plenty and I'm certain Maestra Greta would love to see you."

Ciro returned her smile and shook his head. Sofia frowned at him.

"Signore Corallino, is something the matter?" she asked. "You don't look your usual self."

Ciro found he couldn't answer her. He only shook his head.

"Signore ... Ciro, I'd feel better if you came back with me," Sofia told him, awkwardly wrapping her arm around his while still holding the brown package. "I insist. I'll make you a coffee myself, no matter if Maestra Greta doesn't like the smell."

Left without a choice, Ciro walked back to Greta's workshop. Sofia deposited him in one of the large armchairs by the window, called out to Greta and went to sort out the refreshments.

Ciro sank into the armchair with his head bowed. He couldn't bear to face any of them, but here he was.

Greta came over and greeted him warmly, but paused when he didn't look up.

"Ciro, whatever's the matter?" she asked in concern.

He looked up at her, saw the concern etched in lines on her forehead and slumped even further down into the chair.

"I don't suppose you'd like to purchase some more of those corallo balls you seem to like so much?" he asked, pulling out the two boxes from his wicker basket.

"I could always do with a few more," she said, taking the boxes and looking inside. She tilted the boxes one way and then another. "This looks to be at least eight gold coins worth. Are you certain you can part with so many?"

Ciro nodded, not trusting himself to speak. Sofia came out with a cup of coffee and a glass of water on a tray with a plate of cinnamon and apple scrolls. She put Ciro's portion down on the little table and went to hand out scrolls to everyone else in the Sarta workshop, leaving the two of them alone.

When Ciro didn't move to take anything, Greta picked up the coffee cup and passed it to him. He reached out to take it automatically, his body knowing what to do even if his mind was shutting off from the world.

She didn't force him to speak again, but waited patiently for him to drink his coffee, then pressed the scroll into his hands followed by the water. He felt a little better after the refreshments.

"Now," Greta said, taking his glass away, "tell me what's happened, and don't you dare tell me everything is fine because I won't believe you. And if you try it, I'll just go and ask Seppe and you *know* he'll tell me. So, what is it?"

Ciro finally looked up at her and took a deep, shuddering breath.

"I've been stripped of my Guild Marks," he said softly. "The Mercantili Guild must have found out about the deposit I made somehow and sent the Amministratori to my workshop."

Greta gasped and clutched his hand. "I'm so sorry, Ciro. Those ash-suckers get worse every month. I don't think I made things any better for us during the Alchimista trials."

He frowned, not understanding what she was talking about. She paused and patted his hand.

"Tell me what you need. Do you own your workshop?"

He shook his head.

"When do you have to give it back?"

"By the end of the weekend," he told her.

"And the equipment – is it hired or yours? Have you made arrangements to move everything?"

"It's mine," he said. "I've arranged to give it to Loredana. Anna said she'll find somewhere to keep it until her apprenticeship is over."

Greta put her hand over her heart. "Oh my! Of course. You lost Loredana. And Anna took her in, yes?"

Ciro nodded.

"Well, that's a blessing at least. So she'll organise to move everything?"

"I ... don't know," Ciro admitted. "We only just agreed on it. And she'll hire Seppe as a..."

"Skilled worker." Greta helped him out. "That's at least a silver a day. That will help with rent. Have you found somewhere yet?"

Ciro shook his head. "We're selling everything we can today to see how much money we have."

"But what about your recent sales? Ciro, you must have enough to purchase something outright if you wanted, something small anyway."

"No. They've frozen my assets," he explained. "The Amministratori wanted to seize my assets, but the Gioiellieri Guild won't let them. Either way, I have nothing."

"Maestra?" Sofia came up to them, biting her lip. Greta looked up at her expectantly. "We still have a spare room, even with Domizio renting one. Couldn't Ciro and Seppe rent the other one?"

Greta reached up to pat the girl's shoulder and whispered softly, "*This* is why you're my favourite."

Sofia grinned broadly and returned to her workstation. Greta turned to Ciro, eyebrow raised.

"It's yours if you want it," she told him. "I'll only charge two coppers a week if you help with the meals or deliveries."

"I couldn't possibly accept," Ciro said, without pause.

"Why not?"

"Well ... I ... don't know," he said, lamely. "It's too generous."

Greta waved a hand dismissively. "Nonsense. I insist, unless you have somewhere else in mind."

Ciro shook his head.

"Then it's settled. I'll come around with Domizio on Riposidi to help you move your things. I'm sorry I can't offer any earlier, but we have almost more orders than we can cope with for the Guild Ball. Now, wait a moment while I put these away and fetch the coins to pay you."

Ciro was swept up in the whirlwind of her words and ended up just nodding as she walked off. Within a few minutes, he was back out on the street with eight more gold coins in his pocket. That made a total of eighteen gold and another thirty promised.

And a place to stay.

He breathed a little easier.

Now for the difficult part. He began the long climb up to Signora Loyola's villa. With the restrictions placed on him, Ciro wasn't certain he could deliver on his promised carving for Signora Loyola and had no way to return her money. He tried not to think about it as his chest tightened.

By the time he'd reached the luxurious villa, he was sweating heavily and breathing hard. He could have taken the Funicolare up the hill, but could not bear to part with the copper to pay for it. Ciro fought to catch his breath as he stood on the doorstep. When his heartbeat had slowed down and he could breathe properly, he rang the doorbell.

The same unpleasant maid opened the door.

"Yes?" she asked indignantly.

"Good afternoon, Signorina. Could you please tell Signora Loyola that Ciro Corallino is here to see her?"

"She ain't here," the girl replied as though he should've known better.

"Well, could you please let her know I came and ask her to call on me at her earliest convenience. It is a matter of some importance."

"Fine," the girl said, inspecting her fingernails. "Does she know who you are?"

"Indeed," Ciro replied, beginning to get angry with the arrogant maid. "If she forgets, you can remind her about the bidding war she attended last week."

"Alright, fine."

The door was closed in his face. Ciro's anger bubbled over and he made a rude gesture at the door before beginning the long walk back home. Along the way, he stopped in at a bakery and the food markets to get everything they would need for that night's meal, spending as little as possible to stretch their funds.

Chapter 27 – Riposidi 15 Sarti 230 Years After Implosion

Despite his efforts to please Loredana regarding lunch, Ciro had already passed by Anna's workshop to inform her he wouldn't be available that week. She'd wrung a promise from him to attend the next week and he'd had no choice but to accept.

It hadn't taken him and Seppe long to pack their possessions – there were precious few of them. Some clothes and personal items, several pots and pans, and just as many dishes and cups. Even including several framed portraits of their families, everything fit into just three medium-sized baskets. The final basket was for his remaining portable tools, and the materials he hadn't yet sold or promised to Loredana.

Yesterday, two Gioiellieri Guild Amministratori had come to collect the larger machines for Anna, the corallo statue they'd been working on and the wooden panels. At Ciro's insistence, they'd also taken the clay model for Anna to work from. He doubted she'd be able to finish it by herself in time, but that task was no longer his to fulfil.

Seppe helped him put everything into the last basket.

"You should give this to Loredana," he said, handing Ciro her sketchbook. "I don't know if Anna is getting her to draw every day, but if she isn't, at least the sketchbook might prompt the girl to do it herself. And here's her letter book."

Ciro took the two books and fought back the tears stinging his eyes. He'd so loved being Loredana's Maestro. Her love for the work of a Corallina was an echo of himself in his youth. She'd been the missing piece in his life, one he'd never quite understood was missing until she arrived. And now that she was gone, the ache inside him was almost unbearable.

"Next week, Seppe. I can't face it today."

Seppe nodded. "Yes, we've enough to do today. What time is Greta coming?"

Ciro looked at his pocket watch. "She'll be here any minute now."

They busied themselves packing the rest of their things. If Seppe noticed that Ciro hadn't given away *all* of his blank cammeo shells, he said nothing about it. Instead, he cleared Ciro's favourite workbench of the unfinished projects atop it and put them carefully in the basket. There were four cammei stuck with wax on the top of wooden sticks and five finished carvings, without metal trimmings.

They were meant to be Parting Gifts for the Guild Ball. Now, Ciro didn't know what to do with them. He couldn't finish them properly or sell them. Sadly, he watched Seppe make room for them in the basket. It was almost full now, and the room was practically empty.

Ciro took a last look in every drawer, on every surface. All that remained were his sketchbooks and drawing box, and the large corallo trunk which had been the catalyst of all his problems – and the one thing he'd been looking for his entire Guild life.

"Signora Loyola never came, did she?" Seppe asked, also looking at the corallo trunk.

Ciro shook his head. "Her maid seemed rather indifferent to me. I'm not entirely certain the message was passed on."

"You should write a note," Seppe told him. "Not just for her, but for any of your customers. Telling them you've shut up shop but can be found at Greta's workshop if need be."

"I doubt anyone will come looking for me," Ciro told him. "Especially when I'm forbidden from making anything for them."

Even so, he tore a page out of his sketchbook and wrote the note in large letters. He was just affixing it to the inside of a window when Greta pulled up in her blazermobile.

Domizio hopped out and opened the back door. Seppe brought out the baskets and handed them to the Copper Sarto. He took each basket carefully, ensuring any precious possessions would not be ruined. It didn't take long to load the blazermobile.

"Ready?" Greta asked, walking into the workshop. She paused and looked around. "This feels so much worse than when I left my workshop, and that was *my* choice."

Ciro didn't reply, but looked around the empty room, trying not to let his emotions get the best of him. He felt like a pendulum swinging between despair and anger, never quite settling on either.

"What's happening with that?" Greta asked, pointing to the corallo trunk.

Ciro shrugged. "Can we take it with us? Signora Loyola hasn't returned my call, and I don't know what to do with it."

"Yes, but there won't be room with all the baskets. I'll ask the girls to come back with us to pick it up, then we can pass by the Gioiellieri Guild for you to drop your keys off."

The keys. Ciro patted his pocket. He'd had these keys for nigh on forty-five years. He'd begun renting the workshop soon after Seppe arrived in Tor'Esint. They'd lived here happily together ever since. It seemed unfair they should be forced to leave the only home they'd ever shared together, even if Ciro was no longer part of the Gioiellieri Guild. Though, he admitted, they'd never be able to afford it on just Seppe's new wages from Anna. It was a blessing that Greta had offered them a room at such cheap rates.

"Let's go," he said, shaking his head.

He tried to move, but his feet wouldn't take him. Greta noticed and took his arm. With her gently tugging him along, he managed to leave the workshop.

"I don't think I can do it," he said, once in the blazermobile and staring at his empty shop windows with tears in his eyes. He reached his hand out for

Seppe's and squeezed tightly. "I can't go back in there again."

"It's fine, Ciro," Domizio told him. "The girls and I will be able to lift the corallo trunk ourselves. It'll be heavy, but we'll manage. If you give me the keys, I'll even drop them off for you so you don't have to."

"No." Ciro shook his head. "You can have them for now, but I'll take the keys back to the Guild Hall myself tomorrow. Just in case there's any final paperwork for me to sign."

He handed the keys over to Domizio with a heavy hand. He didn't have the strength to do any more. His eyes found Seppe's as he sat back. The misery he felt was mirrored in his companion's eyes. They held each other closely, both shaking with the effort of unshed tears.

***

When they arrived at Greta's house, the apprentices came out to greet them and take everything inside. Ciro didn't have to carry a single basket himself. He and Seppe followed them up the stairs and into their new bedroom. The girls deposited the baskets along the far wall and left them to get settled.

It was a much more spacious room than their old bedroom. The bed was large enough for the two of them, but didn't even take up half the room. There was a set of drawers on one wall, with a wardrobe next to it. On the other wall, a dressing table with a mirror atop it. Seppe set about putting their clothes away, like it was the most natural thing. Nothing ever seemed to slow him down.

Ciro wanted to tell him to stop, to yell at him to not be so calm and complacent about their change in circumstances. But he didn't. It would be unfair. Seppe was only trying to make the most of a terrible situation. With a sigh, Ciro got to his feet to help him. Together, they packed away their clothes. The kitchen things were left to one side – they wouldn't be needed here.

The last remaining items were Ciro's Corallini treasures. He looked at them morosely. Seppe lay a hand on his back.

"You may as well lay them out here. You'll have nothing else to occupy you while I'm at work all day. Even if you can't sell them, there's nothing to stop you working on them. They can't actually take that away from you. *This* is not the work of a Gioielliere."

Without giving Ciro a chance to protest, Seppe pulled out the cammei he'd been working on with the tools he'd need for them and put them on the dressing table. Finally, he pulled out the small wooden rack with large notches carved into the top. He carefully arranged the unfinished cammei against the notches and placed a soft rag beside the tools. Everything was laid out exactly as it had been on Ciro's favourite workbench.

"What would I do without you, Seppe?" Ciro asked, his voice trembling slightly.

"Die of boredom?" Seppe shrugged. "Now, I need a coffee. Let's find out where they keep everything."

And like that, they were moved in.

Sofia was quick to give them a tour of the upstairs living quarters, pointing out the coffee and tea stores. She even showed them the secret stash of biscuits, which were apparently not very secret. To prove her point, she gave one to each of them and took another for herself, with a wink.

"The entire house is yours except for the other bedrooms," she told them. "Annika, Marta and I share the largest room. I think the most important rule of the house is no naked flames anywhere but the kitchen. We've plenty of glass lanterns and friction lights to go around. If you want to work late at night, Greta purchased a Liquid Sunlight machine. It's set up downstairs. I don't recommend bringing it upstairs, but I'm certain Greta won't mind if you turn it on downstairs whenever you like. If you'll excuse me now, it's my turn to make dinner."

"I'll help," Seppe immediately offered. "I've nothing else to do and I'm the cook in our household."

He gave Sofia no choice, but she didn't appear to mind. She led Seppe back to the kitchen and left Ciro alone. He heard voices downstairs and went down to join them. The corallo trunk was being carefully hidden at the back of the workshop, behind the dressing curtain, away from the view of idle eyes. It looked so out of place among bolts of fabric.

"We thought it would fit best here," Greta told him. "Just until Signora Loyola tells us what she wants to do with it. Better than taking it up to your room and having to bring it back down again if she wants it at her house."

Ciro nodded unhappily. "Yes, that seems the best idea. I may try calling on her again on Ramedi if I don't hear from her tomorrow. It's a shorter walk from here."

"Nonsense," Greta told him with a quick shake of her head. "If you're going to visit her on Ramedi, I'll drive you. That hill is tortuous and besides, if the reason she hasn't called on you is because of her maid, I'll give that girl a piece of my mind and make sure she doesn't try the same thing again.

"Now, Domizio has instilled in me an awful habit of taking Riposidi as an *actual* rest day. So if you'd like to join us for a game of cards or a round of checkers, please do. You might just have the skills to beat Annika. We'd no idea she was so gifted until just a few weeks ago! Now, it's a contest to see who can best her first. The prize is a small item of clothing of the winner's choice, which Annika will make."

"Well, I *am* quite partial to cards," Ciro admitted with a small smile. "We often play at Serafina's house on Riposidi after lunch."

Greta frowned. "But ... that's *today*."

"They knew not to expect us today. But Seppe and I will usually go there on Riposidi, if you don't mind."

"Of course not," she reassured him. "You're under *no* obligation to please us while you lodge here. You pay for your room and all I expect is that you keep it clean. Other than that, you're free to come and go as you please. Though, should it please you to dine with us, you'll always be welcome."

There was an awkward pause. The apprentices looked at each other, and Domizio raised his eyebrows at Greta.

"What game are we playing then?" Ciro asked. "Scopa, Quindici?"

"Quindici," said Annika before the others had a chance to respond. "To lose."

"I beg your pardon?" Ciro tilted his head to the side. "What do you mean, 'to lose'?"

Annika grinned. "Apparently, it was getting too difficult to beat me, so Maestra Greta taught us a new version Maestro Ranieri taught her when she was his apprentice. Everything works exactly the same way, including the points, except you have to try to lose. Get as few points as possible. When someone gets to fifteen, the person with the least points wins."

"Well then, deal me in," Ciro said, rubbing his hands together.

Annika led them to the downstairs kitchenette and began shuffling the cards. "Who else is in?"

Marta and Domizio sat down to play. Ciro made to offer Greta his place, but she seemed more than happy to sit by Domizio's side, head on his shoulder.

Ciro waited until Annika had dealt three cards to each player and placed four others face up on the table. He then picked up his cards and looked between them and the cards on the table. He quickly realised it would be near impossible not to make a total of fifteen and be forced to pick up, so he settled for trying to gather the least important cards to minimise his score at the end.

By halfway through the round, they were all laughing uproariously. Ciro hadn't laughed so hard in such a long time – tears were beading in the corners of his eyes. In the end, Annika won, as everyone had told him she would, but Ciro didn't mind at all. It had been a fun game and taken his mind off his current situation. At least temporarily.

In the pause between games, his melancholy returned with a vengeance. He forced a smile and got to his feet.

"If you'll excuse me, I think I'll retire to my room for a while. The game tired me out more than I realised."

It was a lie, and everyone in the room knew it. Ciro didn't know what he'd have done if they'd said anything to him. Thankfully, they didn't, so he slunk off up the stairs and into his room.

He closed the door behind him, covered his face with his hands and cried. He cried until there were no tears left and he felt empty and numb inside.

Chapter 28 – Gildadi 16 Sarti 230 Years After Implosion

"I don't have to go," Seppe said, sitting on the bed as Ciro lay still under the covers. "Anna doesn't need me. She's only doing this as a favour."

Ciro set a hand atop Seppe's leg. "She'll have more than enough work for you and Loredana will be so happy to see you."

Seppe huffed. "No, she won't. Loredana will be so angry we didn't go to her house yesterday that she won't talk to me for hours."

Ciro knew it was a joke, meant to make him smile, but he couldn't help but feel the sting behind the words. Loredana had every right to be angry. Serafina and Tania too. He'd barely seen them recently – especially since Tania had started going to Telchide's house to play with Teresina rather than staying in Ciro's workshop with Loredana. There could be no excuse for his absence and Ciro knew he'd have to make up for it. But not today.

"Well, we need the money," Ciro said, finally sitting up. "And I've got to return my keys to the Gioiellieri Guild."

"I know," Seppe said quietly. "Are you sure you don't want me to come?"

Ciro shook his head. Seppe had never come with him to the Gioiellieri Guild Hall before. It would feel strange for him to do so now.

"Fine, then. I'll be back after trading."

"I'll be here," Ciro said morosely.

He could tell Seppe wanted to say something, but his companion only shook his head and left the room, closing the door behind him. Ciro lay back down for a few minutes more, listening to the household start the day – Domizio greeted Seppe in the hallway, the girls chattered away in the kitchen, Greta raced down the stairs to begin working.

Ciro stayed where he was, staring at the ceiling, until he heard the last of them walk down the stairs to the workshop. He didn't want to see any of them right now. He hadn't realised quite how much he valued his own space until, suddenly, he didn't have it anymore.

Quietly, he opened his door and peeked down the hall. It was empty, and still. Ciro padded softly to the kitchen and saw a plate on the table with a slice of bread and a dish of butter and a pot of jam beside it. There was a little note beside the plate explaining how to use the heating rod on the bench top.

Ciro picked up the heating rod, twisted the top three times and held it over the bread. It browned, right before his eyes. He didn't realise in time how quickly it would work and burnt the tip of the slice. The other side of the bread turned out better. But the heating rod didn't cool quickly enough for him to place it on the bench. Instead, he put it in the metal sink, hoping it wouldn't do any lasting damage.

He buttered the bread and spread a thin layer of jam atop it. The jam was a luxury he didn't usually afford himself at home. He sighed. *This* was his home now. But he felt guilty eating the food. Surely the paltry amount he was paying Greta could not cover even the cost of their food, let alone the rent for the room itself.

Ciro tried not to think of Greta's charity as he ate her food and sat at her table. It was difficult. The bread stuck in his throat, even as he tried to wash it down with a glass of water. All he really wanted was a cup of coffee, like Seppe had made him every morning for over forty years. He closed his eyes against the tears that threatened to well up and finished his bread in tiny mouthfuls. He washed and dried the plate and opened cupboard doors until he found its home.

He made short work of making himself presentable to visit the Guild Hall. Even if they'd thrown him out of the Guild, he wouldn't show his face there looking like a pauper.

***

Greta had insisted on driving him, but Ciro had insisted even more forcefully on walking to the Guild Hall himself. It hadn't taken long for her to realise it was a matter of pride for him, but when she did, she immediately backed down.

Now, at the steps of the Gioiellieri Guild Hall, Ciro felt his knees buckle slightly. It wasn't because of the walk – most of it had been downhill and really it wasn't so far from Greta's workshop – but he pretended to himself that was the reason nonetheless.

He gave himself a few breaths before heading up the stairs and into the Guild Hall, possibly for the last time ever. The thought took the breath out of him, and he stumbled just inside the doorway. A passing Amministratore reached out and caught his arms, holding him steady. Ciro thanked the lad and released his grip.

Yvette was at the reception desk. He put the key down in front of her. She looked from the key to Ciro.

"What's this?" she asked with a frown.

Ciro cleared his throat. "My key."

"I don't understand," she said, not touching it. "Why are you giving it to me?"

"I'm not part of the Guild anymore, Yvette," he told her. "I was told to vacate the premises before the end of the week. I moved out yesterday, but, well, the Guild isn't open on Riposidi. So..."

He pointed to the key, but she didn't take it.

"I'll get Rosalina," she told him, looking from him to the key and back again. "I've never done this before. Not when the person was still alive. No, that's not what I mean. It's just that we don't usually get keys back from anyone while they can still work... But of course, you can't. I mean you can, but you can't. Oh Ciro!"

Before he could move, she got up and threw her arms around him.

"I'm so sorry!" she said, her voice uncharacteristically thick with emotion. "They shouldn't have done that to you! How did they even find out about it?"

"Sorry?" he asked, suddenly confused. "What do you mean?"

Yvette drew back from him. "We're very careful with our financial records, to keep them out of the Mercantili Guild's grasp. I don't know how they found out about your deposit. That's never happened before. You're not the only one to have ever made such a large deposit."

Ciro turned her words over in his mind, trying to make sense of it.

"Are you saying there's a spy in the Guild?" he asked in a whisper.

Her eyes darted around the room as she nodded.

"But who?"

She clenched her fists by her side. "If I knew that, they wouldn't still be here. But when I find out, I'll wring their necks!"

"Thank you, Yvette." Ciro placed a hand on her shoulder, touched by her concern. "Now, if you don't mind, I'd like to hand in my key and finalise any paperwork I may need to sign."

"Yes. Yes, of course. Just a moment."

She took his key, quickly found a replacement Amministratrice for the desk and went to find Rosalina. Ciro didn't walk the hall as he usually did. Instead, he took a seat and waited patiently.

Rosalina came and sat beside him. "Ciro, I've been so worried. I wanted to help you find somewhere to live, but Luca forbade it. With good reason I suppose, but it almost killed me not to be able to help."

He held her hands in his. "Don't worry. We found a place, with Greta Sarta. She's renting out a spare room to us at very reasonable rates. I think she'd not charge us at all if she thought we'd accept that."

"Greta Sarta," she said slowly. "Isn't she the one who was in the Alchimista Trials?"

"So I've been led to believe," Ciro replied. "I confess, I didn't really follow the trials."

"It was a huge scandal," Rosalina whispered, making sure no one was close enough to listen. "The Mercantili Guild tried to use the Sarti and Inventrici to sabotage the Alchimisti Guild. Only, it backfired on them. I heard Greta turned the tables on them so that Ministro Ercolano ordered the Mercantili books audited to ensure *they* weren't the ones importing the famously alchemically-dyed fabrics which had caused multiple deaths.

"The Mercantili Guild were furious with her but she protected herself so well that there wasn't anything they could do to touch her. How did you get involved with such a woman?"

Ciro shrugged. "She's one of my customers. Bought some pendants for her apprentices and a cammeo for herself. Once she heard of my misfortune, nothing would please her until Seppe and I agreed to board at her house."

He neglected to mention it was a trade for shirts rather than an outright purchase, or the fact that she'd repeatedly purchased corallo balls from him to decorate her gowns, or that she had helped him organise the bidding war.

Rosalina eyed him suspiciously. They'd known each other long enough that she knew he was hiding something, but Ciro would not tell her any more.

"Is there anything else for me to do here?" he asked, suddenly uncomfortable being in the Guild Hall any longer than necessary.

Rosalina shook her head. "It's all done. We only need to sort out the issue of your finances. I'll continue to refuse to release your assets to the Tor'Esint Amministratori. I don't know how I'll manage to release the balance to you, but I'll try to find a way."

"Thank you, Sali. Really. It means more than you know. Not for the money, but for the friendship."

Rosalina hugged him tightly and kissed him on both cheeks.

"Don't be a stranger now," she told him, wiping a tear from her eyes.

Ciro nodded, though he had no intention of ever returning to the Guild Hall. Not if he wasn't a Corallino.

"Sali, one more thing," he said, reaching out before she walked away. "I was forbidden from any work to do with the Gioiellieri Guild, but if they claim my carving had nothing to do with a Gioielliere, then I can continue carving, yes?"

Rosalina bit her lip. "Correct. There's nothing preventing you from carving, but you cannot sell any items at Guild prices. It wouldn't be worth your while."

Ciro thought of the basket of blank cammei shells and smiled slightly. "I don't suppose it would, but it will keep me busy at least."

He walked back to Greta's workshop with purpose. Once inside, he waved a quick greeting to his landlady and trotted up the stairs to his room. There, on the dressing table, was everything Seppe had set out for him. Ciro sat down to work on a cammeo like he'd done so many days in his life, carving and refining the details, letting the world melt away.

He was still working on the cammeo when Seppe arrived back from his first day working for another Corallina.

"How was it?" Ciro asked, not looking up from his work. "Did Anna give you enough to do? Did Loredana ignore you?"

"Yes and no." Seppe kissed the top of his head. "They were both so happy to see me, they barely stopped talking to me all day. Loredana insisted on showing me all her sketches from the previous week and proudly wrote her name for me. She's coming along quite nicely. And Anna found any excuse to give me something to do. She'd have run me off my feet if I wasn't sitting down to cut and polish all day! What about you? How did you get on?"

Ciro shrugged. "I gave back my key. My assets are still frozen. But I'm technically allowed to carve, as long as I don't sell at Guild prices. Mind, I don't know who would buy cammei without backs, but at least it keeps me busy. Look at this one!"

He wiped the shell dust off and showed Seppe the cammeo he'd been working on since he'd returned from the Guild Hall. It was a tiny view of a smoking Sentigura Caldera from the sea, just as he'd always wanted to carve into a corallo trunk, but it worked well on the cammeo. It needed less of the fine detail, but there was enough for everyone to recognise it.

"It's beautiful!" Seppe said, taking it and studying it closely. "How do you keep getting better?"

Ciro huffed happily and took back the cammeo, continuing to work on it.

"Have you eaten anything today?" Seppe asked, sitting on the bed.

Ciro pointed to the place where an empty plate had been. He noticed, with some surprise, that it was no longer there.

"Sofia brought me a plate when I didn't stop for lunch. Such a lovely girl."

"Mm hmm," Seppe agreed. "Well, I need a coffee. Will you be much longer or shall I bring it in here?"

"I'm almost done," he told Seppe. "I'll meet you in the kitchen."

A few minutes later, the smell of coffee drew Ciro's attention from his work. He wiped the cammeo down with his cloth, then used it to wipe his hands of the shell dust.

Sofia passed by his room on her way to the kitchen and paused when she saw him.

"Are you finished with your project?" she asked, trying to peer past him to the makeshift workbench.

He smiled and invited her in, passing the cammeo carving to her. She took it reverently and delicately ran her fingers over the carving.

"What do you think?" he asked.

"It's gorgeous! Who's it for?" she asked, handing it back.

Ciro shrugged. "No one, really. I can't fashion it into a brooch or pendant, so I doubt anyone would want to buy it." He put it back on his makeshift workbench and walked with her to the kitchen.

"It keeps me busy. Otherwise, I'd be down in your workshop bothering everyone and not letting them get along with their work. I doubt Greta would appreciate that very much."

"I suppose," Sofia replied sadly, "but it seems such a shame to keep it hidden from the world when it's so beautiful. And it won't even be the only one if you're going to do that all day, every day. Surely you can do *something* with them."

Seppe handed Ciro a cup of coffee and the two of them sat at the table as Sofia pulled out the flour and filled a jug of water. They sipped and watched as she made a small mound of flour and created a small hole in the middle.

"Will you be dining with us tonight?" she asked them. They nodded and she looked at the makings of a ball of dough in front of her. "I think I'll make a bit more. You don't mind pasta, do you?"

"Of course not," Seppe replied immediately. "In fact, I insist we help you with it. What are you making?"

"Just gnocchi today," Sofia replied, as though it was the most boring thing in the world. "We usually have gnocchi during the week because it's the quickest pasta to make. I'll see if I can't find some herbs to make a pesto sauce, otherwise, there should be bottled tomatoes somewhere around here."

Ciro exchanged glances with Seppe.

"I'll help with the pasta, Seppe will make the sauce. He'll tell you himself, I'm hopeless with cooking. But I don't mind getting my hands dirty with pasta. Now, do you have butter paddles or are we using forks?"

Sofia looked at him in confusion. "What for?"

Ciro's smile broadened. "Well, I say. This will be a treat. Do you have butter paddles?"

"No, but there are plenty of forks."

She pointed to a drawer next to the stove. Ciro ushered Seppe out of the kitchen to purchase ingredients for the sauce then went to fetch two forks, a knife and a plate. By the time Sofia was ready to begin, so was he. She cut portions of dough off the main ball and began rolling them out into long, thin sausages. As each one was finished, Ciro floured it and began chopping it into finger-width sections using the plate as a chopping board. When Sofia had rolled all the sections into sausages, Ciro handed over his knife for her to cut the remaining sausages into cubes. He then took the fork and rolled each cube of dough along the grooves and gently flicked them off the end, ensuring they all landed on a floured section of the table.

Sofia grinned as she saw the ribbed effect on the gnocchi. As soon as she was finished chopping all the sausages into small cubes, she picked up the other fork and joined him. It didn't take her long to get the hang of it, and she only flicked a few onto the floor.

They were almost done by the time Seppe came back with the ingredients to make his basil pesto sauce. Just the smell of the basil made Ciro smile – he loved pesto! Marta and Annika joined them just as Sofia plopped the pasta into the boiling pot of water. She ushered them away from the stove, not wanting to ruin the surprise for them. The four of them set the table as Seppe worked on the sauce, adding lemon, cheese and salt by turns to the paste he'd made of basil leaves, pine nuts, garlic and oil. Each of the girls tasted a teaspoon of the sauce, telling him what else needed to be added to make it perfect.

By the end, Ciro suspected they were only asking him to add more things so they could have extra tastes of the sauce. He'd never known Seppe to be so uneven with any of his ingredients before.

Soon enough, the pasta was ready. Sofia ordered Annika and Marta down to fetch Greta and Domizio while she sauced the pasta and ladled it out into seven plates. Ciro helped her lay the table with a plate for each person. She refused to let the others in until everything was perfect.

"Come, Sofia," Greta opined, "I have work to do. Don't make them call me up if it's not ready."

Sofia crossed her arms and glared at Greta. "It is ready. I just wanted to make sure everything was perfect. I'll bet you've never seen gnocchi like this in your life!"

She finally allowed them access to the kitchen, her cheeks dimpling as everyone cooed at the unique shape of the pasta.

"How'd you do this?" Domizio asked, spiking a ribbed gnoccho with his fork and turning it round and round.

Sofia grinned. "Guess."

"Knives?" Annika suggested.

"Fingernails." Marta guessed.

"No," Sofia laughed. "Forks! Ciro showed me how. And Seppe made the sauce. Buon appetito everyone!"

"Buon appetito," everyone replied before digging into their plates.

Ciro was pleased that their assistance with the meal was so greatly appreciated. If they could help like this most evenings, he wouldn't feel as bad about the tiny amount they were paying in rent.

Chapter 29 – Argentodi 18 Sarti 230 Years After Implosion

"Where is he?" Signora Loyola's imperious voice travelled up the stairs to Ciro as he worked on another cammeo.

Last night, he'd convinced Annika and Marta to sit for him so he could sketch them. Annika had willingly obliged and fussed with her hair and neckline so much Ciro almost regretted asking. She was a terrible model – she kept moving around, trying to peer over his paper to see how the sketch was coming along.

Marta was better. She only asked Sofia to make sure she didn't have hair sticking up everywhere before sitting still the entire time. He sketched them both in enough detail for any design he wished to use them for. He doubted the girls had even realised why he'd asked them to model. Seppe had helped him feign not wanting to lose his sketching skills, knowing all the while he was gathering new inspiration for his cammei.

Unfortunately, the one he wanted most was Sofia, but she had demurred to the point where Ciro was forced to sketch her under the pretence that he was drawing a flower. If she'd had any idea what he had really been doing, he was certain she would've fled the room in discomfort.

Today, he was working on a cammeo of Annika, tomorrow would be Marta. He had already decided to leave Sofia's one until last. That way when she got cross at the fact that he had secretly sketched her, she wouldn't be quite so mad – and he was quite certain she would, in fact, be jealous of her fellow apprentices' cammei and would want one of her own.

"I know he's here, Greta," Signora Loyola shouted again, tearing him out of his thoughts. "I saw the sign in his window. Now, fetch him down immediately."

Ciro put the sketchbook in his drawer and placed the cammeo against the notched rack.

"Signora Loyola, how lovely to see you," he said, entering the room via the large staircase. "I confess, I expected to see you last week at my former workshop."

Signora Loyola huffed angrily. "That ash-sucking maid of mine didn't think it worth telling me until this morning! At least the note in your window led me here. What in Caldera's smoke is going on? And *where* is my corallo trunk?"

Ciro noticed the customers in the shopfront staring at them openly. This was decidedly *not* a conversation for them.

"Signora, perhaps we might discuss the matter in private?" he suggested, attempting to lead her to the kitchen.

She stood firmly where she was and glared at him. "Signore Corallino, I outbid every one of my friends fair and square. You had better not be about to tell me I can't have my carving."

"Signora, *please*."

He took her gently by the elbow and instead led her to the back corner of the workshop where the corallo trunk had been secreted. At the sight of it, she visibly relaxed.

"Now, I do have some unfortunate news. I am no longer a..." He swallowed and paused. "Corallino."

For the first time, Signora Loyola looked at him, truly seeing him. Her fingers covered her lips.

"They didn't!" She looked him up and down for his Gold Guild Mark pin. "Did they?"

Ciro spread his hands helplessly. "I'm afraid they did. I've been stripped of my Guild Marks and forbidden from performing any work becoming of a Gioielliere."

Signora Loyola went suddenly pale. Ciro pulled up a chair for her.

"Why?" she finally asked. "Surely they gave you a reason."

"Ah, yes, well, after the event that evening, all I had left in my workshop was your corallo trunk and some unfinished cammei. No jewellery." He took a deep breath, trying not to need to take a seat for himself. "They claimed I was performing the work of an Artista rather than a Gioielliere."

"But that's absurd! Unless you have a Guild all to yourself, you'll always be between the two."

"Indeed. And it's never really been such a problem before. Not until the Mercantili Guild's edicts were pronounced. Since then, I'm afraid it was only a matter of time until they found a way to do this. I only hope they don't manage to do it to Anna as well – she inherited my apprentice, and I couldn't bear Loredana suffering again."

Signora Loyola reached out a hand to him, anger and sadness warring on her face.

"Well, at least you have my fees to keep you going a good long while. But I must insist you carry out the work you promised me. If the corallo carving is the reason they stripped you of your Guild Marks, then there's nothing stopping you from continuing. Correct?"

Ciro rubbed his arm, not able to look her in the eye.

"I made certain of that myself. I can finish your corallo trunk, but I'm afraid after that, I'll be done."

"I don't understand. Surely, with my fee, you'll be able to purchase another corallo trunk, won't you?"

He shook his head, stamping down the anger rising like lava within him.

"Signore Corallino ... Ciro. What aren't you telling me?"

"It's not your concern," he told her, politely refusing to divulge his entire misfortune to her.

She eyed him closely. He tugged at his collar under such close scrutiny.

"You deposited the money in your Guild vault, didn't you? And the Amministratori confiscated it, yes?"

"Signora, please. My finances are of no concern to you."

"They are when the lack of finances might stop you from performing work I've already paid you to do."

Ciro shook his head. "It won't stop me. I have my tools. All I lack is the space to carve, and your inspiration. Have you given any thought to what you'd like me to carve?"

"In truth, I've no idea," she admitted. "I was hoping you might have some of your own."

"Oh, I think I can come up with an idea or two."

He couldn't help smiling. The prospect of designing something for such a magnificent canvas was exhilarating despite the circumstances. If he didn't have a stash of blank cammei upstairs, it would be the only thing keeping him sane.

"Well, then, if Greta has no objections, I'll leave the corallo trunk with you until we decide on a design. In the meantime, I'll clear a room for you. I'll have the corallo trunk moved and you can bring any tools you need to work on it."

Ciro scratched the back of his neck. "Signora, you *do* understand that it may take months to carve such a large corallo trunk. Are you certain you can spare a room for so long?"

"I am and, in fact, I insist on it. You see, I'm quite a stickler for privacy. I don't like anyone seeing my commissioned projects until they're complete."

"That's true!" Greta called out from her workbench. Ciro turned to see her still working on a dinner jacket. "And I don't mind how long it stays here. It doesn't take up too much space back there."

Signora Loyola stood up.

"It's settled then. Come and pay me a visit when you have some designs for me to see. If I'm not there, my addle-brained maid has been given a long enough tongue-lashing that she'll certainly pass on the message in a timelier fashion."

Signora Loyola shook his hand and kissed Greta's cheeks in farewell. Ciro took the vacated seat and stared at the corallo trunk. Such a large canvas. So many possibilities.

Eventually, he went back up the stairs to work on the cammeo of Annika. The ideas would come to him, as they always did, while he was working on something else. His sketchbook was close at hand for any brilliant strokes of inspiration. More likely, though, he would go through a dozen designs before settling on the two or three he thought suitable. Just as happened with the smaller corallo trunk.

He fretfully wondered what would happen with that. Would the Gioiellieri Guild still want it as a centrepiece? Or would it only cause the downfall of the rest of the Corallini and Loredana?

Chapter 30 - Mercatodi 21 Sarti 230 Years After Implosion

"Marta, Annika, I have something for you," he told them over breakfast. He passed them their cammei. "Now, I can't promise, but if you take them to one of the other Corallini, they may agree to make them into pendants or brooches for you. It shouldn't cost more than two silvers. If they try to charge you more, you let me know and I'll give them a piece of my mind, understand?"

The girls nodded excitedly and took the cammei from him. They showed each other and then everyone else. Ciro saw Sofia's forced smile. She was crestfallen, as he'd hoped she'd be. He caught a glimpse of Greta's injured frown in time to shake his head at her. She turned to hide her disappointment.

"Now, Sofia, if you've got time before you set up for the Mercatodi stall, I'd like to show you something I've been working on."

She looked at Greta for permission and her Maestra gave a short nod.

"Very good then, at your leisure," he told her. "I'll be in my room most of the morning."

Seppe joined him as he left the kitchen.

"A little cruel not to give her the cammeo you made," he whispered.

Ciro raised an eyebrow. "You know me better than that. I just didn't want to give it in front of the others in case she didn't want them to see it. Though why she wouldn't is beyond me – it's one of the finest cammei I've ever made. She makes such a wonderful model."

"That's only because you've never made one of me," Seppe huffed.

Ciro turned to him in surprise. "You wanted me to? You never said."

Seppe shook his head. "Well, what would I use it for anyway? I don't see any other signori walking around with cammei. But you've never even sketched me and now, well, I look like a grape left out in the sun too long. Who'd want to look at that all day?"

Ciro flinched at the sudden outburst.

"I would," he replied, but Seppe had already walked away – off to run a Mercatodi stall for Anna while she continued working. Ciro had promised to stop by at some point, if only to see Loredana and reassure her they'd come to lunch tomorrow.

Ciro tried not to take Seppe's words to heart. *Of course* he'd sketched Seppe, so many times over the years, but he'd never shown him because it hadn't seemed like Seppe was interested in having his portrait done. In the end, he'd kept an entire private sketchbook just for Seppe's face. He'd been careful to be the one to pack it away when they'd moved so Seppe wouldn't be even more overwhelmed than he had been that day.

Back in his room, Ciro pulled out his current sketchbook, turned to a new page and drew the shape of the corallo trunk lightly in pencil. He was halfway through drawing a cascading waterfall when Sofia knocked on the door.

"Ah, Sofia, come in."

The girl bit her lip and walked in, hesitantly. "What did you want to show me?"

Ciro watched her carefully. She wasn't quite ready yet.

"I've done a few sketches for the corallo trunk downstairs and wanted your opinion on if any of them are worth their salt."

He flipped back to the first sketch, careful not to go back so far that she would see herself in the pages. Sofia took the book and studied each picture with intent interest.

"I like the birds taking flight," she told him. "But the one you're working on now looks like it'll be nicer. Is it a waterfall?"

"Indeed. You've got a good eye for detail there. No wonder you're Greta's favourite."

The girl quickly passed back the sketchbook and shook her head. "Maestra Greta doesn't really have favourites."

Ciro raised his eyebrow at her. "Hmm. Neither do I, which is why I thought it unfair not to give you this."

He took her hand and put the cammeo in it, closing her fingers around it. Sofia unfurled her fingers and froze.

"I didn't sit for you," she said, sharply. "How did you do this?"

Ciro shrugged, quite pleased with himself. "A Corallino doesn't need his model to look at him while he sketches. In fact, the best sketches are often those where the model is unaware of the artist working. Do you like it?"

"It doesn't look a thing like me," she replied, trying to hand it back.

When Ciro refused to take it, she placed it on his workbench. He stared in confusion as the girl walked out of his room without the cammeo. He'd never had anyone refuse one before. It left a strange, unsettled feeling in his stomach.

"What was that about?" Greta asked, popping her head in. "Sofia ran downstairs so fast it looked like she was fleeing."

Ciro pointed to the cammeo. "I tried to give her that."

Greta picked it up and smiled.

"You've captured her essence," she said. "But Sofia is a humble girl, she doesn't see herself like this. She doesn't think anyone else does either. It's possible she thinks you're mocking her. Just give her some time. She may come around and accept it from you. Not today though."

Ciro slumped down into his chair.

"And here I thought I was doing her a good turn, that she'd be pleased. Should I apologise?"

Greta shook her head. "Best not to mention it. Even an apology will make her uncomfortable. Don't take it to heart, Ciro. You've only known her a few days really."

Ciro shrugged with feigned nonchalance and took up his sketchbook, not knowing what else to do, and continued working on the waterfall.

***

Later that morning, he went out to face the Mercatodi stalls in the Piazza. In the crush of people, he would never have found Anna's stall if Seppe hadn't told him where it would be.

Seppe and Loredana were happily chatting with each other between customers. Ciro watched them from a short distance away. They had a nice system all worked out. Loredana, attired in her finest work dress from Greta Sarta, would charm the customers with her enthusiasm and understanding of the Corallina's art, and Seppe would point to the items which suited those customers the best. He would then wrap up the item in a small white box as Loredana conducted the financial transaction.

Ciro approached them when they were finished with their latest customer. Loredana crossed her arms when she noticed him, her brown eyes narrowing.

"Good morning," Ciro greeted them. "Looks like you've been busy."

Loredana glared at him. "Why haven't you come to see me?"

Ciro spread his hands in confusion. "I'm here. To see you. And to let you know we'll be coming tomorrow. I promise."

Her features softened slightly. "That's not what I meant. Why haven't you come to see me in my new workshop? You only came that one time to bring my things. I haven't seen you since then."

Ciro rubbed his forehead and knelt by her side. "I'm not your Maestro anymore. Anna wouldn't appreciate it if I dropped by unannounced whenever I felt like it. She'd feel like I was checking up on her because I didn't think she could teach you. It wouldn't be fair on her."

Loredana's bottom lip trembled. "But that means I'll only ever see you on Riposidi, and only if you come."

A small tear ran down her cheek. Ciro wiped it away and hugged her tightly.

"Well then, we'll just have to make the most of those days," he told her. "Bring your sketchbook home so you can show me everything you've been working on, and I'll bring mine to show you what I've been working on."

She jerked up at that. "*You've* been working on something? But I thought you weren't allowed. Seppe said..."

"It's nothing official," Ciro reassured her. "But you know me – I'd get bored if I had nothing to do all day."

"True." Her eyes sparkled mischievously. "Alright then. See you tomorrow, with our sketchbooks."

They shook on it and Ciro bid them both farewell.

Chapter 31 – Riposidi 22 Sarti 230 Years After Implosion

Ciro tucked his sketchbook under his arm and hurried down the stairs. Seppe was already dressed and ready to go.

"We're going to be late," Seppe told him. "Are you finally ready?"

Ciro nodded. "We just need to get desserts on the way."

"You're lucky I'm a working man now, or we wouldn't be able to afford it."

It was a joke and Ciro knew it, but that didn't stop the sudden ache in his chest. He took a deep breath and strode out the door.

Seppe easily caught up to him on the street and linked arms, forcing them to walk at the same pace.

"You know I was joking," he said. "I don't mind working with Anna. She only asks me to do the same as you ever did. Only difference is she makes me coffee instead of the other way around."

"I know," Ciro replied, looking sideways at him. "But I miss working with you every day. It's not the same without you there. I know it's selfish of me to say it, because you'd be bored at Greta's all day – but that doesn't stop it from being true."

"Just wait until you start working on the corallo trunk. Then I'll barely see you," Seppe retorted, "but not because I'm at work – because I know what you're like when you have a project like that to work on."

***

They arrived at Serafina's apartment late, as Seppe said they would. The midday clocks had stopped chiming before they'd started climbing the stairs. Serafina lived on the fourth floor. It would still take them a few minutes to ascend. With a great sigh, Ciro motioned for Seppe to go up before him – they'd both need the bannister to lean on.

Seppe barely knocked on the door before it was opened by Tania.

"Seppe!" she squealed and squeezed him tight around the middle.

"Tania, for Caldera's sake, let them in!" Serafina called out from within.

Tania let Seppe pass and hugged Ciro as he manoeuvred past her. It was only when he was inside the apartment that he noticed Adamo, sitting at the table with Loredana. She was showing him her sketchbook – as she was meant to be doing with him. Ciro suddenly felt foolish thinking Loredana would only want to share her works with him. She should be proud of them and want to show everyone. But why was Adamo even here?

"Ciro, so good to see you," Adamo said, standing to shake his hand.

"Yes, you too," Ciro replied automatically. "I didn't expect to see you here."

"Mamma invited Adamo to dine with us when he passed by to make sure I was happy with Anna."

Adamo resumed his seat across from Loredana.

Ciro hesitated, but went to kiss the top of Loredana's head.

"It's good to see you again," he told her. "We can look through the sketchbooks later. I'm going to say hello to your mamma now."

Loredana nodded and caught his hand to press his fingers against her cheek, like she used to do when she was much younger. Ciro smiled and patted her cheek, breathing a little easier.

He joined Seppe in the kitchen, where Tania barely allowed his companion to deposit the desserts before dragging him out for a game of cards. Serafina looked up at Ciro's entrance, stopped what she was doing and wiped her hands clean.

"Well, hello stranger," she said, embracing him tightly. "We'd almost forgotten what you looked like."

Ciro hung his head sheepishly. "I'm sorry, Rafi. Things have been ... difficult."

"I know, but you seem to have landed on your feet without any help from us." She returned to the salad. "The girls miss you, Loredana especially. It was so difficult for her to agree to change maestri. She cried all night long when they stripped you of your Guild Marks. Adamo sat with her for hours. She didn't want to go with Anna, but he eventually convinced her it was what you wanted."

Ciro looked back into the family room. Loredana certainly seemed at ease around the Gioiellieri Maestro. It was a fortunate position for her, to be close with him.

"Yes, she appears to like him a great deal," Ciro said, turning back to Serafina.

She gave him a dour look. "Yes, Zio, she does. He's been very kind and helpful during this time. I'm not sure she'd have agreed to switch maestri without him. He's even organising for Loredana to move in with Anna, as a normal apprentice, after the Guild Ball."

"So soon?" Ciro asked, his heart aching at the thought.

"It will help," Serafina said quietly, looking very intently at the tomato she was chopping. "The girls are growing and eating more every day and Giulia will be coming back to work soon, so I'll have even fewer shifts."

"I'm sorry, Rafi." Ciro lay a hand on her shoulder. "I'm sorry I can't help you more. I would have before, if you'd have just let me. Now, all I can offer is to watch Tania for you while you work but, even there, I think she prefers the company of Telchide's little Teresina more than me."

Serafina grunted in reply. "They've become fast friends. Loredana can't stand Teresina. She tries to hide it, but every time Tania talks about her, she goes silent or leaves the room. I can't blame her. The Inventore's daughter doesn't think about other people's situation when she speaks. She shows Tania all the marvellous inventions her papà creates, half of which are specifically for her, and doesn't realise it makes Tania want those things and that we can never afford them."

There was nothing Ciro could say to that. He knew it as well as she did.

"What of Adamo?" he asked more softly. "Are things going well between the two of you?"

Serafina peeked out into the family room where Adamo was now playing cards with Seppe and the girls.

"He's a lovely man and the girls adore him."

"That's not what I asked," he said. "It's been years since your Gianni died and then Cetti. I haven't seen you so happy since you moved to Tor'Esint and your girls seem quite attached to him already."

Serafina looked at him sharply. "It can't hurt them to have a friend in high places."

"A friend? Is that what he is?" Ciro asked. "Friends don't generally ask one another to the Guild Ball mere days after meeting them. Friends don't stay for hours convincing children to switch maestri. Be careful with this Rafi or your girls will soon see him as a papà, rather than a friend. Just be certain that's what *you* want."

Serafina put down her knife and turned to face Ciro.

"My affairs are none of your concern. I like Adamo well enough, and I'll spend as much time with him as I like. The girls know very well that he's not their papà. No one can replace him, for me or them, but it's good for the girls to have Adamo around. They're happier and he likes spending time with them. I won't have you judging me for it."

Ciro tried to piece it together, to understand if she actually cared for Adamo or not. The way Serafina spoke of him was quite different to the picture Loredana painted of them together.

"I'm glad you're happy," he said and left it at that.

Lunch was a noisy affair with both girls talking far too much, asking questions, then asking more before the first were fully answered. Ciro found he had missed their noise. It was different from that of the Sarta workshop, though there were more people there. None of them were children. None of them had the exuberant excitement of a child.

After lunch, Ciro sat with Loredana at one end of the table with their sketchbooks, as the others played cards with Tania. Her drawings had improved.

"I see you've been trying your hand at more portraits," he said, looking at the pages filled with faces.

Loredana nodded. "Maestra Anna lets me sketch her customers at the same time as she does, or she gets me to sketch her and Seppe over and over. I'm getting better with Anna, but not so much with Seppe. I can't figure out what to do with the wrinkles." She whispered the last.

Ciro covered his chuckle by turning over the pages of his own sketchbook until he reached the page full of images of Seppe.

"I've been working on these in secret. I want to make him a present. The trick is to think of everything that person is and try to bring that out. It doesn't matter if they're old or young, beautiful or plain, or have the longest nose you've ever seen. Your job, as a Corallina, will be to bring out the best in that person."

Loredana ran to her room to fetch a pencil and immediately began copying the pictures Ciro had drawn of Seppe. He sat beside her, doing the same, encouraging and advising her through the trickiest sections.

"What are you two working on?" Seppe asked, feeling their eyes on him.

"Nothing," Loredana said, snatching her sketchbook up to her chest. "Just portraits."

Seppe raised an eyebrow. "Just make sure you don't do my portrait. These old wrinkles don't need to be immortalised."

"You can do *my* portrait," Tania said, bouncing in her seat.

"Very well, Tania. I'll do your portrait," Ciro told her. "Mind that you don't move too much!"

"I'm going to do mamma, and Adamo if I have time," Loredana whispered to him.

Ciro watched for a moment as she began, then set to work on Tania, beginning on a fresh page. He didn't want Seppe knowing what he was up to or the surprise would be ruined.

By the end of the game, Loredana had sketched both Serafina and Adamo. Ciro had sketched everyone there, including Seppe again on his own personal page.

The two of them showed off their portraits to everyone. Tania exclaimed loudly at how grown up he'd made her look. Seppe tried to growl at the wrinkles Loredana had purposely left out of his visage. It didn't fool anyone.

It was an altogether pleasant afternoon. Adamo was a gentleman to Serafina and caring towards the girls. Ciro had almost expected him to ignore the girls, in an effort to spend more time with Serafina herself, but he didn't. He was grudgingly pleased to see it, though he couldn't suppress the pang of jealousy at the attention Adamo stole away from him with his nieces. Now if only he was certain Serafina cared for Adamo the same way.

"You will come again next week, Zio, won't you?" Serafina asked him quietly before they left. "I missed you almost as much as the girls."

Ciro nodded. "It was only that one week, Serafina. We had to move in a hurry. I *did* apologise for it."

She searched his face, looking for the lie, but it wasn't there. "Next week then."

"Will Adamo join us then as well?"

"I haven't decided yet," she said, peering back over her shoulder at the Gioiellieri Maestro entertaining her daughters.

Ciro smiled fondly at her. "It's not every day you find a person willing to embrace an entire family rather than only the object of their affection. Whatever decision you make, I'm sure it'll be the right one."

"Ciao Zio." She hugged him tightly and kissed him on both cheeks. "Ciao Seppe."

Chapter 32 – Ramedi 24 Sarti 230 Years After Implosion

Signora Loyola showed him into a large, empty room. The floor to ceiling windows on the north side let in so much light, there was no need for lanterns.

"Will this do?" she asked. "I can arrange for a table, chairs, anything you need."

Ciro looked around and tried not to laugh. The room was almost as large as his old workshop without the added clutter of workbenches.

"Yes, of course. A table and chair would do nicely too, though I may ask for the corallo trunk to remain on the ground until I'm up to the lower sections," he told her. "Will you arrange to have it picked up yourself?"

"Of course," she said, with a shrug. "Once we've decided on a design. What have you drawn so far?"

Ciro handed her the sketchbook, open to the beginning of the corallo trunk drawings. She leafed through the pages, pausing at a few to consider them.

"The waterfall, I think. Though are you certain it will work with the shape of the trunk? The branches are so spaced out."

"It would be difficult," Ciro conceded, "but not impossible. The alternatives are a flock of birds taking flight or a volcano erupting into plumes of smoke and fire."

She flipped further along to see the volcano and her eyes lit up.

"This is it!" she cried, pointing to the picture of the volcano. "*This* is the one I want. Can you really do this?"

"Certainly," Ciro replied. "I'll make it from clay first, so if you want any changes we can work it out before I begin to carve the corallo."

He looked around the room. "Could I do that here? I doubt Greta would agree to let me work with wet clay in her Sarta workshop."

She nodded. "As soon as I can arrange to bring the trunk here, you can begin. Unless you need me to transport the clay as well?"

Ciro rubbed the back of his neck. It would be difficult to transport it himself.

"I'll talk to my supplier. For such a large quantity, he may agree to transport it here himself."

Signora Loyola clapped her hands together.

"Well then, that's settled. Is it premature to ask when this project might be finished?"

Ciro startled at the question. "Signora, these things take time. I've never worked on a piece of corallo so large, and certainly not without other distractions. It could be weeks; it could be months."

She held up her hands placatingly. "That's not a problem. We'll discuss it again once you've begun the actual carving. I'll need to organise a dinner party, with at least a few weeks' notice. And I'll insist you be present.

"If the Tor'Esint Amministratori can strip you of your Guild Marks and remove any way for you to make a living through that, I'll ensure the elite of Tor'Esint is fighting hand over fist for the opportunity to have you create such a marvel for them. We won't let them win."

Ciro was overcome by emotion. He tried a smile, but his lips wouldn't move.

"I ... don't know what to say." He paused, shook his head. "Thank you, Signora."

She took a deep breath. "The Mercantili Guild's ridiculous edicts have caused trouble for everyone, not only for the Guilds themselves. We, those of us with more independent means, must do all we can to help those without. And eventually we will find some way to end this situation. Ruining the Mercantili Guild in the process would be a bonus."

Ciro's shoulders sagged at the weight of her words. "Signora, it's obvious now, we can't fight the Mercantili Guild. I somehow managed to find myself stripped of my Guild Marks for doing what I'd done my entire career. Others I know have been thrown in prison. I've even heard of disappearances." He shook his hands in front of his face. "I'm sorry, Signora. But I cannot have any part in this. They've already taken so much from me. I can't afford for them to completely ruin me."

He watched as her face fell slightly, but then assumed a steely façade.

"We'll fight these edicts any way we can," she told him firmly. "If your statue becomes a part of that, so be it. I won't let you stop me from fighting them. I had hoped you'd come up with an ingenious idea, like finishing the statue in time for the Guild Ball and presenting it to the Gioiellieri Guild as a gift from me, in front of the Mercantili Guild, to shove it in their faces and let them know they can't stop you from doing what you do best. That you have friends in high places who look out for you, as we'd do for any we can.

"But if that's not for you, I'll settle for throwing a party with the most influential people I can find and have your statue as the centrepiece. I'll show them I don't care if their edicts have ruined your career – I won't let it stop me from associating with you."

Her words were rousing and her tone hard to resist. Ciro felt ashamed – he shouldn't have dismissed her offer outright. He bowed his head slightly.

"I'll think about it. That's all I can promise for now."

Her face lost its icy hauteur and thawed into a smile. "That's all I can ask for Ciro. For you to think about it. Now, off you go and talk to your clay supplier. I'll organise to have the corallo trunk picked up and transported here."

Ciro left her house feeling much as he did when Greta spoke – swept up into the storm and spat out onto dry land, gasping for air.

He walked slowly back down the steep hill back to Greta's workshop. They'd been living there for a week and a half now, but Ciro still couldn't think of it as home. The room that he shared with Seppe, yes, that felt like home, but the rest ... it felt as though he were an intruder.

Silly for it to matter, but it didn't help that Sofia still hadn't accepted her cammeo.

Ciro had tried wrapping it in a handkerchief and setting it at her place on the table, but she'd taken one look inside and pushed it back to him. Since then, he'd left it, wrapped in the same handkerchief, on a corner of his makeshift workbench. It never moved. He knew he shouldn't be disheartened, especially after Greta's explanation, but he couldn't help it. No one had *ever* refused a gift from him.

To appease his own feelings, Ciro had spent more hours than he should have working on a special cammeo for Seppe. It had two visages facing each other – both Seppe. One as a young man, another as he was now. Of course, Ciro had smoothed out some of the lines, making it more flattering. But, if he'd had his own way, he'd have created the image just as Seppe was now: every wrinkle near his eyes, showing the times he'd laughed, the furrows in his brow from concentration. Seppe's face was a map of his life and Ciro wouldn't change it for the world.

When he arrived home, he raced up the stairs to put the finishing touches on the cammeo before Seppe returned home from work. He intended to keep it in a safe place until the time was right to give it to him.

***

It was still light enough when he finished working on the cammeo to pay a visit to Federico di Enzo. He sold the most reasonably priced art-grade clay in Tor'Esint. Ciro stuffed his coin pouch with only as much money as he was willing to pay for the amount of clay he needed. He didn't have coin to waste.

The walk down to the clay yard was not so difficult from Greta's workshop. It was on the south side of the harbour, further from the docks and nestled in between Zone Fabbri and Falegnami, which made a certain kind of sense. Each of those areas produced pungent smells and sounds.

Federico's warehouse was damp and exuded a strong earthy scent. The first time Ciro had come here, the smell had been so overpowering, he'd gagged throughout the entire transaction. Now, he found it a comforting scent, homey. He looked around for Federico and gave a big wave when he finally spotted him.

"Federico, it's so good to see you," Ciro said, shaking his clay-encrusted hand. "I need to place a large order for clay, but tell me, can you deliver it for me? It's a little more than I would usually ask for."

Federico frowned and looked closely at Ciro's shirt.

"It's true then, that they stripped your Guild Marks?" he asked bluntly.

Ciro took a step back. "Well, yes."

Federico shook his head. "Gives me even more reason then. I can't sell to you."

"What?" Ciro asked, flabbergasted. "Why not?"

The clay seller pointed to a sign on the wall.

Ciro looked over and read it.

By order of the Mercantili Guild, the art-grade clay sellers shall not deal with any persons other than members of the Artiste and Fabbri Guilds.

"But that's ridiculous!" Ciro said angrily. "You sold to me just a month ago and I've *never* been part of the Artiste Guild."

Federico shrugged. "Things change, Ciro. I ain't going against the Mercantili Guild's orders. If they find out I sold to you, I don't even want to think what they'll do to me. I ain't got a Guild in the first place – it'd be prison or *disappearing* for me."

"Preposterous!" Ciro shouted, causing more than just a few people to glance in his direction. "Where am I going to get my clay from if you won't sell it to me? I may not be a Corallino anymore, but that doesn't mean I'll never want to carve anything ever again."

"Sorry, Ciro, but it wouldn't matter – Corallini aren't Artiste. Look, I've got a family," Federico replied, his tone softening a little, though unapologetic. "I can't help you. Maybe you can get some of that lower-grade stuff down the road."

Without bothering with him further, Federico walked away, leaving Ciro standing alone in the large doorway. Everyone else ignored him. Ciro stood there for a minute, trying to come to grips with this. Eventually, he was bustled out of the way by delivery boys heading out with trolleys full of clay.

Ciro shoved his hands in his coat pockets and walked until he found himself on Corso delle Gilde. He followed the road lined with Guild Halls from the Fabbri Guild Hall all the way to the docks, where the Tor'Esint Town Hall stood side by side with the Mercantili Guild Hall, growing angrier by the minute. How dare the Mercantili Guild impose so many restrictions on every other Guild? How dare the Ministro of Tor'Esint allow this to continue? It was outrageous!

By the time he reached the Mercantili Guild, his anger had overwhelmed him and erupted into a furious rage. He picked up a large rock and aimed it at the Mercantili Guild door. It missed and smashed through a window instead. The sound of crashing glass was so satisfying that he picked up rock after rock and hurled them at every Mercantili Guild window he could.

It was only when a troop of Mercantili Guild Amministratori exploded furiously from the Guild Hall that he came back to his senses. Ciro dropped the rock he was holding, dusted off his hands in the hopes they wouldn't realise he was the one responsible and began walking towards Greta's workshop and the relative safety of his new home.

"Stop! Vandal!"

The cries drew closer but Ciro kept walking, head held high, fists tightly clenched in his pockets. Strong hands grabbed his arms, pulling him to a halt.

"What do you think you're doing?" one of them yelled at him, red in the face.

Ciro looked at him innocently, trying to shrug free of their hold. "I beg your pardon signore, but would you mind unhanding me?"

The grip tightened and Ciro was dragged back to the Mercantili Guild Hall. He protested the entire way, but they paid him no heed.

Severino, the head Mercantili Amministratore, was on the stairs, arms crossed and waiting for them when they returned. Ciro glared at him angrily. His rage had intensified, once again, the closer they'd brought him to the Guild Hall.

Severino stared down his nose at him.

"You're Ciro, formerly Corallino, aren't you?" he asked in an offhand manner.

"My name is now, and will *always* be, Ciro Corallino. You can't take that away from me!"

A cruel smile crept onto Severino's face.

"Oh, but I'm afraid we already did. We would have been content to leave it at that, but now it appears you've added vandalism to your list of crimes. You realise you'll need to pay for the damages, whether or not Ministro Ercolano decides to imprison you."

Ciro felt the blood drain from his face. "Imprison me?"

"Well, as I say, *that* will be up to Ministro Ercolano," Severino said casually. "In the meantime, you'll be kept in custody until we've worked out the damages. I do wonder, though, how you'll ever be able to pay for it when your assets have been frozen. Such a shame." He tutted as if to a child. "Come along now. Let's find you a cell."

Ciro was man-handled to the Tor'Esint Town Hall and handed over to the Tor'Esint Amministratori. They handled him with a little more care but that didn't stop them from leading him into a small, spartan cell. There was a wooden bench with a blanket along one wall and a clay chamberpot in a corner. Ciro pushed back against the hands as they shoved him in. His feeble protest went unnoticed as they locked the metal bars behind him.

Left alone, Ciro shouted, his voice becoming more and more hysterical – he could hear it, but he couldn't stop it. Eventually, an Amministratrice came along.

"What're you in for?" she asked, frowning.

Ciro shook his head, refusing to answer. What little dignity he had left was quickly fleeing. He tried to grasp the final strands.

"Could you send a message for me? My family will be wondering where I am if you hold me much longer."

Her lips twitched as she considered his request. Eventually, she took out a small notebook and handed it to him through the bars. He held out his other hand for a pencil. The woman sighed heavily but passed that to him as well.

Seppe, they've imprisoned me in the Town Hall cells. Let Signora Loyola know not to expect me. I do not know when they'll release me.

He ripped out the sheet of paper and folded it in quarters.

"Please, could you have this delivered to Greta Sarta's workshop on the corner of Via Corallino and Piazza Mercantile?"

The Amministratrice frowned. "Greta Sarta? What's she to do with you?"

"I'm a boarder in one of her spare rooms," he told the woman through clenched teeth. Like it was any of her business. "My companion will be there, expecting my return."

She took her notepad and pencil from Ciro and placed the folded note in her pocket.

"I can't promise to have it delivered before my shift ends, but I'll see what I can do."

Ciro paced his cell, but eventually his legs grew tired. He gave in and sat on the wooden bench, wrapping the scratchy, but warm, blanket around his shoulders. Someone would come for him soon. Surely, this matter would be resolved and he would be let out of this cold and unwelcoming cell. Surely.

He fell asleep, still waiting for that time to come.

Chapter 33 – Argentodi 25 Sarti 230 Years After Implosion

The sound of something metallic scraping along the stone floor woke Ciro. He opened his eyes and felt stabbing pain all down his arm. With a groan, he sat up and rubbed life back into his stiff limbs. He searched the cell for the source of the sound. A bowl with thin soup and a thick slice of bread had been pushed through a small gap at the bottom of the bars of the cell.

His fists clenched at the sight of such meagre food, but his stomach rumbled. In the end, his hunger won out and he picked up the bowl. There was no spoon – did they think he could dig his way out? – so he drank the soup straight from the bowl, mopping up the dregs with the bread.

A short while later, a small contraption scuttled along on spidery metal legs, stuck out a claw and waited. Ciro looked at it curiously. The claw opened and closed a few times before he realised it was waiting for the bowl. With a healthy amount of scepticism, Ciro touched the bowl to the claw. It instantly took hold of the bowl, snatching it away to stack it on the pile of bowls on the little wagon behind it.

The metal spider scuttled down the hall, presumably collecting more bowls as it went. Soon after, another spider came along with a wagon full of wooden cups. The spider stopped in front of his cell and extended a cup of water through the metal bars. Wary as he was, his thirst was greater. Ciro downed the water thirstily, realising he hadn't had anything to drink since before his incarceration. The spider trembled impatiently for him to return the cup and then scuttled away.

Gritting his teeth, Ciro relieved himself in the clay chamberpot, which hadn't been emptied since he'd used it the previous night. As a foul whiff stirred in the air, he wondered how often it got emptied.

He listened as the Guild Hall clocks struck a quarter measure, though which hour it was, he had no idea. The light was a pale yellow, so he could only assume it was still early morning.

Though the cell across from him was empty, Ciro could hear other prisoners talking to each other along the echoing hall. He did not try to join their conversation, clinging to the hope that he wouldn't be here long enough to want to.

With nothing else to do, Ciro sat on the bench, as far from the soiled pot as possible, and waited.

And waited.

In the distance, he heard the thud of heavy boots approaching. Slowly, he rose and walked towards the metal bars. An Amministratore stopped in front of his cell and consulted a notebook.

"Ciro, formerly Corallino?"

Ciro drew in a deep breath. "Apparently."

The Amministratore raised an eyebrow at his tone but did not rise to the challenge.

"Says here they've calculated the damage at five gold per window and you smashed twelve of 'em. That's sixty gold coins."

"Sixty?" Ciro asked incredulously. "Where am I going to find *sixty* gold coins when they've frozen my assets?"

The Amministratore shrugged. "If you can't pay immediately, a court date will be set for you to work out a payment plan. If a payment plan is not possible, they'll determine how long to keep you imprisoned."

Ciro shook his head in disbelief. "Of course I can't pay immediately. I only have five gold coins on me. Tell me, did my note get delivered yesterday?"

"What note?"

"For Caldera's sake!" Ciro threw his hands up in the air. "The note I asked the Amministratrice yesterday to deliver for me to Greta Sarta's workshop, to alert my family of my incarceration."

The man shrugged again. "Dunno. Mebbe."

He walked away, leaving a stunned Ciro behind. He was in prison, where he would potentially stay until he paid off his sixty gold coin damages fee. It seemed an unreasonably steep price. He should've known better. No one fought the Mercantili Guild head on and won. What made him think throwing a few rocks could possibly result in anything other than *this*? How could he have been so reckless?

***

It was a quarter past three when Ciro heard clicking footsteps approaching with the thud of heavy boots. He knew it was a quarter past three because he'd been listening to the Guild Hall clocks all day – there had been nothing else to do.

"Ciro?" a familiar voice called out. "Where are you?"

Prisoners up and down the hall called out, pretending to be him.

"Greta?" he cried loudly, sticking his arm as far out of the cell as it would go. "Greta, I'm here!"

She took his hand as she reached the cell, her eyes taking in every detail. Finally, she looked at Ciro himself. Her eyes lost a bit of their fire, replaced by sadness. She turned to face someone Ciro couldn't see.

"Thank you. You can leave us. I'll find my own way back out." She turned back to Ciro and waited for the footsteps to retreat. "What happened?"

Ciro squeezed her hand, relieved beyond reason to see her.

"I ... had a moment of madness," he replied shamefully. "I lost my temper and smashed some windows in the Mercantili Guild Hall. Twelve, to be exact."

Greta leaned in, as though she hadn't heard. "*Twelve* windows?"

Ciro shrugged and nodded. "As I said, I lost my temper. Doesn't happen often."

"I see," she said slowly. "And may I ask *why* you lost your temper? Not that you shouldn't have, but I would've thought being stripped of your Guild Marks would have caused the most anger and that was weeks ago now."

Ciro tried to look up and down the hall, but couldn't get a good view.

"We're alone. No Amministratori," she told him. "What happened?"

"I met with Signora Loyola yesterday morning, to discuss plans for the, erm, special project." Who knew if any of the prisoners were spies for the Amministratori. "She was going to organise to pick up the special item and I was going to purchase some art-grade clay for the planning stages. Only, when I went to the clay yard, they refused to sell to me because of a new restriction imposed by the Mercantili Guild.

"I *need* that clay. And I couldn't think of a way to get it. I was on my way home and just got angrier and angrier until I reached the Mercantili Guild Hall. Then, I don't know, I erupted. I saw a rock near my feet, and I picked it up and threw it. I didn't even mean to hit the window, but it felt so good when I did, I just couldn't stop." He gripped her hand tightly, remembering his fervour. "Now they say I owe *sixty gold coins* to fix the windows or they'll leave me locked up until Ministro Ercolano thinks I've paid off my debt!"

Greta's face grew sharper and more determined as he spoke. When he was done, there was not a shadow of softness there.

"I'll sort out this matter," she told him in a calm voice. "You'll be back with us by dinner time."

Ciro tried to keep a hold of her hand, but Greta forcefully detached herself and strode off the way she had come.

***

It was over an hour later when she finally returned. Ministro Ercolano was with her, as was Severino Mercante. Ciro rose quickly to his feet and stood tall in their presence – he refused to be cowed by the upper echelons of society.

"I don't know why you think coming to his cell will make any difference," Severino said snidely. "He was caught red-handed throwing stones at the Mercantili Guild Hall windows. He must pay his debt before being released."

Ciro crossed his arms angrily, but bit his tongue so he couldn't make matters worse. Greta seemed to have no such inhibitions.

"I'm not denying that he must pay his debt for breaking your precious windows," Greta told him. "All I'm suggesting, with Ministro Ercolano as a witness, is to request the funds be taken from Ciro's Guild vault."

"As you've so kindly pointed out before, those assets are frozen," Severino said.

"Why?" Greta and Severino whipped their heads around to look at Ministro Ercolano. He raised his eyebrows. "Why are his assets frozen?"

"The Tor'Esint Amminsitratore who came to strip me of my Guild Marks said my assets were to be confiscated by, well, *you*," Ciro told him. "My Guild refused to release the funds as I hadn't caused harm to anyone, so they froze my assets instead."

Ministro Ercolano looked at him in surprise. "Why should your funds have been transferred to me?"

"Well, I don't mean *you* personally, I mean the Tor'Esint Amministratori."

"I still don't understand why," Ministro Ercolano told him. "If a Guild Member is stripped of their Guild Marks for any reason, they're to pay damages to any wronged party, and the rest of their funds are to be transferred back to them or held in safekeeping by the Guild as decided amongst themselves. The Tor'Esint Amministratori have nothing to do with that."

Ciro listened in disbelief. Out of the corner of his eye, he saw Severino turning an unbecoming shade of red.

"Is it at all possible that the Mercantili Guild is behind this order of confiscation?" Greta asked Severino pointedly. "If Ministro Ercolano knows nothing of it, I can only presume what everyone else must be thinking – that the Tor'Esint Amministratori are in your pocket and the seized assets are being transferred directly to the Mercantili Guild."

"Nonsense!" Severino shouted. "The Mercantili Guild would never stoop to such low measures."

Greta crossed her arms. "Indeed, just as the Mercantili Guild would never stoop to accusing the Alchimisti Guild of knowingly trading in toxic alchemically-dyed materials to try to shut down the entire Guild."

"That reminds me, I must check how my auditors are coming along," Ministro Ercolano said, turning to Severino. "They must have gone through a great many of the Mercantili Guild accounts by now. I wonder if they're as clear and innocuous as you suggest, Severino. You'd better hope they don't find that Greta's assumption regarding confiscated funds is true or there will be a lot of explaining to do."

Severino paled. "That has nothing to do with the matter at hand. *This* man owes the Mercantili Guild sixty gold coins to pay for damaging our windows."

"Sixty gold coins is a bit steep, Severino. I had a window replaced in my villa just the other day and three gold coins is all it cost. So, Ciro, do you have thirty-six gold coins in your Guild vault?" Ministro Ercolano asked him. Ciro nodded. "Very well then, Severino, you shall release this man *immediately*. I will write you out a chit for reimbursement at the Town Hall. In the meantime, perhaps, Signora Sarta, you could accompany us to the Gioiellieri

Guild so we can sort out the matter of the frozen assets. Severino, fetch an Amministratore to unlock the door. Immediately."

Severino clenched and unclenched his fists over and over until he suddenly turned on one heel and strode off to do as he was bid.

"What just happened?" Ciro asked, afraid he'd misunderstood.

Greta grinned and took a sidelong look at the Ministro of Tor'Esint. "Some small measure of justice. Now, if only we could restore your Guild status."

"Ah, no, Signora." Ministro Ercolano held up his hands at that. "The assets, fortunately, were within my control. But *that* I cannot help you with. Guild status is a Guild matter and always has been. The Tor'Esint Amministratori have no say over it."

"You must see what they're doing?" Greta hissed in a quiet voice. "Surely you can do *something*."

Ciro felt sorry for the man. It was difficult to stand tall under Greta's scrutiny.

"Signora, I fear you think my political power is unlimited," he told her. "Let me disabuse you of that notion. It is not. As it is, I'm sure Severino will find some way to make my life just that little bit more miserable in return for putting my foot down. And, I must say, if you weren't quite so persuasive, I may not have done so. It's usually more bother for me than it's worth."

Ciro choked back a cough. "May I just say then, I'm glad Signora Sarta was persuasive enough for you to help me out of the predicament I find myself in."

Ministro Ercolano sighed heavily, his shoulders slumping miserably. "You must think I don't care about the people who've been hurt by these edicts – all the ridiculous impositions – but that isn't the case. I hear about each and every one, including the people who mysteriously disappear. But if I stood up for all of them, I would soon lose the little support I have. After rattling the Mercantili Guild with the Alchimisti Trials, it's become ... difficult to stand up for the smaller injustices."

"Smaller injustices?" Greta hissed. "This man is the finest Corallino in Tor'Esint and because of a minor technicality, which has always existed, he finds himself stripped of his Guild Marks, his assets frozen..."

"And is only surviving due to the kindness of his friends," Ciro added. "Though I fear Signora Loyola may soon cease to be one of those friends. She paid good money for my services and I now find myself unable to provide them."

Ministro Ercolano looked at him sharply. "Signora Loyola? What does she have to do with this?"

At the sound of footsteps approaching, Ciro shook his head and stepped back from the bars. Severino approached with an Amministratrice close on his heels – the same one who Ciro had given his note to the day before.

"Letizia? Letizia di Bibiana, isn't it?" Greta asked, hesitantly.

The Amministratrice jerked her gaze towards Greta. "Signora Sarta, what are *you* doing here?"

"Signora Sarta is helping to right a wrong," Ministro Ercolano told her. "Now, if you don't mind releasing this man, I'll sign the paperwork."

Ciro held his breath as the key turned in the lock, opening the metal bars. He stepped out of the cell so quickly, his foot snagged on a bar and Greta caught him as he stumbled through. She looped an arm through his and patted his hand reassuringly. It was strange how much safer he felt with her by his side.

The cell was locked once more and Letizia di Bibiana led the way back up to the ground level of the Town Hall. Ciro stood with Greta against one wall of the Amministratori Hall while Ministro Ercolano signed all the papers Letizia and Severino shoved under his nose.

With an exaggerated sigh, the Ministro set down his pen and stretched out his back. Severino snatched back his piece of paper and read it closely, nodding to himself with a small smile.

"Severino," Ministro Ercolano said, waiting for the Mercantili Amministratore to face him before continuing. "I don't want to hear of any further trouble with Ciro. I've looked into his case. He's been a law-abiding resident of Tor'Esint since he arrived to take up his apprenticeship at the age of thirteen. Let's not make a further example of such a well-regarded and long-standing resident of our city or it may not go according to your plan. Do I make myself understood?"

Severino's eyes narrowed. "Of course, Ministro Ercolano. If you'll excuse me, I've urgent matters to attend to."

He tucked the chit into his pocket as he walked away. Ministro Ercolano waited until he'd left the room before approaching them.

"Now, what's this about Signora Loyola?" he asked Ciro.

Letizia di Bibiana looked up sharply from her desk, the movement catching Ciro's eye. He didn't feel all that comfortable around her.

"If you're going to accompany us to the Gioiellieri Guild Hall, I'd rather speak of it there, behind closed doors."

Ministro Ercolano followed his gaze to Letizia. He sighed and nodded. Without bothering to say anything further, he simply ushered Ciro and Greta out of the Town Hall and into Greta's blazermobile which was parked right near the front steps. It wasn't far to the Gioiellieri Guild Hall, but no one proposed they walk there instead.

Ciro hopped into the blazermobile, making space for Ministro Ercolano. He still could not quite believe he was literally rubbing shoulders with the Ministro of Tor'Esint, in a blazermobile of all things! Seppe would have a fit when he found out.

"Seppe!"

Greta paused in the process of pouring blazer solution into the engine.

"He's worried, Ciro. We *all* were. I sent him off to Anna's workshop so he wouldn't spend all day fretting about you. We'll pick him up on the way home. I promise."

The ache in Ciro's chest eased fractionally. He closed his eyes and breathed deeply, trying to slow his racing heart. The roar of the blazermobile's engine blocked out everything else.

It was an extremely short drive to the Gioiellieri Guild Hall. Again, Greta parked near the bottom of the steps and secured the blazermobile. She hopped out on one side as Ministro Ercolano stepped out of the other. He held the door open for Ciro and helped him down from the vehicle. It was strange that such a simple action made him seem more a man and less the Ministro in Ciro's eyes.

As they ascended the stairs, Ciro couldn't help but think of the last time he was there handing back the keys to his workshop. He'd thought that would be the last time he ever set foot inside. Perhaps this time, with the release of his assets, really would be the final time.

The Hall of Great Works was full of people coming and going, more than usual, but it was always that way when Guild Balls approached. As Ciro led Ministro Ercolano and Greta to the reception desk, a small opening widened before them. People had recognised Ministro Ercolano and were making way for him with curious glances at Ciro. By now, everyone must know that he'd been stripped of his Guild Marks – it was no secret.

Yvette looked up as they approached. Her jaw dropped open when she saw who accompanied Ciro. Blinking quickly, she rose to her feet and curtsied.

"Ministro Ercolano, to what do we owe the pleasure?" she asked in the sweetest tone Ciro had ever heard her use. It was disconcerting.

Ciro motioned for him to take the lead. The Ministro stepped forward and Ciro took his place next to Greta instead. The way she slipped her arm into his was so natural and comforting, Ciro couldn't believe the extremes of his ever-changing fortunes.

"Good afternoon, Signora Gioielliera," Ministro Ercolano said with a curt nod of his head. "Would you mind finding the Maestri for me? I've a matter of some urgency and importance to discuss with them. All of them, if possible, but I do understand if only one or two are available."

Yvette bobbed up and down in front of him. "Of course, Ministro. Of course. Please, come this way."

She motioned for another Amministratrice to take her place and led them to what Ciro now surmised must be the waiting room. It was the same room in which Ciro had discussed Loredana's apprenticeship, twice, and where they had stripped him of his Guild Marks. Such mixed emotions made it difficult for him to enter. He hesitated at the door, but Greta gently drew him inside.

They were not left alone for long. Yvette returned shortly with a tray laden with three cups of tea and three of coffee, a tiny jug of milk and a sugar pot. A few minutes later, she appeared again with a small plate of biscuits. Her flustered actions sent butterflies swarming through Ciro's stomach even though he felt nothing else could possibly go wrong today.

"Yvette, *please*, stop fussing," he told her. "When will the Maestri come?"

Spoken to directly, she instantly regained her composure.

"They're finalising a few of the Parting Gift transactions. Perhaps another quarter hour."

"Thank you, Signora," Ministro Ercolano said with a smile. "I think we'll manage by ourselves until they arrive. You've brought us enough refreshments to last that long."

A smile tugged at the corner of Ciro's mouth. The words had been said with such sincerity, that if Ciro hadn't seen the eye roll beforehand, he mightn't have realised how insincere the comment was.

Finally left alone, Ciro sugared Greta's tea and passed it to her. He looked questioningly at the Ministro who shook his head and picked up a straight cup of coffee. Ciro fought the urge to comment – a straight coffee was too bitter for his taste. He sugared his own cup and sat down to enjoy it.

"Now, Ciro, will you finally tell me how Signora Loyola is involved in any of this?" Ministro Ercolano asked, taking a seat beside him.

Ciro shifted to make room for the Ministro and told him the abridged version of events that had led to his Guild Marks being stripped and then his imprisonment. Ministro Ercolano listened attentively for the most part, only asking a clarifying question here and there. By the end of the tale, his face was set in an angry scowl.

"There are so many questions I barely know where to begin," he said, leaning back in his chair. "With such secrecy surrounding the bidding war, how did the Mercantili Guild find out about it in the first place? We can only assume it was from when you deposited the unusually large sum of money. That tells us there's a rat in your Guild. Any ideas who?"

Ciro shook his head. "The only ones who knew about it were Yvette and Adamo. Unless I spoke too loudly when requesting the form to make a deposit. And I suppose any of the Amministratori have access to the books to look up whatever information about any of the Guild Members they like."

"Are there any you don't trust?" Greta asked. "Any you've had your differences with?"

Ciro shrugged. "No. Nothing memorable. Yvette is usually the gruffest of the Amministratori, but she's a no-nonsense person, fiercely dedicated to the Guild. I can't see her approaching the Mercantili Guild to rat me out. How could it possibly benefit her to do so? Especially when I was working on the centrepiece for the Guild Ball."

He saw Greta shift uncomfortably in her chair. She shook her head and bit her lip as though to stop herself from speaking. He caught her gaze and held it until she spoke.

"It may not have been an Amministratrice at all. Not that they wouldn't stoop to that – Caldera knows some would – but there are other people more likely. How many Corallini are there, including you?"

"Four," Ciro replied easily.

"And were all of you approached to create the centrepiece?"

"Of course. But Simone refused because we weren't to be paid for it as the material was being provided."

"That still leaves three of you," Greta pointed out, "and you only mentioned Anna was working with you."

"Yes, that's true, but Sabrina was involved as well, in a way." He scratched the back of his neck uncomfortably. "Well, until Anna's design was chosen over hers by the Maestri. But she was given the larger corallo branches to work with, to place around the centrepiece. I don't think she'd have sabotaged me over that and besides, she didn't know about the bidding war."

Ministro Ercolano raised a finger. "Excuse me, but neither of them needed to know about the bidding war beforehand, and who could stop tongues from wagging afterwards? Once they'd heard about it, it'd only be a matter of time before either of them figured out whether it was you or Anna at the centre of it. From there, a few discreet enquiries and the job is done."

Ciro was still trying to work his way through the implications when the door opened and the three Gioiellieri Maestri walked in. They exchanged pleasantries with Ministro Ercolano and were introduced to Greta all while Ciro tried to convince himself that none of his fellow Corallini would have done this to him.

"Now, what's this matter of urgency?" Rosalina asked, sitting down with a cup of coffee, leaving the tea for Adamo and Luca. Neither of them touched the cups.

Ciro sat up straighter, ready to reply, but Ministro Ercolano lay a hand on his arm to stop him.

"There appears to have been some confusion regarding Ciro's assets. Apparently, the Amministratore sent here to deal with the matter of the Guild Marks was under the impression that Ciro's assets were to be confiscated by the Tor'Esint Amministratori. He was mistaken. I'm here to personally inform you that Ciro's assets are *not* to be confiscated and are now unfrozen. If you're willing, his assets may remain in your vaults."

The Maestri exchanged surprised glances.

"I'm glad to hear it," Rosalina finally said. "Since you're here, there's a matter we've been wondering about that perhaps you can help us with, assuming you know all the Guild, erm, secrets."

Ministro Ercolano raised an eyebrow and looked pointedly at Greta. She looked at him innocently then huffed.

"I suppose I'll just wait in the Hall of Great Works then, shall I?"

Ciro rose to open the door for her, but she waved him back to his seat, before she exited and firmly closed the door behind herself.

"Would this have anything to do with patent fees?" Ministro Ercolano asked in a quiet voice.

"As you say," Rosalina agreed. "Should Ciro still receive patent fees for his Great Works or not? And if not, can he nominate someone to receive his patent fees, as is now the case for any deceased Guild Member?"

"What was that?" Ciro blurted out.

"I admit, I'm not familiar with this particular clause," Ministro Ercolano replied with no little hesitation.

"We've only just begun the paperwork to implement it," Adamo told him. "It was an idea initiated by Ranieri Sarto years ago, but only discovered a few months previously upon his death and the reading of his testament. Greta, who you just dismissed, could tell you more. I believe she's the one who inherited everything from him."

Ministro Ercolano looked at the door, as though he were about to ask Greta back in, then shook his head.

"How does it work then?" he asked Adamo.

"Well, technically, a Guild Member may nominate a family member or apprentice, former or current, to receive their patent fees for a certain amount of time after their death. The timing is rather technical, but it means the Guild Member's family won't be left destitute after their passing, or a Guild Member may choose to give a helping hand to a worthy apprentice." Adamo glanced at Ciro then back to Ministro Ercolano.

"What would generally happen with Guild Members is that they continue to receive their patent fees until they die, even if they're too old to work. After their death, the new clause kicks in. As it's such a new clause, we've yet to discuss what happens in the case of a Guild Member being stripped of their Guild Marks.

"The first question is, do they still continue to receive their patent fees? After all, they worked hard to earn them no matter what else transpired afterwards. If the answer is yes, then we'll assume they can include their patent fees in their will. If not, can they immediately activate the patent fee clause?"

Ciro learned forward so far he almost fell off his chair. "Loredana," he said instantly. "I give my patent fees to Loredana."

Adamo shook his head. "Even if you can activate this clause, you can't choose Loredana – she isn't your apprentice anymore. She's Anna's now. You could choose Seppe or Serafina."

"Serafina then," Ciro answered easily. "With my assets unfrozen and Seppe working with Anna, we'll get by. Serafina won't."

"Well, wait just a moment," Ministro Ercolano spoke up. "What has the Mercantili Guild said about this new clause?"

Rosalina grinned. "As far as we're aware, the Mercantili Guild doesn't know about patent fees because of how their Guild works. Therefore, the Maestri of the other Guilds saw no reason to discuss it with them."

Ministro Ercolano laughed loudly and long. "*This* is clearly a Guild matter. Discuss it with the other Maestri, but I'm happy to abide by your decision. Perhaps it will be decided that the manner in which a Guild Member is stripped of their Guild Marks comes into the decision of the ongoing patent fees.

"If they caused their Guild any harm, I would assume the Guild would feel no obligation to continue the patent arrangement. Otherwise, I don't see why patent fees should discontinue. However, as I say, it's a Guild matter. I only ask that you inform me of any decisions made. I do like to keep myself well abreast of these things."

Ciro listened to it all curiously. He'd been so angry with the Ministro for not putting a hard stop to the Mercantili Guild's nonsense, but Ciro was now grudgingly forced to accept that he did all he could behind the scenes to help the other Guilds and their members. If not for Ercolano, Ciro would still be in prison, his assets frozen, his patent fees at an end.

True, the Ministro did not have the power to give him back his Guild Marks, but he'd done everything else possible to help him. Now, it was Ciro's turn to repay his kindness.

"As my assets have been unfrozen, I need to make a sizable withdrawal," Ciro said. "Ministro Ercolano helped me earlier today. I now owe him thirty-six gold coins."

Rosalina's hand flew to her chest. "*Thirty-six gold coins*! Ciro, that's an absurd amount of money. What's going on?"

Ciro shrugged, ashamed of his anger and the destruction it had wrought. "What's done is done. It's not important now. May I make a withdrawal please?"

Rosalina looked like she would protest, but Ciro shook his head at her. She backed down and Luca took Ciro with him to withdraw the coins. He took no more than was required, preferring to keep the rest for emergencies, as usual. The rest turned out to be quite a decent amount, still over three hundred gold pieces.

If his fortunes hadn't changed so drastically, Adamo was right – he'd have been able to hire, or even buy, a larger workshop fit for a Corallino with an apprentice. He shook his head, trying not to think of the gaping hole in his life. He was still a Corallino, but without the Guild he had nothing. It wasn't fair. He'd had so many plans. So much to teach Loredana. So much that even Anna wouldn't be able to show her. Things only *he* was proficient in. Skills he'd so badly wanted to pass on to her. He'd had eight years to look forward to doing just that, and now, it was all gone.

His shoulders slumped and Ciro felt a tear run down his cheek.

"Ciro?" Luca called out. "Are you unwell?"

"I think I'm just getting old, Luca. Old and sentimental." He took a deep breath and straightened his spine. "Let's get back to the others."

Ministro Ercolano was waiting for him with Rosalina. She exchanged glances with Luca who took his cue to leave.

"Ciro, I understand you're working for Signora Loyola on a special project?"

He nodded, trying not to scowl at the Ministro for letting slip his new working arrangements.

"I'd be honoured to see this project when it's complete. Do you know how she plans to reveal it?"

"I may not be in a position to complete the project."

"Whyever not?" Rosalina asked, confused.

Ministro Ercolano interrupted her. "I believe the matter can be resolved if Signora Loyola employs an Artista to purchase the clay for her. They don't need to know why and no questions will be asked at the clay yard."

"Ciro, really, *what* is going on?" Rosalina asked, grasping his hand tightly. "It's not like you to be so secretive or find yourself in so much trouble."

Ciro laughed. "Perhaps that was my problem all along. Not being secretive enough. Then, perhaps, I'd not have found myself in so much trouble."

"I worry for you, Ciro," she said gently. "You were the best of the Corallini. It's a great loss to our Guild not to have you as one of us anymore. An even greater loss for Loredana not to have you as her Maestro."

Ciro gritted his teeth. "I'm sure she'll do just fine under Anna," he said, not believing a word of it himself. "She'll learn as much with her as she would have with me. And if she's smart about it, she can learn almost as much from Seppe."

Ministro Ercolano coughed. "I think I'm missing something here."

Rosalina turned to him with an air of composure. "Ministro, you may not be aware, but we only had *four* Corallini in the first place and all of them at least in their fifth decade. None of them had an apprentice until Ciro took on his niece, Loredana. Now that he's been stripped of his Guild Marks, she's been taken in by Anna. But that still brings our total Corallini down to three until she finishes her apprenticeship.

"It was already a dying art before this catastrophe. Now, it's almost dead. Imagine if Loredana is the only apprentice. There will be *one* Corallina in all of Tor'Esint. With the recent events, I doubt either of our other Corallini will be eager to take on their first apprentice. Do you?"

Ministro Ercolano glanced at Ciro and shook his head.

"I won't forget this," he told them emphatically. "I'll think of a way to fix it. Somehow."

Ciro shared a cynical look with Rosalina as she got to her feet. Everyone followed her lead.

"We appreciate it, Ministro. But if even *you* can't allow us to give Ciro back his Guild Marks, there's nothing to be done and, please, let me stop you before you suggest the Corallini create their own Guild. The last Guild was created over fifty years ago with a lot more money than the four of them would have combined. It just isn't possible."

Ministro Ercolano huffed. "You've thought of everything then. Perhaps there isn't anything I can do, but I *will* try."

"Of *that*, I am certain," she told him, hand on his arm. "Thank you for helping Ciro with his financial difficulties, but we must ask you to leave now. The Guild Ball is just over a week away and we've much to prepare."

Ciro hesitated a moment. "How's Anna going with her special project? Will it be ready in time?"

Adamo cleared his throat. "I'm not certain it will be. I've been going to check on Loredana periodically and though the project is coming along, it was always going to be too much for one person in the timeframe we had."

Throwing caution to the wind, Ciro offered his services. "I can help her. If you'll let me. If *she'll* let me. I don't want my failure to bring the entire Guild Ball down in standing. I'll even give you my Parting Gifts. I was working on them anyway. No sense in keeping them for myself."

Luca put up his hand at that. "No. We can't officially have any dealings with you and that includes giving any of your cammei as Parting Gifts."

Well, there were ways around that, Ciro knew. He would just have to be careful about it.

They left the inner sanctum of the Gioiellieri Guild and met Greta in the Hall of Great Works. She was halfway down the corridor, looking at the Corallini section.

"Ciro, are these yours?" she asked, as they walked over to her.

He glanced over and nodded, the tightness in his chest returning. Even Ministro Ercolano paused to peruse them.

"You're a very talented man," the Ministro said appreciatively. "If my companion saw these, she'd scoff at the cammeo I had commissioned for her on our Commitment Day."

Ciro frowned for a moment. "That was Simone's work, wasn't it? Cammei are not his forte. If your companion is willing to sit for me, I'd be only too happy to carve a cammeo for her. Another Gioielliere would have to set it for you, but that shouldn't be too difficult to organise. I'm certain Anna Corallina would be willing to oblige you."

Ministro Ercolano tore his gaze away from the Great Works. "Ciro, I appreciate the offer, but I don't want to cause more trouble for you. If the Mercantili Guild discovers you carrying on the work of a Gioielliere after you've been stripped of your Guild Marks, I won't be able to save you again."

Ciro couldn't hide the smile tugging at the corner of his lips. "The Gioiellieri Guild have confirmed that carving corallo, or shells for cammei, are not the work of a Gioielliere, and I have plenty of that material to work with. I may not be able to charge Guild prices for my work, but the joy of creating them can still be mine for as long as my money lasts. Which, thanks to you, will now be longer. Assuming, of course, that Signora Sarta is still willing to keep me and Seppe as lodgers."

Greta gripped his arms tightly. "Of course I am. I fear Sofia has grown quite fond of you and would be distraught to see you go. I can't do that to her."

Ciro smiled at the thought. Perhaps Greta's workshop was more than just a lodging now. Perhaps it really was home.

"In that case, I accept. Viviana will be only too pleased to sit for you. But we have a more pressing matter," Ministro Ercolano told them. "You're promised to do work for Signora Loyola and we must help her find a way around this or she'll never let me hear the end of it."

"Did you tell her?" Ciro asked Greta. She shook her head. "Well then, I'll have to go and explain the situation to her and hope she understands."

"I'll go with you to explain the situation to her if you like," Ministro Ercolano offered, as they walked out into the street.

It was already getting dark. Ciro shook his head.

"I thank you, but no. I'll explain myself tomorrow. I'm starving and sorely tired. Besides which, I'm missing my companion more than words can express."

Ministro Ercolano looked ready to object, but Ciro noticed a glare from Greta stopped him. He struck out his hand instead and shook Ciro's heartily.

"I'll see you at the Guild Ball then."

"No," Ciro replied immediately, "you won't. I'm not a Guild Member anymore."

"Well, neither am I, but that never stopped me. I'll buy you and your companion a ticket. You'll be my special guests. I won't take no for an answer."

The thought of going to the Guild Ball struck Ciro speechless. He'd thought he'd left that world behind. Been thrown out of it for good. But everything and everyone kept forcing him back into that path. He couldn't reply, but nodded. That seemed enough for the Ministro. He took his leave and left Ciro alone with Greta.

He turned to her, meaning to smile, but instead, his knees trembled and he pitched sideways. She caught him with surprisingly strong arms and helped him back to the blazermobile.

"It's alright, Ciro," she told him as she bundled him in. "You're safe now. As far as the Mercantili Guild is concerned, you're untouchable unless they want to start a real war with Ministro Ercolano. As long as you don't provoke them unnecessarily, you know, by throwing more rocks at their windows, you should be fine."

She closed his door, ran around to her own side and shuffled in beside him. It was strange how much safer he felt now than he had in a long time. He was no longer destitute. He had friends in high places. Strong friends, who weren't afraid of a fight. The knowledge made him come to a decision of his own.

He *would* offer to help Anna with the statue so the Gioiellieri Ball went off without a hitch, in secret if necessary. Then he'd take Signora Loyola up on her offer to showcase his work with her corallo trunk in a way that would shove it right in the Mercantili Guild's face. But that could all wait until tomorrow. Right now, all he wanted was to see Seppe. To be home.

Greta drove slowly back to her workshop. The dwindling light meant that more people were out and about, getting ready for the evening's engagements. Lamplighters were already out, activating the friction switches on each corner which, in turn, made the street's metal spiders climb the lamp posts to turn on the gas and light the flames. Even the less affluent areas had gas lamps, only fewer than in other areas. Ciro loved the yellow glow they gave the streets, like a little touch of sunlight.

Before long, they were back at the workshop. The Guild Hall clocks chimed a quarter hour, but Ciro had stopped keeping track. He knew it was late – past trading, and Seppe would be home. Greta helped him up the stairs and into the workshop.

It was so brightly lit, his eyes hurt. The Liquid Sunlight and every glass lamp in the house was lit in the workshop. Every occupant of the house, including the hired Sarti, were sitting around the two armchairs occupied by Seppe, with Loredana curled up on his lap, and Anna.

"Seppe. Reda," Ciro whispered softly, his voice catching in his throat.

It must have been loud enough, though, for they both looked up immediately. Loredana jumped off Seppe's lap and ran straight to Ciro. He knelt and hugged her tightly, her tears mingling with his own.

"Oh Zio, I was so scared for you!"

A few moments later, Seppe lay a hand on his shaking shoulder. Ciro got to his feet, tears still streaming and threw his arms around Seppe, kissing him over and over, trying to believe that he really was here, safe in his home with his companion.

"You scared the smoke out of us! What happened?" Seppe finally asked, drawing Ciro to the armchair and forcing him to sit.

Anna watched him quietly from her chair as Loredana went to stand beside her.

"It's a long story," Ciro said, finally.

"We've nowhere else to be," Anna said firmly. "We've been at our wit's end since you disappeared. Now you tell us what happened or, so help me, I'll throw you into the Caldera myself!"

Ciro took a deep breath and began his story, from when he'd left home to see Signora Loyola, right up to Ministro Ercolano's insistence that he and Seppe join him at the Guild Ball. The only detail he left out was about the patent fees. That was *his* business, and he insisted on keeping it so.

By the time he finished, Sofia had filled his coffee cup twice and pressed him to eat a segmented orange while he spoke. He didn't miss the happiness and relief in her eyes. It filled him with such pride and contentment to know so many people loved him.

"So that's it, then. You've got your money back and the Ministro's protection," Anna said, pursing her lips. "You don't need Seppe to work anymore so I suppose you'll be keeping him all to yourself again."

"What?" Ciro blurted out. "Of course not. Anna, we still need you. You still need Seppe. I wouldn't do that to you. Besides, I have a few propositions of my own for you. We'll need to be clever about it, but I think we can help each other out."

He looked around at the sea of faces and stopped talking. Greta saw his hesitation and clapped her hands loudly.

"Right, Nicolina, Pietro, we'll see you tomorrow morning. Everyone else, all hands on deck to make dinner tonight. Anna, Loredana, you'll be joining us of course. No, don't try to argue. I won't hear it. Come upstairs when you're done talking and you can lend a hand if we aren't finished."

The room erupted into a flurry of activity at her words, eventually leaving Ciro alone with Seppe, Anna and Loredana. He waited until he was certain no one would overhear them, then he leaned in close to the others.

"My first proposition, and hear me out before you say no, is to help you with the rest of the corallo statue. I know you're behind and the Maestri are desperately hoping you'll finish on time. I'll make sure you do. This needs to be the finest Guild Ball we've ever thrown. Which brings me to my second proposition.

"I've been working on the Parting Gifts, even though I needn't have bothered. I'll keep doing those in my spare time and give them to you to finish off so that there will be enough to go around. You can keep the money for those yourself. You've done more than enough to help me."

Anna raised her eyebrows. "Anything else?"

Ciro took a deep breath. "When this is all over, and after I've finished working on Signora Loyola's project, would you perhaps consider working with me unofficially? I plan on continuing with my cammei, but for that to be a viable option, I need to be able to send people to a Gioielliere or Corallina to finish the work. Would you be happy to do that?"

Loredana looked up at her with big eyes. Anna glanced at her, and then at Seppe. She chewed on her lip until Ciro thought it would bleed.

"I have a proposition of my own," she said, not answering him directly. "My workshop is more than big enough to split into two sections. If this arrangement is to work, I'll insist on you carving in my workshop so Loredana can watch and learn from you. I may be as good as you at corallo jewellery, but no one is better than you at carving cammei. Loredana deserves to learn from you as she supposed to."

Ciro's eyes blurred. He wiped away the unshed tears and looked from Anna to Loredana and back again. Their faces were so eager, so earnest.

"I can't put your livelihood in danger," he said softly. "I won't do it."

"Livelihood be damned, Ciro," Anna retorted hotly. "It could have been *me*. If Antonino had decided to sell his corallo to the first customer he had rather than his favourite, I could have been stripped of my Guild Marks, losing everything. Do you think I don't know that? I lie awake at night, sleepless because I know it could have been me."

"Anna, I..."

She waved him into silence. "Only tell me this – if our situations were reversed, wouldn't you have done everything you could to help me? Before and after? Of course you would have – that's just who you are. Well, I'm telling you now, you need to let me do the same for you. Seppe has already proved invaluable in the workshop and is worth more than he allows me to pay him. With you there too, we'll have a nice little setup. You can't get in trouble for carving and that's all we'll let you do. You know it's what you like doing best anyway, so that's settled. Yes?"

Ciro held a hand against his mouth, trying not to show his incredulous smile, trying not to admit how pleased he was. Finally, he nodded.

"Yes, it's settled," he agreed. "The stars only know how we're going to pull it off."

"But we will."

Anna smiled and nudged Loredana towards him. Ciro held out his arms for her again and buried his face in her shoulder. He could barely contain his happiness. She might not be his apprentice, but he'd still have a hand in her career.

***

That night, when everyone else had gone to bed and the lights were all but extinguished, Ciro closed his door and was finally alone with Seppe. The glass lantern on the dresser showed Seppe's hands were trembling as he sat on the bed, eyes downcast. They'd not stopped shaking the entire evening. Perhaps no one else had noticed, but Ciro had.

He sat beside Seppe, took his hands and kissed them tenderly.

"I thought they'd killed you." Seppe's voice quavered. "I thought I'd never see you again. Greta tried to tell me I was wrong, but I couldn't stop myself from seeing you lying in a gutter somewhere, the life draining out of you. Or your bloated body washing up on shore only to be found by some poor child like Loredana or Tania."

"But they didn't," Ciro said, taking Seppe firmly by the shoulders and forcing him to look him in the eye. "They didn't and they won't. I'll be with you every day until the Guild Ball and then again after I finish Signora Loyola's statue. I promise."

Seppe threw his arms around Ciro and clung to him tightly, nodding to himself. Ciro couldn't believe how lucky he was to have such a companion by his side.

Chapter 34 – Legaramedi 26 Sarti 230 Years After Implosion

Ciro woke early that morning, breakfasted, shaved his beard as close as he dared and put on his best work clothes, apron and all. He was in the process of selecting which tools to bring to Anna's workshop when Sofia stopped at his door, looking in. Ciro followed her gaze to the handkerchief on the edge of his dresser, still wrapped around the cammeo he'd made for her. He selected his final tool then beckoned her in.

She hesitated, but finally crossed over to him.

"I wonder if perhaps *now* you might accept my gift?"

He took the handkerchief, unwrapped the cammeo and held it out to her. Sofia looked at it longingly and ran a light finger over the image of herself.

"It isn't me," she said. "Not really."

Ciro withdrew his hand, looked at the cammeo closely then held it up against her face.

"This is what I see when I look at you," he said with a shrug. "That's all Artiste and Corallini do – they draw what they see in someone."

Seppe walked in at that moment and nodded.

"It's true. If Ciro doesn't like the person, you can be certain their cammeo won't be his best work. Mind, it'll still be better than anyone else's, just not what the customer wants."

Ciro wrestled with himself for a moment then opened his drawer to take out another cammeo.

"Sofia, will it make you feel better if I give another unasked for cammeo to someone today?"

She nodded curiously but Seppe shook his head.

"I've told you, Ciro, people don't like it when you do that," Seppe said, reproachfully.

"Well then, I guess you don't want this?" Ciro asked, holding out the cammeo.

Seppe took it with trembling fingers, shaking his head all the while. Sofia looked over his shoulder and drew in her breath.

"That's magnificent," she exclaimed. "Is that you, when you were younger, Giuseppe?"

Seppe grunted. "Then and now. What'd you do this for, Ciro? I *told* you no one wants to see a wrinkled vecchietto in a cammeo."

"I do," Ciro said firmly. "And if you'll notice, I didn't put in *all* your wrinkles. Didn't want you getting mad at me. Now, we'll need to get pins for you both. Anna can help with that."

Seppe's lips curled slowly into a smile as he stared down at the cammeo. Ciro handed Sofia hers. She tried to suppress a smile, but Ciro saw it nonetheless. He patted her cheek like he'd so often done with Loredana.

"Seppe, I need a quick word with Greta before we go to Anna's."

Seppe nodded absently, admiring the cammeo in his hand. Downstairs, Ciro found Greta already at work. She paused and looked up as he approached her workstation.

"I wonder if you might be able to deliver a note to Signora Loyola for me? She needs to hire an Artista to buy the clay for our project. With everything that happened, I didn't get a chance to tell her."

"Of course," Greta replied easily, taking the note from his outstretched hand. "Leave it with me. I'll organise everything with her, including when she can come to pick up the corallo trunk."

Ciro thanked her. "It's in the note, but if you could let her know that I'll be there to begin work on it after the Guild Ball, I think that would work best. I've promised Anna to help her finish the Gioiellieri Guild's centrepiece."

Greta clenched her fists involuntarily. Ciro saw the motion and took a step closer.

"I owe her that much, Greta. And I can't get in trouble for something I was kicked out of the Guild for in the first place."

"Be careful, Ciro," Greta warned him. "Ministro Ercolano can only protect you so much. Don't play with fire to find out the limits of that protection."

Ciro raised an eyebrow at her and spoke softly. "Wasn't it *you* and *your Maestro* who played with fire in the first place? Correct me if I'm wrong, but I believe the new patent situation is being negotiated because of your Ranieri. And the Mercantili Guild's records are being audited as a result of your comments during the Alchimisti trials. Or have I mistaken you for another Greta Sarta?" He chuckled to himself. "I had no idea who you were when we first met."

Greta smoothed her skirt over her knees and tilted her chin up a notch.

"Point taken," she said shortly. "I'll have your message delivered today. Don't be back late tonight or we just might send out a search party for you."

Ciro only winked at Greta. His attention was quickly distracted by Seppe and Sofia coming down the stairs together, both proudly puffing up their chests.

"Let's go, Seppe," Ciro said. "I don't want to be late on my first day back in a workshop."

"Maestra, could I have two silvers to get a pin for this?" Sofia asked, holding out her cammeo to Greta.

Greta took both Sofia's and Seppe's cammei to admire them. "Ciro, these must be some of your best work!"

Ciro took the compliment in his stride but glowed at the grins on Sofia's and Seppe's faces.

"Fia, ask Annika and Marta to bring theirs as well. Ciro, can you take them all and tell Anna I'll pay for the backs for all of them?"

Ciro nodded easily and waited for the small collection of cammei to be gathered before leaving. He walked down the street, hand in hand with Seppe. It was the oddest feeling to be going to someone else's workshop where they were both to be employed in the work they'd done most of their lives.

They walked through the Zone Inventrici and Alchimisti, marvelling at the windows which showed just a peep of the workshops. Ciro had always found it fascinating to watch others at work, no matter which Guild they belonged to. Seppe hurried him along.

"Anna prefers I arrive before trading to help set up the shop," he told Ciro. "I think she's quite liking having more people in the workshop than just herself all day long."

They arrived well before trading began. Loredana was already inside, practising her letters. She waved excitedly when they walked in, but did not stop to greet them. Anna had bought her a chalkboard and Loredana quickly filled up the slate, wiped it clean and started again. Ciro thought it was a good idea. Paper was becoming more expensive the longer the Trading Edict lasted.

Seppe set to work tidying things from the day before and setting up his own work for the day without any instruction from Anna, just like he used to do in Ciro's old workshop. Ciro's chest tightened momentarily, but he took a deep breath in and released his anger with the Mercantili Guild and the anonymous traitor along with his breath. He refused to dwell on what was. He was fortunate with what he had and was determined to be grateful for it.

"Well, Anna, let me see the statue then," he said, walking behind the wooden panels that had once stood in his workshop.

He stopped and stared at it, shocked. She'd had the corallo trunk for almost two weeks and not made nearly as much progress as she should have. Ciro rubbed a hand across his face and through his thinning hair.

Anna looked at the statue mournfully. "I don't think we'll get it done, even together."

"Nonsense," said Ciro. "We've a week left and the two of us to work on it. Seppe! Man the shop all day – no distractions for us. Loredana, help Seppe and organise food and drinks today. And put these cammei in a safe place until after the Guild Ball. They're for Greta's girls and Seppe."

"Yes, Zio."

"Yes, Ciro." Seppe and Loredana chorused from the workshop.

"Where do you want me to start?" Ciro asked Anna, unpacking his tools and laying them on the workbench.

"Why don't you work on the tentacles reaching up to the boat? I'll keep working on the boat itself and then we can work on the monster at the bottom together."

Ciro shrugged his agreement. It was a bad plan. Anna should have offered to work on the tentacles herself. They were less intricate and would be much easier and faster for her to carve than the boat itself – Ciro knew he would work more quickly on the more intricate sections. But it was no longer his project and his lead. He sat down across from Anna and began work, letting the rest of the world melt away.

***

He paused when Loredana brought him a panino, and each time she came out of the kitchen with cups of coffee or water, but otherwise, he worked relentlessly through the day. When the Guild Hall clocks struck four, Ciro was halfway through his second tentacle. Anna was still working on the boat.

"I'm going to walk Loredana home. Should I pass by here on my way back to Greta's or will you be staying later?" Seppe asked, popping his head around the wooden panels. He looked at the progress and huffed to himself. "I'll tell them not to wait on you for dinner at Greta's. Don't stay too long, Ciro. You'll need your rest for tomorrow."

Ciro nodded without looking up. Only after the door closed behind them did Anna speak.

"Seppe's right, you know. You shouldn't stay too late. Tongues might wag."

He paused his work to glare at her. "If tongues wag, then they are seriously misinformed. And who cares if they wag anyway? If we don't work every available hour on this, it won't be done in time. I don't know about you, but I don't want to be mere hours away from finishing it when the Guild Ball begins and then berate myself for not having worked more on it. Do you?"

Anna's shoulders slumped. "No."

"Good then. Let's keep going. I want to at least finish this tentacle today."

Without another word, they picked up their tools and worked in complete silence, other than the Guild Hall clocks chiming every quarter hour. It was late when Ciro finally left. Every gas lamp had been lit and diners were already thronging the ristoranti dotting the streets.

By the time he got home, Greta and Domizio had already eaten, along with the rest of the household, and were back at work on the final gowns and suits for the Guild Ball. The pressure was on everyone, it seemed.

Chapter 35 – Argentodi 4 Musicisti 230 Years After Implosion

It was the day before the Guild Ball and Ciro felt that everyone's lives had been thrown into chaos. Greta and her entire staff, including her apprentices, had been working around the clock to get all their orders finished in time. There seemed to be a constant stream of people coming and going for fittings or to collect finished orders, even outside of trading hours.

Aveline had appeared one evening, well past trading, in tears because most of her gowns no longer fit, including the one for the Guild Ball. After a calming cup of tea and many soothing words, Greta had managed to get her into the fitting room to resize her. They'd agreed Greta would only fix one work dress and the Guild Ball gown until the Ball was over. Ciro had heard the entire thing from upstairs, as had everyone else. Aveline had been in hysterics over it, which seemed so unlike her, it struck their minds as decidedly odd behaviour.

Ciro himself had been working extra-long hours at Anna's workshop, trying to get the corallo statue done in time. They were close, but not finished yet. Today, he'd left home earlier than usual with a small wicker basket of carved, but unfinished, cammei. Each night for the past week, before going to bed, he'd continued working on them to have the required fifteen done in time. He'd barely slept at all. There would be time for sleep later.

He rapped on the door repeatedly until Anna finally opened it. Ciro stared uncomprehendingly at her thick woollen gown, slippered feet and dishevelled hair.

"What're you doing answering the door like that?" he asked, almost angrily.

Anna raised her eyebrows at him. "What are *you* doing here so early? It's not even seven o'clock yet!"

He barged in past her and set his wicker basket down on the nearest workbench. "I've finished the last cammeo. Now, why don't you work on the backing for these today while I finish off the corallo statute? Have the Maestri already organised with you when they're going to pick it up?"

"Tomorrow, midday. That gives me a few hours to sleep and recover before the ball," Anna replied, sifting through the cammei. "Ciro, when did you have time to make these?"

"Greta has these fantastic lights in her house. I've been making good use of them every evening," he replied with a dismissive wave of his hand. "Midday – that's good. Gives us a few extra hours tomorrow. We might need it. Let's get to work."

"*You* get to work," Anna said firmly. "*I'm* going to eat breakfast and get ready. Don't rush me!"

"Bah!" Ciro threw his hands up in the air and disappeared behind the wooden panels. This was the first, and perhaps only, time he'd have the corallo trunk all to himself since it had been confiscated from his workshop. It was time to fix Anna's mistakes and smooth out the rougher edges without her peering over his shoulder.

He stood back to inspect the statue. The boat was done – well, it was Anna's version of done. The tentacles were entirely finished, and the sea monster's body was more than half done. Ciro debated what to work on first. If he began with the boat, he might run out of time to do the body. If he began with the body, he might not have the time or the privacy to work on the boat. It was a difficult decision, but he settled on fixing the worst of the problems with the boat and leaving the fine tuning of it until after the main body of the sea monster itself was finished.

Once Anna was ready for the day, Ciro effortlessly blocked out the sounds of the fire-gun as she began work on the backings for the cammei. It would be a hard ask to do all of them today, but it had to be done. He barely noticed when Seppe and then Loredana arrived to begin work. Loredana insisted on sitting with him behind the panel as he worked on the corallo trunk.

"If you must sit there, then I will insist you sketch the statue. Otherwise, begone with you!"

"I knew you'd say that," Loredana said mischievously. "That's why I've already got my sketchbook and pencil."

She sat down and opened her sketchbook to draw. Ciro grunted approvingly and glanced over every now and then to offer guidance on her sketch. She really had come quite a long way since her first sketch weeks ago.

They worked together for most of the day, Loredana finding any excuse to stay and watch or work with him. Every hour or so, Ciro sent her into the workshop to see how Anna was getting along. The fourth time, Anna sent Loredana back with such a tongue lashing even Ciro heard it. Neither of them suggested she check again.

"She's making a really long strip of twisted gold," Loredana whispered. "Do you think she's going to use it as the border for all the cammei?"

Ciro nodded. "Makes sense to do it like that. It's probably the fastest way. Then she can make loops for pendants if she has no time to make brooches. Does she have moulds for the larger part of the backing?"

Loredana shrugged as Anna called out gruffly from the front workshop.

"What are you two whispering about back there?"

Ciro put down his tools and stepped out from behind the wooden panels.

"Please tell me you have pendant moulds to make the backings of the cammei faster!"

Her frown told him everything. He rolled his eyes and looked over at Seppe. His companion thought for a moment.

"I put them with the smaller items we gave to Anna in the first place – the things for Loredana when she finishes her apprenticeship."

They both turned to Anna. Frazzled by their sudden intense looks, she hesitated for a moment then pointed to a large wicker basket in the corner of the workshop. Seppe reached the basket before Ciro and searched through it for the required items. He pulled out a box wound shut with a piece of twine.

"This one?" he asked, holding the box out to Ciro.

Ciro untied the twine and looked inside. He kissed Seppe's forehead and brought the box over to Anna. Loredana was already standing by her side, keen to see what had caused such a commotion.

"What's a pendant mould?" she asked, looking to all of the adults for answers.

Anna looked curiously in the box. Her eyes flew open as she pulled one out. "These are magnificent! How long have you had them?"

Ciro shrugged. "Years. Decades? I don't know. Long enough anyway. Seppe can help you melt the metal and pour it into the moulds. You just need to size them up to choose the right ones for each cammeo. Then leave them to cool for a while before putting on the twisted cord."

"But what about the pendant loop?"

"Yes, yes." Ciro waved a hand dismissively. "The moulds have the first loop there for you. All you need to do is make a loose hanging loop to go through them. Do you need help, or can you get on with that while I keep working on the corallo trunk?"

She laughed, actually laughed, out loud. "Yes, Ciro, I can get on with it with Seppe's help."

"Loredana, you can watch and maybe even help them. I don't mind," Ciro told her when he saw the burning curiosity in her eyes.

She grinned at him and nodded. Ciro disappeared behind the wooden panel again and resumed his work in peaceful solitude.

***

By the time the Guild Hall clocks chimed four to signal the end of trading, Ciro had done the bulk of the work. The sea monster was carved, but not refined. He'd managed to fix the worst of the problems with the boat and refined the tentacles. He put his tools down and stretched out his back. It had been a long day. In fact, it had been a long week, and he was tired.

He stepped into the main workshop, where Anna was still busily working. She'd used the moulds for all fifteen cammei and was now fusing the twisted metal onto the backings to create a lovely border. Seppe had found the right sized boxes for each of the cammei and placed them to one side. He was showing Loredana how to line them with cotton wool for the cammei to lay on.

"I'm almost done," Ciro told Anna. "I can stay another hour or so to refine everything, or I can come back tomorrow morning. It's up to you."

Anna looked up wearily and rubbed a wrist across her sweat-beaded brow. "You're still coming tomorrow night, aren't you?"

Ciro nodded. "Ministro Ercolano has insisted on bringing me and Seppe as his personal guests. I don't know how well that's going to go down with the Mercantili Guild, but there you have it."

"Just finish it now. Then you don't need to come back tomorrow at all," she told him. "I'll try to get these all done tonight so I can sleep in tomorrow. If you're happy with it, I'll ask the Guild to deposit the money from the cammei into your vault. No, just wait before you argue. I still owe you thirty gold coins from the blank cammei you sold me. Either you take them back or the money from these ones go straight to you. *Your* choice now."

Ciro shook his head. "I don't need the money anymore. You keep it. And with the blank cammei, they can stay here for my future works. If you use them, just pay me a tiny commission for each one. Agreed?"

They shook on it, firmly. Ciro turned to see Loredana with a thoughtful expression. She followed him back behind the wooden panels.

"You're a good person, Zio. I mean I always knew you were with us, but I didn't realise you were like that with everyone. I want to be just like you when I grow up."

She grinned and allowed herself to be drawn in for an embrace.

"That, and be the best Corallina in Tor'Esint, of course."

Chapter 36 – Legaramedi 5 Musicisti 230 Years After Implosion

Ciro woke to a kiss from Seppe. He smiled and opened his eyes.

"I'm going to Anna's. She gave me the day off, but I just want to make sure she doesn't need any more help before tonight."

He kissed Ciro again and left the room, closing the door behind him. Ciro closed his eyes and was asleep again in minutes.

***

A loud shriek awoke him. Ciro hastily checked the time on his pocket watch. It was almost eleven o'clock. He'd slept half the day! It was little wonder with the hours he'd been keeping lately.

"You've ruined it!" the shrill voice screamed.

Ciro hastily dressed himself and hurried down the steps to the source of the screeching. Marta pulled him into the downstairs kitchenette on his way to the workshop.

"I wouldn't go in there if I were you," she whispered. "Looks like something went wrong with one of the orders for tonight and the customer's furious."

Ciro peeked through the same crack in the door the apprentices were using. An overweight, overheated matron stomped her foot and pointed to a plain girl with tightly curled dark brown hair and watery hazel eyes.

"I said I wanted a *gold* gown with *green* trimmings, not a *green* gown with *gold* trimmings! This is *disastrous*! Now everyone will think we couldn't afford the gold material. How could you make such a mistake?"

Greta stood beside the girl, smoothing down her skirt.

"That's not a good sign," whispered Annika. "She only smooths down her skirt when she's nervous."

"I watched her take the order myself," Marta said. "It definitely said gold gown with green trimmings. It's not like her to make a mistake like that."

"Quiet!" Sofia hissed. "I'm trying to hear them."

"Mamma, *please*. I'm the one who asked Signora Sarta to change it," a quieter, but no less shrill voice said. "When I came for my first fitting, she showed me what the colours would look like together and it was so tacky. I didn't want to look like a gaudy statue at the ball."

The woman opened and closed her mouth over and over, eventually settling for shaking her head.

"I'm *not* paying for this. It's not what we agreed on."

Greta grasped her hands together so tightly, her knuckles went white. "If you'd rather your daughter wears last year's dress for the Guild Ball, then be my guest and leave without paying. But if you'd stop shouting for a moment and *look* at her, you'll realise the reversed colours work much better with her complexion and hair. She'll stand out in a much nicer way in this gown, all the more for being happy with the dress that *she* chose."

"Please, mamma," the girl said, clutching her mother's arm. "It's such a beautiful gown and fits me perfectly. Please don't make me go in last year's gown. Everyone will make fun of me. Paulo will snub me, and my dance card will remain empty. *Please*."

The mamma's eyes widened as she realised the implications. "No, dear. Paulo won't snub you. We won't have that. If you *really* prefer these colours, then I'll pay for the dress. But next time, talk to me before you make such a rash decision."

"Thank you, mamma," the girl gushed and hugged her mamma fiercely.

The woman melted under her daughter's gratitude and counted out her coins for Greta.

"Thank you, Signora," Greta said with a tight smile. "Now, Maria, let me help you out of the dress and we'll fold it into a nice white box for you."

"That's our cue," Sofia said and opened the door before Marta and Annika were ready.

The two girls almost tumbled out into the workshop, but Ciro held onto their arms and steadied them. They thanked him and went to help Sofia find the perfect box for Maria's dress. Such a fuss over a ball gown!

Ciro went back up the stairs and helped himself to a slice of bread, toasting it with the heating rod. He'd finally gotten the hang of it and could usually make breakfast without burning an entire side. By the time Maria and her obnoxious mamma had left, Ciro had made himself presentable for the day. He walked around his room at something of a loss for what to do.

A flurry of activity in the kitchenette drew him downstairs. Domizio, Nicolina and Marta were trying to organise lunch for everyone but with the stream of people in and out of the workshop they weren't getting very far. The two Copper Sarti kept being called out.

"Let me help," Ciro offered. He looked around at the scant supplies. "Are you making panini for everyone?"

Marta nodded gratefully. "I've got to toast the bread. Haven't had a chance to go out to the pasticceria for fresh bread."

"Put this away," Ciro told her. "It won't do for such a busy day. Give me fifteen minutes."

He checked his pockets for coins and quickly exited the workshop amid a flurry of activity, women and men calling for their orders to be brought to them before all others. It was complete and utter mayhem.

Out in the piazza, Ciro headed to the northern side where it wasn't quite so busy. The tables along the footpath and spreading out into the piazza were full. He looked until he found a pizzeria which had no customers waiting on their pizze, walked in and ordered eight pizze with simple but varied toppings – too many pizze were always going to be better than too few.

As promised to Marta, fifteen minutes later he was walking back with boxes of pizze stacked one on top of the other. He could barely see where he was going and was surprised to hear Serafina's voice ahead of him.

"Zio, I've opened the door, just walk straight in."

He did as he was told and walked carefully up the stairs to the workshop. Marta raced up to him, took the top four boxes and pushed open the kitchenette door with her back. Ciro followed suit and placed the pizze on the bench where Marta had placed hers. When Ciro realised Serafina had not followed them in, he walked back out to find her.

"Rafi, what are you doing here?" he asked.

She hesitated and glanced between the multitude of customers and the rows of gowns lining the front of the workshop.

"I've come to collect the gown for tonight," she told him. "Only, I'm not sure I'll be needing it."

"What? Why?" Ciro asked, pulling her to one side. "Did something happen?"

Serafina's eyes filled with tears. "I'd asked Giuseppina to watch the girls, but she's come down with a terrible cold. I don't know who else to ask at such short notice and I can't leave them for hours by themselves. Not at night."

"Come with me." He pulled her into the kitchenette where Marta was setting out plates and serviettes. "Marta, will the three of you be staying here tonight, when Greta goes to the Guild Ball?"

"Of course," she said with a shrug. "Where else would we be?"

"Well, there's a copper in it for each of you if you agree to watch my nieces, Loredana and Tania, for the night."

"Zio!" Serafina cried out. "You can't do that."

Ciro nodded to himself. "You're right, one copper isn't enough. Tania can be a handful at times. Two coppers each. What do you say?"

Marta's eyes lit up. "Absolutely! We'll do it. I'm sure Fia and Annika will agree. Will they stay all night or will you pick them up after the ball?"

"All night I think," Ciro said, without consulting Serafina. "It's not right to wake them so late and make them walk all the way back home. And I'm certain Serafina could use a night off, can't you Rafi?"

"Well, yes, but..."

"Then it's settled," Ciro said. "I'll come and pick them up at four o'clock. I should be back an hour before the Guild Ball then."

Serafina shook her head. "Not a chance. Adamo is coming to pick me up at five. We'll bring the girls past here on our way to the Guild Hall. I promised to help with any final preparations for the big night and I won't have you tired out before the ball even begins."

Ciro waved his hand dismissively. "Fine, fine. As you please. Now, let's go and find your gown. And Marta, for Caldera's sake, make sure all the Sarti eat something."

***

The shop closed at a quarter past two. Greta put up a sign that said they were closed for anything but Guild Ball orders to be collected. She left her apprentices in charge and promptly went to bed.

Seppe arrived not long after and followed her cue. It had been a long week for all of them. While he was napping, Ciro took the liberty of setting out their clothes for the Guild Ball. He now regretted not allowing Greta to make them finer clothes, but at least they both had new shirts.

He found Sofia and Marta in the downstairs kitchen, taking the rare opportunity to play cards without Annika around.

"You wouldn't happen to have one of those new iron boards I've heard so much about, would you? Our suits are looking a little crumpled and I want to get them ready before Seppe wakes up."

He held up the wrinkled suits helplessly. Their jaws dropped at the state of the clothes.

"Ciro ... you can't wear those tonight," Sofia said in an agonised voice. "Even if we could iron out all the wrinkles, those suits are *years* out of fashion, not just a season or two."

Marta nodded her agreement, mouth open. Ciro looked at the suits again and shrugged.

"Well, these are our best. At least we have the new shirts Greta made for us. Perhaps they'll take attention away from everything else."

"They won't, though," Sofia insisted. "They'll only bring *more* attention to the older clothing. Why didn't you tell us these were your best suits?"

"I thought they'd be fine," Ciro mumbled. "We've used them for ... years."

The girls shared a look and nodded. They bustled him into the workshop and began taking his measurements.

"Girls, there's no time to make suits now," he pointed out incredulously.

They ignored him and conferred about the numbers with each other before splitting up. Marta headed towards the racks of pre-made clothing, Sofia ushered him towards the change room. He tried to resist, but the young apprentice was quite forceful when she wanted to be. By the time he'd undressed, two suits had been hung up inside the changing room by Marta who had pushed aside the curtain only far enough for her arm to reach through and not for anyone to see Ciro in his underclothes.

"Try on the pants first and let me know how you like the colour," Marta called out. "Sofia will go up to get your shirts so we can see everything together with the jacket."

Ciro did as he was told. It felt odd putting on clothes that weren't his. He hadn't ever bought secondhand clothes and Greta was the only Sarta he'd ever heard of to have such an interesting option for her customers – pre-made to purchase more cheaply or to rent for an evening or a week.

The first pair of pants he tried were just a little too snug around the waist and, though a perfect length, he found the style unappealing. The second pair fit him almost perfectly – the legs were a touch too long, but the style was much more to his liking.

Sofia returned with his shirt and sleeves already laced together and passed it through to him.

"Seppe will be joining us in a few minutes. How are the pants?"

Ciro pulled the shirt over his head and hastily tucked it into the pants before stepping out of the change room. The girls were instantly around him, inspecting the pants.

"We can lightly take them up around the hem, enough to last for tonight, at least," Marta told him. "How's the colour? Have you tried the jacket for size?"

"I like these light pants," Ciro said, pulling on the jacket.

It was rather tight.

"Stop!" cried out Sofia. "You'll rip it. Marta, get two sizes up and in navy. That'll go well with the pants."

She turned at the sound of Seppe walking in and immediately took to him with a measuring tape. Ciro smiled at the bewildered look on his companion's face.

"Sofia, dearest. I just woke up and, I might add, that's only because you made me. What's all the fuss about?"

"Seems our suits are not fashionable enough for tonight. The girls are determined to make us presentable," Ciro warned him.

Marta raced over to Ciro with two navy jackets, one with long tails, the other with short tails. "Try these on and we'll see what works best. Now, Seppe, do you want matching colours or are you looking for something different?"

"You choose, Marta dear," Seppe said sleepily. "I really can't pretend to be more knowledgeable about fashion than you. But I will say one thing – I insist on wearing my new cammeo. Anna finished it this morning, along with all of yours, so it needs to match that."

Sofia jumped up at that, her eyes aglow. "I have just the thing."

She disappeared amongst the racks of clothing while Marta fussed with Ciro's jackets. She assessed them critically.

"You're quite tall, Ciro, so the long tails look very nice indeed, if you're happy to wear them. What do you think?"

She showed him to the mirror just outside the dressing room and turned him from side to side so he could admire himself. It was quite a stunning ensemble – much finer than anything he'd ever owned.

"But Marta, we haven't even asked Greta if I can wear them for the night. And the pants are too long."

Marta waved her hand dismissively. "Greta won't mind. That's what these clothes are here for. As for the length, it won't take me more than twenty minutes to take them up for the night. Mind, if it was to be a permanent fix, it'd take longer, but just for tonight, I can do something to make it hold. Let me take the measurement before you change out of them."

She fussed with the hems, pinning needles all around both legs before warning him to be careful when he took them off. He didn't need to be told twice. A needle in the foot was not something he was keen to experience.

Sofia drew him to one side while Seppe occupied the dressing room with the outfit she'd picked out for him. Ciro took her hand and squeezed it gently before releasing it again. She looked at him with a dimpled smile.

"Thank you, Sofia," he said quietly.

She brushed away his thanks. "Well, we couldn't have you turning up to the Guild Ball in anything other than a splendid suit. Everyone who's anyone knows you're lodging with Greta Sarta, so it's not just *your* reputation on the line. Not to mention the fact that you're Ministro Ercolano's particular guests and your most recent patroness is *the* Signora Loyola.

"You've got to face it Ciro, whether you're a Guild Member or not, you still move in very influential circles. Imagine what people would say if they knew this and saw you turn up in ... those."

She pointed to his crumpled old suit, which had been discarded on a chair next to the dressing room. The disdain on her face was laughable. Only an apprentice Sarta could express such a wealth of feeling over another's clothing he thought.

He found he was mistaken when Seppe emerged from the dressing room. The tan pants and chocolate brown jacket were perfect and would set off the cammeo quite beautifully.

"Well, how does it look?" Seppe asked, looking down at himself.

Sofia stood him in front of the mirror and watched as he fell silent.

"Now, *that's* a suit," he finally said. "Ciro, why didn't we ever get any like this before?"

A loud rapping at the door prevented Ciro from answering. Serafina was already there. It must be close to five o'clock. Less than an hour before the ball.

"Zio! Seppe! You look amazing!" Loredana gasped.

Tania came running in to hug them, but was stalled by Marta.

"Let's stay over here, Tania, just while Sofia helps Seppe with his suit. We don't want to ruin it for tonight, do we?"

Tania tilted her head from side to side, then finally shook it. "No, we don't."

"Those suits are perfect for you," Serafina said from beside Adamo.

Ciro couldn't help but smile at the praise, as though he'd made them himself.

"Well, no more perfect than that gown is on you. Suits you wonderfully." Ciro said, careful not to mention anything about it being hired.

Adamo might not know, and Serafina might wish to keep it that way. After all, money had been a sensitive topic with her ever since Gianni had died and she'd been the only earner in the family. Serafina blushed lightly, and then more colourfully when she realised Adamo was admiring her as well.

Sofia came past and nudged Ciro into the dressing room. He heard Marta talking with the girls. Tania already seemed taken with her, though, to be fair, Tania was taken by anyone who had anything to do with the finest fashions or newest inventions in Tor'Esint. It would be expensive tastes for her to grow up with. Ciro fervently hoped she would join a Guild when she was old enough, and work hard at it, or she would be constantly disappointed in life.

Once he had successfully removed the pinned trousers and changed back into his regular clothes, Ciro vacated the dressing room for Seppe. Serafina was still there, fussing over the girls.

He handed his clothes to Sofia and walked straight over to his niece.

"Rafi, if you don't leave this minute, you'll make Adamo late and then he'll be blamed if anything goes wrong with the ball. Out. Now!"

Adamo shot him a grateful smile and swept Serafina out the door.

"I'll be back tomorrow to pick them up," she told Sofia.

"No, you won't," Ciro told her. "Seppe will take Loredana to Anna's and I'll take Tania to Telchide's. Now be off with you. I'll see you tonight."

He locked the door behind them to dissuade any further delays. Seppe emerged from the dressing room and turned over his clothes to Marta. The apprentice Sarti immediately set to work altering the suits.

***

"Greta, hurry up!" Domizio yelled from the bottom of the stairs. "If we don't leave soon, we're going to be late and Ministro Ercolano *cannot* be late."

"We don't have to go together," Ciro tried to tell him. "If you think she'll take much longer."

"Nonsense!" Ministro Ercolano said. "I insist. Listen, I can hear her footsteps now."

Ciro turned to the stairs and watched Greta descend. His eyes widened at the sight. Her dark green bodice and skirt were laced with silver threads and covered by a transparent layer of light green fabric. The effect was amazing.

"Greta, you look..." Domizio stalled, incapable of speech.

"Ravishing," Viviana said. "After tonight, you'll have a line of people down the street begging for gowns for their next dinner party."

Greta smiled demurely at Ministro Ercolano's companion and took Domizio's arm.

"If *that* happens, I may need to hire more Sarti."

Domizio faltered at her words. "Don't you think three is enough?"

Greta shrugged. "That's a thought for another day. Let's just enjoy tonight. I can't wait to see so many of our gowns and suits in one room."

They walked out together and bundled into the blazermobiles.

***

As they pulled up in front of the Gioiellieri Guild Hall, Ciro's stomach tightened. Seppe covered his hand and squeezed gently. It was as much reassurance as he could give. They both knew it was a risk coming tonight but, as Ministro Ercolano's particular guests, they would be afforded as much security as was possible in the situation.

Ministro Ercolano turned to them from the front seat of the blazermobile. "Ready?"

"As I'll ever be," Ciro answered.

"You deserve to shine tonight, Ciro," the Ministro told him. "I've heard what you did for Anna – the glory for whatever we find inside should be yours as much as hers."

"Cola, don't do anything brash now," Viviana warned him. "If you put this man in any further danger, you'll have more than just the Mercantili Guild to deal with. Don't forget you promised to commission me a cammeo from him and you can't do that from prison."

Ministro Ercolano gave her a short smile but said nothing. In the awkward silence that followed, the men stepped out of the blazermobile, careful not to crumple their suits, and helped the ladies out with their long dresses.

Ciro entered the Guild Hall ready to be impressed. What he hadn't expected was to be astounded. As he walked in, his attention was immediately drawn to the most fantastic lights he'd ever seen. An entire string of them decorating the ceiling in the pattern of the Gioiellieri Guild Mark. They shone so brightly, no other candles or lanterns were necessary. He looked a little closer and noticed the lights weren't flames at all but something else.

"What do you think?" Telchide came up and nudged his shoulder. "*This* was our secret project."

Ciro glanced at Telchide then stared at the lights again. "How did you do it? Is it a modification on your friction lights?"

"It's still a secret," Aveline said, one hand cradling her now-visibly rounded belly. "We've submitted it as a joint Great Work to our Guild, but the Gioiellieri Maestri were given special permission to use them before our Maestri pass judgement."

"Well, after tonight, I think your Maestri will immediately approve the Great Work," Ciro told them truthfully. It was quite a wonder to have such lights without needing to re-power them, and without fear of them burning down the city.

Seppe pulled Ciro along through the entrance. There was a crush of people in front of them, and no wonder! The table of Parting Gifts had been placed directly in front of the entrance, so everyone was forced to walk around it. Hardly anyone was looking at the gifts, though. They were all admiring the large corallo statue in the centre of the table, a sea monster destroying a boat held aloft from the waves.

The deep red statue had been polished so that it sparkled under the bright lights and showed off every intricate detail. The effect was so dramatic that even though he'd been one of the creators, Ciro couldn't help but stop and stare alongside everyone else. Sabrina's smaller fingers of corallo stood all around the main attraction, a collection of people, a few fishing boats and handful of birds and fish, but they paled in comparison.

Seppe kissed his fingers. "Now everyone will know the Mercantili Guild can't keep you down. *This* is a Great Work of epic proportions."

Ciro's eyes felt damp. He quickly dried them with his kerchief as he was jostled out of the way to allow others to view the area. On both sides of the room, long tables had been set up with delicacies from the most famous pasticcerie in Tor'Esint as well as an array of antipasti, pizze and arancini.

Spidery metal servants glided through the room bearing trays of sugar-rimmed glasses filled with vermouth. Other trays held red and white wines, and fruit nectars. Each tray had a single brightly coloured drink in the centre.

Seppe took two glasses of vermouth and handed one to Ciro. The spiders reminded him of the ones serving him in the prison. A shiver went up his spine. He sipped the vermouth trying to forget it.

"The spiders are on loan from the Inventrici Guild," Ministro Ercolano whispered, oblivious to his discomfort. "The Gioiellieri Maestri had to get my written promise that it did not constitute inter-Guild relations if they purchased or hired items from other Guilds for the event."

Ciro nodded and smiled politely, wishing the Ministro could give every Guild member a similar exemption.

"Ciro! We did it! Just look at that crowd."

Anna appeared, resplendent in a rather conservatively cut corallo-coloured gown and clapped him firmly on the back. He'd never seen her smile quite so broadly. Ciro kissed her lightly on the cheek. She did not pull back from him, nor scoff at him as she would have mere months ago.

"Thank you for letting me help you in the end. It was an honour to be a part of something so magnificent."

She didn't get a chance to reply before the Musicisti on stage played the traditional entrance song for the host Maestri of the Guild Ball. All heads turned to the entrance where Rosalina and Luca emerged arm in arm, with

Adamo following close behind with Serafina tightly holding his arm. A pathway cleared for them all the way to the stage.

Serafina stood to one side as Adamo ascended the stage. Ciro was too far away to reach her without causing a commotion, but he needn't have worried. Greta was instantly by her side and took her arm as though they were the greatest of friends. It warmed his heart to know that his niece now had some security – even if something should befall him, she would still have good people looking out for her.

The music stopped and Rosalina stepped forward. Though the three Maestri of every Guild were technically equal, everyone knew Rosalina was the real head of the Gioiellieri Guild.

"Fellow Guild Members and honoured guests, welcome to the ninety-ninth annual Guild Ball. This is the thirteenth time the Gioiellieri Guild has hosted the ball, and we are honoured to have you join us on this delightful night.

"As is customary at the Guild Ball, we have sourced the best each Guild has to offer and brought them together for your entertainment. This one night of the year, the Inter-Guild Edict has no effect. *All* Guilds are here to celebrate the year together – their successes, their creations, everything.

"We've asked our favourite Musicisti to play for you tonight, the most innovative Inventrici to lend us their newest and most splendid creations, the most talented Alchimista bartender to provide a limited number of alchemical drinks and so much more.

"Eat, drink and dance. Every member of the Gioiellieri Guild has worked hard to create enough Parting Gifts for everyone. At the end of the evening, they will be handed out at random – no exceptions.

"Should you wish to peruse the gifts throughout the evening to find the creators of your favourite pieces, the Guild Amministratori will be on hand to assist you with their names so you can commission something directly from them at a later date. Now, let the festivities begin!"

There was a loud bang, and the front of the stage suddenly lit up as though it was on fire. By the time the fires burned out, the Maestri were off the stage and on the dance floor. The music began again, to a round of wild applause, and the Gioiellieri Maestri and Serafina began the night with dancing.

"Might I have the pleasure of dancing with the most talented Corallina in Tor'Esint?" Seppe asked, holding out his hand to Anna.

She nodded and took his hand. Ciro stood back and watched them together on the dance floor with the Maestri. They were swiftly joined by other couples, vying for space. It was the largest ball the Gioiellieri Guild had ever hosted. Ciro took the opportunity to peruse the table of Parting Gifts. As a member of the Gioiellieri Guild, he wouldn't have received a Parting Gift unless there were some left over at the end of the evening. However, that was no longer the case.

Yvette stood by the table, with half a dozen other Amministratori. Each of them held a sheet of paper with a list of names and numbers. The creations were grouped together around numbered tokens. Each number was assigned to a Gioielliere for ease of identification. Ciro looked for his cammei to see if they had been grouped separately to Anna's or together with hers.

The Corallini Parting Gifts monopolised the corners of the table. Simone and Sabrina's were on one end, separated by a narrow gap. Anna and Ciro's creations were on the other with no such gap, though to the trained eye, it was obvious they had still been arranged in such a way that Ciro's were to one side and Anna's the other.

Ciro took the time to look at all of the other Parting Gifts. It was clear to him who had spared no expense and who had stuck to the two gold per piece limit for reimbursement. He smirked at the fact that it did not necessarily mean the more expensive ones were better, just more expensive. A decent portion of the less expensive items were, in fact, quite intricate in their designs – earrings with gold and silver filigree, brooches with jewelled floral sprays. They really were quite a sight to behold.

He was not the only one inspecting the table. It seemed the elite of society had walked straight past the table on their way in, not wanting to be pushed for space, but were back again to inspect the items in peace. Ciro nodded to Signora Loyola, who returned his silent greeting. She pointed out the corallo statue to her gathered friends.

"See how magnificent this is? *My* corallo statue will be even more so. I absolutely insist you come for a dinner party when it's complete." She looked across the table to Ciro's patron for the evening. "You too, Ercolano, and Viviana. You simply *must* see how talented Ciro Corallino is."

Ministro Ercolano coughed loudly. "I think we can all already see how talented he is. I've never seen such a carving in my life – you can hardly tell there were two sets of hands involved."

Viviana shook her head and pointed to the boat. "Here. There were two sets of hands here. You can see how one carved and the other smoothed it over. The same with the boat. The only section that had a single set of hands, to my eye, are the monster's tentacles."

Ciro stared at her in surprise. She turned a raised eyebrow to him.

"Am I incorrect?" she asked.

He shook his head, mutely. She bowed her head to the light smattering of applause from the elite. A moment later, they were all consumed with finding their favourite Gioielliere and taking their cards from Yvette and her fellow Amministratori.

Viviana stepped closer to Ciro and tilted her head towards Anna's cammei on the edge of the table. "I believe the most talented Corallino in Tor'Esint's work is right here on this table. It's a shame his name isn't alongside it."

Ciro ran a hand over his lightly stubbled face.

"Signora, you truly are a connoisseur of fine things. How did you develop such an eye?"

She shrugged. "I was an apprentice Artista in my early years, but circumstances prevented me from finishing my apprenticeship."

"That was a great shame, I think," he told her truthfully. "From what I've seen, your eye is so attuned to detail, your own works would have outshone every other apprentice in your time."

She shrugged again. "It was a long time ago and there's nothing that can be done about it. Who in their right mind would take me on as an apprentice now? I've lost too many years to ever regain any hope of being a successful Artista. That's not to say I don't dabble now and then in the privacy of my own home, but none of that ever sees the light of day."

Ciro cleared his throat. "I believe you're due to sit for a cammeo with me. If you're happy for me to come to your residence for that, I would be honoured if you'd show me any of your dabblings."

Viviana smiled shyly.

"They really aren't that good," she warned him. "I only ever show Ercolano, and his eye is not very fine at all. He thinks fishbones make beautiful lines."

Ciro laughed loudly causing many heads to turn. He apologised with a short bow but continued to chuckle quietly.

"Signora Viviana, would you care to dance?"

Ciro saw the hesitation in her eyes, the quick look to Ercolano and his nod to her. But when she placed her hand in his, it was with certainty and grace. He led her out to the dance floor, just as the first song finished. They took up their place near Seppe and Anna and danced the next two dances together before their own companions came to find them.

Ciro danced three rounds with Seppe before begging a rest. They found their way off the dance floor and over to the food and drinks table. Nestore was there with a host of his regular patrons, clamouring for his latest drink.

The Mercantili Guild were out in full force – not obviously listening in on conversations but straying close enough to other Guild members to make them uncomfortable. Ciro felt the oppression as much as the next person. The only difference was they had no way of hurting him further. They'd already done everything to him they possibly could. Now, he was protected by the Ministro himself.

At least the music did its part to raise spirits. The Musicisti played almost non-stop, taking only very few short breaks. It was during those breaks that the oppression was felt the most. Without the sound of loud instruments and dancing to cover conversations, the Mercantili Guild could hear everything.

Rosalina took the stage and raised her arms. The room quickly quietened into relative silence.

"If all the Guild Maestri would like to gather near the front, it's time to hand out the Guild Awards for the most impressive submissions this past year."

There was a great deal of shuffling as the Maestri from each Guild gathered at the front of the room. Ciro spotted his closest group of friends and joined them with Seppe. He was surprised to find their number now included Inventrici and Sarti as well as Gioiellieri. Even Telchide's friend, Filippo Falegname, was with them.

"Good luck, my friends," he whispered to them.

The only ones he knew for certain had submitted anything were Telchide and Aveline. It had been years since he'd submitted his last Great Work, but he could still remember the excitement and nerves that came along with it.

"I call on the Mercantili Maestri, Mauro, Carlotta and Enza to present their award."

The three Mercantili Maestri ascended the stage to a round of scattered applause, though they did not appear to mind. Mauro stood at the podium while Carlotta and Enza found the award on the table at the rear of the stage.

"The Mercantili Guild Award is presented to the person who generated the most income for the Mercantili Guild, through fees or otherwise. This year, the award goes to Fabrizio Mercante for a total of three thousand, four hundred and eight-seven gold coins generated this year. This is a new record and should be greatly celebrated."

Fabrizio Mercante strode up the stairs and over to the Maestri with a smug smile. His robes were a rich red with gold trimming covering the material in such a gaudy fashion, even Ciro scrunched up his nose at it. He accepted his award to a smattering of applause, mostly from the Mercantili Guild itself.

"How could he have set a new record?" Ciro muttered angrily. "I hardly know anyone who still trades outside the city."

"It's the barricades," Matteo whispered back. "Every fine they hand out goes directly to line the pockets of the Mercante involved. Fabrizio is notorious for sending out as many boats as he can to join the barricade. His mamma is Carlotta Mercantessa, and he has all her resources at his disposal."

"Hush, Matteo. They'll hear you," Lidia warned him.

"It's true, though," Filippo stated, clenching his metal fist. "Fabrizio didn't even want to be a Mercante when he was younger. He wanted to be a marinaio. As if Carlotta would ever have let him throw his life, or her fleet, away like that. Now she'll do all she can to ensure their fleet succeeds."

Ciro crossed his arms angrily. This was *not* what the Guild Awards were meant to be about – and reminding people of their misfortune while congratulating the ones who caused it – it was unconscionable.

Rosalina resumed her place when the stage was free of Mercantili. Ciro could see how much she fought to control her temper.

"Next, we have the Alchimisti. Please join me in welcoming Catiana, Azzura and Onorato to the stage."

The applause was much louder this time. Catiana, Azzura and Onorato took the stage, found the award and stood together at the podium.

"This has been a trying year for many of us," Catiana began. "Not only have we been continually hampered by the Inter-Guild Edict and its ever-increasing list of restrictions, but we've weathered the storm of the Alchimista trials."

Ciro heard the angry grumbling from both the Mercantili and Alchimisti Guild members at that. Even his own group of friends muttered their opinions to each other. Telchide and Aveline shared a look with each other but said nothing. Ciro didn't want to know what the two of them had gotten into with the Alchimisti Guild other than Telchide's dealings with Eduardo.

"Nevertheless, there were some outstanding submissions for the Alchimisti Guild Award this year. In the end, it came down to three finalists – Piera, Albino and Lucrezia. The winner, by an incredibly small margin, is Lucrezia Alchimista for her creation of the quickest working healing ointment ever developed for physical injuries. We have tested it on various injuries and are proud to present this award to Lucrezia for her last-minute submission."

The crowd erupted into loud whoops of cheering as Lucrezia ascended the stage. The Alchimisti Maestri hugged her and handed her the award for the Alchimisti Guild Award. She turned to the crowd and curtsied, holding her precious award aloft. Ciro tried to find the source of the person hollering so loudly over the crowd that Lucrezia blushed deeply, but couldn't pick him out. The crowd was still cheering when the Alchimisti left the stage.

Rosalina waited patiently for the hall to fall silent again before calling up Lorenzo, Mattia and Pasquale. They ascended the stage together, but Lorenzo was the one who held everyone's attention.

"You would think, in a year like this, with so many trials and tribulations, that our Guild would flounder. That our members would be reluctant to submit anything for fear of being accused of inter-Guild relations, as is so often the case with our Inventrici," Lorenzo told them. "Well, you would be wrong. Our Inventrici have worked within the restrictions and managed to submit inventions of epic proportions despite the challenges. The three finalists were Ubaldo, Aveline and Telchide. In the end, we decided to acknowledge all three finalists. Ubaldo wins the Guild Prize for his mechanical spider servants, which are already in use at the Tor'Esint Town Hall and have been serving you all evening. He receives his Silver Guild Mark for this Great Work.

"We also wish to present both Aveline and Telchide their *Gold* Guild Marks tonight for the brilliant lighting system they've developed that functions without the need for flames or constant friction winding. This will revolutionise lighting in Tor'Esint and provide safety for our town with its predominantly wooden architecture. On a more personal note, we wish to congratulate them on the impending birth of their child and wish them every happiness with their new family."

Ciro's party of friends cheered so loudly his ears hurt. Everyone tried to hug the two Inventrici, which resulted in a huddle where everyone was part of an embrace. Eventually, Aveline and Telchide managed to break free to take the stage and accept their Gold Guild Marks. When they returned, they beamed so brightly they could barely contain themselves. Ciro clapped Telchide on the back and hugged him closely.

"Your parents would be so proud!"

"Congratulations to Ubaldo, Aveline and Telchide. We wish you much success and happiness in the future." Rosalina held her hands up for silence when the cheering began anew. "Next, I'd like to invite Adamo and Luca to join me in presenting the Gioiellieri Guild Award."

She waited for them to arrive on stage before continuing.

"This has been a difficult year for us in particular. In being forced to strip Ciro Corallino of his Gold Guild Mark, we lost the most talented Corallino Tor'Esint has ever known. We can only hope his niece inherits his skill as she trains with another Corallina."

There was a long, quiet pause during which Ciro felt everyone's eyes on him. He hadn't expected to be mentioned at a Guild Ball – not ever again. He squeezed Seppe's hand firmly and stared at Rosalina, not allowing himself to look anywhere else. She held his eye and smiled fondly at him.

"Now on to the good news. We had quite a variety of Guild Award submissions this year from our younger Guild Members. The finalists, Alessia, Liliana and Arlo all received their Silver Guild Marks earlier this year for their submissions. It was a difficult decision, but the Gioiellieri Guild Award goes to Liliana for her exquisite use of gold filigree in a bracelet. Never before have we seen filigree used in such a way to create decorative balls in a chain. Quite extraordinary, Liliana. We congratulate you!"

Ciro tried to join in the applause for Liliana but found his heart wasn't in it. He excused himself and went to stand at the back of the hall. Seppe followed him only a moment later.

"It's permissible not to be happy for others, and to allow yourself a moment of sadness, Ciro. Just remember that they mentioned you so that everyone knows what happened and everyone can mourn the loss of your status together."

Ciro leaned into Seppe's shoulder silently and listened as Rosalina continued to call Guild Maestri to the stage.

"From the Sarti Guild, I call Carlo, Michele and Rosa."

They ascended the stage and Carlo took the podium.

"My fellow Guild Members, this year we too lost one of our most respected members – Ranieri Sarto. Ranieri was an innovative Sarto who would have been a fine Maestro for the Guild but for the fact that he could not stop himself from designing and producing exquisite garments. He was survived by his favourite apprentice, Greta Sarta, who herself has become a well-respected and highly sought after Sarta. I spy many of her designs here tonight and encourage her to submit something for the next Guild Awards.

"Our finalists for the Sarti Guild Award are Cassia, Filippo and Lucia. The award goes to Lucia for her introduction of ruffles to men's shirts. It was a bold move and appears to have paid off, as we see here tonight with a number of men."

Ciro watched young men adorned with the aforementioned ruffles preening themselves like peacocks. It was an embarrassment. He sincerely hoped he'd never behaved like that in his youth. Lucia went up to receive her award with a wave to her patrons.

Rosalina waited patiently for her to receive her award and for the Sarti Guild members to vacate the stage once more to introduce the Musicisti. Ciro sighed at how long the ceremony was taking. The Guilds were always called in the same order – the order of the months.

Luisa, Ludovico and Gabrielle ascended the stage to much applause. In their time, they had been the most famous Musicisti in Tor'Esint. On occasion, they still played or sang, but from the stories Ciro had heard, it was generally only at private parties for their closest friends.

As Luisa stepped forward, Ciro looked at her dress and recognised it as one he'd seen in Greta's workshop these past few weeks. Luisa waved her hands along with her fellow Maestri until the applause died down.

"To the Musicisti Guild, music is the source of life, we breathe it every day of our lives and celebrate our members who feel the same way. It is our greatest pleasure to name our three finalists this year. Claria with her most angelic voice, Santo for his outstanding performance of Ludovico's most difficult piece, and Angela for her latest composition.

"The award goes to Angela. Rarely have we seen such talent in one so young. We look forward to your career with great enthusiasm."

Angela took to the stage and Ciro started at how young she was. Like all the others, Angela received her award, acknowledged the crowd and returned to her friends. Ciro barely paid attention to the other awards, though he politely clapped along with everyone else at the appropriate time.

At the end of it all, Rosalina motioned to Adamo and Luca. Ciro saw them scanning the crowded hall and moving out into it, but kept his attention on Rosalina.

"There is a tradition at the Guild Ball, to acknowledge a Guild member who continues to exceed all expectations even after achieving their Gold Guild

Mark. This tradition has fallen by the wayside in recent years, but this year we have decided to revive it.

"This year has seen many of the Guilds suffer losses. Members have been stripped of their Guild Marks for mere technicalities, or imperfect understandings of the history of the Guild and what is permitted.

"Our own Gioielliere Guild has many facets which could cause confusion to any trying to police the Inter-Guild Edict. We all work with gold and silver finework, yet are not Fabbri. Most of us work to cut and set precious gems sourced by our Mercantili at great risk and expense."

She waited patiently for the loud whoops from Mercantili members to die down before continuing.

"One of the oldest forms of jewellery making that we practise in Tor'Esint is that of the Corallini. The rare and delicate shells and corallo sourced from the waters around Beltigura are carved with great skill into the much-desired cammei, the distinctive corallo necklaces and the decorative sculptures as you will find at the entrance of our Guild Hall.

"The skills of the Corallini have always sat uneasily between the craft of the Gioiellieri and the Artiste. Not only do Corallini create unique jewellery using corallo and the occasional gem, but they also hone their artistic techniques to allow them to sketch images and create clay models before they carve cammei and sculpt corallo branches.

"Since our inception, the Corallini have *always* belonged within our Guild, and this should not come into question. And despite the actions the Mercantili Guild has taken to force us to strip his Guild Marks on this technicality, we believe it is still our right to award one of our fallen Guild Members with this highest of honours.

"Ciro Corallino, our most senior and talented Corallino, continues to surpass expectations in the execution of his craft. We wish to express our gratitude and bestow the Tor'Esint Guild Award of the Year to Ciro Corallino for his unsurpassed work on the most elaborate corallo statue Tor'Esint has ever seen. Ciro, we hope to see a good many corallo and cammeo carvings from you in the future."

The blood rushed from Ciro's face at the deafening roar of cheers. He staggered and leaned back against the wall. Adamo and Luca were instantly by his side, linking their arms with his and escorting him to the stage. Ciro couldn't think for the pounding of his heart in his ears. Rosalina kissed both his cheeks and hugged him tightly before pinning a jewel-encrusted brooch of the Tor'Esint Crest to his jacket.

Ciro stared down at the brooch, lost for words. It seemed impossible that this was happening.

"Just let them try to touch you now," Rosalina whispered fiercely in his ear. She turned to the crowd and held her arms up for silence.

"As holder of this brooch, you are *exempt* from all Guild restrictions. Though you may no longer have a workshop of your own, or even an apprentice to call yours, we have obtained a special licence from Ministro Ercolano to establish the very first Sub-Guild – the Corallini Guild!

"All Corallini will now belong to this Sub-Guild, set under the jurisdiction of the Gioiellieri Guild, and are hereby *protected* from the stripping of their Guild Marks for practising skills common to both the Gioiellieri and Artiste Guilds. Though it will be small to begin with, we hope, Ciro, that you will agree to run a school for apprentice Corallini to boost our numbers."

If Ciro thought the cheers were deafening before, he was sorely mistaken. The very glass of the windows shook in their frames at the roar coming from the crowd. He could hardly comprehend his change in fortunes. It was beyond belief.

Which was clearly just what the Mercantili Guild thought. The Mercantili Maestri shouted from the foot of the stage, shaking their fists at Rosalina, Carlotta loudest of them all. The Mercantili surrounding her were red-faced with anger, and their fury increased as she shouted scornful words at the Gioiellieri Maestri.

Ciro watched in horror as the Mercantili Guild began to riot right there in front of the stage. As the members of every other Guild cheered loudly, the Mercantili turned on them, furious and with fists flying. Ciro searched the crowd frantically, trying to see Seppe and Serafina.

He lost sight of it all when projectiles were flung at the stage, and something hard hit him in the face. Adamo and Luca bundled him and Rosalina off the stage and to safety as the Mercantili Guild grew bolder and began to attack other members of the crowd in earnest. In the confusion, Ciro saw other Guild members fighting back – the men throwing punches and some of the women pulling out hairpins and using them to jab any Mercantili who got near them.

Rosalina swiftly took charge once they exited the hall and sent Adamo back inside while she and Luca led Ciro to the safety of a private Guild room and locked the door behind them.

"What have you done?" Ciro asked in horror, staring down at his now bloodied crest and shirt.

He touched his nose – his fingers came away sticky and red. Luca handed him a kerchief and helped him to a chair as he dabbed at his bloodied nose. Ciro looked from Luca to Rosalina.

"What in Caldera's toxic smoke have you done?" he cursed at them.

They shared a resolute look.

"We took the first in a long line of steps that need to be taken to end this accursed Inter-Guild Edict," Rosalina told him. "If the Mercantili Guild is going to play unfair, then we're going to change the rules on them so their policies have no effect."

"They'll murder us!" Ciro yelled. "They'll actually hunt us down and *murder* all of us for this. They would've killed us up there on stage if we hadn't left. You haven't helped us. All you've done is put us in more danger!"

"Ciro, please try to understand," Rosalina said as she took his hand. "We did this to help you."

Ciro wrenched his hand free of her and shook his head in disbelief.

"No. You've done this to help *yourself*. You'll make a martyr of me now when the Mercantili Guild finds a way to destroy me even with all your supposed protection." He stood up and paced the room furiously. "I was *happy*! I had a corallo statue to carve, three times the size of the one out there. I had an arrangement with Anna where I would create cammei in her workshop and she would finish them off. I was going to help train Loredana in the privacy of her workshop, safe and hidden. Now you've ruined any chance I had of hiding in the shadows. You've ruined any chance I had of a quiet life. You've ruined *everything*."

Rosalina tried to go to him, but Luca kept her away. They sat together on one side of the room, while Ciro paced the other side, for what felt like an hour. Eventually, a complicated series of knocks sounded at the door. Luca rose to open it and admitted Adamo.

"Where's my niece?" Ciro asked him immediately. "Where's Serafina?"

"She's safe, Ciro," Adamo reassured him. "I sent her home with Greta and Seppe. I thought she'd be safest there."

The fire in Ciro calmed slightly.

"How did it end?" Rosalina asked eagerly. "Was it as we expected?"

Adamo, nodding tiredly, sat and wiped his brow with his kerchief. Ciro stared at them in horror.

"As you expected? *You expected a riot?*"

Rosalina shrugged unapologetically. "We expected that the Mercantili Guild could respond violently, which is why we organised for loyal Tor'Esint Amministratori to be stationed unobtrusively inside the hall."

"Why?" Ciro asked, once again in a blind fury. "What is wrong with you?!"

"Calm yourself, Ciro," Luca said in a loud voice. "Creating the Corallini Guild was important and necessary. Had we not done so, the art well and truly would have died out with the four of you, because I can guarantee you, they wouldn't have left things alone long enough for Loredana to finish her apprenticeship and then where would we be?

"But in creating the Sub-Guild, we couldn't ignore the fact that the Mercantili Guild would respond aggressively and, perhaps, violently. It gave us the perfect opportunity to arrest as many of them as possible in one swoop. We had the full support of Ministro Ercolano. The Maestri didn't throw any punches themselves but they incited their Mercantili to riot. I wouldn't be surprised if half their Guild was arrested."

Ciro stopped pacing and stood behind a chair, his hands gripping its high back.

"Exactly how long have you been planning this?" he asked them, more calmly than he felt.

The Maestri shared guilty glances with each other. He stared at them until Rosalina huffed loudly.

"Since the day Ministro Ercolano came to sort out the problem with your frozen assets."

Ciro did the calculations in his head.

"That was over a week ago! Why didn't you tell me? Why didn't you *ask* me?"

"Would you have said yes? Knowing full well what would ensue?" she asked him. "Of course you wouldn't have. Better to do what we knew was best than to ask your permission for something you had no control over anyway. You *will* be the head of the Corallini Guild until such time as there are more members. At that time, we suggest Anna as your second, then perhaps Sabrina as your third when numbers are sufficient."

"Why not Simone?" Ciro asked suspiciously. "Not that I'd want him. But why don't you want him?"

"We ... are not at liberty to discuss it," Luca said quietly. "Simone will be given the option of either abandoning everything to do with Corallini and becoming a Gioielliere or of joining the Corallini Guild alongside Anna and Sabrina, but he will *never* be given the option of becoming a Maestro in the Corallini Guild.

"Should he refuse these options, he will be given the opportunity to hand in his Guild Marks rather than have them publicly stripped from him."

Ciro held his tongue. All his earlier thoughts of Simone being the saboteur came flooding back to him. He found he was pleased that there would never be the opportunity to put Simone in a position of power over anyone. Silence flooded the room for long minutes.

"I'll take you home now, Ciro," Adamo told him. "Your entire household will be anxious to have you safely back with them. We've posted four loyal Tor'Esint Amministratori to guard Greta's workshop. Two of them will escort any household members who need to leave the workshop for any reason. This arrangement will remain in place until we feel that you are no longer under any threat from the Mercantili Guild."

There was nothing he could say to that. Ciro nodded morosely. This should have been the happiest night of his life and, though he had been honoured in front of all of Tor'Esint's Guild Members and elite society, his spirits were lower than he could have ever imagined.

"Sali, we'll need to organise for the Parting Gifts to be delivered over the next week. The Amministratori ended the Ball and sent everyone home without them. Can I leave that with you two?" Adamo asked.

She nodded. "We'll make sure it happens. Take Ciro home now."

Ciro waited for Adamo to unlock the door and exited without bidding Rosalina and Luca his usual fond farewell. He couldn't swallow his anger at them enough for that.

Chapter 37 – Orodi 6 Musicisti 230 Years After Implosion

The kitchen was full of noise and laughter the next morning. Ciro lingered awkwardly in the hall. Greta and Domizio were regaling the girls with stories from the previous night. Tania wanted to know all about the gowns, Loredana about everything else. The apprentices were listening in with interest, especially to the Guild Awards. Only Serafina wasn't there. Adamo had taken her home last night, after bringing Ciro back to Greta's.

Seppe had cleaned up Ciro's injuries from the previous evening, but there was no way to disguise the cut on his nose or the swelling under his eyes. Ciro put on a brave face and walked into the kitchen. All eyes turned on him. Loredana gasped and quickly covered her mouth with a hand. Ciro ignored the looks and stood by the benchtop to drink his morning cup of coffee without a word.

Greta motioned for the girls to stay seated and took up the thread of the conversation again, drawing attention away from him and they got to the end of the awards. Ciro was conscious of the worried glances the girls were throwing his way, but he refused to meet their eyes.

"But what happened then?" Sofia asked. Loredana was so upset that Sofia had thrown a comforting arm around her shoulders. "Why didn't Ciro come back with everyone else? What happened to his face?"

Greta glanced at Ciro, but he only shook his head. He didn't want to talk about it – he was still furious with the Maestri for making decisions about his life without even discussing it with him.

"Well, there was a surprise announcement. Tor'Esint is to have its first ever Sub-Guild," she told them. "And the Mercantili Guild didn't react very well to the announcement. There was a bit of a ... scuffle."

"What's a Sub-Guild?" Marta asked, frowning.

"It's a small Guild which sits within a larger one," Greta replied. "Really, I think Ciro will have more details for you as the new Guild will sit within the Gioiellieri Guild."

Loredana slammed her palms down on the table in anticipation.

"Is it ... did they ... No, they wouldn't!"

She held Ciro's eyes with a piercing gaze, her trembling lower lip the only sign of how distressed she was. Ciro knew it wasn't just because of his injuries, but for how unpredictable her own life had become with all these changes.

"They've created a Corallini Guild and have made me the Maestro of it," he told her. Everyone was listening, but Loredana hung on his every word. "In an attempt not to let the art die out, I'm to run a school for apprentices, as many as they can attract. Anna and Sabrina will be in the Guild too. And you, Reda. You'll be the first apprentice in this new Guild. I'll be able to teach you, along with anyone else who wants to learn."

Loredana didn't answer immediately. Though the others loudly exclaimed their excitement and congratulations, the only person in the room he wanted to hear from was his niece, his hope for the future. Yet she was the only one not speaking.

"I was to move in with Anna today," she said quietly. "Are you saying she isn't my Maestra anymore and that mamma has to keep me at home and continue to pay for me when she can't afford me? And what if the Mercantili Guild stops this Sub-Guild? What then? I go back to Anna again or everything to do with Corallini gets destroyed?"

Ciro's shoulders slumped. "This wasn't my decision. They didn't even ask me about it. I've been thrown into this as much as you have. And, believe me, I'm as angry and scared as you are.

"I don't know what their plan is for the apprentices. Perhaps you stay half a day with me, training, and the rest of the time with Anna, still living with her. I'm not sure they've even thought about it. For Caldera's sake, I don't even have a workshop anymore. I wouldn't know where to train you. For now, we just go on as we thought we would – you and Seppe go to Anna's workshop with a Tor'Esint Amministratore escort, and I go to Signora Loyola's to work on the corallo statue."

"No." Greta shook her head. "You stormed off to your room as soon as you returned last night, but Adamo left instructions that you should return to the Gioiellieri Guild this morning to begin sorting out paperwork. I'll arrange for a message to be sent to Signora Loyola, but I doubt you'll be working on the corallo statue today."

The Guild Hall clocks struck half past the hour. Greta stood and clapped her hands.

"I know it's been a busy few weeks for everyone, but the shop will still open today. Domizio, take the blazermobile and drive everyone where they need to go, with the Amministratori escorts.

"Annika, I want you to focus on your Copper Great Work from today. You're ready. Marta, Sophia, pick one of our orders and start on a copy for our pre-made clothing rack, with different material and trimmings. Let's go."

She clapped her hands again and everyone scattered. Seppe joined Ciro in their room to prepare themselves for the day ahead.

"Loredana has a point, you know," Seppe said gently. "It was difficult enough being torn away from you and then making the decision to go with Anna. You're asking her to leave all of that again to join you. I'm just saying, it's not an easy decision."

"*I'm* not the one asking her to do this," Ciro retorted angrily. "I wasn't consulted at all. Do you think I *wanted* this? That I wasn't already happy with the small bit of peace we'd carved out for ourselves? I didn't know what they were planning and I would've put a stop to it if I did. They knew that. That's why they didn't ask me or give me a choice. They made this decision for me – for all of us – and now we've no choice but to follow the path they've laid out."

Seppe nodded knowingly. "Yes, you said. But your anger, your uncertainty about it all – that's all she's seeing. Not the rest of it. She's just a child, Ciro. She can't possibly understand all the changes that have been forced upon her and the danger she's in just for being an apprentice Corallina.

"In her mind, the most difficult thing should've been to have the Guild agree to let her apprentice with you before her time. After that, there shouldn't have been any problems. In her mind, at least. Try to see it from her point of view."

Ciro pulled on a clean shirt, belatedly realising he hadn't tied on the sleeves yet. Seppe came over and tied them on for him.

"Just talk to her. Reassure her. That's all she needs right now. She needs that as much as you do."

"I will, when I know more." Ciro looked fondly at Seppe and kissed him. "What would I do without you?"

Seppe finished the laces and laughed. "Live a lonely and bitter life, blaming everyone else for the things you can't control." He frowned at Ciro's injuries. "I'll see if I can pick up some of Lucrezia's new healing ointment for you today."

Before he let Ciro leave the room, Seppe pinned on the new brooch that had been gifted to him the night before – the blood that had spilled on it had been wiped off. The brooch was a heavy weight, not only on Ciro's shirt.

***

Domizio dropped off everyone else on the way to the Gioiellieri Guild. The Tor'Esint Amministratori refused to let Ciro out at any of the stops on their trip. He farewelled his family from the blazermobile with a promise to see them on Riposidi for lunch. It cut Ciro to the bone that Loredana barely acknowledged him as she alighted from the blazermobile.

One Tor'Esint Amministratore accompanied Ciro into the Gioiellieri Guild Hall, the other accompanied Domizio back to Greta's workshop. It was frustrating to think they would be shadowed until things calmed down. That could be weeks, months, even years! Ciro tried not to think about it as he was escorted down the Hall of Great Works.

A wave of silence flowed around him as people realised just who was walking down the hall. Ciro tried not to shy away from the hostile stares thrown his way. There were more than a few of them. But surprisingly, more people came up to shake his hand and congratulate him on his new status and the creation of the new Sub-Guild. Questions were fired at him one after the other. Ciro barely had time to take in one before the next was asked. He couldn't answer any of them.

The Tor'Esint Amministratore by his side cleared the admirers away and took Ciro up to the reception desk. Yvette swiftly whisked them into the inner workings of the Guild, up the stairs, further into the private rooms than Ciro had ever been allowed before. All the while, the Tor'Esint Amministratore stayed by his side, as though even Yvette was a threat.

Finally, she led them into an oversized room where the Gioiellieri Maestri were seated around a large table, waiting for him along with the Maestri of every Guild other than the Mercantili Guild. Even Ministro Ercolano was there.

Ciro looked around the room warily, thinking he surely must have walked into a trap. He turned to the Tor'Esint Amministratore, but the man was already standing with his back against the door to ward against any intrusion. Perhaps he'd already been briefed on today's procedures. Everyone else seemed to know more than Ciro. It was high time a stop was put to it.

"Greetings Maestri, Ministro."

Ciro saw the only empty seat was between Adamo Gioielliere and Carlo Artista, a Maestro of the Artiste Guild. He walked over, with more confidence than he felt, and took it.

"Maestro Ciro," Ministro Ercolano boomed from the other side of the table, "it's my honour to be here today, to witness the official creation of the Corallini Guild. I look forward to the many changes this will bring about within the Tor'Esint Guilds."

"I'm glad one of us is looking forward to it," Ciro muttered under his breath. Adamo elbowed him sharply in the ribs. Ciro sighed and added in a louder voice, "You honour me, Ministro Ercolano. I can only hope I live up to your expectations."

The Ministro nodded and beamed at the other Maestri, gesturing for them to get on with proceedings.

Rosalina held up a sheet of paper. "To create a Sub-Guild, we require the approval of at least six Guilds, including our own. Most of you have indicated your support for this plan. All that remains is to put your signatures to it. Once done, Ministro Ercolano must sign off on it to make it official. We've gathered you all here today to ensure this is formalised with the minimum of fuss.

"The Corallini Guild will be bound by the same rules as every other Guild, with associated procedures for apprentices and Guild Works. As it is a Sub-Guild with no money of its own, we are willing to assign two Gioiellieri Amministratori as Corallini Amministratori and pay their wages ourselves until such time as the Sub-Guild is financially independent.

"From this point onwards, all yearly Guild Fees paid by Corallini will go directly to the Corallini Guild. The Maestro, or Maestri when it's larger, will have full control over how that money is to be invested in the future of the Guild.

"We nominate Ciro Corallino as the first Maestro of the Guild, with others to join the ranks when there are enough members. We propose to advertise the new Sub-Guild to orphanages and in Piazza Mercantile to attract new apprentices."

The Maestri had all been nodding along easily. Ciro realised they all already knew the terms and were merely here as a formality. He cleared his throat and raised his hand. Rosalina turned to him with a raised eyebrow.

"Forgive me, but including myself, there are currently only four qualified Corallini in Tor'Esint, and only three who I would support having an apprentice. I don't currently have a workshop and, even if I did, I wouldn't have room for the number of apprentices you seem to be proposing. Even if we took our full complement each, the three of us together could only take nine apprentices and I very much doubt any of us would agree to three teenagers in our homes at our ages. Do you have an alternative proposal?"

"This part was *my* idea," Ministro Ercolano said excitedly. "Viviana and I have a rather large villa with many empty rooms. If enough apprentices apply, we thought to take them into our own home at the end of the day. They could learn with you, in your workshops or anywhere else that suits your purpose, then we can look after them ourselves."

Ciro shook his head in confusion. "I don't mean to be difficult, but how will that ever work?"

Adamo lay a calming hand on his arm. "It would only be for a few years, Ciro. Until the first of them achieve their Silver Guild Mark. Then the apprentices can begin to be housed with Corallini the same as with other Guilds. The only difference, at first and possibly forever, is that they will learn all together rather than only be taught by their direct Maestri."

Ciro chewed on the inside of his cheek as he thought the matter through.

"I have an alternative proposal," he told them. "What if the apprentices attend the school for half a day and spend the rest of the time with their Maestri, to learn from them and help in the workshop as all apprentices should do. This could continue indefinitely, so that the older and more skilled Maestri can pass on their skills to more apprentices.

"I'd insist that the Maestri would get to choose if any of the apprentices live with them, rather than with Ministro Ercolano and Viviana. My Loredana has been uprooted too many times now. I refuse to do it to her again. And until you have more apprentices for me to teach, I insist that I be allowed to assist in Loredana's training in Anna's workshop. It would be unfair to do it any other way, especially as I have no workshop of my own."

All eyes turned to Rosalina.

"Agreed," she said with a firm nod. "However, I think the half days should begin immediately. You may teach Loredana for half the day, then return here to continue with the paperwork and sourcing a suitable workshop for your needs."

Ciro stared at her, baffled. He hadn't actually expected them to agree to it.

"One more thing. I want you to make Giuseppe di Antonio a Corallino. He's been working with me every day for over forty years and can create the most marvellous corallo beads you've ever seen."

"No, Ciro," Rosalina said quietly. "We will not begin this Guild by bending rules."

A crushing weight fell on Ciro's chest.

"I will, however, allow for Giuseppe to be hired by the Corallini Guild as an instructor for that particular skill, if and when the apprentices grow too numerous for you to manage. Just as I will allow for Gioiellieri to be hired as teachers for their particular skills as needed."

It was probably less than Seppe deserved, and Ciro wished he'd been able to negotiate more for him than that. At least it was a recognition of his skills.

"Agreed," he sighed.

Rosalina amended the paperwork to include the agreed changes while the other Maestri spoke quietly amongst themselves. Once completed, she waved the paper a few times to dry the ink, then passed it around the table. Each Guild's Maestri read the changes and chose one of their members to sign the paperwork. Ciro's eyes moistened as he realised there would not be only the six required signatures, but eleven. Eleven Guilds backing him. Eleven Guilds certain in the knowledge that he, Ciro Corallino, was the best choice to lead this new Guild and teach an entire generation of apprentices.

The Mercantili Guild was the only one missing, and they would never have signed it anyway. In fact, had they been present, they would have tried to persuade everyone against it.

Finally, the paperwork was passed to Ciro. Blurry-eyed, he read and signed it. A round of applause brought the tears out and down his face. He couldn't help it. Despite the anger, the frustration, the *fear*, Ciro realised he was happier than he'd ever been in his life. More secure in his trade than ever and able to fulfil his lifelong dream.

Before leaving, some Maestri of the other Guilds shook his hand, others hugged him, a few kissed his cheeks – all congratulated him. When they were all gone, Ciro sank back down into his seat and stared again at the paperwork in his trembling hands.

"Now, Ciro, one last thing for today," Rosalina said. "We didn't want to discuss it with the other Guilds here in case they do things differently, but it's a matter of patent fees. You may not be aware that a small percentage of each patent fee paid for each Great Work is kept by the Guild as an Amministratori fee.

"From this day onwards, all of these fees will be deposited directly into the Corallini Guild Vault. It's not as much as with other Guild Submissions because the four of you have such different styles, you rarely use anything the other has created first. But it's something at least. It will still be years before the Corallini Guild can stand on its own two feet as most of your funds will come from annual membership fees and, for the moment, there are only four of you. If you can think of any way to grow your funds, feel free to run them past us so we can assist in your endeavours."

Ciro nodded, a little of the wind taken out of his sails.

"What of my equipment? The machines I handed over for safekeeping for Loredana. Will we be able to use those in the new workshop? Can we commission more of them? I'm willing to pay for them myself if need be."

Adamo clapped him on the shoulder. "All in good time, Ciro. We'll give Anna, Sabrina and Simone the choice of moving into the Corallini Guild or dispensing with it entirely and remaining part of the Gioiellieri Guild. Tomorrow morning, we'll begin the search for a suitable workshop for training a group of apprentices. Anna and Sabrina will be welcome to come along if they so desire.

"For now, take the rest of the day to discuss the matter of Loredana with Anna and organise anything else you need to in your private life. Such a significant change is bound to have unforeseen effects."

Still stunned, Ciro thanked them all and left with his Amministratore escort.

***

Later that morning, Ciro found himself walking along Corso delle Gilde, closely followed by his escort. He'd intended to go straight to Anna's workshop to tell them the news, but the more he thought of his change in circumstances, the more change he saw in his personal life and turned towards home. What he really needed was to talk to Seppe, but to do that, he'd need to involve Anna and Loredana or wait until the end of trading.

"Nothing for it," he muttered and turned back the way they had just come and headed towards Anna's workshop.

Along the way, he bought a handful of pastries and panini as peace offerings for another interrupted work day.

Seppe looked up from his work as Ciro entered the workshop, his eyes flicking to the Tor'Esint Amministratore waiting outside the door. His smile calmed Ciro's nerves, as it always did.

"What news?" Seppe asked. "Are you officially the Maestro of the Corallini Guild?"

Anna and Loredana looked up from their work at the question. Ciro nodded.

"Congratulations, Ciro," Anna said, walking up to kiss him. "Of all of us, you deserve it the most. Tell us everything."

Ciro handed her the box of pastries and panini and related the changes that had been agreed to that morning. When he got to the part regarding apprentices, he looked only at Loredana.

"It means you can stay here, Reda, with Anna, and learn from both of us. Half a day with me, half a day with Anna. *You* are the most important member of our new Guild. You will be the first member to go all the way through with us."

A small smile crept to her face. Suddenly, she lunged up and jumped into his arms.

"Thank you, Zio. Thank you so much!"

He hugged her fiercely, then set her down gently.

"And you, Seppe, they wouldn't let me make you a Corallino," Ciro began.

Seppe shook his head. "I never expected to be one."

"You didn't let me finish," Ciro chided him. "They wouldn't let me make you a Corallino *but*, when there are enough students, they've agreed I can hire you as a skilled instructor to train the apprentices in cutting and shaping corallo beads. That is, if you want the position."

Anna clapped Seppe on the back and Loredana hugged his waist. Ciro smiled at the tears in his companion's eyes. The recognition that he was as skilled as other Corallini in this was worth more than gold. It wasn't a Guild membership, but it was enough.

"Anna, I left the best for last. If you sign over to the Corallini Guild, you may take your full complement of apprentices as soon as we find some. They don't all need to live with you and Loredana. Ministro Ercolano and his companion, Viviana, have agreed to have all the Corallini apprentices board with them until such time as there are enough Silver Corallini to take in apprentices themselves. They'll be bound by the same training as Loredana. Half a day with me, half a day with you."

Anna frowned. "Would I need to compensate them then? If they don't board with me? Or would I need to compensate Ministro Ercolano?"

Ciro shook his head. "There was no mention of compensation. I believe Ercolano and Viviana have long wished to make use of their empty home and are keen to help our new Guild. The Gioiellieri Maestri will have more information for you regarding that. They'll be here later this afternoon to discuss matters with you.

"I've organised, from tomorrow, to continue training Loredana for half of every day here in this workshop until we have another site. The other half I'll be out of your hair, dealing with other matters. Now, if I might have a private word with Seppe? Perhaps the two of you could start on the panini and pastries."

He pointed to the box he'd brought as an offering. Anna rolled her eyes, but led Loredana into the kitchen to sort out the food. Ciro waited until they were out of hearing before turning back to Seppe.

"Well, Ciro, you've managed to turn the situation around to your advantage, I'd say," Seppe said.

Ciro sat at his regular stool and beckoned Seppe over. They sat in silence for a long moment before Ciro found the courage to speak.

"I don't know how to say this. I know how fond you've grown of Greta's girls, but I don't know if we can continue to stay there. Greta only offered us a room out of charity. Now that my assets have been unfrozen and the Gioiellieri Guild is going to help us find a suitable Corallini workshop for our school, we aren't in need of her charity."

"Out with it, Ciro. What exactly do you mean?" Seppe said bluntly.

"I don't want to overstay our welcome. If the Corallini workshop has living quarters, we might need to consider moving in there or finding our own place. What do you think?"

Seppe huffed and looked away from him. Eventually, he turned back with quivering lips.

"All my life, I've followed you. Let you dictate our entire lives. Don't get me wrong – I'm grateful I get to spend my life with you. Every day of it. But this time, I'm putting my foot down.

"I *like* living in Greta's home. The rooms are filled with laughter and life. If anything is to change, it should only be that we insist on paying full board. But we stay there. As long as Greta will have us. As long as her apprentices are happy with us. It feels more like home than the tiny quarters above your workshop ever did. I don't want to lose that at this time of life. I'll talk to her myself if you prefer."

Ciro took his hands and kissed them.

"I'll talk to her," Ciro said in a trembling voice. "I'll do it. I'm sorry if I ever made you feel less important than me. That your wants or needs came second. I never meant to do that. You know I treasure you more than anything else. I'd do anything for you. I just don't always know what you want."

To emphasise his point, he touched the cammeo Seppe wore so proudly on his shirt. A cammeo it had taken him years to create because he didn't know it was wanted.

Seppe took a breath, as though he would say something but instead, he just leaned forward and kissed Ciro.

"Come have lunch. Better to have that conversation on a full stomach."

***

Ciro and his escort arrived back at Greta's workshop just past two in the afternoon. The workshop was full of people. The apprentices were run off their feet taking orders, while Greta and her hired Sarti dealt with more difficult customers.

For any other request, Ciro would have waited until the end of trading to discuss it. But he'd promised Seppe and he intended to have the matter sorted before the end of trading, so Seppe would know he could call this place home for as long as Greta would have them.

He caught Greta's gaze and pointed to the upstairs kitchen, not wanting any interruptions or eavesdroppers. She nodded and held up 10 fingers. Good. Enough time to make a pot of tea and a cup of coffee. He hurried up to get everything ready.

By the time Greta walked in, he had everything prepared, including a pot of her favourite tea with a cup already poured and cooling. He sat on one side of the table with his coffee and motioned for her to join him.

Greta smoothed down her skirts – a sure sign she was flustered. Tea would help. Ciro pushed the cup of tea to her usual seat. She smiled at the gesture and sat down.

"I have a rather important matter to discuss with you," he told her. "Can you spare the time?"

"If I don't spare it now, I never will," she replied tiredly. "Who knew the favour of Signora Loyola and the gowns and suits we made for the Guild Ball would have us taking orders and having a waiting list months long? Now, tell me what this important matter is."

Ciro sipped his coffee and cleared his throat.

"I would like to renegotiate the terms of our boarding."

Greta froze with the teacup on her lips. She forced herself to take a sip and carefully place the teacup back on the table.

"Yes, well, your fortunes have changed quite considerably," she said carefully. "I suppose you'll be moving out as soon as you've found a new place to live. It's been lovely having you. I'm sure the girls will miss you terribly."

Ciro reached out across the table and took her hand in his. "Greta, you've done more for us than anyone could ever have expected and we've grown so fond of your household. Seppe and I would dearly love to remain as your boarders. I can't tell you how we've enjoyed it. However, I do not feel comfortable with the current rates."

"You ... wish to stay?" Greta asked hesitantly.

"Indeed, for as long as you'll have us. But I will not rely on your charity any longer than necessary. Which is why I insist on paying you a gold coin a week for our continued arrangement."

Greta shook her head. "A gold coin is ridiculously excessive. One electrum a week will be sufficient."

"One electrum for each of us, I'll grant you," Ciro conceded. "So two electrums a week. We'll help with meals every evening when we're here and spend Riposidi with my family. Agreed?"

Greta shook her head, about to protest. Ciro squeezed her hands.

"Agreed? *Please*, Greta. It would mean the world to Seppe and, I confess, I'd dearly miss living here if we can't agree on this."

She hesitated but eventually nodded.

"Can I make an amendment to the agreement though? Do you think Serafina would agree to lunch with us one Riposidi a month? She and her daughters made quite the impression on my girls, and I confess it would be lovely to have a reason to regularly invite Aveline and Telchide over. We're all so busy these days, if we don't deliberately set aside time to spend with each other, we never will."

Ciro smiled. "That's a fine idea. I'm sure we can arrange that."

In the back of his mind, Ciro worried about how Loredana so despised Teresina, but he was certain one day a month of association would not kill her.

"I've got to get back to the shop," Greta told him. "If you can help me organise the invitations, we'll have our first lunch here this Riposidi as a celebration."

Greta waited for his agreement before draining her tea and leaving the room. Ciro sat at the table a while longer, enjoying his coffee and the extraordinary change in his circumstances.

Chapter 38 – Riposidi 8 Musicisti 230 Years After Implosion

The big day arrived. Greta's household was a flurry of activity. Sofia had requisitioned Seppe, Ciro, Marta and Annika to help her make gnocchi for their guests. Greta and Domizio were on cooking duties for everything else until others were free to help them.

Greta had invited Ciro's family and her entire staff of Sarti, including Nicolina's mamma. Telchide and Aveline's entire households were coming, as was Signora Loyola, Ministro Ercolano and Viviana, Anna, Sabrina and the Gioiellieri Maestri. In total, there were to be twenty-eight people.

Ciro was baffled by how the guest list kept expanding. He'd argued with Greta over it dozens of times, but she'd insisted on each addition and would not budge.

"Where will we seat everyone?" he'd asked, when the guest list had blown out of proportion. "How will we feed them all?"

She only explained they could reposition all the workbenches downstairs to seat everyone and bring all the benches and chairs from the kitchens. It would have to do.

By half past eleven, the cooking was well underway, the gnocchi were finished and covered the entire upstairs kitchen table. They would need to cook it in batches. Thankfully, they didn't take long to cook and by the time one batch was drained, sauced and taken downstairs, the next batch would be almost cooked.

Half the household was reorganising the Sarta workshop to have enough seats for everyone. Aveline, true to her character, turned up early with Nevio. She attempted to assist in the preparations, but everyone kept ushering her to sit instead. At four months pregnant, she was now visibly with child. Greta had done a marvellous job with her outfits, to extend them enough so that Aveline could wear them comfortably, but nothing in the world could prevent people from seeing the bulge.

Ciro spent his time between the kitchen, helping Seppe and the apprentices, and down in the workshop, helping to arrange tables and chairs for the approaching celebration. There was too much to do. As soon as Telchide's party arrived, Greta ordered them into action. When it was clear there wouldn't be enough seats, Aveline insisted the apprentice Inventrici bring chairs from her own workshop to make up the difference.

The final few details were sorted out and the tables set just as the Guild Hall clocks struck midday. The doors stood wide open to receive the host of guests. One after another, they arrived and were seated. Mere minutes later, the first plates of gnocchi were brought down the stairs. Ciro headed towards the stairs to help, but Marta firmly directed him back to the table.

"It's *your* celebration, Ciro. Time for you to become a guest rather than a host."

There was polite chatter amongst the guests until all plates were at the table and everyone was seated. At that point, Greta tapped her glass of wine with a teaspoon and rose to her feet. All eyes turned on her.

"The past three years have been difficult for so many of us. But with the changes brought about these past few months, it feels like we're finally making a difference. Let the creation of the Corallini Guild be the beginning of an uprising against the Mercantili Guild. To Ciro Corallino and his new post as the Corallini Maestro."

Her words caught Ciro off-guard. He stared at everyone in bemusement as everyone raised their glasses and drank to his success.

"Buon appetito!" Sofia called out and the meal began.

***

Late that afternoon, long after lunch, and after Annika had thrashed almost everyone in various card games, Ciro took the opportunity to talk to each and every one of the guests, even the Inventrici apprentices he'd barely said two words to before. It was fortunate for Telchide and Aveline that their three apprentices got along with each other, and Teresina, so well.

"You make the most wonderful companions," Ciro told them fondly, watching how Telchide doted on Aveline.

Aveline seemed startled at the comment.

"We're not companions," Telchide explained. "Aveline, well, we see each other often and work with each other sometimes, and the apprentices share things with one another when we share meals, and Teresina's taken to spending every other day in Aveline's workshop. But we're not companions."

Ciro frowned.

"Having a companion is not about a commitment ceremony. Seppe and I have been companions for years without any such formality. Everyone with eyes can see you love each other. Why shy away from the label?"

Seppe joined them.

"It's not for you to understand, Ciro. Their life is their own to decide. And look, they seem happy, so leave them be."

Aveline graced Seppe with a grateful smile. He was right. Aveline didn't shy from Telchide's arm around her shoulders in public. Their relationship was plain for all to see. Only their living arrangement potentially begged for improvement.

Serenita, who Ciro had seen watching the conversation from her corner of the table, came over.

"*I* won't leave them be," Serenita said firmly. "I'm sick of this arrangement myself. And it'll only get worse when the baby arrives."

"Serenita, please, not here," Aveline begged her, as though for the hundredth time.

"No, hear me out," Serenita said firmly. "You both have your Gold Guild Marks now, and Telchide is finally getting the business and charging the prices he deserves. No small thanks to you there. So I'm certain he can afford to help me rent a small room nearby, where I can have my own space, but still come to visit Teresina. And, most importantly, you keep your workshop, like Chide said Kesida told you to do anyway.

"I'll be out of your hair and out of the house."

Aveline glanced uncertainly at Telchide, who beamed from ear to ear.

"I think that's a wonderful idea, if you agree," Telchide said to Aveline. "I know Teresina will be happy with that, so then we've only to ask the boys."

Ciro reeled from the tension he'd caused with his unthinking comment. Aveline looked exhausted, as though she'd had this conversation too many times. Ciro took a step back. On the other side of the room, Signora Loyola stood to one side, trying to catch his eye. Ciro gratefully took his leave from Telchide's party and walked over.

"I'm sorry, Ciro," she said with a sigh. He frowned in confusion. "That I sent you down to the clay warehouse by yourself. I should've known the Mercantili Guild would do something to make things difficult for us. When you didn't return that afternoon, or the next day, I should have realised something was wrong and tried to find you myself. I'm sorry I didn't help. I didn't know..."

"Signora," Ciro said, laying a hand on her shoulder, "you could not possibly have known. The fault was *not* yours."

He paused, not quite knowing how to continue.

"There *is* something we need to discuss, though. It may take a few weeks to find and set up a new workshop for the Corallini school. In that time, I'm dedicated to teaching Loredana half days and dealing with Guild matters the other half.

"I propose, if you're willing, to have some of Loredana's lessons at your home so she can watch and learn as I work on your corallo statue. You know, she's already seen all the sketches for it and is so involved in the process, I couldn't bear to have her miss out just because of our combined changes in circumstances. Would you allow that?"

Signora Loyola looked around him. Ciro followed her gaze and smiled fondly at the sight of his niece speaking with the Gioiellieri Maestri and Anna.

"I think that's a fine idea," she agreed. "In fact, I'll have my blazermobile pick you both up every Gildadi, Argentodi and Orodi morning and bring you back to your destinations in the afternoon. I won't have you walking all that way every other day."

"Thank you, Signora. Your offer is most generous."

Signora Loyola waved a dismissive hand. "Nothing to the generosity of allowing you to display the final masterpiece in your Hall of Great Works when you have one, after my dinner party, of course."

Ciro raised his eyebrows in astonishment. "Of course!"

She really was a most generous and thoughtful patroness.

Rosalina came up from behind and took Ciro by the arm. "Signora, I apologise, but I must steal Ciro away from you for an urgent Guild matter."

"Already?" Ciro asked in surprise.

Rosalina smiled tightly and drew him away. She refused to say a word until he was safely ensconced with the Gioiellieri Maestri, Anna and Sabrina.

"We haven't had a chance to tell you yet, but Anna and Sabrina have now signed over their membership to the Corallini Guild. Ciro, you'll need to design a Guild Mark and we'll have them made up for all of you. Of course, all three of you will have your Guild status transferred over, so we'll only need to make three Gold Guild Marks for now, but we thought it would be a good idea to make at least one of each of the others for when we begin recruiting apprentices.

"Some adolescents can be so vain when it comes to which Guilds they'll apply for – they won't even consider those that they don't like the Guild Mark for. So make sure it appeals to the true Corallini within you. Loredana would be a good test subject for it. If she doesn't like it, it likely won't work."

Ciro nodded along to the plans. They all sounded reasonable enough, but as he churned over the words in his mind, he realised something was wrong.

"What about Simone?"

Adamo and Luca coughed uncomfortably and shared meaningful glances with Rosalina.

"Simone's been stripped of his Guild status and can jump in the Caldera for all I care," Rosalina said hotly.

Ciro's shoulders slumped. "It was him, then?"

Adamo nodded. "It took a while, but we traced the connection back to him. He barely qualified as a Corallino rather than a Gioielliere in the first place, but his anger at the three of you working on the corallo statue together when you wouldn't be compensated for it was enough to spur him into action.

"He took it a step too far, though. Somehow, the ash-sucker didn't think they'd try to strip *all* Corallini of their Guild Marks. We hear he spun a pretty little speech to the Mercantili to convince them not to strip his own Guild Marks and that he even resorted to bribing them if they'd only leave him alone and then attack Anna and Sabrina after you."

Ciro shook his head angrily. "Simone never liked us. It had nothing to do with the statue. His Maestro was the worst of their generation but even *he* complained to my Maestro about Simone. How did he ever get so far in the Guild?"

"It's our fault," Luca said unexpectedly. "Not ours personally, but the Gioiellieri Maestri of the time. Corallini were never our Guild's strong point.

Without one of the Corallini as a Maestro of our Guild, how were any of us to know what qualified for a Great Work of any level for Corallini?

"It will be one of the biggest benefits of having this Sub-Guild. You can police your own members and will know, without a doubt, if their Great Works are good enough for the next Guild Mark. I'll wager you think Simone should never have moved off his Silver Guild Mark, but when there were only four of you left in the city, holding one back may have seemed more than a little unfair."

"Unfair?" Sabrina asked angrily. "He tried to ruin our livelihoods, our Guild status, and you say it would have been *unfair* to keep him where he belonged? Such soft spines!"

Ciro saw Anna roll her eyes and bit his tongue to keep from laughing. Sabrina's temper often got the better of her. He was glad she wouldn't join the ranks of Maestri of the Corallini Guild for a good few years to come. He didn't think he could deal with her so closely.

He begged their pardon and went to sit in his favourite armchair by the window. Seppe soon came over, kissed him on the top of his head and sat in the opposite chair. It didn't take long for Loredana to join them and snuggle up on Ciro's lap. He kissed her forehead and held her tightly.

"My little one, Loredana Corallina, I can't wait until the day when I get to bestow you with that name and your Copper Corallini Guild Mark. I don't know how I could ever be prouder of you than I already am, but maybe that will do it."

Loredana smiled up at him and kissed his cheek.

"I love you, Zio. I'm so glad I get to be part of your world, forever now."

Ciro's heart ached with happiness. He glanced over at Seppe who seemed to feel exactly the same way. All three of them would be part of the new Guild in one way or another. All their skills and potential were finally recognised for what they were – the future of the Corallini Guild.

Chapter 39 – Legaramedi 12 Musicisti 230 Years After Implosion

As the Guild Hall clocks struck half past twelve, Ciro walked along Corso delle Gilde with his Amministratore escort. He'd spent the entire morning with Loredana at Anna's workshop, listening to her reading and sketching alongside her. It was a relief to know that sketching was an integral part of the Corallini Guild and they could never be accused of doing the work of Artiste.

"You sure you want to do this?" Ubaldo asked.

Ciro raised an eyebrow at him. "I need to sketch the Guild Marks so I can create my own for the Corallini Guild. So, yes, I'm sure I want to do this."

Ubaldo shrugged. "Seems an unnecessary risk to take, standing right there in front of the Mercantili Guild, scribbling away. You know there's only one of me. What're you going to do if we're attacked by half their Guild?"

Ciro hesitated. "Well ... I don't know. But hopefully we won't have to find out."

He felt uneasy at the thought of going past the Mercantili Guild Hall again, especially after what had happened last time. But it was different now – he wasn't a Corallino in the Gioiellieri Guild. He was the first, and only, Maestro of the new Corallini Guild. He was virtually untouchable. Unless, of course, they managed to get past his Amministratore escort.

Ciro shook his head. There was no point thinking of what *might* happen. They began at one end of Corso delle Gilde, where the Fabbri had set up their Guild Hall. All of the Guild Halls had likely started the same way, but over time, a few of them had gained in wealth and popularity, allowing their expansion. There was no way to spread out, so the prosperous ones went up. The Alchimisti, Inventrici, Gioiellieri and Sarti had all added extra levels to their Guild Halls. But the Mercantili Guild had gone even further, making their own Guild Hall taller than the Tor'Esint Town Hall.

Ignoring the twitch of annoyance at the thought, Ciro stood on the dock side of the street and carefully sketched out every detail of the Fabbri Guild Mark. With an anvil and hammer, Ciro found it uninspiring. Perhaps it appealed more to the Fabbri Guild members, perhaps not. One thing was certain – it was unmistakable for any other Guild.

Once he was done, he moved along to the Calzolai. Ciro looked at it sceptically. It was even simpler than the Fabbri Guild Mark. It was a shoe on a last. It wasn't even an elaborate shoe, just a plain lace up.

As they walked along the street, pausing at every Guild Hall, Ciro became more and more despondent. Each Guild Mark was no more inspiring than the first. All of them were easily recognisable for what they were, but none of them were exciting. None would make an apprentice jump out of their boots to join any particular Guild. The Gioiellieri one was more delicate than the others, but so it should be for the type of work they did.

"Did you ever think of joining a Guild?" Ciro asked Ubaldo, as they made their way back to Piazza Mercantile.

Ubaldo shook his head. "Couldn't be bothered with an apprenticeship. I worked at the docks until I was old enough to become an Amministratore. The work was probably just as dull, but at least I earned a living the whole time."

Ciro frowned. It had never occurred to him that any apprentice might begrudge the fact that they didn't earn any wages.

"Yes, but your Maestro or Maestra would have provided your food and lodgings, even your clothes."

Ubaldo shrugged. "My parents provided my lodgings and the little I spent on food and clothing meant that I had a tidy amount saved by the time I joined the Amministratori. I earn even more now, so my parents can work a little less.

"If I'd joined a Guild, I wouldn't have been able to help them at all until I was on my Silver Guild Mark at the earliest. I've enough friends who joined a Guild to know that it isn't an easy thing to do if you aren't especially skilled or have money behind you. I'm thirty-four now and half my Guild friends are still on their Silver Guild Mark with no hope of ever moving past it. So, you tell me, what's the point of joining a Guild?"

Ciro stared at him, dumbfounded. He'd never before understood why anyone wouldn't want to join a Guild. It hadn't occurred to him that the only reason he'd fared so well was because he was so skilled. But Ubaldo was right. If the Corallini Guild had existed when the four of them were going through their ranks, Simone would never have moved past Silver and even Sabrina mightn't have moved past Electrum. He could only say with certainty that he and Anna would have reached their Gold Guild Mark. Did that mean Simone, and perhaps even Sabrina, would never have earned enough to live comfortably?

It was an arresting thought, and made Ciro appreciate Greta's set up even more. He'd overheard enough conversations to understand that she was giving her hired hands enough time to create their Great Works, while paying them enough to live on. It would ensure their loyalty more than any other action possibly could.

Perhaps there was something in that idea. He would need to think more about it.

***

Late that evening, Ciro stared at his sketchbook, tiredly, while the others took turns playing cards against Annika. Creating a Guild Mark was no easy feat. What was so different between Corallini and Gioiellieri, or even

Corallini and Artiste? He'd sketched a dozen ideas, but the only ones simple enough to work were the ones that could be mistaken for another Guild. They couldn't have that.

Sofia peered over his shoulder. "You're overthinking it," she told him. "What are the first things Corallini learn to make, or the simplest?"

"Corallo balls, polished branches, small pendants and..." Ciro paused. "You know, it's been so long since any of us were apprentices, I can barely remember."

"The balls won't work," Greta said, without looking up from her cards. "They could easily be mistaken for glass or wooden beads."

"Pendants won't work either," Seppe added, unhelpfully. "That could still be the Gioiellieri Guild."

"Branches, then." Sofia said decisively. "Only Corallini work with them and they're easily identifiable. Try drawing one in a circle."

Ciro huffed, but did as directed. Not quite content with the first one he drew five different branches in circles in a matter of minutes. He firmly placed the sketchbook on the table, for any casual eye to see.

"Well, one of them must be good enough," he said to himself, loudly enough to be overheard.

He tried not to notice if any of them were taking the time to look, but he couldn't help it. This meant more to him than he'd imagined. It was a heavy weight. The decision was his, and his alone. Not even Anna and Sabrina were to have a hand in it. The Gioiellieri Maestri had insisted. *They* weren't Maestri of the Guild, so it wasn't their decision.

Seppe made a big show of putting down his cards and peering at the sketchbook.

"The fourth one," he said decisively. "It's the most distinctive and the most interesting. Can't be confused for anything else."

"But it's imperfect, with smaller branches coming off both sides," Ciro protested, not really happy with any of them.

"Corallo isn't perfect, Ciro. That's what makes it beautiful." Seppe explained patiently. "But don't believe me, ask the others. Ask Loredana – isn't that what the Gioiellieri Maestri told you to do?"

Ciro raised his eyebrows in agreement, then looked around at the others. None disagreed with Seppe.

"Tomorrow then," he huffed, packing away his things. "Now, let's see if I can't win a game against Annika for once."

Chapter 40 – Orodi 13 Musicisti 230 Years After Implosion

The next morning, Ciro sat in Signora Loyola's blazermobile beside an excited Loredana. Every time they worked at the villa, Loredana looked subtly different. Perhaps she took more care with her hair, or to smooth out the wrinkles in her work dress. Ciro didn't know what it was, but she always looked just that little more presentable.

Today was no different. Though Ciro noted she had a small satchel over her shoulder.

"What's in there?" he asked, pointing to the satchel.

Loredana rolled her eyes so quickly, Ciro almost missed it.

"Maestra Anna was unimpressed that I came home covered in clay last time, so she sent me with a smock to cover my clothes while we work." She crossed her arms tightly. "I refused to wear it out in public. It's *embarrassing*."

Ciro clamped his lips shut to stop from laughing. He remembered Anna from her apprenticeship years – she always took such care with her appearance.

"Well," he coughed. "Yes, it's not a bad idea. We've at least another week of working with the clay model before we begin on the corallo itself."

Loredana leaned into him as the blazermobile rounded a corner.

"I don't get to help then, do I?" she asked, a hint of annoyance creeping into her voice.

Ciro hesitated. It was potentially the only time he would have such a large piece of corallo to teach her with. On the other hand, he wasn't certain how lenient Signora Loyola would be if Loredana made a mistake, potentially ruining the piece.

"We'll find something for you to do," he said, patting her knee. "Don't worry."

Loredana sighed loudly. He couldn't blame her.

The blazermobile's engine roared as it whizzed up the hill to the luxurious villas on the crest of Tor'Esint. Ciro was getting used to these trips. He no longer held onto the rails for dear life. It probably helped that Greta wasn't the one driving. She drove the way she spoke – like a storm, all speed and no respect for the consequences. Most times she offered to drive him; he insisted on walking unless Seppe was with him.

None of them would soon forget the day Greta allowed Seppe to drive her blazermobile. Every horse along Via Mercante had reared up and run away, carriage or no, with their owners caught unawares. That was also the *last* day Greta had allowed him to drive her blazermobile. For everyone's sake.

"We're here!"

Loredana grabbed for the handle, but their Tor'Esint Amministratore escort was faster than she was. He gave her a stern look until she withdrew her hand,

and only allowed them to alight when he was certain no Mercantili Guild members were around.

She crossed her arms in annoyance. "How much longer will you need an Amministratore to escort you everywhere?"

"I don't know," Ciro replied. "Until they're satisfied we're safe."

Loredana frowned. "But there haven't been *any* attacks on us and it's been over a week since the Guild Ball."

Ciro shrugged. "Perhaps our escort is the reason why there haven't been any attacks. Besides, how would Ministro Ercolano feel if he withdrew our escorts and only then we were attacked?"

"I suppose," Loredana relented. "Doesn't mean I have to like it."

"No, it doesn't," Ciro agreed. "Let's go inside now. I have something important to show you."

They walked through the villa, unescorted. By now, Signora Loyola's household staff knew to expect them and to trust them. Only when they were behind closed doors, with their Amministratore escort standing guard in the hall, did Ciro open his notebook to show Loredana his Guild Mark sketches.

Before showing her his ideas for the Corallini Guild Mark, he went through each of the others, to give her some perspective. He didn't want to get her hopes up for something intricate and impossible. Finally, he turned to the Corallini Guild Mark sketches and bit his tongue. He did not want to sway her one way or the other. He hadn't even removed the initial sketches that he'd already dismissed as implausible. Loredana's opinion in this matter was important to him and he didn't want it tainted by him or anyone else.

"Oh Zio, these branches are *perfect*!" she said in delight.

Ciro frowned. "No, they're rather imperfect."

"But that's what makes them perfect. This one looks like one I found with Tania last month," she said, pointing to the fourth one.

Ciro laughed. "That's exactly the one Seppe chose."

Loredana smiled infectiously. "Well, there you have it then. The fourth one it is. It really is perfect, Zio. Everyone will know it's the Corallini Guild from this. There's no mistaking it for anything else."

Ciro hugged her. "I guess it's settled then. I'll have the mould made up and order all the Guild Marks we'll need for now."

"Three gold." Loredana said, with certainty.

"*Four* gold," Ciro corrected her, "as well as an electrum, a silver and a copper. The Gioiellieri Maestri want one of each to show prospective apprentices at the orphanages."

Loredana frowned for a fleeting moment, but Ciro didn't miss it.

"I know that look. What's the matter? And don't tell me 'nothing'."

She hesitated and bit her lip. "Well, if you get anyone to sign up within the next three years, which, of course, you will, then I won't be the first apprentice to gain their Copper Guild Mark. Even if I was the first apprentice. And before you say it, yes, I know how silly that sounds."

She abruptly burst into tears, burying her face in her hands. The sobbing grew louder until Ciro thought his heart would break. He held her closely and waited for her breathing to slow back down to normal. Loredana pulled away and wiped her tears with the kerchief he handed her.

"Sorry, Zio. I know it's silly."

Ciro shook his head. "It *isn't* silly though, is it? You said it yourself – you're the first Corallini apprentice. It only stands to reason that you should gain your Copper Guild Mark first, assuming you're talented enough after the five years."

"But you promised the Gioiellieri Maestri that I would be an apprentice until I'm eighteen, just like anyone else."

"Yes, well, that was when you were a Gioiellieri apprentice," he said with a wave of his hand. "You're a Corallini apprentice now and I'm the Maestro of that Guild. I'll plead your case before them and get a new contract for you. After all, you'll need to sign another one now that you're in a new Guild, with new conditions. I'll just ensure the wording is to our liking."

Loredana grinned at him through her tears. She heaved a trembling sigh of relief and handed back his kerchief.

"Let's get messy with some clay then," she said, putting on her smock.

Ciro flipped through his notebook and found the page for the corallo statue.

***

Rosalina looked at Ciro's sketches of the Corallini Guild Mark with a critical eye. She said nothing, but passed the sketchbook on to Adamo and Luca.

"Which one have you settled on?" Adamo asked him.

Ciro coughed, uncharacteristically nervous. "The fourth one. At least, that's what Loredana and Seppe both like the best."

Rosalina laughed and shook her head. "I know we said you should get her opinion, Ciro, but the decision is *yours*. Which do *you* like the best?"

Ciro took the sketchbook back and looked at the five images again. None of them were perfect, but he'd been told enough times now that perfection wasn't the point with corallo.

"I do like the fourth one," Ciro admitted, "but the second one isn't bad either. And it might make a more durable pin, you know. More points of contact."

"Three points of contact are enough, Ciro," Luca pointed out. "If you prefer the fourth one, then go with that. We can have a Fabbro make up a mould of both designs for us to test. You never know how it'll actually look when it's cast."

Ciro waited a moment for them to decide who was going to organise it, then realised they were waiting for him.

"Yes, well, I'll just go to Angela Fabbro to organise it." He coughed again. "Is, erm, this something I pay for myself?"

Rosalina raised an eyebrow. "No, Ciro. This is something the Gioiellieri Guild pays for. Just tell her to bill us for it."

"I'll come with you," Adamo said suddenly. "Until news spreads, people mightn't trust you have the authority to use our account."

Ciro breathed out a long sigh of relief. He hadn't been looking forward to a repeat occurrence of that fateful day at the clay warehouse.

***

They walked to Angela's workshop, trailed closely by Ciro's Amministratore escort. Adamo kept taking in sharp breaths as though he was getting ready to speak, but then let it all out in a long breath without a word.

"Out with it," Ciro said eventually. "What are you trying so hard to ask me?"

Adamo glanced sideways at him, but quickly averted his eyes.

"I was wondering if you'd spoken to Serafina lately," Adamo said. "Since the Guild Ball, I mean."

Ciro frowned. "Well, of course I have. You were there too, at the lunch Greta hosted for me."

Adamo nodded thoughtfully. "But not since then? I mean, she hasn't spoken to you about ... anything?"

"Should she have?" Ciro asked, a sliver of concern creeping up his spine.

"No."

The reply was too quick.

"Adamo, did something happen?"

The Gioiellieri Maestro pursed his lips and shook his head.

"Why don't I believe you?" Ciro asked sardonically.

He watched as Adamo looked skyward and sighed heavily. "I asked if she was happy. With me. When she said yes, I asked her to move in with me. With Tania, of course, and Loredana if anything changes in her circumstances."

Ciro huffed out a silent laugh. "Let me guess – she didn't answer and hasn't spoken to you since?"

"She makes Tania answer the door and say she's busy or sleeping, when I know she isn't," Adamo replied mournfully. "I can't even leave a letter with Tania because I know Serafina can't read. I don't know what to do."

"That sounds like my Rafi," Ciro agreed. "She's worked so hard to keep her girls fed and clothed since their papà was lost at sea. Even I am barely allowed to help her. She's just too proud to accept more help than she thinks necessary – she thinks it's charity and she hates people thinking of her that way."

"But that's not why I asked her to move in with me!" Adamo spluttered. "It has nothing to do with charity. I love her."

Ciro missed a step and stumbled. Adamo immediately reached out to steady him and looked him directly in the eyes.

"I *do* love her, Ciro. I've tried to tell her that, but she doesn't want to hear it or she doesn't believe me. I don't know how to convince her that I won't leave her, or her children."

For a moment, Ciro thought to keep out of it. But he was the only family Serafina had left. The only one in Tor'Esint who had known her more than a few years.

"You won't be able to convince her of that," Ciro told him. "You'll never be able to promise her that because it's out of your control. You might not want to leave her, but I'll wager neither did her first companion. Then he was lost at sea, and then her mamma passed away. She lost too much, in such a short time. She's scared. She doesn't want to lose you too."

Adamo shook his head. "But isn't she losing me by shutting me out?"

"No. That's her closing off her heart. Trying to protect herself. Trying to protect her daughters, before it's too late." Ciro tried to explain, but knew, even as he said it, that there was no way Adamo could understand it.

"But it *is* too late!" Adamo shouted, startling the people walking past them. Ciro watched his expression soften as he struggled to bring himself under control. "She already loves me – I'm sure of it. And poor Tania looks so sad every time she sends me away. It breaks my heart. She wants me to stay as much as I want to stay."

Tears sprung into Adamo's eyes. Ciro saw him blink them back, saw him grapple with himself.

"You could talk to her," Adamo suggested. "She'd listen to you."

Ciro laughed. "Oh, it's nice you think that. But she won't." Adamo opened his mouth to protest and Ciro stopped him with a raised hand. "I'm not saying I won't talk to her, but don't go expecting a miracle."

Adamo drew in a deep breath, and Ciro with it, enveloping him in an embrace. Ciro hoped he hadn't raised the poor man's hopes. Serafina was as stubborn as Cetti had been, and there had been no stopping Cetti once she had made up her mind.

Chapter 41 – Riposidi 15 Musicisti 230 Years After Implosion

Ciro and Seppe picked up Loredana from Anna's house on their way to lunch at Serafina's apartment. Halfway up the stairs, they heard Tania wailing loudly. Ciro sent Loredana up ahead of them, certain she was just as curious as he was to find out what had caused the commotion.

By the time Ciro and Seppe reached the apartment, the wailing had fallen silent, Tania was nowhere to be found, and Loredana stood facing her mamma, hands on hips, while Serafina refused to meet her eyes.

"What's going on?" Ciro asked, placing the usual desserts on the empty kitchen table. He peered through to the kitchen, where preparations for lunch hadn't even begun yet. "Rafi, what's happened? Is everything alright?"

Serafina glanced up at him and quickly darted to the kitchen. "I'm sorry, Zio. We'll have to eat out today. My treat, of course."

Seppe gripped Ciro's hand tightly. They both knew Serafina could barely afford to treat herself to a meal out, let alone all five of them.

"*Our* treat," Ciro told her firmly. "After all, what would people say if the new Maestro of the Corallini Guild expected other people to pay for him! Now, Loredana, you go and get Tania ready, while we decide where to go with your mamma."

Loredana turned a stony face to him. "Tania won't leave her room. Not when she's in one of these moods."

Ciro rubbed the stubble on his cheek, trying to find a way around the problem.

"Loredana, you come with me," Seppe said in his quiet voice. "We'll find something nice and bring it back here. Then maybe Tania can eat it when she's feeling better."

Ciro kissed Seppe fondly and surreptitiously handed him a gold coin.

"Make it something nice," he whispered. "Something to coax Tania out."

Seppe closed his fingers around the coins and nodded. He held out a hand to Loredana, who only hesitated for a moment before taking it. She didn't spare a glance for her mamma before leaving.

Ciro quietly closed the door behind them and walked into the kitchen where Serafina was still hiding. He set about making a pot of coffee as she stood as far away as she could, in a corner of the room, refusing to meet his eye.

"We've got an hour at the most before they return," Ciro said casually. "Less, if they find a pizzeria and Loredana twists Seppe's arm."

Serafina only shook her head. Ciro didn't press her, yet. He put the caffettiera on the stove and set out two coffee cups. Only then did he turn to his niece again.

"What happened with Tania?" Ciro asked her.

"She's a child," Serafina answered simply. "She got angry with me and refused to help with lunch."

"That doesn't explain why Loredana's angry with you," he said gently.

Serafina pushed back her shoulders and raised her chin. "Loredana doesn't know the half of it. We only see her once a week now that she's Anna's apprentice."

"Rafi, please, I know Loredana's apprenticeship isn't the problem."

"What would you know?" Serafina said sharply. "I see *you* even less than I see Loredana! You've no idea what's happening in my life."

Ciro took a deep, steadying breath. "I know Adamo asked you to live with him after the Guild Ball and now you refuse to even see him. I know you've been making Tania send him away, rather than face him yourself. So, what happened today? She realised you weren't allowing him to come for lunch, even with all of us around to shield you?"

Serafina's mouth opened slightly in shock. "How do you know that?"

"He cares for you, possibly more than you know," Ciro told her. "I see him most afternoons, dealing with Guild matters. He puts on a good face for the others, but when it was just the two of us, he broke and begged me to speak with you."

"There's nothing to speak about," Serafina said, crossing her arms tightly. "And how dare he bring you into it? This has nothing to do with you!"

The coffee bubbled, forcing Ciro to attend to it. He took his time in turning off the gas stove, sugaring and pouring the coffee before setting a cup on the bench nearest Serafina. She didn't make a move to take it. Ciro shrugged and gently blew on his, sipping it slowly.

"Serafina, I know I'm not your papà, but I'm the only family you have left. I know you better than anyone else and that's why I can tell that you're terrified."

She looked at him sharply. "I'm *not* terrified."

"Oh, but you are," Ciro replied. "You're terrified that if you let this man into your life any further, you won't cope if he leaves you too. Never mind the fact that you're causing yourself the same amount of hurt by cutting him out of your life now. Never mind the fact that your daughters clearly love him, or the fact that *you* love him. You refuse to even think about that because if you let yourself, you'll realise what a huge mess you're making of things.

"Adamo loves you, and you love him. Not only that, but he loves both of your children. Just think about what will happen when they realise you've torn him away from them. They won't thank you for it. They'll resent you. Their papà was taken by the sea and there's nothing you could have done about that. But Adamo is being taken away by you. They won't understand you're trying to protect them, to protect yourself. They're *children*."

Tears were running down Serafina's face now. Ciro turned at a sound behind him and saw Tania's tear-streaked face peering around the door.

"I'm scared too, mamma," she said. "I'm scared I'll never see Adamo again, or see you smile."

Serafina put a trembling hand to her lips, to stifle the sob. She looked from Tania to Ciro, hopelessly lost.

"I'll smile again, Nia, and so will you."

Tania's angry spark returned. "I'd smile a whole lot quicker if you would just let Adamo back in our house! I miss him, mamma. I know you do too. Why else would you cry every time he comes and you make me send him away?"

"I'm sure Adamo will survive, and we will too," Serafina said quietly.

"You don't see his face every time I send him away. You don't see his tears, or get to hold his hand and see how much he doesn't want to let go. I think you're too scared to see all of that, and that's why you make me do it instead. Well, it's just plain mean! I won't do it anymore. If you want to send him away, you do it yourself!"

Tania ran away. Ciro flinched as the door to her room slammed shut. He risked a glance at Serafina.

"Don't look at me like that, Zio," she said defensively. "I'm only doing what I think is right for my family."

Ciro shook his head, frustrated. There was no talking to Serafina when she was like this – just like her mamma.

Instead, he set the table and dealt out cards for them to pass the time until the food arrived.

Chapter 42 – Gildadi 16 Musicisti 230 Years After Implosion

A package was waiting for Ciro at the Gioiellieri Guild Hall when he arrived that afternoon. He took it with him and walked through the inner rooms to where he was now accustomed to meeting at least one of the Gioiellieri Maestri every day.

Luca was waiting for him in the large study, an array of papers spread out before him. He looked up as Ciro entered.

"Have you decided on a property for your Guild Hall yet?"

Ciro put the package down on the large wooden desk and walked around to see the papers from Luca's side.

"I liked these two the most," he said, pointing to two sheets. "They both have a sizable room for the main teaching area, and enough extra rooms for private meetings or individual tuition, should that be required."

Luca examined the two sheets. "Neither of them are near the Gioiellieri Guild Hall. This one is cheaper to purchase, but it's near the clay pits and your students may not appreciate the smell. This other one is more expensive, and right in the heart of Zona Sarti. I believe you live there now?"

Ciro nodded. "If it's too expensive, I can choose another."

"We've already approved all of these properties." Luca waved a hand dismissively. "You just need to decide on one. Zona Sarti is a good location. If you have a display area for customers, you'd attract wealthier clientele closer to the spine of Tor'Esint there."

Ciro took the paper from Luca's hand and examined it closely again. "Could we look at it again, before we agree to it?"

"Indeed. But first, don't you want to see your Guild Marks?" Luca tapped on Ciro's package. "Angela Fabbro delivered them herself this morning. She seemed quite proud of her work."

Ciro's fingers trembled as he opened the package. Inside were seven shiny new Corallini Guild Mark pins, four gold, one electrum, one silver and one copper.

Luca picked up a gold one and pinned it to Ciro's shirt, next to his jewel-encrusted Tor'Esint Crest. "There, *now* you're truly the Corallini Maestro. How do you like it?"

Ciro smiled in disbelief as he turned up his collar to inspect the pin. It was perfect in a completely imperfect way.

"I think it will do nicely."

Luca repacked the rest of the Guild Marks and handed them to Ciro. "I believe these belong to you now. Give one each to Anna and Sabrina when you get a chance. We can keep the rest of them in your Guild vault until your Guild Hall is ready, but for now, take them home to show your family. I'm certain they'll be delighted to see them."

***

After visiting the potential new Guild Hall and co-signing the paperwork with Luca to secure it, Ciro headed home. It was only a short walk from Viale Ignazio to Greta's workshop.

His Amministratore escort, Ugo, allowed him to divert into a heavenly pasticceria on the way home. He knew it was Greta's favourite and he wanted to treat everyone after the successful day he'd had.

He pushed open the door to Greta's workshop with his back, hands laden with a multitude of desserts. Sofia was instantly by his side, taking charge of the packages, but her brow was tightly creased. Ciro allowed her to take them from him as his eyes took in the situation.

Serafina, of all people, was pacing up and down in front of the workbenches, wringing her hands in front of her. She caught sight of Ciro.

"It's all your fault!" she yelled hysterically. "She's gone and I can't find her!"

Ciro stared at his niece with incomprehension as she threw her hands over her face and descended into tears. He looked around to the others, eyebrows raised. Greta gently drew him aside and explained.

"It appears Tania's missing. Serafina went to pick her up from Telchide's workshop early this afternoon, as a treat, only to find she wasn't there."

Ciro frowned. "Chide just let her go off by herself? That doesn't sound like him."

"We don't know." Greta shrugged. "Serafina only arrived a few minutes before you."

Ciro patted Greta's arm and went to the sobbing Serafina.

"Rafi, come and sit. Tell me exactly what happened. Then we'll go and find her."

He motioned to Annika for a tea – coffee would only make things worse – and led Serafina to one of the large armchairs at the front of the workshop. She allowed him to, taking his offered handkerchief.

"I took Tania to Telchide's house on the way to work, as I usually do these days. She refused to speak to me the entire walk." Serafina said with a bit of her usual fire returning. "In fact, she hasn't spoken a word to me since you allowed her to shout at me yesterday."

Ciro bit his tongue. This mess was not *his* fault.

"When I went to pick her up, Telchide told me she'd left earlier that afternoon because *I* wanted her to meet me at the pasticceria today. It's a load of hot ash! I never organised that with her so I came here because I thought if she was too angry to see me, she might've come to see you instead."

She looked up at him hopefully, tears in her eyes. Ciro's heart ached at the sight.

"I'll find her, Rafi. I promise," Ciro said, holding her hands. "I have a few ideas. You just leave it to me."

"And me," added Sofia. "If you'll let me come with you."
Ciro glanced over to Greta who quickly nodded.
"It's settled then. I've already bought enough dessert for two families, so you'll stay here for dinner tonight. Sofia and I will bring Tania back in time to eat."
He almost added the dangerous "I promise", but thought better of it just in time. He could not promise that. Not yet.

***

Out in the piazza, Sofia held tightly to his arm.
"Where first?" she asked.
"Telchide's workshop."
Sofia missed a step. "Telchide's workshop?"
"Yes, I have a feeling that little girl of his will know more than he did. Is there a problem?"
"Not at all," Sofia replied, looking a little flushed.
They walked arm in arm, with Ciro's Amministratore close on their heels. In less than ten minutes, they'd arrived. Sofia quickened her step as they approached.
They walked through the door and were immediately accosted by an apprentice.
"Signore Corallino, you've brought a smile to my face with the beautiful Sofia!"
Sofia blushed brightly. "Florio, Gaspare, it's lovely to see you both again."
"You see, Rio, she's just as happy to see me as you," Gaspare called out across the room from Telchide's workbench.
Telchide looked up at the fuss and quickly rose to his feet. "Ciro! What an unexpected pleasure! What can I do for you today?"
Ciro left Sofia with Florio and walked over to Telchide.
"I'm looking for Tania. She's missing."
Telchide's eyes grew round. "What do you mean, missing? She said she was going straight to her mamma's pasticceria. Florio, didn't you take her there?"
"Of course, Inventore," Florio replied, pulling himself away from Sofia's gaze. "I took her to Pasticceria Delfina, just like she asked me to."
"Delfina?" Ciro repeated in confusion. "Serafina works at Pasticceria Mario, over in Zona Musicisti."
The smile dropped from Florio's face. "I'm sorry, Signore Corallino, but I didn't know that."
Sofia joined Ciro. "Signore Inventore, perhaps we might have a word with Teresina? We think she may know more about this than anyone else."
Without being asked, Florio ran up the stairs and came back moments later with Teresina, her lips pressed together tightly.

"Teresina, where's Tania?" Ciro asked her.

"Florio took her to see her mamma, of course," Teresina replied easily.

Sofia narrowed her eyes. "And where did she tell *you* she was going?"

Teresina flinched slightly, but her smile returned quickly.

"She told me she was going to see her mamma," Teresina replied in a rehearsed tone.

Ciro clenched his fists at his side. This girl was lying, and they all knew it. Before he could say anything, Sofia had taken charge.

"Do you know what could happen to a young, unaccompanied girl in Tor'Esint? Serafina will be furious when she learns from me that you helped Tania romp around the city all by herself. In fact, she might be so scared for the safety of her daughter that she'll refuse to let Tania out of her sight, even to play with you." Sofia threw the words into the air so sternly, Ciro wondered what might have happened to her in the past.

"You wouldn't," Teresina said uncertainly.

Sofia shrugged. "Of course, if you tell us where Tania really went, I may be able to put in a good word for you. That's if Tania's found unharmed. So, what's it to be?"

All eyes were on Teresina. The girl began to crumble under their combined gazes. She let out her breath in a big sigh.

"She went to see Adamo at the Gioiellieri Guild Hall. Pasticceria Delfina was the closest one we knew there – that way she didn't have to walk far by herself," she added as an afterthought. "We *did* think of her safety, you know."

"Teresina, how could you do this?" Telchide asked angrily. "After all the trouble we took to find you a new friend, and *this* is how you repay us?"

"I'm sorry, papà," Teresina said quietly, "but Tania missed Adamo so much and her mamma won't let..."

"What her mamma will and will not let her do is none of your concern," Ciro said loudly enough to drown out her words. Serafina's private affairs did not need to be aired in public. "If Serafina ever allows Tania to come here again, it won't be until after you've apologised for purposely deceiving everyone.

"Come, Sofia. Let's go to the Gioiellieri Guild and see if she made it there. Good afternoon, Chide, boys."

He didn't bother saying anything further to Teresina. She didn't deserve the courtesy. Sofia waved a shy farewell to Florio as she walked out the door.

Out on the street, Ciro quickened his step.

"Loredana's right," Ciro said angrily. "That Teresina is a little brat. She thinks of nothing and no one but herself."

Sofia coughed beside him. "That's not entirely true, Ciro. She must have been thinking of Tania when the two of them concocted this plan. Maestra Greta says Teresina's never had a friend her own age before. She must've felt so bad for Tania that she thought lying for her was the best thing."

He could see that Sofia was right, the child was only six after all, but he wanted to stay angry with Teresina – because then he wouldn't have room for his anger with Tania, or Serafina herself, for causing all this pain. He walked in furious silence with Sofia by his side, and his Amministratore escort a few steps behind.

By the time they'd reached the Gioiellieri Guild Hall, his anger had settled to a low simmer.

As they walked down the Hall of Great Works, Ciro could see Sofia eyeing the submissions. On any other day, he would have taken her for a slow tour of the artworks. But not today. Today, he walked quickly up the hall to Yvette.

"I need to speak with Adamo. Is he here?"

Yvette looked at him quizzically. "Didn't you already see Luca about your Guild matters?"

"Yvette, this is important. Where's Adamo?"

She frowned and checked her pocket watch. "At this time of day, he ought to be in his study. You know where it is, but she'll need to stay here."

Ciro made to argue, but Sofia shook her head at him.

"It's fine, Ciro. I'll look at the Great Works and see if I can't find yours."

He kissed her gratefully on the cheek and promised to return quickly.

Adamo's study was on the top floor of the Guild Hall. Ciro walked up as quickly as his tired legs would allow him, fear beginning to make its way through the fading anger. He knocked on the door.

"Enter," called out Adamo from within.

Ciro opened the door and looked all over the room, his eyes finally coming to rest on Adamo's wooden desk – large enough to hide an errant child.

"Is she here?" Ciro asked, not bothering to explain himself.

A guilty looking Tania peeked out from under the desk.

"Tania, what are you doing here?" he asked, ignoring the Gioiellieri Maestro completely.

Tania scrunched up her lips, scrambled out from under the desk, and stood tall. "I wanted to see Adamo, so mamma said I could spend the afternoon with him."

Ciro raised an eyebrow at that. He turned his stare on Adamo instead.

"That's what she told me when she arrived." Adamo frowned. "Tania, did you lie to me?"

Tania didn't reply.

"Don't feel bad, Adamo. You're not the only one she's lied to today." Ciro held out his hand. "Tania, come with me. Your mamma is beside herself with worry."

"No," Tania said quietly but firmly. "I won't come."

"Tania please." Ciro wrung his hands in front of him.

"I want to spend the day with Adamo," she insisted, more loudly. "It isn't fair that I can't see him just because mamma is scared he'll disappear on us too. She should have banned him from our house *before* she fell in love with him."

Adamo coughed loudly. "She fell in love with me?"

Tania turned a withering gaze on him. "Of course she did. Otherwise, she wouldn't be so scared of you leaving us."

Adamo looked to Ciro for confirmation. "Is this true?"

Ciro's shoulders sagged. He was too old to get mixed up in other people's relationships.

"I believe it is, though she didn't use those exact words with me," Ciro admitted. "But that still doesn't excuse your behaviour, Tania. After this, I don't even know if your mamma will allow you to visit Teresina. The two of you planned the entire affair and lied to everyone involved to get what you wanted. Now, let's go."

"I'm *not* coming!" Tania stamped her foot on the ground.

Ciro was close to losing his temper with her, but Adamo held out a placating hand.

"What if I come with you, little one?" Adamo suggested. "Then perhaps your mamma will be angrier with me than with you."

Tania considered it with a frown. "Why would you want that?"

Adamo shrugged. "She's already not talking to me. What difference would it make at this point if she's angry with me as well? Perhaps, at least, she might agree to let you keep visiting Teresina."

A tear rolled down Tania's cheek as she went over to hold his outstretched hand. "But she still won't let me see *you*, and that's what I really want."

"I know, little one. I know." Adamo kissed the top of her head and looked at Ciro with mournful eyes. "Let's go then. We'll take my blazermobile. No need to let Serafina fret any longer than necessary."

***

A short ride in the blazermobile took the party of five to Greta's workshop once more. Tania sat silently in front with Adamo the entire trip. She didn't even complain when they had to wait for Ciro's Amministratore escort to check for danger before allowing them to alight. Ciro saw how white her knuckles were as she held tightly to Adamo's hand, the fear of being ripped away from him plain for all to see.

Ciro walked into Greta's workshop ahead of the others but couldn't see Serafina anywhere. Greta pointed upstairs.

"She worked herself into hysterics. Marta's force feeding her chamomile tea to calm her nerves."

Adamo walked in as Greta explained.

"Perhaps I should go up and talk to her first," he suggested.

Ciro shook his head. He could only imagine how that would go.

"The three of us will go up together. And Tania," he said looking down at her, "don't even think of lying to your mamma. Do you understand?"

Thankfully, the girl nodded silently. Ciro rubbed his forehead with two fingers, trying to stave off the headache he could feel coming on. He led the others up the stairs to the large kitchen. Serafina was seated at the table, head in her arms, sobbing uncontrollably. Marta sat by her side, stroking her hair.

"Mamma?" Tania called softly from the doorway.

Serafina looked up through bloodshot eyes.

"Tania? My Tania! Where have you been?"

She held out her arms to her daughter, but Tania stayed where she was.

"Go to your mamma," Ciro told her with a not so gentle nudge forward.

Tania looked up at him with tight lips. "No."

"Tania, you had me so worried," Serafina said, getting to her feet and walking over to them. "Where did you run off to?"

"She came to see me," Adamo said, stepping into view. "Apparently, she and Teresina concocted the plan together and tricked us all."

Serafina took a step back, hand immediately covering her mouth. Ciro looked from one to the other and shook his head.

"Marta, why don't you get Tania to help you in the workshop? She can sort through your buttons or beads. I'll go out to get us all some dinner. I'm sure everyone will be joining us at this point."

Before Serafina could object to being left alone with Adamo, Ciro bundled Tania and Marta out of the room.

"What did you do that for?" Tania asked at the top of the stairs.

Ciro patted her on the head. "They need time to talk, Tania, without *you* or anyone else there. Now, you stay here with Marta and make yourself useful or you won't get a single one of the cannoli I bought for after dinner."

Tania's eyes widened at the news of a treat, and she turned to await instructions from Marta. Ciro left them to their devices, carefully deposited the new Guild Marks in his dresser and descended into the downstairs kitchenette.

"I need a coffee," he mumbled to himself.

"Well, it's a good thing I know you so well," said Sofia, pouring out a cup for him.

Ciro walked over and gave the girl a squeeze around her shoulders. "What would I do without you, Fia?"

Sofia laughed lightly. "Don't say that with Seppe around or he'll think I'm replacing him!"

"It'll be our little secret." Ciro sipped the coffee and sighed loudly.

"So how did it go?" she asked.

Ciro shrugged. "I left the two of them to talk it out. The situation can't continue like this. If Serafina can't sort out a solution herself, then maybe they can find one together. I've assigned Tania to Marta for the rest of the day. Hopefully that will keep her out of trouble."

"I can certainly help Marta keep her occupied." Sofia grinned. "Oh, and Ciro? That's a lovely new pin you've got there."

Ciro looked down in confusion. With the commotion caused by Tania, he'd all but forgotten about his new Corallini Guild Mark.

"Do you think so?" he asked, genuinely.

"It suits you more than the Gioielliere one ever did. Congratulations." Sofia squeezed his hand before walking out to join Marta.

Ciro sipped his coffee by himself in the kitchenette, quietly admiring his pin. It was lovely.

***

An hour later, Ciro left Greta's workshop to stroll around Piazza Mercantile in search of dinner for the household and their unexpected guests. He'd guarded the stairs against Tania, who kept begging for the water closet, or some other reason she just *had* to go upstairs. Her requests fooled no one, and, by the end of trading, Marta had wised up to her antics enough that Ciro felt safe in leaving her completely in charge of the young girl.

The piazza was already filled with tables and chairs ready for the evening's diners. He walked around the entire piazza, searching for something suitably extravagant for that evening's celebration of his new Guild Marks, but found nothing other than extravagant prices. It had been weeks since he'd dined with Lidia and Matteo in Zona Gioiellieri, where all his favourite ristoranti were. The narrow alleyways housed hidden treasures. Perhaps the same was true for Zona Sarti.

His Amministratore escort kept pace with him as Ciro walked up Viale Despina. He spotted a perfect little ristorante with the most mouthwatering aromas wafting out of it. The waiter caught Ciro's eye and rattled off the menu from the top of his head:

Spaghetti alle Vongole
Fettuccine Boscaiola
Penne Arrabiata
Tortellini Esinto
Risotto Marinara
Ravioli di Zucca

Ciro's head spun with the promise of flavours. He ordered a dish of each to take away and waited at a table with his escort. With so many orders, the food was taking longer than Ciro had expected.

"I need the water closet," Ugo told him, squirming slightly in his seat. "How much longer do you think it'll be?"

Ciro shrugged. "Use the water closet. I'm sure they won't mind."

Ugo glared at him. "I can't leave your side, remember?"

"I'll be fine," Ciro assured him. "There aren't any Mercantili around. Unless they've been following us all day, they can't possibly know where we are."

Ugo looked up and down the narrow street hesitantly, clearly torn between his duty and his urgent need to use the water closet.

"You stay right there," he said, pointing to the chair. "I'll be quick."

Ciro chuckled to himself as Ugo hurried inside the restaurant. Ugo was certainly his favourite of all the Tor'Esint Amministratori assigned to protect him.

He sat there for a minute or two. Then, suddenly, the world went black. Ciro cried out and struggled against the cloth over his head, trying to fend off his attacker as he was pushed to the ground and punched in the stomach over and over again.

"Stop! Ruffians!" Ugo shouted, his heavy footfalls running towards them.

The blows stopped. Ciro heard a muffled curse and suffered a swift kick to his stomach before he heard footsteps running away.

Ciro struggled to get the cloth off his head as Ugo's bulky form ran past him. He gasped for air as someone rushed to help him. The cloth was deftly pulled away from his head and a glass of water thrust into his hands. Ciro held the glass with trembling fingers for a moment before it slipped from his grasp and shattered on the cobblestone path. He reached out his hand towards the shards, but was held back by strong hands.

"No, Signore, don't worry about it," one waiter told him. "We'll clean it up. Andrea, get the broom."

Another waiter nodded and disappeared inside as the first waiter sat beside Ciro and filled another glass with water. This time, he held it to Ciro's lips himself. Much as it made him feel even older than he was, Ciro was grateful for the help.

Andrea soon returned and swept away the broken glass. As he finished, he glanced down the street.

"Here comes the Amministratore, Davide," Andrea said.

Ciro turned to see Ugo walking furiously up the street. Alone. His heart sank.

"I'm sorry, Ciro. He got away," Ugo told him needlessly. "Did you see a pin? A Mercantili pin on the attacker?"

"He threw that cloth over my head before I even knew he was there," Ciro replied, in a strained voice. He took another sip of water, unassisted by Davide.

"What about you two?" Ugo turned his attention to the waiters.

They both shook their heads.

"We came out when we heard the ruckus, but his back was turned to us," Davide told him.

"Didn't even see his face," Andrea added. "But that wasn't how Mercantili dress. If it was them behind it, they hired someone to do it."

Ciro touched his ribs experimentally. They hurt, but not enough to be broken. He looked up to Ugo with fear.

"Don't tell my family what happened," he pleaded. "They don't need to know. I don't want to worry them."

Ugo looked at him with large, pitying eyes. "I won't tell them myself, but I do have to tell Ministro Ercolano. You know how he can be. He won't let it stay a secret. Besides, they took your pin. Your family will notice that."

Ciro looked down at his shirt and fingered the tear in his collar where his new Corallini Guild Mark pin had been just before the attack. An overwhelming sense of loss erupted inside him. They'd taken his identity, the very thing that made him who he was. A Corallino.

"I can fix that," Ciro said quietly. "I have spare ones at home. They don't need to find out."

"Signore, your food's ready."

Two large waxed-cardboard boxes of pasta were set on the table. He peeked inside to see each type separated by a high cardboard divider. Ciro handed over two gold coins and got to his feet. The boxes were rather larger than he'd expected – he wasn't certain he could carry even one by himself in the state he was in.

Davide noticed his hesitation.

"Signore, if you'll permit us, we can help you. Andrea, get the spiders."

Ciro was in no mood to argue. He was in no mood to celebrate either, though his family was now expecting it. How sour would the mood turn if they realised what had happened?

Revulsion swept through Ciro as a horde of mechanical spiders flooded the cobblestones. He took a step back as Andrea and Davide placed the boxes of pasta on top of the spiders.

"You hold this and they'll follow you home," Davide said, handing him a disc with an alchemical solution floating inside it. "When you're done with them, give the disc to one of the spiders and they'll come straight back here. Marvellous invention, no?"

Ciro took the disc hesitantly. He didn't want the mechanical spiders following him anywhere, but could not refuse the kind gesture from the restaurateurs.

"Very thoughtful of you," Ciro said half-heartedly.

Davide grasped his shoulder in sympathy. "It's the least we could do. Safe journey home, Signore."

Ciro smiled out of habit and began the slow and painful walk home with Ugo, straightening his clothes and running a hand through his hair to try to make himself presentable again. Evening revellers in their glamorous outfits made way for them with gasps of delight and wonder. Everyone was used to the mechanical spiders that lit the gas street lanterns every evening, and some may have seen their use at various other functions such as the Guild Balls, but sightings in these numbers was rare indeed.

As they crossed the piazza to Great's workshop, Ciro turned to Ugo.

"Not a word, remember."

"Greta Sarta is not my employer. I've no obligation to tell her," Ugo replied easily. "But you should tell her. And Seppe. They've a right to know. What if one of them was with you when it happened? You think they wouldn't have been attacked alongside you?"

Ciro missed a step. He hadn't even thought of that. "You don't really think they would stoop so low, do you?"

Ugo raised an eyebrow. "They stooped low enough to beat a vecchietto, didn't they?"

"Vecchietto indeed," Ciro scoffed. "I'm barely seventy."

Ugo whistled through his teeth. "As old as that, really? Well, you take my point, then."

Ciro sighed. "I'll think about it. But if they're going to find out, *I* want to be the one to tell them. Not you. Understand?"

Ugo held up his hands in defeat. It was a foolish argument and Ciro knew it. His ribs ached so much he couldn't breathe deeply – there were bound to be bruises all over his torso. There was no way Seppe would miss that when they went to bed.

The door opened and Loredana ran out to greet them, cooing over the mechanical spiders.

"What are you doing here?" Ciro asked, startled at the sight of her.

"Greta sent Domizio to pick us up for dinner. Anna's here too."

"Well then, make yourself useful and take the pasta inside. Good thing I bought extra."

Loredana called for help and Tania came running with Marta and Sofia at her heels. Together, the four of them took the boxes inside. Ciro couldn't help but notice Ugo keenly watching the piazza for further signs of attack. For the first time, he didn't think it was a waste of time.

With a heavy sigh, Ciro handed the circular disc to the closest mechanical spider and watched as they scurried away across the piazza, startling onlookers with their unpredictable movements.

"Send Ubaldo out," Ugo instructed Ciro as he walked up the stairs. "One of us needs to alert Ministro Ercolano of the attack. Don't be surprised if you end up with more escorts after this."

Ciro nodded unhappily. As he entered the workshop, he caught Ubaldo's eye and signalled him to go out. Thankfully, it was a fairly regular routine for the escorts to come and go from the workshop and no one paid him any attention. With the commotion brought about by extra visitors, only Seppe and Sofia took any notice of Ciro – the others were already heading upstairs. His companion's eyes went straight to his ripped shirt collar, and Sofia's weren't far behind.

"Greta let you out with a ripped shirt?" Seppe asked in surprise, giving Ciro a kiss.

Sofia stood back, arms crossed. "No, and his new pin's missing."

Seppe pulled back from Ciro and eyed him closely. "What happened, Ciro?"

"It's nothing," Ciro said, waving his hand impatiently. "Let's go upstairs. I'll quickly wash up and join you for dinner."

At that moment, Ubaldo re-entered the workshop, locking the door behind him, and began closing all the blinds. Seppe raised an eyebrow and turned back to Ciro.

"Don't give me *nothing*," he said angrily. "Something happened. What was it?"

"Some ruffian stole my new pin is all," Ciro lied. It felt so wrong, but he didn't want to worry them.

Seppe kept his eyes firmly on Ciro. "Sofia, be a good girl and go upstairs. Tell them we'll join them momentarily. I'll help Ciro make himself presentable."

Ciro could see she wanted to stay, but no one could withstand the polite firmness of Seppe when he was in one of his moods. They waited in silence until Sofia was out of earshot.

"I've spent almost my entire life with you, Ciro. Do you really think I don't know when you're lying?" Seppe asked angrily. "If something happened to you, then I want to know. I have a *right* to know. So you tell me, and you tell me now. You hear me?"

"I was attacked," Ciro told him quietly. He watched the blood drain from Seppe's face, leaving it a sickly shade of grey. "Let's go upstairs so I can change."

He walked slowly up the stairs and left the door to their room slightly ajar for Seppe to follow him. Painstakingly, Ciro took his ripped shirt off and lay it on the bed. He'd need to ask someone to fix it. Perhaps Sofia would ask less questions than the others. Perhaps she'd want to ask more, but she wouldn't – not if he asked for her silence.

"Why would you lie about something like this?" Seppe asked, locking the door behind him. "And where was Ugo when it happened?"

Ciro chose a new shirt from his dresser, trying not to catch a glimpse of his quickly bruising torso in the mirror in the corner of the room.

"It happened so fast," Ciro said, buttoning his shirt. "Ugo only stepped inside the ristorante for a minute or two. Even the waiters didn't have time to react before the attacker was on me."

Seppe sat on the edge of the bed, fists clenched uselessly by his side.

"Was it the Mercantili Guild?"

Ciro shrugged. "Probably. Otherwise, why would he have stolen my pin? But Ugo didn't catch him, so I suppose we'll never know."

"And you wanted to hide this from everyone, from *me*?" Seppe asked incredulously. "Have you not understood, after all this time, how much you mean to me? Did you really think this was something you could hide? Just look at your chest, Ciro! Look at the fear in your eyes. You think I can't see it?"

Ciro's fingers trembled as he struggled with his buttons. Seppe stood in front of him, buttoning his shirt, covering the bruises.

"I see everything, Ciro," Seppe said quietly. "You can't keep things like this to yourself. Aside from the fact that concealing this would allow the Mercantili Guild to get away with it, not telling everyone close to you could put us all in danger. I know you don't want that."

Ciro opened the dresser drawer and pulled out the box containing the new Corallini Guild Mark pins and showed Seppe.

"Tonight was supposed to be a celebration. I got my new pin, and I was going to give Anna and Sabrina theirs tomorrow. I didn't want to bring the mood down."

Seppe chose a gold Guild Mark and pinned it to Ciro's shirt.

"It will still be a celebration. Look how rattled the Mercantili Guild is getting and you are part of that. Surely, this can only mean we're getting closer to the end of these smoking edicts." Seppe cupped Ciro's face in his hands. "Now, let's join the others. You can give Anna her pin, and order a new one for Sabrina tomorrow."

Ciro held Seppe's hand against his cheek and leaned into it. Somehow, no matter how bad things got, Seppe was always there, talking reason to him.

"What would I do without you?" he asked.

Seppe scoffed. "Don't you give me that – I know you say the same thing to young Fia now."

Ciro smiled. Even with the chaos surrounding them, Seppe could always bring some semblance of calm and normality to their lives.

***

The kitchen was a hive of activity. Plates changed hands as they were filled with the different pastas. Chianti flowed into glasses for the adults and fruit nectars for the children and apprentices.

Ciro looked around the room, full of his closest family and friends all getting along together. The people he now couldn't imagine living without. Even Serafina and Adamo must have reached some sort of agreement. They weren't sitting next to each other, but only Tania separated them. Loredana chose to sit next to Sofia. Ciro was glad the two of them got along so well, despite the difference in age.

"Ciro, Seppe, we made up plates for you," Greta told them, pointing to the last two free seats.

Before joining Seppe at their places, Ciro walked over to Anna and pinned her new Gold Guild Mark to her bodice. The room fell silent, as everyone tried to get a look at the newest Guild Mark in Tor'Esint.

Ciro sat at his seat and received a pointed look from Seppe. He sighed heavily and squared his shoulders, regretting the action as he winced in pain.

"Today, we celebrate the creation of the new Corallini Guild Mark," Ciro said to a round of applause and cheering. He held up his hand for quiet. "As joyous as this moment is, I should let you know that I was assaulted this evening. Ugo has gone to alert Ministro Ercolano, and he assumes our protection will be doubled."

There was a long and deafening silence.

"I'll need to alert the other Gioiellieri Maestri. Was it the Mercantili Guild?" Adamo asked.

"Never mind that." Anna waved aside the question. "Were you hurt?"

Ciro shrugged. "Bruised is all. And they stole my Guild Mark pin. Sorry, Adamo, but we'll need to order another gold one for Sabrina."

"Then it *was* the Mercantili Guild," Adamo said, his fist slamming on the table. "We won't stand for it!"

"Did you see their faces?" Greta asked. "Can we prove it was the Mercantili?"

Ciro shook his head. "Listen, I don't want to dwell on the attack. It won't happen again, especially if our security is doubled. The more important news is that we've chosen a site for the new Corallini Guild Hall. It should be ready in a few weeks. Two at the most."

"That's exciting," Loredana said, with a forced smile. "Where is it?"

Ciro loved her for trying to lighten the mood.

"Not far from here, actually. If Anna agrees, you can come to see it tomorrow morning. I'll be spending every afternoon there, making sure the Falegname does everything to my exact specifications."

Loredana looked across the table at Anna with large, pleading eyes. Anna grinned and shook her head.

"I suppose we can take a quick look tomorrow morning, before trading."

"I'll send my blazermobile around for you and Loredana," Adamo offered. "Then he can take you all back together for your morning's work."

"That's not necessary," Anna said, shaking her head.

"I insist," replied Adamo firmly. "I couldn't possibly live with myself if the two of you were attacked on the way to the Corallini Guild Hall without an escort, so soon after an attack on the Corallini Maestro."

Ciro didn't miss the small smile on Serafina's lips at the care Adamo took of her daughter.

"Very well," Anna agreed. "We'll be ready for your blazermobile at seven o'clock."

"Then it's settled," Greta said with a clap of her hands. "Now, let's finish this pasta before it gets cold. And I can see Tania already eyeing the cannoli."

Chapter 43 – Ramedi 17 Musicisti 230 Years After Implosion

Ciro unlocked the doors to their new Guild Hall and let the others in. Anna had insisted that Sabrina be shown as well, but Ciro had refused. She would only have been annoyed at the fact that Ciro and Anna both had their Gold Guild Marks and, because of the attack yesterday, she was still without her own. As soon as he'd made that point, Anna had backed down. They both knew what Sabrina was like.

"It's ... a bit bare," said Loredana, her voice echoing around the room, "and a bit small for a Guild Hall."

Ciro tried to see it from her viewpoint. It *was* much smaller than other Guild Halls, but there were only the four of them for now, three without counting Seppe.

"This room will be split into a few areas including the display area, equivalent to the Hall of Great Works in other Guild Halls. I'll discuss it with the Gioiellieri Maestri, but I think it would be best to bring the Great Works of all Corallini here, not just ours. What do you think?"

Anna startled at the question. "Well, yes, if you think you can convince them. It makes sense. But how will the room be split? Will you have cabinets built?"

"No, I thought to put up a wall," Ciro replied uncertainly. "Do you not think that the best idea?"

Anna shrugged. "That's up to you, and the Gioiellieri Maestri of course. It would be more expensive than cabinets. What will be on the other side?"

Ciro moved into another section of the room. "I thought to put a row of workstations here and then line up the machines on the wall there, so they'd be out of the way. There are private rooms for meetings or more specific training back there."

His mind was a tempest of ideas, each vying for his attention. There were endless possibilities, and the decisions were all his to make.

"That sounds like a lot of work," Anna ventured.

Ciro rubbed behind his neck. "Yes, well, we've been doing something every day to get things ready. Now that we have our building, we can put all of our plans in motion. I hope to have it up and running in two weeks, three at the most. All the other Guilds are dropping everything else to help us. They all see it as their way of sticking it to the Mercantili Guild."

Ciro paused, suddenly feeling suffocated, like the cloth was over his head again. He couldn't breathe – couldn't see. He felt Seppe's hands holding his own.

"You're safe, Ciro," Seppe's calm, reassuring voice told him. "Ugo and Ubaldo are standing guard at the door. The Mercantili cannot get you here."

Ciro listened to his words and fought his way back to the surface. He blinked and saw Seppe's light brown eyes focused on his own. A deep breath, then another, and he steadied himself.

Anna had bundled Loredana to another part of the room, but his niece was peeking at him from behind her maestra, sharp concern written on her face.

"Zio, what did they do to you last night?" she asked, her question echoing off the walls.

"Not enough to stop me," Ciro said, more bravely than he felt. "I think it's time we headed back now, or we'll miss our time together this morning."

***

A pair of Tor'Esint Amministratori arrived at Anna's workshop, just as Ciro was leaving.

"What's this?" Anna asked, coming to the door.

"Ministro Ercolano's orders," Ugo informed them. "From now on, two Tor'Esint Amministratori will guard the Corallini workshops and Greta Sarta's workshop. Another two will shadow Ciro at all times."

Anna placed her hands on her hips angrily. "That's ridiculous! The Mercantili Guild wouldn't dare attack our workshops."

"I thought they wouldn't really attack me either," Ciro said quietly. "I'm sure Ministro Ercolano just wants to keep us safe, Anna. At least until this whole situation settles down. I wouldn't be arguing against it if I were you. Not now."

Anna looked him in the eye and her resolve melted. All of them had thought the protection was unnecessary. All of them had argued against it in the first place.

"Very well," Anna relented. "Just mind you don't scare off my customers."

The new Amministratori brushed off her comment and turned to face the street. Ciro felt happier leaving Anna's workshop with them there. He hadn't realised until this morning just how much the attack had rattled him.

***

All three Gioiellieri Maestri were waiting for him at the Guild Hall. So was Ministro Ercolano. Ciro's heart caught in his throat at the sight of them all looking so grim.

Ministro Ercolano came forward and grasped his hand tightly. "It's so good to see you, Ciro. When I heard about the assault, I feared the worst."

"I'm sure Ugo exaggerated when he explained," Ciro waved aside his concern. "It was nothing." He tried to glare at Ugo, but the Amministratore refused to meet his eye.

Adamo coughed. "Ciro, I saw how rattled you were last night. It was not *nothing*."

"I admit, the attacker caught me unawares, but they only left behind bruises, that's all."

"And they stole your Gold Guild Mark pin," Luca pointed out. "The one that only just arrived yesterday. They must be spying on us to know that."

Ciro nodded. There was no point denying it.

"I suppose we'll need to order a new one. I can pay for it myself. After all, I'm the one who lost it."

"You'll do no such thing," Rosalina said firmly. "We'll order another gold pin and charge the Mercantili Guild for it."

Ercolano coughed. "Sali, I know we all suspect the Mercantili are behind this, but we have no proof. If we did, then there'd be a more severe punishment than simply paying for a new pin."

She clenched her fists tightly. "Then what do you plan to do about it? Increasing their protection won't solve the problem, Ercolano. The Mercantili need to know they won't get away with this."

"What about the Alchimisti Trials?" Ciro asked, recalling something Greta had mentioned. "Did your accountants find anything in the Mercantili ledgers regarding the alchemically-dyed material?"

Ercolano sighed heavily. "Not yet. There are so many Mercantili records. We managed to stop them from destroying any records within the Guild Hall, but if any of them kept records at home, they'll be lost to us by now.

"Every day, my accountants spend hours poring through their records. If there's something there, they'll find it. I hope."

"Hope is not good enough," Rosalina told him. "We need a way to end these edicts, to end their stranglehold on Tor'Esint. The Guilds aren't the only ones in their grip, you know. Prices for everything but fish seem to have soared. How is anyone to afford the cost of living?"

Ercolano stared at her in shock. "I hope you're not implying that I can be bought. After everything I've done to help! Have you any idea how dangerous it was for me to stick my neck out during the Alchimisti trials? Or to release Ciro from prison and support the creation of the Corallini Guild?

"Don't you dare suggest I'm not doing enough! I'm doing more than my fair share. Maybe the Guilds should be doing more to help their own situation."

Adamo caught Rosalina's hand before she managed to slap Ercolano.

"Sali, he's doing all he can and so are we," he added pointedly. "There's little more the Guilds can do."

Ercolano pursed his lips. Ciro could tell he wanted to say more, but perhaps he couldn't.

"I have an idea," Ciro said slowly, "but it might be best to keep it within the Guilds. Sorry, Ministro, but I don't want to implicate you in anything."

Ercolano gave him an odd, approving look. "Then I'll take my leave. Don't plan anything illegal. I'd hate to have to arrest you."

Ciro grinned and shook his hand. "You have my word. And tell your lovely companion that I'll be asking her to sit for me as soon as our new Guild Hall opens."

"I'm sure she will be pleased to hear it," Ercolano said, smiling broadly.

Ciro waited for him to leave before discussing his plan with the others. It wasn't really his plan at all, but now that he was in over his head with Guild matters, he had no choice. He only found it strange that he was the one initially against any action and now he was orchestrating it all.

Chapter 44 – Orodi 20 Musicisti 230 Years After Implosion

Ciro waited in Signora Loyola's foyer for the others to arrive. He'd purposely kept it a small gathering. This was only to gauge interest and potentially organise something bigger. He was the first to admit the idea wasn't his. In fact, when he'd told Signora Loyola that he'd changed his mind, she'd been so surprised that she'd almost dropped her coffee cup. All those weeks ago, when she'd first mentioned the idea of planning something, he'd immediately shied away from it.

"They're late," she snapped impatiently. "Doesn't this matter to them at all?"

He ignored her outburst. She knew as well as he did how important this was to *all* of them. If they were late, there would be a reason for it.

The doorbell rang, but Signora Loyola did not move to answer it.

"Where is that wretched girl?"

"You gave her the night off, remember?" Ciro said.

Signora Loyola rolled her eyes and stood to answer the door. Ciro followed, a step behind. Solidarity was important at times like this.

Quickly and quietly, their guests entered, cloaked and hatted in dark garb. Caution was essential at a time like this.

"Come through," Signora Loyola instructed them. "Cloaks and hats can come through to the dining room. I've given my useless maid the night off."

"You should give that useless maid the boot," Greta replied, none too softly.

Signora Loyola turned sharply. "If she weren't the daughter of my loyal chef, I would."

"I like Greta more and more," Lucrezia said, from behind Aveline. "Why don't you ever invite us out together?"

Aveline grunted audibly. "Crez, you grate on so many people, it's a wonder your workshop is always as full as it is. Why would I inflict you on my closest friend?"

"I'm the best Gold Alchimista in Tor'Esint," Lucrezia sniffed. "I can afford to grate on as many people as I like, especially if I think they're ash-suckers."

"You think everyone's an ash-sucker until you get to know them," Telchide pointed out.

Signora Loyola raised an eyebrow. "I assume this means you all already know each other then?"

"I thought it best to only invite those whose loyalty was without question," Ciro told her. "The five of them have proven their loyalty to one another, and to me, time and again. I would trust them with my life."

Signora Loyola sniffed. "What about with your career?"

"If you doubted that, you wouldn't have agreed to this meeting," Ciro pointed out.

Filippo Falegname came in last and closed the door behind him. Signora Loyola stared at him for a long moment.

"I assume Carlotta doesn't know her companion is conspiring against her?"

It was more a statement than a question. All eyes turned to Filippo.

"Carlotta and I barely speak anymore. Too many Guild secrets could be revealed. It was bad before I became a Maestro, now it's ... unbearable."

"And yet you stay with her," Loyola noted.

Filippo shrugged. "At least this way, I have a better chance of seeing how our actions affect the Mercantili Guild. She spent days trying to secure the release of all her Guild members after they were arrested at the Guild Ball, and she accused me of conspiring against her by signing the agreement to ratify the Corallini Guild.

"I tried leaving her once, years before all of this started. Problem was, I loved her too much to stay away. She's a different person now, but I have to hope I can bring her back to who she was. At the heart of it all, she's just trying to secure the future of her Guild, in a horribly twisted way."

"Filippo has already proven himself to us," Ciro reminded them. "He helped us minimise the damage when Telchide had Sebetine declared dead. I trust him implicitly."

He held out his arm to Signora Loyola and escorted the lady of the house through to her dining room. The others followed close behind, with stifled gasps of wonder. Villas like Signora Loyola's ran all along the spine of Tor'Esint, but only a few Guild members were affluent enough to live in some of them. Mostly, they belonged to non-Guild members and were passed down through families.

As they shed their cloaks and hats and took seats around the dining table, Ciro noticed the only ones who did not look ill at ease were Aveline and Filippo. He didn't know much about Aveline, but the ease with which she moved around such a luxurious room, Ciro knew exactly where she'd come from. Telchide, of course, had never mentioned her wealth.

Each place setting had a sugar-encrusted glass filled with vermouth, a slice of lemon balanced over the rim. Ciro picked up his and ate the lemon with relish, then took a slow sip of his drink. This was luxury. Ciro had never been poor, but he attributed that to always being so careful with their money. It meant they rarely ate out or bought themselves treats.

"Careful Ciro, or you'll be drunk before we start," Greta whispered, with a light touch on his arm.

Ciro frowned and looked at his glass, surprised to see half the vermouth was already gone. He put the glass back down and looked around the table. No one was talking. Everyone appeared to be waiting for someone else to start.

"I suppose you're all wondering why we invited you here tonight," Ciro began.

"It had better have to do with how to stop these smoking edicts or you're wasting our time," Lucrezia replied, none too quietly.

Ciro was taken aback. He'd not had much to do with Lucrezia before. The only reason he'd agreed to invite her was because Greta, Telchide and Aveline swore to her loyalty.

"Indeed," Ciro continued. "I should've agreed when Signora Loyola first asked me some weeks ago, but I stubbornly thought the Mercantili Guild would eventually leave me alone. The fact that I was recently assaulted has proven this is not the case. The Mercantili won't stop until every threat to them is quashed. I wouldn't be surprised if they wanted to dismantle every Guild but their own and it's time we do something about it."

"Assaulted?" Filippo started. "If the Mercantili Guild attacked you then why hasn't Ercolano done something about it?"

"The man got away and was not from the Guild itself. There's no evidence to charge them with."

Lucrezia rolled her eyes, but before she could make another snide comment, Signora Loyola jumped in.

"The biggest problem we have in attempting to take on the Mercantili is creating the opportunity for enough Guild members to come together without fear of a Mercantili raid. There, we may have a solution." She glanced at Ciro and raised her eyebrows. He nodded in reassurance. "Ciro assures me the corallo statue he's working on will be done in a matter of weeks now that his work to set up the new Corallini Guild Hall is almost complete.

"When it is ready, I will be hosting one of my famous dinner parties. I propose to invite as many Guild members as we can get away with to work on our strategy. But first, we need a plan."

Ciro saw the look Aveline shared with Greta and Telchide.

"You three already have a plan, don't you?" Ciro asked her.

Aveline shrugged. "It's a long-term plan, and would take a strong commitment from everyone, but we believe it could work."

The conversation paused as the chef entered the room with a steaming tray of lasagna to sighs of delight. Generous portions were served on gold-edged plates.

"You've outdone yourself again, Luigi," Signora Loyola told the chef. "It's a wonder none of my friends have managed to snatch you away."

Luigi chuckled and waggled a finger. "Don't think they haven't tried. Some have even offered twice what you pay me, but I've refused every one of them. I doubt they would give me the freedom to cook whatever I like every day."

"Ah, but that's when you do your best work," Signora Loyola told him fondly. "Now, let us enjoy tonight's creation."

She waited until he'd left before turning to Aveline.

"Right, let's hear this plan then."

"The easiest part is asking all Guild members to stop ordering goods through the Mercantili Guild, only sourcing their supplies from Tor'Esint where possible," Aveline began.

Filippo coughed. "That's the easiest part? How are we meant to stop ordering goods through the Mercantili if we need things from outside the city? Did you not hear how much Fabrizio made through the blockades?"

"There are ways," Greta said with a grin. "Don't worry about that part."

"Next comes the difficult part," Aveline continued. "We need to ensure that the Mercantili Guild wins the bidding war to host next year's Guild Ball. It'll be the centenary, a landmark occasion indeed, so they'll be itching to get for themselves."

Signora Loyola drew in a sharp breath. "Why would we want to do that? They're insufferably smug as it is. I don't want to give them more fuel for their fire."

"Well, this is where Telchide has come up with a brilliant plan," Aveline told her. "We ensure they win the bidding war, and goad them into making the ball spectacular, though they probably don't need our help for that. Then, and this is the important thing, not a single person buys a ticket for the ball. They'll have sunk so much money into it that they'll be ruined if we don't attend. And, if not ruined, at least severely crippled. What do you think?"

Ciro listened with growing hope.

"That could work," he said excitedly. "Even the Gioiellieri Guild spent a fortune on the Guild Ball. The Mercantili Guild would be guaranteed to spend more. The difficulty would be ensuring they win the bidding war and convincing everyone to boycott the event without alerting the Mercantili Guild."

Signora Loyola waved a hand. "The first one's easy. Ministro Ercolano judges the bids for the next hosts. A quiet word with him would ensure the Mercantili Guild wins."

"And we can ensure the other Guilds boycott the event," Greta said confidently. "All we need to do is invite Maestri from all the Guilds, save the Mercantili, to your dinner party to set out the plan and they can enforce it within their own Guilds. They could also alert the members of their Guild not to order through the Mercantili Guild unless absolutely necessary."

"Won't the Mercantili Guild get suspicious if they aren't invited?" asked Lucrezia. "They've been raiding ristoranti and bars – even Nestore's Exploding Beakers has been raided. What's to stop them raiding a private house?"

Ciro shook his head. "They weren't invited to ratify the establishment of the Corallini Guild and they didn't find out until it was too late. We can be clever about it. The Gioiellieri Maestri managed to organise that. They could help organise this."

Signora Loyola clapped her hands. "Well, there we have it. Ciro, you work your fingers to the bone to get that corallo statue done. I'll have a word with

Ercolano about the bidding for the Guild Ball. Then, when we have a date, I'll hand deliver letters to each of the Guild Halls for the Maestri."

"I don't think that's a good idea," Greta pointed out. "If you go personally to each of the Guild Halls but the Mercantili, they're bound to notice, especially as their Guild Hall is right in the middle of the others. Why don't you give the letters to the six of us? We'll give them to our Maestri and then they can distribute the rest of them themselves."

Signora Loyola grudgingly accepted Greta's solution and focused everyone's attention back on her dinner party.

After all the food had been served, and everyone had eaten their fill, she led them all to the drawing room to demonstrate Telchide's magnificent music box for them. She wound it up all the way, then held her hand out to Filippo. Ciro mused that they must have known each other quite well for him to accept so easily.

He held out his own hand to Greta and danced her around the room. She was a lovely dance partner. The music box played an entire song before stopping – he'd never heard a music box play such a long tune before.

Without asking Signora Loyola's permission, Telchide walked over to the music box, opened a compartment on the side and started rifling through it until he found what he was looking for. The dancers turned to watch him curiously. A moment later, the music box was playing a different song.

"How did you do that?" Aveline asked him, quickly closing the distance to the music box.

Telchide tapped the side of his nose. "I made a few modifications to the original design. This one can not only play an entire song, but has a selection of songs for Signora Loyola to choose from."

Signora Loyola smiled smugly. "Yes, I only commission items from the most promising Guild members. Now that your new lights have been approved, I expect I'll be the first to have them fitted in my own home."

Aveline grinned like a child and squeezed Telchide's arm until Signora Loyola held out her hand to him for the next dance. Filippo pulled a protesting Lucrezia to her feet, so Ciro took it upon himself to dance the next song with Aveline.

They danced until every song had been played at least once. By that time, Ciro's poor legs were begging for rest. He signalled Greta and she immediately understood it was time to leave.

"Signora, thank you for a wonderful evening," he said, kissing their host on both cheeks. "I haven't had so much fun in years."

The six conspirators left the house under the cover of darkness, anxious not to let prying eyes see them all together.

Chapter 45 – Orodi 6 Falegname 230 Years After Implosion

It had been over a month since the Guild Ball. Ciro had spent every second morning with Loredana in Anna's workshop. After a short discussion with Anna and Seppe, they'd divided up her training with ease. Seppe would teach her how to work with small corallo branches to cut and shape them into branch pendants and corallo balls. Anna would teach her how to carve larger pieces of corallo for brooches, earrings, rings and necklaces. Ciro would teach her to cut and carve cammei and larger corallo statues, like the one he was working on for Signora Loyola every other morning. For the Gioiellieri side of her apprenticeship, Ciro and Anna would work together to teach her.

But today, he had begged leave of Signora Loyola in order to finish setting up the new Corallini workshop. Anna, Seppe and Loredana had all insisted on coming along to help, though he'd made it clear it was his workshop, as Maestro of the Guild, and he would fit it out in the way he thought best.

***

"Well?" Ciro walked proudly through the Hall of Great Works and into the main workshop, spreading his arms wide around him. "What do you think?"

Loredana clapped her hands in delight and ran to see everything. Anna and Seppe moved more slowly, inspecting the benches and placement of machines, the notched stands with wooden pegs all ready to be worked with.

The Corallini workshop was finally finished. There was easily enough space for twenty apprentices, though Ciro had pointed out to the Gioiellieri Maestri that they'd likely never have so many at one time.

"Are these new machines?" Seppe asked, pointing to a row of corallo cutters.

Ciro beamed. "All of mine are set up over here. Loredana, they're still for you when you become a Corallina. But the rest are new. Rosalina insisted that I order everything we'd need, for when we have so many apprentices that you two and Sabrina need to help with them."

Anna stood quietly for a moment, eyes flitting over the workbenches. Ciro walked over to her, anxiously.

"You don't like it?" he asked, in an injured tone.

She frowned and looked up at him. "Like it?" she asked incredulously. "You've ordered things that even Sabrina and I don't have – that we've never even thought of before."

Ciro was crestfallen. "I *knew* we should have asked your opinion, but the Maestri wouldn't let me. They kept insisting *I* was the only Maestro of the Corallini Guild for now, so the decision was mine alone."

Anna laughed. "Ciro, I don't think you understand. It's marvellous! Our apprentices won't want to come back to learn from us in the afternoons. You've done a wonderful job."

At her sudden laughter, Ciro noticed the crinkles around her eyes as she smiled. This wasn't a lie. It wasn't to placate him.

"Seppe? Loredana?"

Loredana continued running around the workshop until she reached Ciro and threw her arms around him.

"Oh Zio, it's magnificent!"

Ciro heaved a sigh of relief, and felt Seppe's hand on his shoulder.

"You've done a good job. It's functional and spacious – enough room for three Maestri and myself to teach all the apprentices."

"When does it open?" Loredana asked, tugging the corner of his jacket.

Ciro stroked her hair fondly. "We can test it out today, if you like. It would be good to work out if we're missing anything, or if a different layout works best before it officially opens on Gildadi. Rosalina said there's a group of teenagers who've signed up from the orphanage and another few they've tempted from the Gioiellieri apprentice waiting list."

"How many in total?" Anna asked, a hint of concern in her voice.

Ciro shrugged. "Six, I think. I'll get the final list this afternoon and organise the details with the Gioiellieri Maestri and Ministro Ercolano. The apprentices will live in his house so we may need to organise for them to travel back and forth from his house to the Guild Hall and your workshops..."

Anna suddenly grabbed his arm. "Our workshops! If we're here, teaching apprentices all day, who will be in our workshops commissioning new works or generally keeping shop?"

Ciro hesitated.

"You hadn't even thought of that, had you?" she accused him. "You don't have your own workshop anymore, so it didn't even cross your mind, did it? I knew this wasn't going to work. I just *knew* it!"

Annoyed and angry, partly with himself, Ciro only crossed his arms.

"We'll figure something out," Loredana said, running over to them. "We're good at changing things. Look how many times we've had to do it, even just with me!"

The girl was a wonder. So much positivity from such a young child.

"You're right. We can figure this out together," Ciro said, holding his hand out to her. "Seppe, can you ask Ugo to bring Sabrina here? Tell him we'll need her the rest of the day and ask if her companion can mind her shop.

"Reda, my office is over there. Be a good girl and fetch a notebook and pencil from my desk. Anna, come, let's figure this out together."

Anna shook her head. "No, not until Sabrina arrives or we'll never hear the end of it. Let's just work with Loredana until she arrives."

Loredana came running back with the notebook and pencil just as Seppe sat down to join them.

"Do we start with how the four of you are going to teach seven apprentices?" she asked excitedly.

"No," Anna told her firmly. "We'll start the way we always do – with your letters. You can use Ciro's notebook if we have nothing else."

Before she could open his notebook, Ciro took Loredana by the hand and over to a cupboard in the far corner.

"Slates and chalk pencils are here. Cloths to wipe them clean are in that drawer."

Loredana reverently took one of everything and sat at a low workbench to begin her work. He left her there and returned to talk more quietly with Anna and Seppe. Anna stared at him, mouth wide open.

"What's the matter now?" asked Ciro, shoulders sagging.

Anna shook her head. "You really did think of everything we'll need here."

"I tried. I'm sorry I forgot about your workshop. It didn't occur to me that you'd still need to trade out of there."

Seppe lay a hand on Ciro's arm. "We'll figure it out. You did a marvellous job getting everything else ready. I never would have thought of slates and chalk."

Anna raised an eyebrow. "You took that idea from me, but the extra cloths to wipe them down was a good idea too."

Seppe clapped his hands together. "There's one thing we can work out without Sabrina. Her companion can keep shop while she's out, but what about Anna?"

"You could hire a shop hand," Ciro suggested.

"Not plausible," Anna immediately retorted. "Most shop hands aren't literate, and an illiterate one would be beyond useless."

"Could you work certain days here and others at your workshop?" Seppe asked. "Or mornings here and afternoons at your workshop?"

Anna shook her head to all suggestions. It was as though she just didn't want to find a solution.

"What's *your* suggestion, then?" asked Ciro, fed up with her attitude.

Anna was silent for a long while, pursing her lips, shaking her head. Finally, she looked at him with certainty.

"I close my workshop and direct people here. Sabrina does the same. We set up a shopfront in the Great Hall and hire a literate shop hand to run it."

"No," Ciro said in a quiet, but firm voice. "This was never meant to change your working lives in such a big way. We'll set up a roster for the three of you to work here with the apprentices so there's always at least two of us here. You and Seppe can take turns coming so that there's always one of you at your workshop and you get at least half the week to work on your own commissions.

"You can even work on some of them here while you teach the apprentices. What better way for them to learn than by watching?"

The front door slammed open and Sabrina strode in.

"What do you mean by summoning me away from my work?" she yelled from across the room. "And for the whole day! Marco was just about to head out when I left. He's furious."

Ciro rolled his eyes at the theatrics. Sabrina could be a very pleasant person when she chose to be, but that was usually when she wanted something from you.

"Thank your lucky stars your shop is open at all today," Anna chided her. "This is *your* Guild too, or would you rather we make all the decisions without consulting you?"

The force of her words were lost on Sabrina as the younger Corallina's eyes darted all over the new workshop.

"Are those ... fire-guns? And corallo cutters? And..."

Sabrina walked around the room, inspecting the various machines and tools. Finally, she joined them at the centre workbench, waving her hand carelessly.

"Well, what did you want?"

Anna visibly bristled at her tone. "We won't bother asking your opinion next time. Ciro and I can make all the decisions without you."

"Don't be like that," Sabrina simpered. "I'm here now, so let's make these decisions together."

Ciro caught Seppe's eye and struggled not to groan.

"You said there's a kitchenette, yes?" Seppe asked, knowing the answer. "I'll make a pot of coffee."

Loredana jumped up from her seat and ran over to them.

"I've finished my letters. I'll make the coffee."

Anna raised an eyebrow at her.

"I promise, I wrote every letter ten times over and read a page from one of the books Zio has in the cupboard there. It has *everything*!" she squealed, jumping up and down before running to the kitchenette.

"Books? Letters? What's she on about?" asked Sabrina. "What does that have to do with anything?"

Ciro shook his head. "Never mind that now. We need to work out a roster. We'll have six new apprentices starting on Gildadi, seven including Loredana. We need to draw up a schedule for them, and a roster for the four of us."

Sabrina stared at him in confusion. "There are only *three* Corallini Maestri, Ciro. They didn't admit Simone, remember?"

Seppe coughed uncomfortably and tugged at his collar. "I'm going to help Loredana with the coffee."

Ciro waited for him to leave. "Sabrina, if you'd bothered being more involved in the new Guild, you'd know that the Gioiellieri Maestri agreed that Seppe can be hired as an instructor for corallo beads."

"I see," she clasped her hands together on her lap, "and will Anna and I be paid for our skills as well? After all, if you expect us to teach apprentices alongside you, our businesses are bound to suffer."

"Rina, why do you have to be such an ash-sucker?" Anna bristled. "Of course we won't be paid. Is any other Guild member paid to take on apprentices? No!"

"But we aren't like any other Guild, are we?" Sabrina pointed out, obstinately. "If I'm not mistaken, these apprentices won't be learning in our workshop, helping us with our own work and increasing our business. They'll learn here, and work on who knows what, but certainly not our things."

"Signore, please, this is no way to start our Guild." Ciro held up his hands for silence. "None of us will be paid to teach the apprentices, me included. We have two choices. Either, as Anna suggested earlier, you both close your workshops permanently and work through here. Or, as I suggested, we work out a roster for at least two of us to be with the apprentices each day which gives you at least half the week in your own workshop."

Ciro watched her expression as she shared a look with Anna.

"I hate to say it, but Anna's suggestion is probably the better one," Sabrina admitted. "Half a week in the workshop is not enough to get my work done. I'm sure it won't be for Anna either, though at least she can have Seppe working there the other half of the week on corallo beads. My Marco can't do more than take orders and sell pre-made items."

Seppe and Loredana returned with a tray of coffee. The conversation stalled with their arrival. Ciro's mind was a swirl of activity as he slowly sipped his coffee.

"No," he said finally. "I won't have you both closing your workshops. There will be seven apprentices in total. Loredana will stay with Anna, there's no question of that. That leaves another six new ones. We'll take two each. Anna, I know that gives you three, but you also have Seppe to help.

"Sabrina, you come, with your apprentices, on Gildadi and Argentodi. Anna, Ramedi and Orodi, with your apprentices. Seppe, Gildadi and Legaramedi. Anna, your choice which, if any, of your apprentices come with Seppe.

"While you're here, you help teach all the apprentices with the new equipment. Whatever they help you make on your days, you can bring back to your workshops to sell. But only what they help *you* to make. Nothing of mine or Seppe's comes back to your shops."

There was a weighty silence as they contemplated the new plan. Ciro watched their faces carefully for any sign of anger or annoyance. To his surprise, Loredana seemed the least impressed with the new plan. He raised his eyebrows at her.

"That means I won't learn with you every day," she said quietly.

"Four days is enough," Seppe told her. "I'll bring you with me on my days, if that's alright with you, Anna."

Anna pursed her lips. "Yes, I think that's a good idea. But I won't send the other two apprentices along with you. I think the older apprentices should stay with their Maestri every day. Otherwise it's unfair on Sabrina's apprentices because Marco won't be able to teach them at all."

Ciro drew up the roster for teachers and apprentices, tore it out of his notebook and pinned it to the wall. He treated them all to lunch in a small ristorante down the road and spent the rest of the afternoon showing them the workshop in detail so they knew what to expect next week. In just a few short days, the Corallini Guild Hall would be open for business. It was an exciting prospect!

Chapter 46 – Gildadi 9 Falegname 230 Years After Implosion

The Guild Hall clocks struck eight o'clock and there was a sharp rap at the door. Seppe, Anna, Sabrina and Loredana were waiting with Ciro. Anna wouldn't stay, nor would her new apprentices, but he'd asked her to be there that morning to meet everyone.

Butterflies in his stomach, Ciro opened the door. Ministro Ercolano and Viviana were there with six new apprentices, four boys and two girls. He smiled broadly and spread out his arms.

"Welcome, welcome all of you to the Corallini Guild Hall. Please, come in, come in."

He ushered them all in, the apprentices looking apprehensively around, Ercolano and Viviana taking in everything with a more critical eye.

"Thank you for escorting the apprentices here," Ciro said in a quieter voice. "Signora Viviana, if you would like to remain, I'd be happy for you to sit for me today. There's no time like the present to begin your cammeo, or perhaps this afternoon, come an hour before trading ends and you can take the apprentices home with you when you're done."

Viviana exchanged looks with Ercolano. "I think this afternoon will do. We'll give you time to settle in with your apprentices this morning."

They showed themselves out and Ciro returned to the main workshop to address his new Guild members. He took a deep breath and went to stand with his fellow teachers.

"Good morning, new apprentices. We're so pleased to welcome you to the Corallini Guild. For the next five years, you will learn your trade from the four of us and submit your Great Works to be assessed for each Guild Mark." He consulted the list of names Ercolano had given him. "Andrea and Grazia, your Maestra will be Sabrina. Carmela and Tommaso, your Maestra will be Anna. Which leaves Aldo and Bruno with me, Ciro Corallino.

"Aldo and Bruno, this will be your workshop every day. The rest of you will spend two days in this workshop and the remaining time in your Maestra's workshop. As you already know, every evening, you'll return home to Ministro Ercolano and Signora Viviana's house. Are there any questions?"

One of the boys raised his hand. Ciro nodded for him to speak.

"Aldo, Maestro," he introduced himself. "Excuse me, but if there are four of you, why are only three of you taking on apprentices?"

Ciro glanced at Seppe. "Well spotted, Aldo. Although Signore Giuseppe has worked with me for forty years, he is not a Corallino. However, you'll be hard pressed to find anyone in Tor'Esint more skilled than him in the cutting and shaping of corallo balls. Signore Giuseppe will teach all seven of you that skill."

"Seven?" asked Aldo, when one of the others nudged him.

Ciro motioned for Loredana to join him. He could feel her racing heartbeat under his hand as he held her close to him.

"My niece, Loredana, was the first Corallini apprentice. She is Maestra Anna's apprentice and, unlike the six of you, will live with Anna as she has done for some time already. She will spend four days a week here, in the Corallini Guild Hall, and the other days in Anna's workshop."

The six apprentices eyed Loredana suspiciously, but none of them said anything further. Ciro thought perhaps the knowledge that she was his niece kept them from commenting.

"Right then, Carmela and Tommaso, you can accompany Anna to her workshop for the day and return here an hour before the end of trading so you don't miss out when I sketch Signora Viviana for her cammeo. The rest of you, come over to the low workbenches."

There was a bustle of activity as everyone did as they were told. Loredana, already knowing the routine, pulled out five slates, chalk sticks and cloths, and handed them to each of the other apprentices before sitting down at the seat nearest Seppe.

"Now, the first part of the day is usually spent with our letters," Ciro told them. "Tell me, do any of you already know your letters?"

All of them shook their heads. It was to be expected – orphans were rarely taught their letters and people on the waiting list were probably not from Guild families and so likely the parents were illiterate themselves. It was a sad, but all too common story. Well, at least he could do something about it within his own Guild.

"Right then, Loredana, you know what to do. Seppe, Sabrina, come help me with the others."

Thankfully, Sabrina didn't object. Ciro wanted all the apprentices to be taught in a similar way, so that none had an unfair advantage over the others. He'd already explained on Orodi what he would expect of her, but was still surprised that she was so willing to agree.

The three of them fell into an easy rhythm of dividing and teaching the apprentices during the day, taking a break at midday for lunch. Ciro sent two of the apprentices out with Seppe to get panini for everyone. They would need a more permanent solution, but it would do for now.

***

As the Guild Hall clocks struck three, Anna's apprentices walked in the door. They instantly went to the other older apprentices to compare notes on their day. None of them spoke to Loredana, just as it had been most of the day. Ciro noticed, but was remarkably impressed by how she hadn't let it get her down.

"Could I have everyone's attention, please?" Ciro called out to them. "Signora Viviana will soon be here to sit for her cammeo. I'd like each of you to get your sketchbook and a pencil from the cupboard, ready to sketch her alongside me. Seppe and Sabrina will walk around to instruct you as you draw. My attention will be wholly consumed by my model."

Aldo was the first to the cupboard, closely followed by Bruno. They took their things and sat next to each other. Soon, the cupboard was overrun by apprentices. Rather than be trampled by them, Loredana stood off to one side, head hung low and hands held together in front of her.

The sight was almost too much for Ciro to bear. He could see how close to tears she was. Then a most unexpected thing happened – Tommaso, one of Anna's new apprentices, came away from the cupboard with two books and walked over to Loredana.

"This one's already got some lovely drawings in it. Is it yours?" he asked kindly.

He held out Loredana's book to her. She took it with a small smile and leafed through it.

"Thank you," she said in a quiet voice. "Zio Ciro got it for me when I began my apprenticeship with him. I have another one at Maestra Anna's workshop now."

They walked together to an empty workbench and Ciro overheard her explaining how her apprenticeship had changed. Tommaso seemed genuinely interested in her, which heartened Ciro, considering they were going to spend much of the next five years together.

Once they were all settled, Ciro drew a simple rose, a bird and a heart on the large chalkboard on one side of the workshop.

"While you wait, I want everyone to draw each of these, ten times over," he instructed them. "Loredana, keep going with the flowers and birds I drew for you last Orodi."

She shifted uncomfortably under the stares of the other apprentices but settled down when Tommaso admired her work. Content that the youngsters were now all sufficiently occupied, Ciro set things up for himself.

He'd placed a comfortable armchair in a well-lit corner of the room, but at this time of day, there wasn't quite as much light as he preferred. Taking a leaf from Greta's book, he asked Seppe to help him position his new Liquid Sunlight so that the bright yellow solution would shine a warm glow over Viviana's face once he inserted the charged friction rod inside it. When he had a moment, he'd talk to Telchide and Aveline about their new lighting system. It appeared less dependent on friction and had lasted the entire Guild Ball.

He went to fetch his own sketchbook and when he returned, Viviana had arrived. Seppe was showing her around the workshop and to her armchair. Her eyes glittered with excitement when she spotted him.

With a buoyancy he hadn't felt in a long while, Ciro got ready to sketch the first patron of his Corallini Guild. He took his seat to one side of her so the apprentices could all see her as well. As with most of his cammeo sketches, Ciro took his time with the details in his first sketch, then did a few more rough sketches in slightly different poses to find the perfect one for her.

"You were to become an Artista, weren't you?" he asked Viviana, finally deciding what would help to capture her essence. He got up to fetch another sketchbook for her. "Why don't you draw something while I sketch you? This may take a little while."

Hesitantly, she took the pencil and sketchbook, but did not open it.

"It's been a while since I drew anything. Even a flower."

"No matter," Ciro reassured her. "It's in your veins. If you can think of nothing else to draw, then there's always the exercises I set for my apprentices to get them going. You could start there."

Without giving her another chance to object, Ciro opened the sketchbook for her and sat down to his own drawings. She was a sublime subject. So full of life and, now that she was beginning to draw a simple design, so confident and happy.

Ciro said nothing further but spent the next quarter hour drawing her in detail once more – this was the perfect pose. Long after he'd finished, Viviana was still sketching, as were all the apprentices. He quietly moved over to the benches with notches for cammeo holders, chose a blank cammeo from the stores he'd tried to sell to Anna and Sabrina and sat down to work. In the end, the Corallini had only kept twenty each and given the rest back to him for the Guild Workshop.

When the Guild Hall clocks struck four o'clock, Ciro had already made a little progress with his work. Viviana came over to see the sketches. Her breath caught in her throat at the sight.

"You took great liberties with my likeness," she chided him. "I don't at all look as radiant as that."

Ciro laughed. "You do when you draw. You should do it more often. Now, show me what you did."

Viviana handed over the sketchbook before she thought better of it. There was an entire page of small sketches, beginning with the rose, flower and heart, evolving into more intricate flowers and ending with sketches of most people in the room, including Ciro himself.

"Tell me again why you didn't finish your Artiste apprenticeship?" Ciro asked, finally closing the sketchbook. "You must be talented indeed if this is what you can achieve in such a short time."

Viviana shrugged. "Life happens. We can't change the past. Now, I must get these apprentices home and settled in. Ercolano has organised a nice dinner to welcome them into our household."

In a matter of minutes, the Guild Hall was empty of all but Ciro, Seppe and Loredana. Sabrina had departed along with the apprentices, ostensibly to check if her companion had kept her shop running adequately in her absence. In truth, she simply looked exhausted from the long day of work. So many apprentices all at once was going to be difficult, but Ciro believed they were up to the challenge.

"Well, I think that went rather well." Ciro clapped his hands together in satisfaction. "Seppe, Loredana, what do you think?"

"They seem like a decent group," Seppe said cautiously. "We'll see if any of them have what it takes for an apprenticeship. But it was a good first day."

Loredana pursed her lips. "I liked it better when it was just me. The others don't talk to me. They probably think I'm too young to be an apprentice."

"Tommaso was talking to you," Ciro pointed out. "He seems to think you are quite talented, not too young at all."

Loredana blushed at that. "Well, he's the only one," she said sharply.

Ciro shared a look with Seppe but said nothing further. It had been a long day, and he was ready to while away the evening playing cards with the girls at home.

Chapter 47 – Ramedi 17 Calzolai 230 Years After Implosion

Trading was over for the day and had been for over an hour. Ciro had taken to spending part of almost every day working on Signora Loyola's corallo statue. She had magnanimously agreed to allow Ciro to work on it in the new Guild Hall rather than at her own home. It had taken a great deal of persuasion on Ciro's behalf. The masterstroke had been telling her how long the piece would be delayed if he could only work on it after hours once the Guild Hall opened.

Most days, he arrived at the Guild Hall at a quarter to eight to organise what the apprentices would be taught that day. Once the corallo statue had arrived, he'd spent the greater part of every day working on that, allowing the apprentices to watch him and work on their own skills in turns. None watched more assiduously than Loredana, nor asked more questions about the process.

Ciro felt it was high time she was given a small piece of corallo to carve. He would bring it up with Anna the next time he saw her. But for now, he was waiting for Signora Loyola while going over the corallo statue with a fine eye, picking out any small detail he thought needed touching up.

Tapping footsteps echoed through the Guild Hall. He turned in time to see Signora Loyola's eyes grow wide at the sight of her corallo statue in all its glory. A terrible volcano spewing forth plumes of ash and streams of lava.

"Is that it?" she asked in an odd voice.

Ciro looked at his work proudly, but caught the odd tone and stood back to examine it from beside her.

"You don't like it?" he asked in concern. "I put everything I had into it."

Without looking at him, she lay a hand on his shoulder. "It's more striking than I could have ever imagined. When we use the unveiling of the most magnificent corallo statue Tor'Esint has ever seen as the reason for my dinner party, not even the Mercantili could say we were lying. Is it ready, then?"

Ciro nodded. "Do you have the invitations ready for me?"

Signora Loyola reached into her elaborately embroidered silver purse and pulled out a large stack of envelopes sealed with her own personal crest. Of course, it was not a Guild Mark, but one that was easily recognisable as hers, since it was her profile.

"Now, we're agreed. You split them with Greta, Aveline, Telchide, Lucrezia and Filippo, take them to your Maestri to be distributed to the other Guilds. I've organised it for this Riposidi, so you'll need to deliver them tomorrow and insist on a prompt reply. Aside from the Maestri themselves, I expect you to be there with Greta, Aveline, Telchide and Lucrezia. No excuses. Six o'clock sharp."

She glared at him, seeming to dare him to argue. He didn't.

"Very good, then I'll organise for the statue to be picked up tomorrow morning. If they don't have a letter with my seal, don't let them touch it. Understand? All I need is for someone else to steal my latest acquisition right out from under me before the unveiling."

Ciro spread his hand wide. "But of course, Signora. If you give me but a moment to lock up, I'll walk you out."

He threw a linen sheet over the statue to hide it from view, put the precious envelopes in his leather satchel, checked the window latches and walked Signora Loyola back into the Hall of Great Works where he'd managed to convince the Gioiellieri Maestri that all Corallini works should be displayed, including those of Corallini past. It made for a small, though still rather impressive, display. Ciro fancied that his works were among the best there. It gave him a little glow of pride every time he looked at them.

Out on the street, Ciro locked the large double wooden doors and held out his arm to Signora Loyola once more. His Amministratori escorts followed them to her blazermobile and waited there until she was safely away.

"Ciro, I don't like how late you're staying at the Guild Hall," Ugo reprimanded him. "The darker it gets, the more easily an attacker will be successful."

"Ugo, Greta's workshop is just around the corner and across the piazza. Look how many people are already out and dining. Nothing will happen."

The Amministratore grunted in reply, but took up his place beside Ciro, with his partner close behind them, and began the incredibly short walk home.

It was a relief when he walked through the door. Greta's workshop now felt like a little sanctuary to him. A place where time stopped and he could enjoy the finer things in life – good company and good food. Sofia greeted him with her dimpled smile and ran to put a pot of coffee on upstairs. At the furthest workbench sat Greta, head bent over her latest project. It seemed she was never without a design to work on, especially since her resounding success at the Guild Ball. Every one of her gowns had been admired by all and more than a few recommendations for her had been passed around.

"Greta, if you have a moment, I'd like a private word with you," Ciro said in a hushed voice.

Greta looked up sharply and then around him at the almost empty workshop. Only Domizio and Annika were left. She put her material down and walked with him to the kitchenette off to the side of the workshop.

"Is something the matter?" she asked him worriedly. "Were you attacked again?"

Ciro shook his head. "Nothing like that. I finished my statue. The dinner party is scheduled for this Riposidi, six o'clock sharp and we're expected to attend. I've got the invitations in my satchel, but we need to divide them amongst ourselves, the Falegnami, the Inventrici and the Alchimisti. They must be delivered tomorrow with prompt replies."

Greta drew a deep breath and nodded. "We can do this, Ciro. It's what we've been working towards. I'll take the blazermobile now for a quick drive to their workshops, Aveline will be at Telchide's this time of the evening. I can give him Filippo's as well. Then each of us can deliver them to our Guilds first thing tomorrow morning."

"That may be a problem." Ciro scratched behind his neck. "Signora Loyola is arranging the collection of the statue tomorrow morning and I must be there."

Greta sighed heavily. "Very well, I'll send Domizio with the blazermobile to pick you up at midday and take you to the Gioiellieri Guild. He can be trusted more than most."

Ciro passed her the lion's share of the envelopes and kissed her on the cheek. "Thank you, Greta. You're too kind."

A slight blush spread across Greta's face as she pushed him gently towards the stairs. "Go, I can smell your coffee from here. If I'm not back before dinner's ready, start without me."

Ciro squeezed her hand in thanks. It was difficult keeping such a large secret from so many people. Especially those close to them. But every one of them would be in danger if they accidentally let slip what they were planning. Even Seppe didn't know. Not the exact details anyway. Ciro suspected he knew something was afoot.

Chapter 48 – Riposidi 22 Calzolai 230 Years After Implosion

At a half past five in the evening, Greta's workshop was unusually full. To avoid suspicion, the invited parties were taking as few blazermobiles as possible, and from as far away from the Guild Halls as they could. In Greta's blazermobile, Ciro would be squashed in with the Sarti Maestri. Adamo had his own blazermobile so had offered it to the Gioiellieri Maestri as well as the Falegnami, whose Guild was next door to theirs. Other similar arrangements had been made amongst various Guild members.

Seppe stood at the top of the stairs, holding Ciro's hand.

"I don't know what you're planning, and I'm not certain I want to, but you'd better be careful. I've already had to see you be stripped of your Guild Marks, lose all your money, be thrown in prison and attacked. I don't think this poor heart of mine can handle anything else."

Ciro looked at his companion's careworn face. Though most of those things had not been his fault, Ciro could understand how Seppe felt.

"Seppe, I love you more than life itself. I promise, I would never do anything to purposely hurt you. But what we're doing tonight, it's important. We're trying to stop more things like that from happening to me, or any other Guild member, again.

"As far as anyone outside the event knows, it's just a dinner party to celebrate Signora Loyola's most recent acquisition and I'm attending as the guest of honour as the creator of the corallo statue. Her dinner parties are famous around Tor'Esint. No one will find this unusual."

It wasn't a lie. That *was* why the dinner party had been organised. No one needed to know what else would happen there.

Seppe kissed him sadly. "Just make sure you come home safely. What would I do without you?"

The question caught him off guard. Usually, Ciro was the one asking it. He held Seppe in a tight embrace and kissed him once more before descending the stairs in his new suit. Greta had insisted on him wearing it tonight to not embarrass her. Everyone who was anyone knew he was part of her household now and if he didn't look the part of a Guild Maestro, she would never live it down.

In the workshop, Ciro was faced with Greta in a stunning forest green gown with silver trimmings and a silver shawl. Her hair was curled, thanks to Annika's use of the curling iron, and piled atop her head in an elaborate fashion with beads threaded through it. She looked the perfect picture of elegance.

The Sarti Maestri, Carlo, Michele and Rosa, were just as elegantly dressed in their suits and gown. Ciro was suddenly intensely grateful that Greta had insisted she sew him a brand-new suit, fit for a Guild Maestro.

"Maestro Corallino, it's a pleasure to see you again." Carlo kissed him on both cheeks. "We're all in great anticipation of seeing your masterpiece. Signora Loyola has been silent as ever on the subject, but we've been told to expect something exceptional."

Michele and Rosa also kissed him on both cheeks. He was a Guild Maestro now, just like they were. It still seemed surreal to him.

"Ciro hasn't even told me which of his many designs Signora Loyola decided on," Greta told them in mock annoyance. "Shall we be off? I don't want the guest of honour to be late to Signora Loyola's dinner party."

At a nod from Ciro, Ugo and Letizia secured their path to Greta's blazermobile and squeezed in with them. Though Greta's blazermobile was larger than some, seven people was still a tight fit. Ciro was grateful that no one complained about the Amministratori escort. There was nothing he would have been able to do about it.

***

As the Guild Hall clocks struck six around the city, they were welcomed into Signora Loyola's house by the great lady herself. Ciro noted that her useless maid was clearly only present to take everyone's cloaks and hang them along the coat rack in the foyer. The lady of the house lavished kisses on her favourite guests and deigned to shake hands with the others. Ciro was surprised when both he and Greta received a kiss on each cheek.

"Don't look so surprised, Ciro," she said in a low voice. "You and I have been through quite a bit now. I didn't realise what a chain reaction I was setting off when I outbid my acquaintances for a corallo trunk. Who'd have thought we'd be standing here now, celebrating your masterpiece with every notable person in Tor'Esint?"

Ciro raised an eyebrow at her. "Tell me you didn't invite Ercolano and Viviana."

"Of course not," she scoffed. "I breakfasted with them last Riposidi to arrange the other part of our plan. Everything is in order."

"Signora, I'm so pleased to see you wearing my gown this evening," Greta said with a broad smile. "It's my favourite one this season."

"And so it should be for all the trouble I went to in order to get it from you," Signora Loyola replied, but Ciro could tell there was no bite behind her words. Instead, she was beaming at the compliment. He looked closely at the dress and was pleased to notice that he could tell it was Greta's handiwork, so familiar was he with her style now.

With the crush of people entering, Greta took Ciro's arm and pulled him towards the enormous dining room which had been completely transformed since their last dinner here. In the centre of the room stood his corallo statue, covered over with a large white linen cloth. Four long tables were arranged around the statue in a square, with chairs facing the statue.

Even Ciro had to admit he was excited for the unveiling, and he was one of only two people at the dinner who had seen the finished product. He covered Greta's hand on his arm and squeezed it gently. She gave him an encouraging smile and drew him over to some of their mutual acquaintances.

"Veli, Telchide, it's so lovely to see you! I feel like we never have time to talk anymore."

Greta's words swept them up in their whirlwind as she embraced them both fondly. Ciro kissed them both and marvelled at Aveline's glowing visage.

"You look much recovered since the first time we met," he told her in all sincerity.

Aveline huffed out a small laugh. "That's because the baby has finally begun to approve of the food I eat and is letting me keep it down. I'm grateful the worst seems to be over."

"Just wait until the birth and sleepless nights," said Lucrezia, joining them from behind. "You'll be wishing for morning sickness instead."

"Crez, why do you always have to be like that?" Aveline asked, swatting her arm lightly.

Telchide joined them. "It's because she's missing her favourite marinaio. You can tell by the way she's wearing the necklace he gifted her."

Ciro looked at Lucrezia closely and recognised his own handiwork.

"Corrado! Corrado Marinaio is your companion?" he asked in disbelief.

Lucrezia's eyes widened at his loud and indiscreet statement. "Of course not! And how do you know about Corrado anyway?"

Ciro laughed long and loud. "He gave me a larger version of that stunning rock a while back and said I could have the entire thing if I would make him a necklace for a special someone. I never imagined he'd actually found someone."

Aveline and Telchide stifled their own laughs behind their hands as Lucrezia blushed deeply.

"Oh my, Lucrezia, I never thought to see you actually speechless," Greta goaded her. "What a sight!"

Before Lucrezia could think of anything to say to them, the sound of a spoon repeatedly tapping a crystal glass rang around the room. Their hostess, resplendent in her blue gown, stood in the centre of the room, next to the corallo statue.

"Thank you all for joining me tonight for the unveiling of Maestro Ciro's masterpiece," she said in a loud and clear voice. "Most of you are aware of the tragedies which have befallen our noble Corallino in the past few months, but such is the force of his character that even *that* could not stop him from creating possibly the most marvellous item I have ever had the honour to commission.

"Without further ado, I give you Ciro Corallino's finest corallo statue ever."

And with that, she swept off the linen cloth to reveal a volcano erupting in all its glory. Even Ciro was caught breathless by the sight. It really was his most wonderful work yet. Unless he got another piece of corallo so big as this, it would likely be his only such creation. He would need to get word to Antonino that he could come back home and start sourcing materials for the Corallini Guild.

Around the room, gasps and whispered words of praise sounded like music to his ears. A few people began clapping and soon the room was filled with the thunderous applause of the Maestri of Tor'Esint. Ciro breathed heavily as the tears coursed down his cheeks. A delayed moment later, he had out the handkerchief Seppe had insisted he take tonight and was dabbing his eyes with it.

Through his tears, he saw even Signora Loyola clapping for him, a curt nod of approval as their eyes met. He returned the nod, still astounded by the reaction of the guests.

Eventually, the noise died down, but not until every single one of them had nudged their way through to Ciro to congratulate him on his work. It was almost more than he could take. By the end, he was leaning more on Greta's arm than she was on his. Thankfully, she realised, and took him to his seat by Signora Loyola's right hand. Greta's own nameplate was on his other side. A wave of relief flooded through him as he realised how little he knew any of the guests other than the Gioiellieri Maestri and Telchide. Even Aveline, Lucrezia and Filippo were acquaintances rather than friends.

With her usual grace, Signora Loyola took her seat and rang a bell. Not a minute later, platters of antipasti were brought in, two per table – asparagus wrapped with prosciutto, tomato and mozzarella bruschetta, marinated artichoke hearts, salami slices and small bowls of olives. Ciro made sure to take one of everything as the platters passed his way. Each portion was sufficient enough for a wonderful taste, but not enough to ruin their appetites for the main meal.

The room went silent as the guests devoured the food with praises called out to their hostess. Ciro watched from the corner of his eye as Signora Loyola took their compliments with due gratitude. He wondered just when she planned on discussing the real reason she'd organised the dinner party, but when the platters of pasta arrived, it appeared she had no intention whatsoever of discussing it until after dinner.

Ciro happily twirled his spaghetti marinara, mopping up the sauce with the crusty bread set out in a basket between him and Greta. Only after every drop of sauce had disappeared from his plate did he take some of the fettuccine boscaiola. The creamy sauce was so rich he was glad he'd only taken a small serving of it. Lastly, he revelled in the veal tortellini with a spicy tomato sauce.

"Pace yourself, Ciro," Signora Loyola warned him at that point. "Clearly, you've never been to one of my dinner parties before."

"I came here just the other week," he said, waving a dismissive hand.

Signora Loyola only laughed. By the time the fish, meat and vegetables arrived, Ciro was so full he could only take a bite of each. There was easily three times as much food as the first time he'd eaten here.

He wasn't the only one who'd made such a mistake filling up on the earlier dishes. Each of the final platters was returned to the kitchen almost half full. It pained Ciro to see so much good food gone to waste. He groaned involuntarily.

"I'll keep some for myself, but the rest will go to the orphanage," Signora Loyola told him in a low voice. He glanced at her in surprise. "I may come from a wealthy family, Ciro, but I know the value of food. Without my patronage, that orphanage would barely manage to feed their children, let alone clothe them."

Greta leaned over towards them. "Why Signora Loyola, if you're not careful, you'll ruin your own reputation as a hard woman to deal with."

"Nonsense," Signora Loyola said, tilting her chin upwards. "Now, you two had better be ready to answer any questions about our plan. It's almost time."

The plates were cleared away and trays of coffee and tea cups were brought out with sugar cubes and tiny milk jugs. Ciro watched on in anticipation as Signora Loyola waited for the room to be empty of the waiters. They must have had orders to close the doors behind them because soon the room was shut off from the rest of the house.

Signora Loyola tapped her glass to get their attention. Silence quickly descended.

"I thank you all for coming tonight, especially at such short notice. We are here to celebrate Ciro's marvellous statue, of course, but there is another reason." Signora Loyola took a moment to glance around the room. "You may have realised that every Guild Maestro and Maestra is here other than the Mercantili Guild. That is no accident. They were the only ones not invited."

There were murmurs around the room at this revelation. No doubt, some of them had assumed the Mercantili Guild had been invited but had snubbed the offer.

"The Trading and Inter-Guild Edicts have gone on for far longer than anyone expected, and the effects are worsening rapidly. It now appears if we don't actively do something about it, the Mercantili Guild could ruin every other Guild in Tor'Esint, not to mention non-Guild business owners, within a few years. If you want no part in what comes next, you are free to leave this room now and we hope you will remain silent about what you've heard so far."

There was a long pause while she waited for any sign of movement. A few Maestri looked pointedly at Filippo but he held his head high and did not move. Ciro found himself holding his breath through the silence. Signora Loyola nodded approvingly.

"Very well then, let's get down to business. It will be announced next week that the Mercantili Guild has won the bid for the hundredth annual Guild Ball." This was met with a number of groans throughout the room, but Signora Loyola silenced them by raising her hand. "I went to some trouble to orchestrate that and for good reason. You all know how much money the Mercantili Guild spends on their Guild Balls and with the triumph of the Gioiellieri Guild Ball, they've got a tough act to follow.

"It's imperative that everyone makes sure the Mercantili Guild knows how excited Tor'Esint is to have them hosting the Guild Ball next year. However, the most important thing will be the most difficult – no one is to buy a single ticket for the Guild Ball. I don't want any of your Guild Members attending the ball. It will begin the crippling effect we need for the Mercantili Guild. They will spend an unreasonable amount of money on the event and will need ticket sales to cover those expenses.

"Of course, you need to ensure complete and utter secrecy in this matter. Far be it for me to organise the entire affair for you, but it might be worth your while alerting your Guild Members that they will be able to purchase their tickets directly from you a week before the Guild Ball. Perhaps each of you could organise your own smaller ball for the festivity, or even an outdoor party on the same night with the townspeople in Piazza Mercantile."

Stunned silence met her proposition. Ciro couldn't tell whether they supported the idea or were overwhelmed by the mere suggestion.

"The most important, and potentially the most difficult, part of our plan is to cease trading through the Mercantili Guild. This should be a subtle, slow reduction of purchases at first. If at all possible, encourage your Guild Members to begin purchasing their goods from within Tor'Esint rather than elsewhere and bypass using the Mercantili Guild."

Gennaro Fabbro got to his feet angrily. "Impossible! We don't have raw supplies of metal in Tor'Esint. How can we get them here without going through the Mercantili Guild?"

Signora Loyola faltered and looked towards Ciro, and then to where their other co-conspirators sat. He stared at her and shook his head. This had been Telchide's plan, not his.

"Can you convince Ercolano to stop the Mercantili blockade?" Patrizia Falegname asked. "You seem to have enough sway with him to do that."

"No," Ciro spoke quietly. Everyone quietened to listen to him. "We will not be asking Ministro Ercolano to stick his neck out any further. If the Mercantili don't shy away from attacking a vecchietto like me, I can't imagine what they would do to a younger man if he tries to intervene with their most lucrative income source.

"We cannot afford to approach this directly, or they will suspect and retaliate. Amongst this group of talented people, surely we can come up with alternative solutions."

"Ciro's right," Luisa Musicista said. "We Musicisti don't need much from the Mercantili Guild. Perhaps a new instrument from time to time if our own instrument makers are too busy, but we can be patient and use our own instrument makers more. Then all we would need to provide is wood, metal and string supplies for them."

"You see!" Signora Loyola sat back happily. "*That's* the sort of thinking we need."

Alessio Ballerino raised his hand. "We use the Mercantili to bring in bulk supplies of ballet slippers. If we can work with a few local Calzolai, then we can circumvent the Mercantili altogether as we already use local Sarti for the outfits."

"We can help you there," Elisa Calzolai immediately offered. "Come to our Guild Hall tomorrow, and we'll talk through the details to find you the Calzolai you need. Of course, that doesn't solve our problem of sourcing the materials necessary. I assume the Sarti have as much trouble as we do with material. The haberdasheries don't always have the quantity or specific materials we need for our specialty items, so we are forced to work with the Mercantili Guild to import them."

Greta smirked at that. "There are ways around the Mercantili if you know the right people. Some of my more regular suppliers have a key to my warehouse and deposit materials there without needing to meet me. True, it's a little more difficult for them to get into the city these days, but there are still ways."

From the raised eyebrows and the amount of people shaking their heads, Ciro wasn't certain others would be as brazen as Greta in their attempts to work around the Mercantili.

"That's too dangerous," Gennaro Fabbro raised his booming voice again over the chatter.

"There are safer ways."

Ciro looked over to see Aveline had risen from her chair.

"There is nothing in the Trading Edict preventing you from writing to your counterpart Guilds in other cities. What's to stop *them* ordering what you need and transporting it directly to your Guild disguised as a gift? The Mercantili Guild cannot possibly interfere when one Guild visits another. In fact, if you make it a point to go to the various Guild conventions and place bulk orders there, your more secretive regular deliveries could be hidden within those bulk orders."

There was a murmur around the room as each Guild's Maestri spoke quietly to one another.

"That could work," Gennaro Fabbro admitted, finally. "It'll take a lot of planning, mind you."

Signora Loyola sighed loudly. "That's why we said it would be a gradual change. If everyone stops trading through the Mercantili Guild overnight, they'll suspect something. But if it happens gradually and then after their Guild Ball you have all stopped trading with them, we'll have dealt them a crippling financial blow. It's the only thing that might convince them to end these ridiculous edicts and allow Tor'Esint's Guilds and tradespeople to prosper as they used to. Now, who's in?"

Another round of murmurs went through the room but, slowly, hands raised around the tables until every single person was in agreement. Ciro raised his own hand and smiled in disbelief at what they proposed to do. It was almost unthinkable, but it just might work.

Milton Keynes UK
Ingram Content Group UK Ltd.
UKHW040111021124
450424UK00005BC/677

9 780648 341680